PENGUIN BOOKS

WHO WAS OSWALD FISH?

A. N. Wilson was born in Staffordshire and grew up in Wales. His first novel, *The Sweets of Pimlico* (Penguin, 1983), was awarded the John Llewelyn Rhys Memorial Prize for 1978. His other novels are *Unguarded Hours, Kindly Light, The Healing Art* (Penguin, 1982), which won the Somerset Maugham Award for 1980, the Southern Arts Literature Prize for 1980, and the Arts Council National Book Award for 1981, *Wise Virgin* (Penguin, 1984), which received the W. H. Smith Annual Literary Award for 1983, *Scandal* (Penguin, 1984) and *Gentlemen in England* (Penguin, 1986). He has also written a study of Sir Walter Scott, *The Laird of Abbotsford*, which won the John Llewelyn Rhys Memorial Prize for 1981, biographies of John Milton and Hilaire Belloc (Penguin, 1986) and the non-fiction work *How Can We Know?* (Penguin, 1986). His most recent novel, published in Penguin, is *Love Unknown*. He has edited Sir Walter Scott's *Ivanhoe* for the Penguin Classics. A. N. Wilson is a Fellow of the Royal Society of Literature.

A. N. Wilson

Who Was Oswald Fish?

And thus the whirlygig of time brings
in his revenges.

Twelfth Night

PENGUIN BOOKS

Penguin Books Ltd, 27 Wrights Lane, London w8 5tz (Publishing and Editorial)
and Harmondsworth, Middlesex, England (Distribution and Warehouse)
Viking Penguin Inc., 40 West 23rd Street, New York, New York 10010, USA
Penguin Books Australia Ltd, Ringwood, Victoria, Australia
Penguin Books Canada Ltd, 2801 John Street, Markham, Ontario, Canada l3r 1b4
Penguin Books (NZ) Ltd, 182–190 Wairau Road, Auckland 10, New Zealand

First published by Martin Secker & Warburg Ltd 1981
Published in Penguin Books 1983
Reprinted 1984, 1987

Printed and bound in Great Britain by
Cox & Wyman Ltd, Reading
Filmset in Monophoto Photina by
Northumberland Press Ltd, Gateshead

For Marilyn Butler

I

Fanny Williams would have been much better off in an opera than a novel. She was too loud and too near forty to provide any of the conventional attractions demanded (even nowadays) of a fictional heroine. From about half past eight to half past nine every morning the house in Tregunter Road was filled with high screams, the Mermaid's Song from Weber's *Oberon*; or Maria Stuarda belting out some passionate duet with Tito Gobbi; or Fanny running her bath, opening her post, or calling the children for their breakfast. If, like Charles Bullowewo, you lived at the top of the house, it was not always possible to tell which sounds were coming from Radio 3 or the hi-fi turntable and which from Fanny's inordinately powerful lungs, particularly since articulation, from such a distance and at such a pitch, tended to be lost in a general piercing shriek, *You'll be flipping well late for school you arseholes* being more or less indistinguishable from *Quando di luce rosea*.

But today the household, swirling and shaking as usual to the romantic tones of Donizetti, could hardly avoid hearing her shout out, *'I've got it, I've got it!'*

Her hair flowing long and brown over her Victorian lace nightgown as she ran about the landing waving the letter, she could easily have been Callas playing the Bride on a good night. Everyone had to be told, everyone. She picked up corgis as she went and announced the news seriously into their foxy little faces. 'Honey, I've got it! Flora, I've got it!' and then, her voice rising to a crescendo, she flung open the bedroom door of her son, Marmaduke.

'Marmie, I've got it! Oh, look at you, you lazy –' and she pulled back the bedclothes. How perfectly sweet, he had a little erection poking out of his pyjamas. 'Good morning Mr Willie,' she said addressing this organ, 'but for heaven's sake, Marmie, get dressed or you'll be late for school.'

Marmaduke, still half asleep, murmured 'Oh Fanny' in the weary tone he always used when addressing his mother. His twin sister, Pandora, was already up and dressed in the next bedroom, vainly brushing her thick brown hair in front of the looking-glass.

'Darling, there are brioches in the oven.'

'What have you got, Fanny? I heard you shouting you had got something.'

'VD, I expect,' said Tracy, emerging on to the landing from the loo in a pair of white silk pyjamas.

'Please!' said Fanny. Tracy, her younger sister, could be extraordinarily coarse at moments. 'No, I've got the church.'

'Oh Christ,' said Tracy, who thought Fanny meant 'I've got religion,' and went back to her bedroom bewildered by life's depressing emotional possibilities. 'That's the last thing I'd have expected,' she said.

'Charles! Charles! Charles I've got it!' Fanny was calling up to the second floor, running upstairs, several steps at a time. She burst into Charles's bedroom and he woke with a start, a huge naked black shape on the pillows. 'Gosh,' she added, 'how spectacularly beautiful you are.'

'So are you.' How marvellous that even when being woken up Charles remembered to be *polite*! She ran over and kissed him on the cheek, rather bumping her head on another body which seemed to be emerging from the bedclothes.

'Oh God,' said the other body.

'Hallo,' said Fanny, 'I didn't see you there.' It was as if she had spotted someone in the corner of the room at a party. No trace of embarrassment could be discerned in her tone of voice.

'This is a friend of mine,' said Charles; then, awkwardly, 'I am most awfully sorry but I never caught your name.'

'The *wonderful* manners!' Fanny screamed.

'David Matheson as a matter of fact,' said the stranger, who had a moustache and rather bad breath; a little elfin man with short fair hair and a drawly, rather toffish voice. Presumably Charles had met him the previous evening in that loo on the Embankment where he made so many friends, and had not had time for formal introductions.

'Do come down and have some breakfast whenever you want,' said Fanny. 'There are brioches and croissants and things. I have been trying to get those children ready for school but I *had* to run

8

up and tell you, darling Charles, that I've got it, I've got it. I've *got it.*'

'Fanny, how exciting.' There was almost something deferential in Charles's tone to Fanny. 'And no compulsory purchase order from the council or anything?'

'Why should there be?'

'Well,' he sat up straight and his face became troubled and serious, 'because, if you remember, your lovely church is smack in the middle of a development area and they are obviously going to pull every string that they can to get that place demolished.'

How reassuring, but how equally troubling, Charles's legal brain could be at times. She would never have had the know-how – plenty of energy, plenty of enthusiasm but not the reassurance which knowledge brought – to have gone ahead over this church business without Charles at her side. It was like Lord Melbourne – or did she mean the Duke of Wellington? – and Queen Victoria. She had spotted the church six months before, in the middle of the most miserable part of the ugliest city on earth – 'just beyond Saltley gas works' someone had directed her – and seen at once that it would make the perfect warehouse. Since that date her obsession had developed. Any building, after all, would have done as a warehouse to store the stuff which she needed for the new branch of her shop which she was opening in Corporation Street. Since first conceiving the idea that she should *possess* St Aidan's, the place had taken on almost mystic significance.

She had no feeling about it directly connected with its former use as a place of worship; no feelings about religion, indeed, had ever vexed her. And it had not been used 'as a church' for several years before she bought it. A repository was all it was; and of course once she had put her plans in motion actually to purchase it, it was dirt cheap. It was owned by the Diocese of Birmingham, or was it the Church Commissioners? Charles had been perfectly angelic writing all the letters, and it was only at a fairly late stage in the proceedings that they realized that there was any opposition to the proposal. It came from the City Council who – 'obviously' Charles had said – wanted to buy the flipping thing themselves. But what could *they* want with a warehouse, with a *church*, she must stop calling it a warehouse? And he had smiled his knowing professional smile and said it was the kind of property which the City Fathers did not like

9

to see passing into 'private hands'. Fanny suspected it was purely personal prejudice against *her*. There had been a hell of a hullabaloo over getting planning permission for her shop in Birmingham – simply because it was beautiful. Brighton had been perfectly sweet when she opened a branch there. Bath had been OK, though a number of fussy people had said, 'This is a *Georgian* city, Miss Williams,' as though horrified by her thoroughgoing devotion to the Gothic; and of course no one had batted an eyelid when she opened branches in King's Road, Chelsea and Notting Hill. Damn it, was her argument, these people should be grateful that she was wanting to put up something *beautiful* for a change. And in *Birmingham* of all places. It was far worse than Swansea, her part of the world. The Bull Ring Centre, with its endless multi-storey car parks, its enclosed shopping areas and precincts, was the most tawdry modern night-mare she had ever seen in her life. And yet the very people (she rather inaccurately averred) who allowed all that to be built were protesting that she had fully gothicized a shop front in Corporation Street – pointed windows; leaded coloured glass in the art-nouveau doors; Gothic drainpipes – fully gothicized the whole flipping thing. People in Brighton had written letters congratulating her when she opened her branch there. There had not been the same sort of encouragement so far from Brum. Still, it was early days yet. The branch in Corporation Street had not yet been opened, and it looked, from the letter she held in her hand, as though the battle over St Aidan's was won.

It was her natural instinct, when anything much happened to her, when she fell in love or the Aga went out or the bank manager wrote her threatening letters (which he still did, even though her shops were *coining* it in) to rush round the house and bawl her secrets to *everyone*. Tracy rather meanly (enviously even) said that it was because Fanny missed not being in the gossip columns any more and so had to be her own William Hickey and Nigel Dempster rolled into one: if so, she chose the more old-fashioned method of conveying the news – the crier not the news sheet.

Tracy, being only twenty-four and only a half-sister, could not very well be expected to judge Fanny's 'past'. After all, when Fanny had begun her dazzlingly successful little career as a model in 1962 (when she was eighteen), Tracy had only been six years old. Think of it. The subsequent 'fame' had not been very spectacular or long-lasting, but it had been enough to seem legendary in the back-to-back terraced house in Neath where Tracy (and Fanny before her) had been brought up.

Was it of Fanny, or of some other starlet in the inky sky of the 1960s, of whom the story had been told concerning the pop idol and the Mars Bar? Tracy had *first* heard of it in relation to Fanny, and that was what mattered. Their tarty mother, who had never got on with her eldest daughter but was scarcely one to talk, had repeated this story all over Neath and said Fanny was a *slut.*

'She needn't think I'm having her back in my house,' Mam had said. To Tracy, aged seven, it had seemed the very height of adventure. To Fanny, aged nineteen when the pronouncement was made, it was sadly unimportant. It was years since she had thought of setting foot in her mother's squalid house (every morning the ashtrays brimming, empty beer cans on top of the television, a mingled smell of pubby things with cat pee and men's socks). A bright future stretched ahead. Contrary to all expectation, Fanny was good at saving/making/creating money. Most of what she earned as a model went into the bank. Her career in the world of Pop was not a success but it 'opened doors' as her odious little agent, erstwhile (how *unbelievable* it now seemed) lover, had put it. Columns in weekly magazines and an increasing desire to inhabit a purely commercial world would have been enough to secure a future of happy independence. If only she had been able to *see* all that at the time instead of being such a bedhopping extravaganza – as Nana Owen (her beloved grandmother) had rather surprisingly once put it. And what bad luck that she had hopped into that *particular* bed – that of her future husband, as it had to turn out – in the spring of 1970. It was pure accident; just as it was wholly fortuitous – not her fault at all – that she happened to become pregnant. Bugger and blast Mr Heath and the swing, she often had cause to say. The man she had been to bed with turned out to be the candidate for a marginal constituency somewhere in the Midlands. A whiff of scandal, in those days when politicians were meant to be inviolate, might have lost him those much-needed few votes. So, they had married (Marylebone Registry Office), and rather than being the Mme Trudeau of Wolverhampton or wherever it was, she had stayed in London while he campaigned during the bright June until Waterloo day. How *extraordinary* it was: because it was not as if she

had ever *particularly* liked him. He was all the things she was not
– English, well bred, serious – and there must have been something
about all this which she had found initially reassuring. But she had
often had lovers who had pleased her more and there were, she felt,
a thousand men in the world with whom she had 'more in common,' whatever that meant. At any rate, within a matter of months,
this comparative stranger had (as a result of two or three bleary-
eyed encounters at parties) become her lover and then (babies)
fiancé/husband, and then (because of the swing and the amazing
decision of the floating voters to have Mr Heath instead of Harold)
the Honourable Member.

The marriage, which had brought along the twins by Christmas,
had lasted about four years and finally been dissolved in 1976.
Sympathetic journalism blamed the late-night sessions at the House
and the pressures of Fanny's 'work' as a self-publicist. More hostile
accounts named Fanny's lovers.

This lover business was perplexing. She had always with one part
(quite a large part) of herself been rather squeamish about such
matters. One of the things which attracted her to the Honourable
Member had been a shared diffidence, though it was sad to find that
he did not share her feeling that this made it all doubly exciting
when they did actually make love.

She envied the Prince Consort and Queen Victoria who, she had
always imagined, had had about the most wildly exciting sex life of
any couple in history. To *be* Prince Albert, and know that the soft,
dumpy little writhing body beneath you, the legs like stiff little
sausages clamped over your back, was Defender of the Faith,
Empress of India etc.: what could be more exciting? And for her, the
sheer exquisite delight of his handsomeness, his wonderful thick
whiskers ...

Anyway, for whatever reason, her sex life had not been able to
hold a candle (even) to Queen Victoria's and, for all the public talk
of motels and the Rolling Stones, her sixties had not been all that
swinging. Although it was a betrayal of all she had been born to,
all she had developed into believing (and for Nana Owen it was
rather squalid to *talk* to a Tory, let alone put up with boring versions
of the missionary position underneath one every week or so) Fanny
rather liked those years of Conservatism. Perhaps, like Queen
Victoria and sex, it was the sense of enjoying something deeply

wicked, but she had felt a warm glow of satisfaction to have an orange-faced, bloated bachelor Prime Minister who obviously over-compensated by guzzling. The Honourable Member was not so sure about this new, radical, biros-and-combs-in-the-pocket sort of Conservatism, but he had worked himself up into a frenzy during the election and now said Mr Heath was a wonderful man and the only alternative was Enoch, who looked so bonkers, hissing about the nig-nogs, with his hair brushed back and his little moustache snarling on his upper lip. Anyway it was fun to be thinking seriously about politics for a change and she had felt really proud going to the House with the Honourable Member when he took his seat on the first day; proud, and in an unprudish way, rather *seemly*. She had worn a little hat and felt like Queen Mary (who, she suspected, had never enjoyed sex with poor George V; just lain there rather stiffly and tried not to murmur until it was all over). The trouble was that Fanny and Queen Mary were such different characters. And although the Hon. Member was sweet and boring and gentle and all that a husband in the missionary position in the dark should be, and although the twins, Marmaduke and Pandora, were a source of wonder and shared delight, the memory of the past still (increasingly) rankled. She began to think rather angrily of the Swinging Time everyone had assumed her to be having during her early career. It wasn't as if she was absolutely Intacta when she first met the Honourable Member. Of course she wasn't. And only half an hour before, at the same party, she had allowed the Famous Novelist (who rather surprisingly was lurking in the bath when she went to the loo) to do something really rather extraordinary. But in spite of little encounters like this she was still what she thought of as *innocent*.

It would have all been perfectly all right had the Honourable Member not been so quietly boring in every possible way. And, when not prosing about politics, so *silent*. His boringness had provoked her to rages and sulks; and her being angry had made him even more silent, more reserved, more frequently working late on committees and such. Yet, as she told successive lover after lover, later on, she was loyal to the Honourable Member for three years – three flipping years – in which she had no 'experience' with him worth the mention and none with anybody else. *Three flipping years. Think of it*, she would say when men went to bed with her. She never knew if they did think of it (it was so hard to know what other people were thinking) but she did. Often.

Those years had been her preparation for life, as she now realized. They were the years when her distinctive resourcefulness, her powers of character and will, became most sharply defined. She had thrown things, broken things, smashed things. On one dizzy evening she had even smashed the eighteenth-century cut-glass decanter (given by the local constituency activists as a wedding present) over the Honourable Member's head. He had taken it all so patiently and *Oh so quietly*. But she had not been disloyal to him, and it was only at a fairly late stage that she had realized that the whole thing was a fiasco and a failure and would have to be wound up.

Her first infidelity was as casual and as heartless as she could make it; with one of the removal men, lying on the bare boards of that house in Tregunter Road, in the brief half hour before the other pantechnicon and the Renault and the Honourable Member and the twins had arrived. She felt in a superstitious way that she had 'christened' the Chelsea house by this profligate gesture. It had happened suddenly and to the removal man's – though not to Fanny's – surprise. He had untied her bun and let her hair fall over her shoulders and while he did that she had, with all the deliberation and expertise of a professional, removed his trousers. The marvellous thing, as she had told someone afterwards, had not been the sensual pleasure (in fact minimal: two splinters in the bum and violent stomach pains for about a week; she had assumed she was preggers with a sweet little piccaninny baby, but the doctor said this often happened when Intercourse had happened after a gap: how embarrassing) – no, not the sensual pleasure so much as the optical: doing it out in the open in that large empty airy room: seeing his sweaty, smiling, excited face contorted with the joy of it all.

Once initiated, it was only a matter of time before she found a lover and when the time came when she really had had *enough* of the Honourable Member she found herself telling him that she was so-and-so's mistress and wanted a divorce.

She had expected him to say, 'But he's a *photographer*.' And he had said this, but as ever, the Member was Honourable, she must do exactly as she thought best. Best for herself. Best, of course, for the children. And then she and the Honourable Member had explained to the not very interested Marmaduke and Pandora that

14

Daddy was going to come and see them some afternoons and weekends, but would from now on be living in a flat off Victoria Street. Poor little bastards (not that the Honourable Member had ever suspected that, but she really *couldn't* have married the Famous Novelist): with what indifference they had received the news. It had hurt the Honourable Member (and, in a nebulous way, Fanny herself) more than she could have predicted.

'I suppose you want to marry this man,' the Honourable Member had said, meaning so-and-so, the photographer. He had spoken quietly, generously, pompously after delivering the children from a visit to the Pandas (gift of the Chinese people to nice Mr Heath. But why oh why did he have to go and abolish the poor old English counties?) in Regent's Park. Until the Honourable Member had voiced the thought, Fanny had faintly supposed so, too. The photographer was, after all, not exactly boring. Working in advertising, as he did, somehow imposed fewer restraints than working in the House, so one had none of the Victoria-and-Albert kind of thrill. Still, count your blessings. Until the moment when the Honourable Member had said it, and then Fanny realized that she did not want to marry randy photographer at all.

'Marry Stephen? What a ridiculous suggestion.'

'Whatever you want. I just thought –'

'You just thought? You just thought? You have never thought of flipping anything. If you had, we might both have been spared all this.'

'Yes.'

'Oh, why are you so *flipping pompous?*'

It was odd that he provoked her to scream like Aïda with her tits caught in a mangle. She was not angry with him so much as with the recognition that he had seen through the photographer idea. And she had watched his face become drawn and hurt and he had quietly said, 'Good-bye, Fanny,' and turned and walked back towards Earls Court Station and she had felt that appalling mixture of grief and excitement which accompanied insulting the Honourable Member. Had she grown up too fast, left home too soon, had too obviously implausible a mother, or what? These were thrills which adolescents should experience when insulting their parents. It had been an oddly revealing conversation, though. In some ways perhaps she *was* still married to the Honourable Member; always would be and no amount of lovers would change that fact. As he walked so stiffly away, not turning, down Tregunter Road and disappeared round the corner to Redcliffe Gardens, she had felt the beginning of her dependence on him. It was the start of their secret and illicit friendship: a friendship which surrounded the children but was also something more than that.

Only that week for instance, the week that Fanny knew for certain that she was the rightful owner of St Aidan's, Purgstall Heath, she had been on the telephone to the Honourable Member every flipping day. Just because Pandora needed a brace on her teeth and had been to the dentist the previous week did not necessitate four telephone calls in as many days. Both Fanny and the Honourable Member realized this. Quietly, almost happily, they luxuriated in their secret: for, having children in common (and after all, it was possible they were his, and he *felt* them to be his which was all that mattered), they had something more precious or intimate than could ever be shared by friends and lovers. Yet with a startling lack (for her) of sentimentality, they kept this semi-reconciliation on the secret, half-spoken and wholly platonic plane it needed for its survival. It was the one subtle feature of Fanny's existence and she treasured it as such. The Honourable Member had long ago found out that Fanny was impossible to live with: she said that he bored her, sexually and domestically, to distraction. It was not long before the Honourable Member had met the girl of his dreams and settled down as a happily married man. But for Fanny it was all much less easy.

The photographer came and went. Marry him indeed! His going threw her back on herself and it was during this period that she thought up the idea of her shops. They, like all that was best about her, were merely an extension of her personality: a personality she had chosen to express by the cumulative accretion of clutter which characterized her house. The room where she had lain on the bare boards with that wonderfully romantic Jamaican removal man did not remain empty for long. William de Morgan tiles were soon enough rampaging around every restored fireplace in the house: Morris and de Morgan papers danced on the walls: knobbly furniture was everywhere, draped in lace. The children equally were encouraged to accumulate clutter of a somewhat artificial kind. Did they really need two rocking horses (three if you counted the broken one, faded and warped from being left out in the garden), four large dolls' houses, dolls'-house food and furniture spilling out over three mantelpieces, a set of five hundred tin soldiers, a clockwork railway ...? Furniture, even though it was a large and spacious house (just as well the Honourable Member was able to buy it when he did before the Boom, which also appeared to be the fault of poor old Ted Heath) seemed to be *crammed* in. Every bedroom had a four-poster in it, most of them draped with appropriate hangings: two or three of the bedrooms also had sofas, draped with antimacassars and surrounded by pots of maidenhead fern on stands, or porcelain figurines of the Prince Consort. And this hectic air of interior clutter spilled over into her social life, her personal life, as well. Lovers, after the photographer, came and went. For some reason they got less and less suitable: almost chosen, like American cars, for their built-in obsolescence. Either they turned out to be happily married to someone else and just looking for a bit of crumpet on the side, or they were poofters, or they fell in love with her and she felt a return of the cold scorn she had felt for the Honourable Member. Anyway, for whatever reasons, the lovers came and went. Their going rarely made much impact on the menagerie Fanny had by that stage collected around herself: Honey and Flora the corgis, and Captain Flint the parrot who lived on the end of a chain in the kitchen and made obscene suggestions to the bread man. And from time to time Nana Owen, Fanny's grandmother, came to stay, and there was a bedroom on the first floor called Nana Owen's room. Fanny's sister, Tracy, twelve years younger and all denims and cowboys and sado-masochism, having trained as a typist, got bored with being a temp and lived in as a permanent P A to her sister, dealing with shop 'business' and supervising the children. Au pairs and chars, like the lovers, came and went. Sometimes they merely changed their status. Everyone had agreed, for instance – except Nana Owen who enjoyed flouting the conventions – that Charles was Fanny's *nicest* lover to date. Handsome, sophisticated, clever, a barrister, an Etonian. Perhaps, as Fanny told herself, her momentary idyll with the Jamaican removal man had been designed as a foretaste to prepare her for the delights of Charles. She had never had a lover who, even in bed, even while writhing about with no clothes on, displayed such perfect manners. He always appeared to be considering her needs before his own and this, combined with almost miraculous 'timing', again and again miraculous – she did not know men *could* so often – made him seem the perfect lover. Moreover he was so practical: so good at managing people. The central heating boiler had not been working for two months when Charles moved in. Within twenty-four hours he had rung up the Quali-Heat people and arranged *everything*. He was wonderful too about filling coal buckets and changing light bulbs and organizing domestic help and compiling shopping lists. It should have broken her heart when he told her the truth, after a number of unsuccessful attempts to patch up and disguise the fact. For, so odd, after that first marvellous night in which he appeared to be capable of doing it any number of times, it totally fizzled. Tiredness couldn't be the reason seven nights running. And she had not really been surprised when he told her; even though she had never formally thought to herself *he is gay* any more than she had articulated the actual phrase *he is black*. How polite and crestfallen and unhappy he had been. Too beautiful to lose, like some Staffordshire figurine or some Mercury cast in bronze, Charles had been added to the collection, told to regard himself as part of the family – or was it part of the furniture? Still, occasionally they had a little toss about in the bed without any clothes on, and evenings frequently ended with their cuddling each other in front of the fire while he told her about his current case or about friends met in some lavatory or other (what a very peculiar way of looking for *lovers*!). But nearly all the old magic had gone and it was hard to see why it was not bitter, as it had been with the Honourable Member.

'Charles Bullowewo, my wonderful surrogate husband' was how she described him, when she remembered the word surrogate and did not mix it up with 'derogatory' or 'suffragette'. And what a noble figure he made at the head of the table, hosting dinner parties. Even without guests – and there were always guests – there would be seven of them most evenings: herself, and Charles, Nana Owen, Tracy and Tracy's boy friend of the moment, Pandora and Marmaduke. Charles was not exactly a surrogate – or did she mean substitute? – husband. Never for an instant had she felt in his company the heavy sense of horror which a husband (her husband at any rate) had been capable of creating. And moreover, above all, it was to darling Charles that Fanny owed the idea of her shops! She had already opened a shop (in the Fulham Road) before she met

Charles. It was called 'Bits and Pieces' and it sold Chinese paper lampshades, terracotta kitchen ware, pine furniture, posters and other seventies paraphernalia. Badges were popular and she had two laundry baskets full of them just by the counter – Simon and Garfunkel piped through the stereo, joss-sticks, silk scarves from India, slipper-socks from Afghanistan – when suddenly Charles, who had come into the shop, hurt her by saying, 'This is like every trendy boutique I ever came into.' The energy, the effort, the *tears* she and Tracy had expended on that bloody little shop. But of course he was absolutely right and then he had pointed out to her that her obsession with the nineteenth century had – was it profit potential or market feasibility? Some amazingly awful phrase that one did not expect to hear on Charles's cultivated lips. And so it was that the 'Fanny' shops had been born, had flourished, expanded, grown to the point where there were three branches in London; one planned in Edinburgh and one in Cardiff; a branch in Oxford, a branch in Brighton, a branch in Bath, and now at last, with the most idyllically beautiful Gothic brick warehouse as well, a branch in Birmingham.

II

When Jessica Owen (Nana Owen to all the family) was packing to go to stay with her granddaughter in London, the handle fell off the cloth holdall into which she had stuffed her few belongings. There was no point, at the age of eighty-three, in going out to buy a new suitcase. Besides, where, in Neath, could a decent suitcase be found?

With tottering steps, Nana Owen made her way up the ladder into her loft and produced from the dusty shadows two heavy leather suitcases, which she managed to drag to the trap door and toss down on to the landing. One was lighter than the other and bounced against the bathroom door, chipping off some paint. But the other exploded in a cloud of dust and burst open. And when the dust had subsided and she had clambered down the ladder from the loft, the landing was covered with little black and marbled notebooks.

'They came down like manna from heaven,' she said afterwards, only manna wasn't black and marbled and it didn't come in a suitcase.

Both suitcases were too heavy for her journey. She relied in the end on two plastic Tesco bags. But as she sat in her Inter-City train she read a selection of the notebooks and realized, with increasing agitation, that she had lighted on her father's diaries.

22.iii.84. Toiled on with hack work for Messrs. C and M. Mr. M. hard at work designing staircase for central library. Yours truly more humbly engaged at present with Edgbaston Pumping Station. Still, as Mr. C. likes to quote,

> A servant with this clause
> Makes drudgery divine
> Who sweeps a room as for thy laws
> Makes that and the action fine.

I try to do all for the glory. Yet, much present drudgery comes to me in the light of penance.

25.iii. Lady Day. A bright radiant morning. I noted daffodils on my way to work. More toil at Pumping Station. Dined with my brother E. and Frances. E., to me, when we were alone together: 'I am never able to forget the total disgrace which you brought on yourself, the near disgrace you brought on the firm and the family by your ... your wickedness.' When E. blusters I can see straight into his nostrils. This is because he tosses his head back. *Lev.* xix, 17 *Thou shalt not hate thy brother in thy heart.* Lord, how have I transgressed against this thy law. *Ex.* xx. 17 *Thou shalt not covet thy neighbour's wife* – how much the more so thy brother's wife! Poor Edmund he knoweth not the truth of his words when he tells me that I am numbered with the transgressors. F. enters the room. Her swan neck, adorned with choker, makes me faint and weak: as do her slender white fingers, extending from her silken mittens. Almost, in my madness, I think I could reach out and touch her hair! Lord have mercy upon me a sinner. Dull talk at dinner. Good boiled mutton. Capers. Parsnips. Mashed potatoes. A ginger suet pudding and hard sauce.

26. ii. The Sabbath Day of the Lord. At Church. Psalm 57 – *Under the shadow of thy wings shall be my refuge until this tyranny be overpassed.* Mr. Twells preached on the necessity of belief in Eternal Punishment. E. & F. asked me to dine with them. I refused. Going there is too upsetting. I feel an uncomplicated jealousy of my brother's wealth and settled prosperity, wallowing behind his carriage drive in Augustus Road, while I flounder in diggings! My own choice, I know, to live in this way, but it irks me for a' that. Then, again, I feel that I could endure my brother's wealth, his vulgar cravat, his diamond pin, his pseudo-gentility, his pretence at keeping up with the learning of the day ('This Ruskin chappy' yesterday. Chappy, forsooth! I own E. never read a word of Ruskin but his *Morning Post* tells him to be on his guard against any seditious nonsense like *Unto This Last*). My brother's sense of superiority, his crude influence over my father, his clear desire to keep me out of my inheritance – all these I could endure. But the enchantress F. is too much for me. Surely if in time I behave well and offer it in all sincerity and truth to the Father of Lights, this tyranny will be overpassed?

27.ii. More work at Pumping Station. Mr. C. next wants me to help him with two police stations in the Venetian Gothic style.

28.iii.84. I failed to win the competition for St. Alban's Bordesley. Needless to mention, it passed into the hands of one of the big-wigs. Pearson of London. The judges wrote that they much regretted &c., &c. I hear he thinks of a grand apsidal affair, rather like the great churches of Caen, Boulogne, etc. So! My hours of drawing foliated spandrels, splendid decorated flying buttresses &c. all wasted. My repeated failures confirm my sense of personal sin and guilt. Truly the Lord visits my iniquity with much grief. I felt sure that I would win his commission if I could avoid looking with lust towards my beloved F. for but 6 weeks. But it was not to be. The devil, as always, held the dominion over me. *Lord have mercy upon me a sinner.*

Weds.29.ii. My designs for the Venetian police stations to incorporate cast-iron balustrades &c. modelled on the Doge's Palace. Mr. C. agrees to use Fish and Son. When I inform my brother of this, he is not in the least grateful. 'I should have thought it was the least you can do,' is his only comment. When I leave him I scarcely dare to look up at F., who is standing in the hall – her rustling blue skirts stirring such thoughts.

Thurs. 30th March. More bright, cold weather. V. blue-skies – as blue as my F.'s skirts as she stood in the hallway. What was the meaning of her half smiles as her eyes met mine? It has always been my private opinion that my great sin of five years ago, the disgrace I brought on poor Annie and the house of Fish and Co. (as it was then) increased my desirability to the fair sex. I know when E. first brought F. home that she knew of it and that it thrilled her. But I try to muzzle such thoughts. For no good can come of them. Such a bright morning as I sat in my tram on the way to the office. The trees in Hagley Road in bud. Thick puffy white clouds scudding across an azure sky. Would that the human race were ever as much comfort to my soul as the weather! Mr. C. crotchety today and complaining of the cold.

31.iii. Worked at police stations with intensity. Plan cast-iron balustrades, drain-pipes, gutters, lamp brackets &c. One day, perhaps, Pa will recognise that I am trying to expiate my guilt and then he will consent once more to receive me into his affections. A partnership in his firm I could never hope for; nor would I desire. I am an architect, not a manufacturer! But only so much as a word of forgiveness. I have shown all the penitence of the Prodigal, Pa none of the liberality of the Prodigal's Father. It is five years to the day since my disgrace and Pa has not since spoken or written to me a single word. And yet we continue to live in the same town; even to dine together on Christmas Day. Five Christmases of exquisite torture and silence; and, of late, for the last three Christmases, only the kindly exchanges of the eye between me and my beloved enchantress. Yet if I continue my battle against principalities and powers I will vanquish my fleshy foes. I have an unpleasant cold in the head, caught from Mr. C.

Sat. 1.iv. Like an April fool I went to the office in the tram even though I felt quite dizzy with my cold. Mr. C. thinks there is too much iron tracery &c. in my police stations: incompatible, says he, with the style of the great Venetian builders.

Sun. 2.iv. Cold too bad to venture out to church. Stayed indoors all day and did not dine with E. and F. At tea-time, as I was sabbath-breaking by perusing a delightful vol. by A. Trollope, there was a knock at my door. Just

22

as I was – tousled hair, streaming eyes and nose, a dressing-gown over my waistcoat and trousers, a blanket tossed over my shoulders, I went to the door. It was F. !!! I was too flustered to notice in all details the delicacy and tenderness of her solicitude. How bright her blue eyes are. The colour of the sea, a deep blue-green. How lustrous her hair, piled up on that noble head beneath a trim little hat from Rackhams! 'You should be in bed,' says she, stirring in me feelings too intense even to be recorded in this too frank volume. And as she said so, her hand – her little lily hand, so white, so soft, such an exquisite piece of ivory – stretches out cool and comforting, and touches my brow. 'I declare you have quite a fever,' says she. What man would not burn with fever when touched by such a nymph? I try to bluster. 'I am right enough,' says I, 'it is nothing that a hot toddy and a day indoors will not cure.' But she, in that calm almost *amused* way of hers, is insistent that I go straight to bed while she in a half-wifely way (O God!) tidies my sitting-room, patting cushions, arranging papers into piles and saying that she will bring me two hot bottles and a jug of camomile tea. I insist that the hot bottles are too heavy for her delicacy to carry; but she shews herself a hardy little worker. When I am settled in bed, and in my nightshirt, my blanket thrown about my shoulder, it is almost a torture to me to know that she will soon come into my bedroom – my bedroom! – as a wife might casually glide in – and yet not as a wife. Presently she enters. 'You will catch cold in your chest,' she says, and with those same delicate fingers she buttons my nightshirt up to the top, her eyes falling on the thick bear-like tufts which protrude between the gaps in the flannelling. Do I fancy it, or does her finger stay deliberately to tease these over-abundant hairs on my chest? The moment passes. She hands me the stone bottles and the tea on a tray; and she has made buttered toast. She stays while I eat it. And then, before I have a chance to beg her to stay a second longer, she is gone! Like a phantom, like a white lady of Avenel! I am a worm, and no man, a sinner, an outcast, a reprobate. For the more I long for that strength from the mercy seat which is promised to penitent sinners (1 Cor. x. 13) yet the Evil One again and again overwhelms me. For several hours after F. had gone I lay in a sort of torrid tempest of lust and fever: half awake, half asleep; half luxuriating in wicked fancy; half horrified at these feelings and pleading with the Lord to assuage them.

The notebook was finished. The train had reached Cardiff. A waiter was coming around offering breakfast. Nana Owen sustained herself with a Welsh cake and a Thermos flask full of tea. She opened another volume, of which only a few pages had been covered, and which bore no date: a very different character emerged from the guilt-ridden Oswald Fish of the earlier notebook. This seemed like a man who had not merely changed, but who had put all memory of his former self behind him, who was writing as if the dark years of grief and selftormenting guilt had not happened, as if the 'disgrace' of – how many? – years ago had brought with it an instantaneous sense of 'pagan' delight and liberality.

> Against his better knowledge, nor deceived,
> But fondly overcome with Female charm.

There must be many enough reasons for saying farewell to the Christian religion in this our day – since Darwin and others have shown the Bible not to be true and the German critics have proved that it was not written by God. When I first embarked on an architectural profession, my early ardour for ambons and roodscreens, for gradines, sedilia and piscinas more than compensated for intellectual difficulties of faith. Intellectual fiddlesticks! I do not believe that a man, or a woman either, adopts a religion because it is rational or discards it because it is irrational. We are not, most of us, creatures of reason. I am not. And it was the Church's infernal insistence on chastity which made me a practising pagan. As I laboured for –, copying drawings, of lintels and spandrels and architraves; mastering the styles, so that sh^d a client require of me columns or capitals; I^d reply certainly sir – w^d you have a sturdy romanesque, serried or thick geometrical design, or a fluted sec. column, or perhaps a floral capital: or could I interest you in the yet slenderer extravagances of Perp? I was, as I say, an enthusiast, but such enthusiasm cannot keep a man going all day long. Since my decision not to join my revered brother Edmund as a partner in the firm, Papa made clear that I w^d have to earn my way as an architect, even though I w^d earn commissions for any business I brought his way. I was therefore in no position, like Edmund, to take to wife a beautiful and rich woman like Frances, and must content me with my lodging at the 'wrong' side of Duchess Rd., with the excellent Mrs. Shakespeare. I was 19 when this way of life started, and I hardly knew the difference between man and woman. With what temptation I laboured and prayed in those days to subdue my flesh. But I was 19 and Annie, the daughter of Mrs. Shakespeare, my good landlady, Annie was 17. When I look back on it all now it is almost unimaginable to me why I should have felt such paroxysms of guilt and shame when our 'sin' – Annie's and mine – was unmasked. All the terrible *boringness*, the tedious and unnecessary constrictions of my childhood – not of hers, I suspect, for her mother was still a comely woman and seemed understanding enough when all was revealed to her – seemed to be shaken off by those magical awakening hours when, in Annie's arms, I discovered the joys of sense. Any religion, it seemed to me, which said that copulation was sinful must be a wrong one. Were Annie's round white breasts, so soft and smooth that I thought they might melt or bleed at my rough touch, were they evil? Were her long strong legs, wound tightly around the small of my back, evil? Was her thick dark hair falling over her rather thin shoulders evil? If so, thought I and think I, damned be the gods who say so!

Why all this preamble about Annie? I have known other women since in the good old biblical sense and never regretted for a moment my departure from the straight and narrow. It was because I saw her today – no less lovely now, though fully the woman, her hair piled up in thick rolls on her head, a little hat balancing on top of the whole, a neat simple, slightly waisted dress, a parasol forsooth! She was walking hastily up Corporation Street and I thought at first she had not seen me, or that she thought, for the sake of respectability or some such damned nonsense, she would not be seen in my company ever again. This after all had been Papa's strict stipulation when it was discovered that Annie was with child. Scandal must at all costs be removed from the house of Fish. Never mind the poor Shakespeares. It did not matter what filth and disgrace attached to the name of Shakespeare. Heaven and the congregation of Edgbaston Old Church, and the membership of the Rotary Club and the shareholders of Thomas Fish and Son Ltd., had no interest in Shakespeares. But disaster would indeed come if it were revealed to the world that the said Thomas Fish's younger son were endowed with the natural faculties common to nearly all mankind. A son of the Fish family with a phallic member? Who ever heard of such a thing? A Fish moreover w. a member that functioned? Disgusting. The fruit of all such aberrations must be passed off out of harm's way. The expense, no doubt, was regrettable – young Master Oswald must be made to pay for his mistake by not being allowed full partnership in the firm when he came of age. But when it was needed to keep unsullied the name of Fish money was no object: and if it taught the young scallywag a lesson, who knows but g^d may not after all come of evil? With such cant rubbish, poor Annie, 3 months pregnant, was found a 'position' in the household of a Yorkshire cousin, and we gathered afterwards that he had taken his mother's name of Shakespeare as was agreed. Annie continued to be paid – 'paid off' was Papa's phrase – but it was fourteen years or more since I had set eyes on her.

Could it even be, I considered, as I saw her scuttle off up Corporation St., that she had not recognised her old lover? I am but $5 + 30$, but age no doubt has worked his ravages on my appearance. My brow is perhaps a little higher than in days of youth – damn it, Oswald, my dear sir, admit it – you are $\frac{1}{2}$ bald! My cheeks, then decently whiskered, are now thick with bushes of hair so abundant that the mere name of whisker can convey only the slightest part of their luxuriance. (I have always derived a sensual pleasure from the feeling of hair, even of my own.) Withal there is perhaps an air of prosperity about my person since she saw me last – Oswald, thy euphemism grows absurd: admit it, sir, thou hast a double chin! Since I have been taken into part partnership of the firm, I have much work to my credit: no church of my own yet, it is true, but extensive restorations at Kettering, Lichfield – where not: as well as having made contributions (the design of altar-rails pulpits, above all ornamental iron *screens*) at St. Saviour's Wolverhampton, St. Anastasia's, Shirley, St. Bartholomew's, Kings Heath, St. Mary Magdalen, Selly Oak; all this is no mean feat and it doubtless leaves the mark of prosperity, nay achievement, on a man's brow.

And yet, as Annie looked up at me, I knew that she knew me. Our eyes met, I knew her, and, by heaven, for all the tightened neatness of her mien, she knew me. Shy of my pate, for all that, I raised my hat to her and smiled, but she hurried on, trying, as it seemed to me, to lose herself in the crowds. This modesty did not become the wench. Let her keep her simpering ways for my brother Edmund (O that scene, in Papa's drawing-room 14 years ago, that scene of blushes and demure innocence – she all but sang 'She was poor but she was honest'). I ran after her and saw the swish of her skirt disappear into a shop. Undeterred, I stepped inside.

It was — the lady's outfitters and I felt not unabashed to be so fast surrounded by a fair crowd of women all engaged in the perusal of such items as a gentleman is not supposed to concern himself with – stays, drawers, bodices, and the like. She stood absently behind two women who were inspecting corsets.

'Good day, Annie,' I said.

'Why,' says she, as though catching sight of me for the first time, 'it is Mr. Oswald.'

'And who else did you take it to be,' says I.

'You are much changed, sir,' says she, and there was a trace of her old coquettishness in the way she spoke as though for 2 pins she would have removed a glove and reached up to stroke the thick growth on my cheeks.

'But Annie never changes,' said I.

'This is scarcely the place, sir,' says she with a blush, the sentence dying on her lips as we became aware of other ladies staring in my direction as though they were startled monkeys whose cage had been invaded by a lion.

'Perhaps, unless you have purchases to make,' says I, 'we should stroll together for a while.'

'But *I do have*' – and she faltered – '*purchases*.' Then said I, 'I shall wait for you outside the shop.'

She kept me waiting a good age and was only carrying a small package when she came out of the shop.

'And how goes it with Annie,' I asked, as jocular as I could manage; for by now the sadness of it all was beginning to send chill into me and I half regretted having forced my company upon her.

'Very well,' she says. 'Mr. Humphrey' – my mother's cousin – 'treats me very proper.'

'Indeed,' says I, raising a lascivious eyebrow.

'Indeed,' says she, 'and I am going to be married.'

'Who is the happy man?' says I.

'A Mr. Trowbridge, sir, he is Mr. Humphrey's gardener.'

'Well Annie,' says I, 'I hope you will be very happy. And how is ... how is the child?' We walked on in silence until I had decided that she had not heard my inquiry and I was about to propose another line of conversation when she said: 'He's a good boy, Mr. Oswald. He's been a good son to me and all. And he has' – the arch smile was very calculated and deliberate – 'He has quite a look of his father.'

I wanted to say something handsome, I wanted to say that, now that Annie was to be married and I was a little more prosperous, I hoped it might be possible for me to help the little chap on his way in the world – even look for employment for him sh^d that be necessary. But her pert allusion to the child's paternity silenced me.

'Mr. Humphrey was only too anxious as how he could stay with us all at Staleymoor and mayhap become a gardener's boy or a kitchen boy,' she said proudly. 'But there was more spirit in Toby Shakespeare.' Toby? I had never heard my son's name before. I felt tears starting to my eyes to think of this incarnation, this existence which had come into being as a result of my conversion to paganism, hedonism and sensual pleasure. Dumbfounded, I ventured, 'If he is not to be a gardener, what is he to be?'

She smiled triumphantly, but her eyes were full of tears. 'A stoker.'

'A stoker, Annie?'

'That's what he is aiming for, sir, still like everything else, as I says to him, I says, you start at the bottom and d'you know what he says to me, he says I'm not proud, mam, I'm not proud but if I work hard you see if one day I'm not a stoker.'

'Do you mean a stoker on the railways, Annie?'

'Lord lumme, what else w^d I mean? Ever since he seen 'em he's been igsorbed in them engines. He used to watch them going past in the distance, standing at the end of Mr. Humphrey's garden when he couldn't hardly walk and he should have been helping me and Nelly collect beans from the vegetable patch.' As she spoke I began to see for the first time the force of Papa's strict injunction that we were never to have any more to do with one another. For the surge of envy and curiosity was intense – envy of Annie for her diurnal involvement with this young fellow, potential stoker; curiosity about him, his looks, his – the many faces of his character which Annie, knowing him as a mother, had by now ceased to notice or had for long taken for granted.

'And does he know, Annie?' I asked.

'Know, sir?'

'Does he know who his father is?'

Looking at me with a steely expression, she said, as coldly as if she believed

27

it and were announcing it as a quite casual fact, 'Oh, his poor father was killed in a mining accident before he was born.' I was shocked by the performance. She obviously half believed her story. By now we had reached an eminence and gazed down desolately together, two parents, at the rich and crowded city. Pugin's St. Chad's and the — being the nearest monuments.

'We sh^d not meet again, sir ' she said, 'like as how Mr. Thomas said we never should.'

'Will you?'

'Will I what, sir?'

'Annie, will you kiss Toby for me? You need not tell him that you are giving him a kiss from his father, but will you kiss him and think of me?' She looked up at me. Her tears had dried now and she was composed, almost stately. She had developed a hardness of feature since the days when I loved her.

'You do not care for us, Mr. Oswald,' she said. 'You have your own life and I has mine and Toby now is old enough to have his.'

'That's a cold saying, Annie.'

'But . . .' she said.

'Yes, Annie.'

'But I will kiss him – and think of you –' and then with a heave of true dignity, neither sir nor Mr., she said my name 'Oswald!' and ran off down the street. I watched her but this time I did not try to follow. Soon she was lost in the crowds.

III

How convincing Fred Jobling would be, on oath, at the Birmingham Coroner's inquest.

'And – I realize this question must pain you, Mr Jobling, but had your wife ever expressed a wish to take her own life?'

'Well, not in so many words.'

'I am sorry, Mr Jobling. I must ask you to be more explicit.'

'She did once say that if anything happened to the cat, she would ... she would throw herself under a bus.'

'If *anything* happened to the cat?'

'That is to say, if it died.'

'Yes, Mr Jobling, I quite understand you. And it was the case, was it not, that – I really am sorry to have to ask you these questions – that your cat did in fact die, mysteriously, was it not? – the day before your wife's unfortunate collision with an omnibus at Five Ways?'

'It was the brakes.' (Heartbroken voice.) 'I kept telling her that the brakes needed mending.'

Most days began with some such half-playful lugubrious reverie, thinking of ways of murdering his wife. The present brain-wave was a good one since it killed two birds with one stone, providing an excuse for poisoning Ping-Pong, their hateful Siamese. A little dexterous unscrewing of the brake blocks on her Raleigh and *wham!* When she careered off on the bike to save petrol, pedalling hard, ears flapping in the wind, next time she felt like a Pastry at the Danish Centre in the Bull Ring.

Fred felt that he could have endured anything dreamed up by whatever malicious fates governed his destiny, anything rather than Jen's teapot-handle ears. A wife with a foreign accent; a wife with a moustache; a wife with lesbian or religious leanings, any of this he could have managed. But the fates had to snigger and produce the ears.

Odd; all those years ago when, mildly lonely in Godalming, he had started to walk out with Jen, he had never really noticed the ears. Perhaps they had always been rather cleverly swathed in her dark, slightly rats-taily hair. What was the year that she gleefully started to reveal them to the world, 1970, 1971? What quirk of psychology explained it? Every morning, she would stand in front of the glass with a dirty great comb and deliberately place her greasy shanks of greying hair behind the offending protuberances. With half-closed eyes, pretending to be asleep, he would watch her, fascinated morning after morning, at her daring. Large, red, flappy things they were, with no charm at all; they were not even pointed enough to be thought elfin. More like vaguely translucent, vibrantly pink little pieces of back bacon which had come to life mysteriously on the side of her head. As often as not, they would have some bright orange wax at the mouth of the cave; she was somehow always careless about keeping them clean. But, to revert to the beginning of his sentence, or train of thought, had anyone told Fred all those years ago in Godalming that fifty per cent of his domestic waking life would be spent thinking furiously about Jen's ears, he would have laughed. This added to the pain of it all, for it was real, localized, physical pain which the ears caused him; a sense of lassitude, combined with aching in arms and shoulders; the contraction of the brows caused a slight headache and there was a sense of sick disappointment in his stomach. Sometimes she would look at him enquiringly and smile and he would say to himself, 'I shall be all right if you just look away.' But she would not look away, and he would say, 'All right then. I will be all right so long as you don't . . .' But already his condition was being broken. Her hand was casually coming up to the hairline, the lank lock which had fallen forward over her forehead was being brushed with the fingers deliberately back behind the teapot handle.

Why was he unable to find it funny? Why did the knowledge that the only acceptable reaction to these sensations was laughter make it all so much more painful? He felt that if he had mastered these matters, he would have achieved a mastery over self of almost Buddhist proportions.

Poor Jen of course never thought about her ears. She had married Fred on the rebound fourteen years before: not her idea, not anybody's idea of Lothario, and much trouble it had brought – his abandonment of that perfectly nice solicitor's office in her dear old Godalming (Mr Finch, Fred's senior partner, played golf with Daddy) and his crazy decision to take up local government; his getting the job in Brum of all places as legal adviser at the Town Hall; his dreams of becoming Mayor of Trumpton.

It was to be near his Dad, after his mother died, she could see that, even if she had never got on with the old boy. Birmingham was not everyone's idea of bliss, any more than Fred was, but they did have a nice house – a huge place in Edgbaston; Fred's father and grandmother shared one third of it (cleverly 'divided up') and Fred and Jen and Sam and Harriet lived in the other two thirds. She knew it was, by today's standards, a palatial house, and now she had a part-time teaching job (French) life was manageable. Although Fred's father had been in the City since the war and Fred had grown up in Surrey, like her, she knew that the Joblings were an old Birmingham family, and that Fred's grandmother had been born in their present house, married there, stayed there still. There was something impressive about this. And Brum was not all multi-storey car-parks and Pakistanis. Edgbaston was wonderfully leafy and full of handsome old houses. When Fred had announced his decision to move there (six years ago it was now) she had been Determined To Make a Go of It. She had developed a devotion to the City Art Gallery and the Barber Institute: went to concerts in St Philip's, found some congenial colleagues at school. A Go, in a fashion, had been Made. But it was this, mysteriously, which Fred seemed so unwilling, so incapable of making. He did nothing but moan about Brum, when it was he who had made her come in the first place and she had sacrificed far more than he had. Really, she could at times have murdered him.

So they lay, side by side, silently pretending to be asleep, and wondering if they could face another Birmingham Monday.

Mondays were less bad, for Fred, than Sundays. There was some consolation at least in knowing there would not be another of those for a week. On Saturdays there was at least the shopping; and on all the other days there were telephone calls, and every excuse to be late back in the evenings, slightly tight. But on Sundays they were thrown back on themselves, and the success or failure of this depended on his own mood or on that of his children. Jen, damn and blast her, contrived to be always the same: the same slow, home-counties, slightly la-di-da voice; the same sallow complexion, the same oval Mona Lisa face, placid beneath the dark fringe, now tinged with grey. Always the same. He liked to think he was capable of being different personalities on different days. Sometimes he brushed his diminishing dark hair sleekly and wore his horn-rims, a future Lord Mayor. On other days he wore contact lenses and a Shetland jersey beneath a tweed coat; a John Buchan hero, or so he felt, in spite of the increasingly inelegant paunch. On some days, similarly, his children were quite genuinely a source of pride and comfort and delight. On other days they simply maddened him.

'They need someone who is always the same,' Jen would say. 'You are up and down like a weathercock.' She had said it yesterday, on Sunday, and he had spent a bitter hour in the garden, making a bonfire and ruminating in obsessive silence on the absurdity of the remark. Weathercocks go round and round, not up and down. He could not stop thinking about it and it made him hate her for it.

And yet there were other days when these feelings could be forgotten; days when he was able to laugh, and not mind the fact that he was imprisoned in a sort of clownishness which made it impossible for anything he did or said to be taken wholly seriously; or when the Jen of the old days seemed to return, the Jen of Godalming before he knew her very well, before he discovered that she saw life as a competition in Morality, before he discerned her passionate, conceited desire to be always in the right, always the virtuous one. And when this horrible lank-haired bosomy Pharisaical mask (a kind of grotesque caricature of her mother) fell away, he derived such fun – still – from her company. She's not a bad old girl, he would laugh, and think how proud he was of her cleverness at languages – and her deep brown eyes and their long lashes would be beautiful for ever, even when the rest of her body had swollen and yellowed and uglified.

But this morning, lying still in the large brass bed which they had bought in Guildford with such anticipation a month or so before their wedding, they shut their eyes and tried to linger out the moments of sleepy privateness.

'Are you awake?' Jen asked, adding snappishly, 'Don't be in a mood, Fred, *please*.'

She could never quite tell whether his sleep at this stage of the day was feigned or real. How she had loved, before the children were born, this hour of the day. The pre-breakfast romp with Fred, often when he was half asleep. The days when he was such fun and not in the least pompous or snappy. He was still a *hoot*, of course, and everyone said how nice to be married to someone who keeps you entertained all the time. But really that Fred wasn't so much in evidence these days, sad to say, and when she woke in the morning she knew there would be no lovemaking; the choice, merely, between silence and some snappy comment.

She heaved herself off the edge of the bed and drew the curtains, bright March sunshine flooding the bedroom. How good that the gloomy winter mornings were behind them. Once up, she felt more exuberant. It wasn't only Fred's BO which made her want to fling open the window and inhale the cold air, listen to the bell tinkling in some distant brick church or the harsh debate of starlings on the telephone wires. But she just said, 'I'll make the tea,' and, as she padded downstairs (one day someone would buy her a pair of really nice bedroom slippers) Fred's sleep became real and dreamless.

In the kitchen, Jen made the children's packed lunches for school, let in Ping Pong and gave him his liver (a task which always made her gorge rise: a boring old puss: if Fred was not so fond of him she would have had him put down years ago and bought a nice cocker spaniel), and thought about the previous day, when the Gladstones had been to lunch.

Neither Fred nor Jen actually liked the Gladstones but for a variety of causes they had Sunday lunch together about once a month. Debbie Gladstone was a tiresome, noisy, badly behaved little girl who, in the Joblings' opinion, brought out the worst in Harriet. Not only was the house in a state of physical chaos after Debbie's departure – broken light bulbs, beds made untidy, lavatory paper festooning stairs and bannisters, etc. etc. – but Harriet and Sam were so over-excited. Still, Harriet was a withdrawn child, shy to a fault, and they had been grateful, when she first went to her new school, for the way that the more extrovert Debbie had brought her out, befriended her, helped her along. That was eighteen months and they did not know how many thunderous tea-parties, smashed cups or tumultuous runnings up and downstairs ago. Debbie's father, Mr Gladstone (one had to call him Jeff but in private Jen and Fred always satirically referred to him as Mr Gladstone), was a perfectly harmless man who was something in components. He spoke with a black-country accent which Fred used to mock. Jen upbraided him for this intolerable snobbery (as she had often noticed even Fred's father had *touches* in his vowels), but she could not refrain from the much more malicious reflection that the wife, Melanie Gladstone, *thought* she sounded county while actually being almost as Brummy as her husband. Such commonly held snobberies held Fred and Jen closely together even though they professed to despise the Gladstones because of their unthinking cliché-ridden Toryism.

At least, Jen had thought, the Gladstones' coming would mean that Fred would not be able to talk about crises at the office. *Little* things had started to get him down of late. This silly demolition business – compulsory purchase order or whatever it was. Anyone would think it was the end of the world and, as she kept telling him, it was only a warehouse. He was obsessed by it though, said it was all his responsibility and got all serious and said it was the first major mistake of his life. She hated it when work distressed him because he became all pompous and red and Mayor-of-Trumptonish. While they had been waiting for the Gladstones to arrive, he had talked about this warehouse business endlessly: the Purgstall Area Development Scheme he called it, shortening it to PADS in a quite serious way. 'If PADS doesn't go through I'm finished,' he had kept saying, instead of doing something useful like peeling a few potatoes or even cleaning the draining board and drying a few plates.

All that had happened was that the City Council wanted to demolish a derelict church in a slummy part of town to make way for what they called a Leisure Park. There was to be more than the usual children's playground: it was to be properly landscaped and would make the hideous surrounding area, all tower blocks and smashed telephone kiosks and black boys with tea-cosies on their heads, slightly more inhabitable. Demolishing churches was easy as blinking – how often she had heard Fred grind on all about it, but she had forgotten the details – they insisted that redundant churches must have a new use found for them within a stated period or else they were compulsorily demolished. Unless *sold* of course. And now the whole of PADS was held up because it turned out that the Church Commissioners did not own St Aidan's, as this hideous little brick building was called. It was owned by a London shop who had bought it as a warehouse. Well, why not buy it from them, Jen had asked a dozen times, and pull it down? She did not really like the idea of pulling old buildings down but she thought anything was preferable to Fred in one of his obsessive moods. And that was just the trouble, he said, because this warehouse – why call it a church, it was a church no longer – was nothing to look at but it was a listed building, grade something or other, and no one would have minded, only the woman who had bought it was a notorious troublemaker anyway.

They had been having PADS day and night for a fortnight but since most of it was hush-hush, Jen had felt fairly certain the Gladstones' visit would shut him up. In they had all come, Debbie bringing with her an atmosphere of instantly hateful, pugnacious badinage. Little Sam had wanted to try out his endless riddles on the company:

'What colour is a red house?'

And Melanie Gladstone had very nicely said all the right answers: 'Red.'

'What colour is a blue house?'

'Blue.'

'What colour is a yellow house?'

'Yellow.'

'What colour is a green house?'

But before Melanie could guilelessly say 'green' (and Jen thought she probably never did get the point of the joke) Debbie had yelled out the real answer really loudly and this had upset Sam and made Harriet over-excited and made it impossible to concentrate on what Mr Gladstone had been saying about gardening.

What he appeared to be saying was, 'Let's face it, Fred, with a garden my size, frankly, I reckon it needs five hours per weekend quite definitely.' After the Gladstones had gone Fred had obsessively repeated this sentence in which you had to admit *was* a rather good imitation of Jeff's voice. He had gone on and on and on, after they had left, about the horrible Terylene trousers Jeff wore and about whether the Gladstones would call them beige slacks. It made him feel, Fred had kept saying, as though his stomach was shrivelling to the size of a golf ball to hear men talk about 'slacks' instead of trousers. (Jen wished his great tum *would* shrivel a bit, but she had not said so.)

Melanie Gladstone was better dressed than her husband. She

wore jeans and a blue sailor's Guernsey; round her neck a red spotted handkerchief. It was impossible to know what it was about Melanie – perhaps the inappropriate goggles: on anyone else these clothes would have looked chic and studenty; on her they looked more screamingly like a rich Birmingham housewife than if she had worn a hat from Rackhams. The goggles did not help though – very thick rims to slightly tinted lenses. They looked like spectacles bought at a joke shop, but with her perm and her not very clever features, her appearance really could not take this venture into the jaunty. Poor Melanie; when the children had been bundled upstairs and Fred was dispensing drinks, she had started the conversation that had made Fred's spirits, low at the prospect of the Gladstones' arrival, plummet to subterranean levels.

'Have you heard that they are going to open a "Fanny" shop in Corporation Street?' Melanie had said. Fred could not very well say he was about to start litigation about the 'Fanny' shops unless they changed their tune about the warehouse. He had gulped down his gin and rudely refilled his glass without offering anyone else the chance of more (a fact that Mr Gladstone had noted by automatically saying, even though he had not been asked, 'No thanks, Fred, really. I'm doing fine.').

Jen had felt the conversation should have gone somewhere after that. Fred was silent. It was up to her to change the subject, she could now see, but at the time she had rather desperately asked, 'There are shops in London, aren't there, I've never seen them?'

Melanie had then explained. 'Oh, they're really fabulous, they are completely authentically Victorian. They're quite big you see, the size of a department store. Would you say they were bigger than Habitat?'

And Jeff had tried to do a rather boring calculation while Melanie continued, 'You can go in and buy anything – lovely Victorian clothes and the Victorian soaps and the real old-fashioned cocoas and Victorian mustard-baths.'

'And a bit of old-fashioned something else,' Jeff had leered.

'I couldn't keep Jeff out of the Erotica section when we went in the King's Road,' quipped Melanie.

'Went! Came, more like,' said Jeff, but, such coarseness falling on silence, he began to pontificate. 'Many people think of the Victorian age as one in which sex was a taboo subject, and yet look at all the

36

prostitutes there were in the big cities like London and Birmingham.'

'I would have thought prostitutes flourish best in places where sex is a taboo subject,' Jen had said. She used to rather like conversations about sex. Now that it was such a rarity between herself and Fred she minded talking about it, as a woman who has lost a baby might mind talking about young children. The Gladstones were evidently (how was it so obvious?) able to keep that side of things going in one of what they called their 'double bedrooms with rad'. Rad? It had taken Jen ages to work out what a rad was, particularly since she had heard it as *rag*. In spite of Jeff's busy life as a rep. or whatever he was, and in spite of those 'five hours per weekend' in the garden, sexual intercourse was flourishing in the Gladstones' unpleasant modern house in Harborne: Jen hated them a little for it.

'You can get anything in the Erotica corner,' Jeff had continued. 'real dirty postcards – French, weren't they, Melanie – and aphrodisiacs ...'

'Have you tried them?' Fred had asked with a sudden burst of interest.

'Jeff doesn't need them,' Melanie shrieked.

'And there's a real What-the Butler-Saw machine,' Jeff had said.

'No,' Melanie had said, 'but it isn't all just filth, is it, love. I mean it's beautifully tasteful and some of the things are just out of this world. They've got Victorian bathroom ranges – reproduction, you know, to the same patterns as they had in the last century – some of those loos and wash-basins! And the clothes section is fabulous. You can get real Victorian stays and corsets.'

Jen had asked, 'Why are they called the "Fanny" shops?' It was an embarrassing name – Fanny was not a word she would ever use to describe any part of her body, either her bottom as it would be in America, or the opposite end as it would be on this side of the Atlantic. She had never given this part of her body a name, and she was always astonished to think of *women* using words like *cunt* and *pussy*. It seemed understandable that men would need to use such words: women, however, not – unless they were going to the doctor, in which case the technical terms which science supplied were surely the least embarrassing.

'It's Fanny Williams who runs them,' it was explained.

Someone else asked, 'Didn't Fanny Williams have an affair with one of the Rolling Stones?'

Why (Fred querulously asked Jen afterwards) had she not brought this tiresome conversation to an end? He could hardly explain that Miss Williams's love life was a matter of indifference to him – or that owing to her interference the people of Purgstall were going to be denied a . . . something of use to the community. A gym perhaps, or a sauna bath. Anything would be preferable to this repository for pseudo-Victorian erotica; underclothes and lavatories; reproduction button-back sofas; children's books, printed 1977 with repro illustrations by Edmund Dulac; parasols; mustard baths; moustache-curlers. Such things might be all very amusing in some emporium in the King's Road, Chelsea; he did not even mind the shop which was gradually being unveiled in Corporation Street. But the idea that PADS should be held up by it all, that old people should be denied their day-centre, yobboes their youth club, the whole community its sports centre, this made his blood boil. They were being denied it simply because of Fanny Williams, a tawdry, commercially-minded self-publicist. So he had raged, after the Gladstones had gone; then he had amused Jen by his imitations of Mr Gladstone saying her apple pie was really delicious: he pronounced all the vowels identically, *reely deeleecious.*

She smiled, thinking back to this bright moment of the previous day. The kettle was coming to the boil and the morning tea-tray was ready now. And she suddenly felt a little stab of sorrow and horror as she thought of Fred lying in bed upstairs. Could it really go on, she wondered, this unsatisfactoriness, for ever and ever? Is that what life was going to turn out to be like – increasing dinginess, increasing absorption in domestic chores, increasing need to keep Fred sweet? He had become like an angry man on the stage, liable to explode at any moment. Not a trace of his character had been visible before they got married. Jokey, funny, rather a one: these were the words used of him. And her mother was so pleased to have her youngest child marry a local solicitor because it meant they would always be nice and near. Her eyes filled with tears now as she thought of Surrey. How she missed it.

Perhaps it had all started when Harriet was born, this irritability of Fred's: the broken nights, the sense all egoists have, when their wives have babies, that they have been demoted in the world's affections. And in some odd way, sex had never quite recovered either. Jen was sure they went together, the sex and the irritability. Fred was in moods all the time for the first six months of Harriet's life because he was not getting enough of it: she was tired: he was tired – anyway, there never seemed to be the moment: the Norland nanny fussing about the place, the interrupted nights, the fact that he obviously found the sight of her feeding Harriet at the breast disgusting. It was odd, male jokes were always going on about boobs and tits and Raquel Welch, whenever you turned on the TV. But Jen had come to the conclusion that a lot of men did not really like tits at all. And Fred had been visibly disgusted by the marks of stretching on the sides of her belly. She hated them too: it was no surprise he did. No amount of slimming or anointing got those nasty grey wrinkly bruises away. Was it just these marks? She could not honestly remember the order of events any more. In the rather depressed state she was in after Harriet was born she had not really wanted it; and then by the time she had bucked up a bit and did want it again, Fred had mysteriously gone off the idea: sat downstairs late, melancholically drinking or catching up on work until he could be reasonably sure she was asleep. Of course things recovered for odd patches; there had been that surprisingly successful week in Milan when Harriet stayed in Godalming with her mother – otherwise Sam would never have been born. Of course things were not all bad. Sometimes Fred was quite good with Sam. But it was that *sometimes*. Up and down like a weathercock. He was no fun to be with any more: only occasionally at least. And to think that she had told herself when she got engaged *he's not an Adonis but he will always be entertaining*: if only she had not foolishly fallen into the habit of pandering to him when all healthy instincts told her that she ought to hit him over the head with a frying pan. And it was all so sad. Viewed from the outside, she could imagine – if anyone were writing a book about them or making a film – it would be funny: her physical clumsiness, for instance, the way she kept spilling or dropping things and the way it never failed to make Fred cross; or the way they saw far more of the Gladstones than they could really bear: all these things were absurd. But how heavily they weighed on her. Jen felt sometimes – she felt today as she precariously carried the tea-tray up the stairs, and wondered if the cup and saucer, wobbling on top of the milk jug, were going to be safe – that if it were not for her part-time teaching job she would be unable to carry on. Should they go to a marriage guidance counsellor? Fred just wouldn't – and besides, *he* was the one who needed counselling, not her. She wondered sometimes whether he was not a bit round the bend. He was so obsessive. She agreed, for instance, that there was something vulgar about Mr Gladstone saying they had 'three double bedrooms' as though their house was a hotel, but Fred had been obsessed by it for weeks. And little things got him down so, things at work. Jen would have been happy if she never heard of St Aidan's, Purgstall, again.

IV

Nana Owen rather liked the new trains. You glided along as if you were in an aeroplane – almost no noise at all. When you wanted to go to the lavatory, you did not have to slide back the door of a compartment and clamber down a corridor. The doors slid back automatically: and it was a rather neat little lavatory, with two nice little bits of green soap which she wrapped in the cellophane which had enclosed her Welshcake and stuffed back into her Tesco bag.

The infernal fires of Port Talbot, belching flames to the sky from the steelworks, had given place to the dinginess of the environs of Cardiff. She normally took rather a lot of notice when she travelled – waylaid a fellow passenger to carry her bags or quarrel about politics. But now she felt stunned. She had never really known her father. His cursory visits to the house in Haverstock Hill had never been happy – although she believed her mother's accounts that there *had* been happier days. She found it hard to remember him during her childhood years. The memory had been overlaid by all the unpleasantness of his last illness, and his turning funny, and that hospital. They had had to put him away, there was nothing else for it, but the thought of his suffering still filled her with irrational guilt. Now the few notebooks she had brought with her (and there were piles more left at home) were unveiling a figure she had never even *imagined*: her father as a young man. The Birmingham 'past' which she had never explored and which she always understood to have been unhappy – its youthfulness, its pomposity, its anger, its utter remoteness from the gibbering old man that she had last seen in a lunatic asylum in Carmarthen – all these things struck chill into her breast as she opened another little notebook. This one was in pencil – again no date – and she was at Swindon before she had got to the end.

It is of course not without paradox that having yearned, yea prayed, in my very early manhood for the chance and opportunity of becoming a

Gothic architect: of erecting a temple to the Lord and singing unto him a song in this strange materialistic land: a monument to faith among the waste of Mammon – having so yearned, I say, in the days of faith, to have my prayers answered when faith is gone is irony indeed. There is no hypocrisy about my entering the competition for the chapel of ease – which is to be called St. Aidan's. It was a pure matter of wishing to advance in my profession, as a seaman would long for his commission or a budding politician a seat in the House. I have assisted other men in their greatness – watched Bidlake hack out church after tedious church for his customers. Why not, I thought, I, Master Oswald Fish? And it was only after I had heard from the Trustees by post this morning that my designs had been chosen, that I was bidden to meet them with the Rev^d Mr Pinchard – Father Pinchard as he styles himself – of St. Jude's in John Bright Street – that the inconsistency of my position threatened to overwhelm me. These men are, after all, enthusiasts: men for whom the bricks and stones which I will fashion into Gothic shape will be a very temple of the living God! A god in whom I no more believe than in the Zeus whom the ancients thought to inhabit Parnassus or that Woden whom our ancestors imagined to haunt Mercia before Christ's name was heard in the bleak plateau which was one day to become dear Birmingham. Oswald, thought I, you are a hypocrite: a Pecksniff, an architect masquerading as a Christian to tout for trade, for it is indeed true that I would no more have admitted my unbelief to Father Pinchard and his friends than I would have revealed to a child my unbelief in fairies. Troubled at my equivocation and duplicity, I betook myself this afternoon to the mean suburbs of this city where my proud St. Aidan's is to be erected – a ritualist edifice, it would appear, if the Trustees have their way, with many a screen and hanging lamp to adorn the interior if the money lasts out. It is 35 years since I was born in this city, but I do not think I have been in these regions above three times – and those lately, merely with the professional eye, to try to discern the imagined effect of my elevations and designs. Now I saw with different eyes, with the guilty eyes of a man. It was father and grandfather, and men like them who had these mean terraces built for 'our' workers to 'live' in. The squalor, the meanness of these streets! I saw half-starved ragged children running over the cobbles with no shoes. I saw red-faced, gin-sodden women slumped against their doorlintels: one was actually lying in the gutter but I was too much of a coward to kneel down and look at her to see if she were dead or alive for fear that I would be robbed or stoned. In some streets I was jeered at for my warm Ulster and my new hat. I felt hostile eyes upon me, more eyes staring from the windows in the little hovels some brute called one day a house, than I would have thought possible to squeeze in. In some of these squalid places – no more, I am certain, than two small bedrooms upstairs, and a kitchen or parlour downstairs – there must have been families of 12 or 14. And it

42

was this – it seemed to me suddenly clear and certain – it was this which the greed of my family had created, which the avarice of my brother Edmund had helped to continue. And I must take my share of the blame, for what had I ever done, in all my five-and-thirty years, to relieve the lot of these poor people? Nothing: nor will I. There is enough self-knowledge in one to know that I can *do* nothing. I am not one to build soup kitchens or preach salvation to the urban poor. It was my idleness, not my idealism, which made me want to be an architect rather than help Edmund to run the works. And I have always been glad to reap my share of the profit as a shareholder on the board. Indeed, after I took to refurbishing and restoring churches I was glad to bring business in the way of the works. Old papa, who had made his fortune from gate hinges and lamp brackets, was not a little disconcerted to think of Fish and Co. branching out into rood screens, sanctuary lamps, communion rails and the like. But Edmund was shrewd enough to see there was money in it: and I was shrewd enough, having brought business their way, to take my commission, and happily watch the works in Porchester Street expand: not only in the ecclesiastical line of course, so that now the name of Fish is synonymous, I might say, with the very words ornamental ironwork: from girders to park benches, from tomb-rails to balustrades, the name of Fish is indelibly stamped in almost every municipality from Wigan (our northernmost customer, I think) to Penzance. Nor am I such a fool as not to feel pleased by the prosperity of my family, nor such a hypocrite as not to be pleased that I have profited by it. And yet, as our factory has increased, so have our houses, our carriage-drives, our parlourmaids, our épergnes and our holidays in Buxton, my brother is married to a 'grand lady' – too grand, Papa believes, for us all. And young Agnes and any other children they have will doubtless be reared as gentlefolk, just as we were reared as semi-gentlefolk. And all the while the poor of King's Heath and Sparkbrook and Selly Oak have grown poorer. The gap between them and my brother Edmund is immeasurable – wider than the gap between Pa and the working people in his day. For grandpapa – though he was always the Gaffer and they touched their cap no doubt when he walked into the works – there was scarcely any gap at all. What a rum thing the 19th century has become to be sure! And, as I walked, fearing for my hat and troubled by my conscience, ashamed to catch a glimpse of my prosperous appearance in the glass window of a corner shop – I saw what Fr. Pinchard and his men and nuns cd. do which I cd. never do. Blessed are the poor, say we, living hidden by our laurel bushes and carriage drives. Blessed are the poor, say Pinchard and his nuns – and by Heaven they mean what they say and strip themselves of the trappings of their class and breeding and education and go to live among the poor like medieval saints, attending their wants, nursing where no professional medical man wd. go, teaching the children, reclaiming the women from bawdy houses and the men form gin-shops. And what have they to put in the place of the sensual pleasure of the bordel, or the hazy oblivion of the gin bottle or the colour and noise and excitement of the music hall? Nothing but their magic shows in church in which they dress up like the Pope of Rome himself, in pageantry and incense and in music, bringing to these poor lives the only shred of Romance that existence cd. conceivably offer them? And will I, for the sake of an over-educated scruple, refuse to bring some of that colour, some of that romance, some of that sheer goodness, into this bleak ugly world? Not Oswald Fish. The Trustees have £6,000 to spend and I am determined to give them as lovely a treasure house as could be found in Bruges or Paris or Torcello. The outside must be mean enough, though I have aimed in my elevations for the simple elegance of the Early English manner. Inside, however, will be another story: I am resolved to fill it with such paintings, such gold, such apparent extravagance as can be cheaply and magnificently provided. And with good management there should be money over for a bell-tower. So it is that without compunction I offer my little pinch of incense on the altar of a god in whom I do not believe to atone for my own sins and the sins of my fathers – *Sancte Aidane. ora pro me!*

After this entry there was a blank page and then the writing continued in ink:

This evening an encounter which will, I have no doubt, change the whole of my life. At luncheon with the Trustees of St. Aidan's, I was told the proud news that I was selected as the architect of St. Aidan's, the chapel of ease. My pride imaginable. Several other notables in the competition against me – Huggs, Twells, even young Bidlake himself and a man called Dawney from Street's office in ِLondon. But, in their excellent wisdom, the Trustees of St. Aidan's preferred O. Fish Esquire: an intelligent choice, as all would agree.

This afternoon, as I have described, I betook me to Purgstall to see the site of the church. And then, thinking to communicate the very cheering intelligence of my election to my brother Edmund, I called at his house in Augustus Road.

I own that my motives for doing so were not unmixed with triumph over poor Edmund who had so often mocked my aspirations – though why he should have done so, I do not know, since my work brought in new orders for the firm Fish and Co., making altar rails for one of these niminy-piminy ritualistic churches! How our old grandfather would have burned with horror, seated proudly in his pew at the Congregationalist Church! But Father had been happy enough for me to bring money his way, and so has brother Edmund. The iron screen at Tunstall; altar rails at St. Saviour's, Wolverhampton; St. Anastasia's, Shirley; St. Bartholomew's, Kings Heath;

gate and railings outside the Church of St. Mary Magdalen, Selly Oak; and the great rood screen at Saltley ... These were all as valuable commissions for the works as were their former dull addiction to brackets, garden gates, lamp pillars and the like. So it was that, I own, I looked forward to seeing my brother throw out his chest and say, 'Well, brother, how goes the world of ecclesiastical knick-knackery' – and to see him shake his head as though poor young Oswald (aged thirty-five!!!) would never learn from his revered elder brother (aged thirty-seven!!!).

But, when I was shown in, I was surprised to discover that my brother was not at home. My sister-in-law Frances was in the drawing-room. As I entered, she was at work with a sketch book and it was only when she looked up that I perceived the moisture in her eyes. Could brother Edmund be ... ?

'I am sorry to disturb you,' I said, 'but I came to tell my brother some good news.'

'He is dining at the Town Hall,' she said, adding, with a touch of sad satire in her tone, 'with his friends.'

'Then perhaps I can tell you.'

'Oh Oswald, is it very good news – you look so happy.' And her face changed inexpressibly, putting its own sorrows by and smiling intently in order to enter into my joy. How beautiful this change of emotion was – this gesture of genuine, sympathetic joy; this concealment of her grief. Her very bright green eyes were still moist, but the whole animated face had leapt to a new life – her ruby lips parted slightly in that exquisite smile, her *retroussé* nose turned up almost comically as though the sense of smell could make you laugh.

'Yes,' I said, 'it is indeed very good news.' And I told her at once about the St. Aidan's Trustees, etc. And she replied, 'At last! A church of your very own, this is so much better than restoration and improvement ...' Seeing thus, at once, why this moment was such an important stepping-stone in my life.

Silence fell as our eyes met and I said: 'But you were not happy, I think, when I came into the room.'

'What makes you say such a thing?'

'Because I can see.'

'I am as happy as could be expected ...'

Did she need to say more? The great mystery – of how anyone as amusing and clever and beautiful and delightful as Frances could ever choose to tolerate the company of my boorish brother – was at last revealed in all its cruel obviousness.

'Is he cruel to you?' I asked, violently. 'By God, I could break his –'

'Please, Oswald, please!' She wrung her hands. Her eyes were dry now and there was no need to dissemble.

'No, he is not cruel. Poor Edmund does not know what torment he is inflicting on me ... How very improper it is to be telling you all this.'

'Not at all.'

'It is. Very. Have you *no* morals?' At first, in her harshness, I heard the tones of The Family who had condemned me so hypocritically over the Annie business years ago. But then I realised that she was teasing me. Her smile seemed so inviting that I approached her where she stood by the hearth and slipped my hands around her pretty waist. She gave a little gasp and said, 'Sssh, such behaviour,' and broke away, but she was entirely unsurprised by my gesture. Now I was in despair – had I offended? No. Evidently not. She paced the room, her velvet dress swishing over the thick Turkey rugs, brushing against the Moorish tables.

'How very improper we are being,' she repeated, in the matter-of-fact tone which might be used of other people's solecisms. 'Presumably, you are improper much of the time. Perhaps you have even mastered the art of impropriety.'

'Frances ...'

'That is to say, your apartments are presumably better suited than mine to the conduct of impropriety. This is your father's house. He is asleep upstairs. At any moment, he will come pottering in here, looking for his spectacles.'

I blinked at the cool, unhurried way in which the plan of our campaign was forming itself in her brain, and being instantly translated into action.

'And presumably,' she continued, 'tomorrow afternoon you could absent yourself from Mr. Chamberlain's offices on the pretence that you have to see the site of St. Aidan's, Purgstall? He might allow you that freedom, only a day after your triumph.'

'And what freedom might *you* allow me?' I asked her. And then, impulsively, she ran to me and said, 'Oh my darling Oswald, I am so pleased for you.' And our kiss was full and long and passionate. Through my waistcoat and her bodices, I felt her breasts pressed to mine and our hearts thumped eagerly together.

Absurdly, all I could think of to say was, 'I want it to be pointed. Early English. It will have to be brick, of course,' when I wanted to say, 'I love you.' But she did all the necessary talking and said that she would come to my apartments in the Hagley Road at 3.00 p.m. tomorrow.

So much in the space of one little day! My mind is dizzy now. I cannot sleep. I cannot even rest. My hand shakes as I write. The turmoil! My plans for St. Aidan's churn in my brain. I begin to imagine myself with great commissions – Town Halls, Cathedrals and Hotels rise in my mind's eye. And then I try to understand Frances's behaviour. She has always, in the nine or ten years that she has been married to my brother, been so *distant*.

I never dreamt of this. I have always, on the other hand, admired her, as a woman.

The Inter-City train was approaching Swindon. Roads, seen from the window, were now filling with rush-hour traffic. Nana Owen sat in a daze. She was beginning to wish that she had not brought the diaries with her, and the thought of piles and piles of them, unread at home, now filled her with dread. She had been so much looking forward to staying in Chelsea, where she had her own room, and a bit of respect, and enjoyed young life going on around her. For all her sixty years in South Wales, she would always be a Londoner.

Her father, her parentage, were Nana Owen's secret. She had always known – her sad, silent, beautiful mother had always allowed her to understand – that there had been 'trouble' with Father's family; that they would have married if they had been able. How nobly she had concealed from her daughter the fact, so obvious to her in later life, that her parents 'lived apart', had bust up, in the modern phrase, years before she really grew to consciousness. How well her mother had concealed the philandering activities of her father, on the other side of London from their dull little house in Haverstock Hill. And how well, she now saw, after eighty-three years, the full family scandal had been concealed from her! Her father had eloped from Birmingham with his brother's wife! Fran, as Nana Williams always called her mother, had been *married* to the family in Birmingham they never spoke about!

Unwillingly, yet compulsively, she turned the page and read the last entry in the notebook. How strange it felt, when all physical passion had departed her tired old body, to meet her parents, as it were for the first time, young and in love.

'You must know that I have always thought you *wonderfully* beautiful.' Frances said these words striding into my room at ten past three as though in answer to a question, and as though she had herself only been gone two minutes.

'And I you,' I said. 'But what . . .' 'What of Edmund?' she finished for me. 'Oswald, I am not behaving wrongly, really I am not. Even Agnes no longer needs me. Edmund and their repellent nanny have somehow made her a stranger to me.'

'Do you often do this sort of thing?' I asked. She stared at me, so wildly.

'What a repugnant question! Please! Of course, I have never committed adultery in my life. But Edmund's behaviour is impossible.'

I conceded he was a little pompous.

'Pompous! It is like being married to a Standing Committee of the City Council. He has more time for them than for me. He talks about their deliberations ceaselessly.'

She looked up at me seriously and said, 'There is very little affection' – it was as if the word was chosen with care – 'between us, you know, Oswald.'

'Very little?'

'None. Not since Agnes was born. and very little before that.'

'But Agnes is nine years old!'

And on saying this, I took her in my arms. Her kiss was not violent and demanding as it was last night. Her head and neck submitted with exquisite gentleness; her legs pressed against my own.

'Will we be disturbed here?' she asked. I assured her not, and she let herself be led towards the bedroom. With what delicacy she withdrew to my dressing-room to avoid the tedious business of unlacing and unbuttoning being a visible impediment to our joys. When she returned, a naked angel, the only remnant of Edgbaston respectability about her was that her hair was piled up in a bun. She stood, trembling a little with fear and with cold, as I undid it and it fell with long tresses over her shoulders and her round white breasts. While I buried my face in its thickness, her fingers the while strayed over my body, stroking my beard, my chest, my *****.

'I have never seen a naked man before,' she said, fascinatedly. 'But you must have seen a naked woman. You must have seen Annie.'

'You are so beautiful,' I said.

'And so are you,' she said. 'I want to show you how much I love you.' And she led the way to my bedstead.

I think she must love me very much indeed.

V

At twenty to nine Fanny had dropped the children at their primary school in Kensington and was driving home for breakfast. Normally she breakfasted at a café in the King's Road, Chelsea, before looking in on her shops and discussing points of sale with the manageresses. But today she had to pick up Nana Owen from the station and she was anxious, before she did so, to have a talk with Charles and Tracy. They would have to be angelic and entertain Nana Owen: she could not resist the idea of driving up to Birmingham to gloat over her triumph.

Charles, immaculately pin-striped, was stage-managing breakfast with punctilious efficiency when she swanned into the kitchen, wishing she could get out of her head the tune of the Chorus of Hebrew Slaves from *Nabucco*. Tracy had either decided not to bother with breakfast, or had been, washed up and gone, for it was just the three of them sitting around the large table for coffee and brioches – Charles, Fanny and Charles's new friend, who had not managed to shave but had obviously had a bath and looked quite respectable.

Charles, standing by the toaster, introduced them with formal little bows, 'Fanny Williams. David Matheson.' One would never have guessed from the way he did so that less than an hour before Fanny had seen them in bed together without any clothes on. For two pins she would have joined them. One heard of men going to bed with two lesboes, so why not the other way around? But perhaps it would make them all shy and crestfallen.

David Matheson was as little as possible like Prince Albert, her ideal of masculine beauty, but he had a nice little face, with a weak smile and a surprisingly thick moustache (perhaps false?) on his upper lip.

'We could sell you a curler for your moustache if you came to my shop,' she mocked, dissolving into tinny giggles which she sort of sucked in at last with the sentence, 'Sorry, I'm not really mocking at you or saturating.'

49

'Satirizing', Charles corrected her. 'David won't need to buy anything from you but he might be able to help you with your new purchase.'

'Not with the church? I hope you aren't a clergyman,' she said it with real vehemence, as if it was the one category of person she was not prepared to have in the house.

'I'm an architectural historian.'

'What a very irritating way you have of speaking with your words joined together so it's impossible totellwhereoneendedandanother begins,' she mocked. 'But do tell me, do you do Victorian architecture?'

'I did my thesis on Vanbrugh.'

'Is he a Victorian?'

David looked at the ceiling as if for guidance and clapped his hands with mirth.

'Fanny has no education at all,' Charles explained.

'I flipping well do,' she replied at once. 'If I'd listened to what my teachers said and if I hadn't left at fifteen I would have been very well educated.'

'Where did you go?' David asked.

'The secondary modern in Neath. You went to Eton, I suppose, like Charles.'

'Winchester, actually.'

'Are *all* the public lavatories in London full of public schoolboys making obscene gestures to each other?' she asked, fascinated.

'I'm longing to know why you need the services of an architectural historian,' David drawled.

'Fanny's bought a church. It's a listed building in the middle of Birmingham and, in spite of pressure from the City Council to have it demolished, the sale has finally gone through.'

'How wonderful! It's a Victorian church? Who's the architect?'

'I've no idea,' she said. 'I don't even know how one would find out. It isn't as if it's St Paul's Cathedral.'

'It'll be in Pevsner,' said David.

Fanny, who had finished her breakfast, pressed the boys to share the last of the brioches, washed down by now cold coffee. She ran to the hall where travel books, maps and architectural guides were crammed into a walnut bookcase, the veneer peeling off because of the central heating.

'Bugger,' she called back to the kitchen.

'Yes, darling,' Charles said.

'No, bugger someone has pinched Pevsner's Staffordshire.'

'Birmingham's in Warwickshire, ducky.'

'Are you trying to fool me?'

She came back into the kitchen with the Warwickshire volume. 'No, really, it *is*. Why have I never known that? Now, churches, here we are, St Agatha's, Sparkbrook; St Agnes, St Aidan – St Aidan – there seem to be at least two St Aidan's. Which one is mine?'

'Let me look,' said David, suddenly seeming quite authoritative. 'St Aidan's, Purgstall Heath?'

'That's the one,' Fanny cried excitedly.

'1894–5 by *O. FISH*. Red Brick E. English, Pointed. *Screen and Altar Rails* also by Fish. (Fish & Co.) *Font* by *Bidlake* (1899?).'

'That doesn't tell us much,' said Charles.

'I'll look up Fish in the index,' said David.

'Poor man, being called Fish,' said Fanny. 'Wouldn't it make you desperate having one of those awful surnames like Cock or Bottoms?'

'See under Chamberlain,' said David to himself.

'Who was Chamberlain?'

'Birmingham architect. Chamberlain and Martin – here we are. They had a firm. Nothing very remarkable.'

'Any relation of the Prime Minister?'

'I don't know. Oh yes, look at all the things they did – public libraries, the Pumping Station of the Birmingham Waterworks at Longbridge . . .' he laughed contemptuously.

'What's funny?' snapped Fanny.

'I just think it's odd that there are some people who actually take all this kind of crap seriously.'

'God,' she said blushing furiously, 'you really are a nasty little prick.'

'Sorry. I didn't mean to tread on any corns.'

'What about O. Fish?' Charles asked.

'He appears under Chamberlain and Martin. Must have been a partner, I suppose. Here we are. Gates and Railings outside St Mary Magdalen's, Selly Oak: altar rails for St Anastasia's, Shirley.' Fanny wanted to beat David over his elfin little head for not taking it more seriously. 'Must have been a metal man. One of these is Fish and Co. I wonder if it is the same bloke?'

'How could one find out?'

'I could find out for you,' said David.

'I thought you said my *beautiful* church is crap.'

'I did. That's no reason why one should not be interested in it. I'm an architectural historian, not an aesthete.'

'I *hate* you!' Fanny screamed, a real Delilah by Saint-Saëns. 'You are so *flipping* pompous.'

'Don't mind Fanny,' said Charles.

'I could find out if you wanted,' drawled David in his reasonable tone of voice, like a British diplomat keeping his cool while the Russians all banged their shoes on the table. 'I have an architectural library, it's my job.'

'Certainly,' said Fanny sighing, 'that would be very kind. Come back here for supper and tell me what you have found out. Now, Charles, I hope you aren't very busy today, because I want you and Tracy to meet Nana at Paddington in – goodness, an hour –because I have been seized by an irresistible longing to see my *beloved* St Aidan's.'

'What – today?'

'Now, this second,' she said, still humming the chorus of the Hebrew slaves, and picking up a Corgi. 'Flora, I am taking you to see my *beautiful* church. Yes, I am. Yes, I am. Yes, I am. *Trac-eeee!*'

Tracy appeared, in tight denim dungarees and knee-length cowboy boots. She made a marked contrast to her sister's piled-up hair and consciously old-fashioned padded shoulders, tightly waisted coat and full skirt.

'I was only in the next room,' Tracy replied. 'No need to shout. Don't forget Nana is coming today, will you?'

'Tracy, can you look after her for the day – I've got to go to Birmingham – you and Charles?'

'I can fetch her from Paddington,' said Charles, 'but I've got to go to work today.'

'She doesn't need looking after,' Tracy said, 'but I can easily spend the day with her, sure.' Her Welsh lilting accent was heavily tinged with approximations to American speech, based on the pronunciation of mid-Atlantic pop stars.

David looked a little baffled. He blinked egotistically, but Charles

52

seemed already drawn into debates about arrangements. Only (he looked at his watch) nine hours before, they had been strangers. Then had followed their encounter, their drive back to Tregunter Road, their delightful night of passion. Already they were treating him as if he were enough part of the furniture to be ignored.

Charles said, 'See you again this evening,' as he planted a big kiss on David's mole-like short hair. But he was soon gone with Tracy. David, hurrying towards The Boltons a few moments later, found himself in tears.

VI

After Reading it was always hard to settle. The landscape was almost wholly dotted with ugly houses; people were rushing past to go to the lavatory one last time (what weak bladders people had; she really did not need to go more than once in a journey). But she could not resist reading the final entry in the notebook in front of her. It was not written on the pages of the book, rather on loose leaves – writing-paper headed HOTEL ANGLETERRE, Bruges, September 10th. This must have been 1896, she surmised from the other, internal evidence of the book:

Every Gothic architect, even a Gothic architect manqué, wants to see Bruges. I felt such intense anger with Frances for her sudden reversal of feeling. her craven kow-towing to all the petty conventions which I had taken her to despise, her fear of reputation, scandal and disgrace, that I longed to be far away from her, and left for London that night. I slept at an hotel in Bloomsbury (a modest enough place, but I was shocked by having to spend as much as seven and sixpence for my room, with a paltry little breakfast of cold meat, devilled kidneys and eggs, weak coffee and dry toast) and I travelled on to Bruges the next day. I have been here three weeks now. Of course, it has been impossible to leave Frances behind in any but a physical sense. Every day I have taken my sketch book out and, with eye and brush and pencil, feasted on every arch and spandrel, every monument and image, every reliquary, every embossed column, every screen of wood or stone, every soaring tower and ingenious arch in this most captivating town. Yet while eye and finger have traced the delicacy of medieval stone-work and metalwork, my heart has been tugged back to her. It did not take long for my anger against her to simmer down, and it occurred to me first as a speculative notion, soon as a certainty, that her rebuff had merely been intended to try me. How often we had by now both told each other that we would never, whatever happened, forsake the vision of joy and love which had been opened to us! And yet, as soon as she had said, with such terrible calmness, that it had come to disgust her to be deceiving 'her husband' – what a chill that formal way of referring to ludicrous Edmund, whom I have known as a stuffed shirt and baboon for the last thirty years and more, struck

54

into my breast – no sooner had she said that her first loyalty was as a wife and that her transgression now filled her with remorse and disgust, than I allowed her her way and like a coward I left the house in silence. How much I risked, if our love were to become public, I do not think she had considered. An ecclesiastical architect, flagrantly committing adultery with his own dear brother's wife? Unthinkable! The Pharisees! I can imagine them, their reverend heads nodding in the chapters, committee-rooms and bishops' palaces where the architectural competitions are assessed and judged. 'Ah, a design by Mr. Fish. Very admirable.' 'Excuse me, my Lord,' and Mr. Dean whispers a dark little secret into the bishop's ear. Ah, yes, poor Mr. Fish. Not quite the man we want to be designing the house of Almighty God! O whited sepulchres! Yet, even while I was prepared to risk the shame, the disgrace, even the destruction of my career itself, for the sake of having Frances, yet she, it appeared, was willing to risk nothing, for fear of upsetting her polite neighbours in Edgbaston. Or so, at first, it seemed. Later it dawned on me as I have said, with certainty, that she was merely testing me: that the natural and manly thing to do when she expressed these fears would have been to insist on our eloping together at once. Instead, like a schoolboy in a fit of pique, I left the house without a word and set off on an architectural jaunt, trying to lose myself in my medieval dream world of gargoyles and stone tracery. Needless to say, I hated myself for this and wrote to her telling her my address, and begging her to forgive me, to write, even, if it is yet possible to reverse our fate, to come out to Belgium and join me. But I have had no reply, and pace the streets with an exquisite melancholy which rather suits the faintly misty autumn weather and the ancient delicacy of the buildings. How fine it all is! Les Halles, with its belfry infinitely finer than any of the imitations I have seen, such as Waterhouse's recent Town Hall at Manchester (fine though that is: would that Birmingham had one which could rival it) ... and the churches! So many intensely varied shades, from brightest candle flame to deepest shadow; candle flame reflected on brass sanctuary lamps. N B for future use: one of the loveliest sights in the world ...

Nov. 13th. Weather quite warm enough to sit out and sketch and cough quite gone. I sat sketching one afternoon on the Quai du Rosaire, struck by the way in which even the row of trees, half bare of their golden leaves, appeared to be aping the Gothic mode and forming a great aisle of column arches. My longing for F., always intense, took a particularly physical form this afternoon. The memory of scenes of the deepest tenderness and intimacy kept returning to me as I worked hard with my sharpened pencil and my India rubber. There was a frankness and a delight in her response to my approaches (until that last fatal day of our estrangement) which was quite new to me in a woman. It must have been innate for I wholly and unshakably believe her account of her life with Edmund as one of innocence until the evening I got the commission for St. Aidan's. (Blessed church! It should be dedicated to some pagan deity who delighted in the flesh rather than to the crabbed old medieval figure of St. Aidan!) Can future generations of worshippers at that shrine ever know the delights experienced by its architect on the night, as it were, of its begetting! The memory of that night flooded back to me this afternoon and I felt impassioned to remember the very sounds, not words, even, which she made while she was in my arms. Her phrases, 'It is so so different. Is it because I'm in love, Oswald?' These questions came back and back into my mind creating a torment of regret and desire. 'Not yet, not yet.' And, as I concentrated on the distant grey of spindly roof-tops across the water, beyond them 'Le Beffroi' chiming out the hour, 'Now. Come, come inside me *now*!'

'*Viens, viens, maintenant!*'

The voice came from the *quai* and not from my own tormented memory; from a coal-black governess or nurse-maid, dressed almost like a nun with a white lace cap, covered with a mantilla, who called out to her charges, some young imps of seven or eight years old. Until that moment I had not thought of gratifying my desire for F. by finding some surrogate. My mood was too elevated to be appeased by a visit to the stews, too anguished to be satisfied by the notion of a new love blotting out the old. Nevertheless, when Madeleine came into view for the first time, calling out to those children, I had an immediate certainty, not only that I desired her (what man would not have done – her very lips would have corrupted a hermit) but that she would, very easily, be mine.

As she approached, I laid down my pencil and raised my hat. She smiled back at me, showing a mouthful of magnificent pearly teeth and closing her lips again in a way which emphasised their moist, tactile, I can only say *kissable* qualities. Her enormous glossy black eyes stared out of a chocolate-brown face which was long and serious and (again the thought occurred to me) nun-like. '*Ils sont toujours méchants, ces petits singes,*' she said, indicating with leisurely dignity the two little Belgians in tweed knickerbockers who, their wooden hoops abandoned, were having a mock swordfight with their sticks.

I asked her if she lived in Bruges and she smiled once more, whether at my question or at my accent, I could not be sure, and replied that she had only lately arrived and that she was waiting in a certain hotel (which she named) until the family who owned the children, diplomats if I understood *her* accent aright, had come from Paris. When she named her hotel and it turned out to be the hotel where I am myself accommodated, it caused me no surprise because, as I have already related, I had decided that fate had meant us for one another – not perhaps, forever, but as strangers and sojourners in a strange land to console one another. When she had collected her charges and followed them off down the Quai, they beating their hoops again with their sticks, she swinging her parasol gently on her arm, I felt inflamed with desire for her and determined to have her before nightfall. I interpreted her large knowing glances as an invitation, her smile, as I had said that I hoped we w^d see more of each other, a confirmation that she too wanted me.

I bided my time, ate in a restaurant, an early dinner, and returned to the hotel at about eight o'clock that evening to find that she had put her boys to bed, eaten a light supper herself, and was sitting down in the little hotel lounge with some embroidery. We were alone in the room and as I pretended to concentrate on the volume I had brought with me – Mr. Ruskin's last – I asked myself whether the attraction of Madeleine lay in the novelty of her appearance, for I have never before been at close quarters with a negress and admired the many little ways in which her features differed from the European. The greater fleshiness of the nose and lips, the larger pores so that one could almost see the glistening skin breathing. Above all the texture of her hair, now bare and unfettered with the nonsense of lace which had encumbered it on her afternoon walk. Such hair – so thick, so black, so wiry that I might almost at that moment have reached out to touch it and run my fingers through it again and again, itself almost an adequate substitute for any grosser intimacies. How did she come to be there – this lovely phantom, this character who could have walked out of one of Hakluyt's voyages or Raleigh's *History of the World?* Birmingham can never have seen a negress – since the days when gd. Sam Johnson's servant took his wife there on the way to Lichfield – & is not likely to see one in the future; who, born in the world that had brought forth this savage natural beauty, speaking of bright sunshine, exotic nature, warmth, luxury, wd. choose to incarcerate themselves in the pernickety narrow confines of modern B'ham? But I digress. I asked her how she, a woman evidently not of Flemish or French extraction, came to be in Bruges and she told me again that she was there as governess to a diplomatic family recently returned from Africa, the Belgian colonies, and that she wd herself be returning to the banks of the Congo before Xmas. Her father, she told me, had had her educated by the missionaries and was himself a teacher in a missionary school. Mention of the missionaries caused my heart to sink not a little since it seemed certain that the missionary's notion of woman's behaviour would not accord with the manner in which I intended to conduct myself for the rest of the evening. She asked me if I were an artist and, to avoid further complications, I said that I was, and that I would dearly love the opportunity of sketching her, so unusual was it to have met a blackamoor at such close quarters. She said that she had no objection to being sketched and asked me where my materials were. When I said they were in 'my apartments', the plural, as I thought, adding respectability to my meagre bedroom, she said it wd.

perhaps be easier for me to sketch her undisturbed if we withdrew there: which indeed we did. I sketched her, while she embroidered, for about half an hour, before suggesting, as casually as I was able, that I would be honoured if she would allow me to sketch her unveiled and nude. She smiled an impenetrable smile, and I thought at first that she had not understood my request. But she stood up and carefully began to unbutton her dress, laying her clothes carefully on the suitcase as she removed each garment. When she had got down to the stage of wearing only her stockings, her suspenders and her bust bodice she asked me how she should pose and I said, firmly, *'Absolument nue, s'il vous plaît.'* How far the pretence that we were still indulging in an artistic evening was one which she wished to perpetuate, I do not know, but she allowed me to approach her, and to begin untying the ribbons which held her bodice in check. When it fell to the floor, her huge breasts were firmer and rounder and more pointed than any that I had ever seen and I could not resist holding them in my hands, smooth to the touch as vast balls of satin. She only began to say *méchant*, a word I sealed with a kiss.

Having conversation afterwards with Madeleine revealed that she did not wish to return to the Congo, and that she dreamed of marrying a European. She told me things about the treatment of women in Africa which I did not understand but which made her cry. She spoke of the cruelty of the Belgians and the power of the witch doctor – if— meant witch doctor. But we passed nevertheless an agreeable evening and it did not occur to me that she was seriously imagining that I was the man who could rescue her from her predicament.

When she had left me and I had fallen into the sort of half slumber which is most conducive to contemplation, I fell once more to thinking of Frances. Madeleine had been unable to gratify my longing for my loved one and I felt at the same time self-disgust for exploiting her weakness and at the same time a cool fascination with her appearance – the way, for instance, in which her hair appeared not to be growing but to be stuck on to her – like black gluey fluff: the way her fingers were longer, the joints bigger than on any European hand – all these things fascinated me. The next day I did not see her in the morning, and I devoted the daylight hours as usual to architectural drawing, taking advantage of the drizzle which drove me indoors to sketch the infinitely sad figures of Charles le Téméraire and Marie de Bourgogne, lying in the cold shadows of the same chapel in Nôtre Dame.

On my return to the hotel after dining, there were 2 letters awaiting me. The one envelope bearing simply my name, was evidently from Madeleine. Being unable at once to summon up the moral courage to open the second missive I read Madeleine's first – it read simply, *'Si vous avez besoin je viens à votre chambre à 9 hres.'* The second envelope was, of course, from Frances. It began abruptly. 'All that I feared has happened. But now perhaps was meant to be – poor Edmund says that for the last sixty years the name of Fish has been associated with all that is noblest and finest about Birmingham. And it is now to be disgraced. But I *do* love you, and I am sorry we parted in that way. I am making my way to Bruges and should arrive not long after you receive this letter.'

Jessica Owen blinked. Could this man be her own father? Emotions crowded in upon her: amusement, shock, disgust, incredulity. What could possibly have happened? Frances had evidently refused to run away with Oswald to London, changed her mind, but he, unable to contain his lust till her arrival in Bruges, had coupled himself with a darkie. How beautiful Madeleine sounded. Jessica wondered what had become of her; surely she would not have been compelled to return to Africa? Perhaps she ran away to America, though that was scarcely better in the last century.

She was so absorbed that she did not notice that she was at Paddington, sitting alone in the compartment. There was a knocking on the window. 'Nana! Nana!' Jessica looked up. Tracy was there. Where was Fanny? She had been so much looking forward to seeing Fanny. And with Tracy, oh dear, that arrogant barrister that she tried so hard to like and simply could not – his large, round black face grinning condescendingly. If only he called her Mrs Williams she felt that it would have been tolerable. It was all right for Tracy and Fanny to call her Nana, she was after all their grandmother. Gathering up her two Tesco bags, her mind halfway between Paddington Station in 1979 and a hotel bedroom in Bruges in the late 1890s, Nana Owen emerged from the train with a spindly elegance. Had she got everything? Spectacles? A change of knickers? Minty cigarettes? Her OAP rail-card? Above all, the diaries?

'Hello, Nana,' said the black man in a fruity, Etonian voice. 'Fanny's got to go to Birmingham for the day, she'll be back this evening. We are deputed to look after you.'

'Tracy, my pet,' said Jessica Owen, and kissed her younger granddaughter.

VII

Jen, barefooted, in the kitchen of her house in Birmingham, had just finished making the early morning tea.

Upstairs, Fred snored his way through 'Thought for the Day'. Along the landing from his bedroom was a door bearing the notice: PRIVATE. NO ADMITTANCE UPON PAIN OF DEATH.

Behind this door lay the Joblings' elder child, Harriet, deeply absorbed in her brother's comic. As she read, her mind was half engaged while its other half contemplated the coming day. A school day, thank the Lord, a day devoted to Debbie Gladstone. At the thought of Debbie, Harriet felt a little twang of happy relief inside her chest, as though someone really had plucked a heart-string. She had heard a lot about heart-strings: she thought of hers locked up, imprisoned, like an old piano, gathering cobwebs in an attic. Only the Gladstones could produce music from it – the Gladstones and, on the days she was allowed to go round, her great-grandmother.

With the Gladstones, particularly with Debbie, Harriet felt free. They were neither interfering like her mother, nor irritating, like Sam; nor an embarrassing mixture of the two, like Fred. Debbie's jokes were actually funny: so funny that you laughed till it hurt. And you didn't get bored so easily at the Gladstones' house. Debbie was allowed to stay up and watch David Attenborough. Debbie had a room of her own, and a microscope, and riding lessons every Saturday morning. Her mother was not embarrassing, and prepared food you really wanted to eat, and you hardly ever saw Mr Gladstone. He certainly did not keep putting his head round the bedroom door, as Fred did, saying things like, 'You OK, you two girls?' with a smile on his face which seemed annoying somehow: as though he was *asking* to be liked. And the other thing was that Debbie could call Mr Gladstone 'Dad' instead of 'Jeff'. Debbie hated calling her father 'Fred' – she was ashamed of doing so and always referred to him when at school, as 'my dad'. She envied Debbie so

much that sometimes she even slipped into called Mr Gladstone *Dad*.
No one seemed to mind this.

She turned the pages of her comic – rather of her brother's comic
– and saw with half an eye that he was awake now. Harriet knew
perfectly well that he did not want to read it at that hour of the day:
it was just dog-in-the-manger. The little boy ran over and roughly
grabbed the comic from her hands before she had even finished
'Desperate Dan'. As he did so, he crushed her knee and slightly
bruised her chest. She struck out at him automatically and said, 'Get
off, can't you!'

'Well it's my *Dandy*!'

'I never said it wasn't.'

And somehow this prompted her (it was an impulsive gesture, she
did not think about it) to grab the comic back and wave it in the
air above his head. The little boy did not reach up for it, as she
expected. Instead, he slipped his hand under her blanket and
grabbed the Family Tree: a large piece of greaseproof paper, which
for the last three or four weeks, Harriet had not allowed out of her
sight.

'Sam, give that back this *instant*!'

'Well you took my comic.'

'*Give-it-back* –' and she tried to control herself, but still, at nearly
nine, she had this tiresome and uncontrollable habit and she felt her
face growing hotter and the tears gushing to her eyes. Furious at
herself, she lashed out at Sam and grabbed the greaseproof, tearing
one corner as she did so.

'Look what you've made me do!' she exploded; the salt water was
now pouring down her cheeks and in at the corner of her mouth,
so that she felt all the shameful taste of it, felt her chest heaving like
a cry-baby. And Sam cried too, a high wail, and ran down the
landing shouting, 'Mum, mum, mum!'

Harriet's tears subsided. She could hear her mother carrying the
teatray up the stairs – she could hear the rattling spoons and cups
and saucers. 'Ping-Pong, you silly cat, get out of my way – you'll
trip me up.' And while her mother said this Sam was repeating
'Harriet hit me,' in a sort of rhythmic chant which had become
ARIER ITMER, ARIER ITMER. Although she had only just stopped
crying herself, Harriet despised the jerkiness of his voice, convulsed
with sobs.

'Oh, Sam, what's the *matter?*' That tone of concern and puzzled amusement. Harriet had long ago noted that her mother only understood about half of what Sam said. 'Wait till Mum has put down the tray or I shall spill hot tea all over poor old Ping-Pong.'

'ARIER ITMER,' he jerkily repeated.

'What, darling?'

'Sneak,' Harriet said aloud to herself. A useful word. Debbie Gladstone used it a lot.

'Harriet what, darling?'

'ARIER ITMER.'

'I can't understand you, pet.'

Harriet had found this so exasperating that she called out, 'I hit him.'

No one heard. She heard Mum say, 'Oh *bother.*' Then the crash of crockery falling from the tray. It was the way Mum carried trays, always at an angle. Separately, in their different bedrooms, Harriet and Fred waited for the next phrase (for this dropping of something from the tray happened at least once a week): 'I knew that was going to happen.'

Harriet said quietly to herself, 'If she knew it was going to happen, why couldn't she stop it?' Fred merely covered his face with a pillow while the voice on the landing continued, 'Milk all over the carpet – never mind. I'll put the tray down and you come and tell me what happened. Mmm?'

Pleased by the noise and mess caused by the milk jug slithering off the tray (the accident *looked* and was less disastrous than it *sounded*) Sam had stopped crying by now and allowed himself to be led into the bedroom.

'Fred's still asleep so don't disturb him.'

'I think Fred's only pretending to be asleep.'

'Well, don't disturb him all the same.'

'Anyway Harriet hit me.'

And the (by now) rather theatrical whimpering and whining began again.

'I expect you did something to annoy her.'

'I didn't. She just *hit* me.'

Sneak, sneak, sneak, thought Harriet.

Fred got out of bed and staggered off to the lav., trying not to catch Jen's eye – or rather, her ears. At breakfast, after breakfast, he might be strong enough for them, but not yet. On the landing, still with his eyes half shut, his spectacles not yet on, he stubbed his toe on the hot tea-pot.

'I should have warned you,' hooted Jen good-humouredly from the bedroom, secretly pleased that he had stubbed his toe and hoping it hurt like billy-oh – 'Oh, and Fred!'

'What is it,' he hissed through clenched teeth. Of all the bloody silly places to leave a tea-pot.

'Now you're up, be a duck and bring up some more milk from the kitchen.'

Harriet, listening to all this with quiet amusement, could not hear whether Fred said anything in reply. He seemed to be muttering something in a low agony. To Harriet, it was a mystery why grown-ups wanted tea in the morning.

Carefully, and hastily, she dressed herself, leaving as much time as possible for the Family Tree before leaving for school. Although other sounds came from outside the bedroom door – someone with a mop and dustpan and a brush, cleaning up the wreckage of the milk jug; Sam and Fred playing a shrieky game, pretending Fred's knees were mountains; some music on the radio – Harriet took no notice.

She had heard the so-called 'facts of life', but although what her mother had told her coincided, roughly, with the information which had been imparted, helpless with sniggering mirth, by Debbie Gladstone, it was still hard to believe. Perhaps Debbie Gladstone's mother and her mother had got together and decided to palm them off with this fairy story – as fairy story it must be, for the simple fact was that it did not work. She had tried it: one evening, when the grown-ups were out and the babysitter was absorbed in the television, she had got Sam to stick his 'willie' (Debbie's word – Harriet preferred the more measured formality of *'penis'*) up her bottom. Of course, as anyone could have told them, it would not go. Harriet had never expected that it would: just as well, for the last thing she wanted was one of Sam's babies. It would only ever remain a matter of academic interest because, ever since being told (again by Debbie) why Mary was called the Virgin Mary, she had decided she wanted to be a Virgin too, though not one who had the bad luck to have a baby even *without* someone sticking penises up her bottom.

If the *means* of procreation failed to hold the attention, however

63

the consequences of it gripped Harriet with an obsession, an obsession which pointed its genealogical twigs all over the piece of
greaseproof paper (normally kept well tucked into her sock). She
stared at it in fascination. There was herself and Sam: above that,
Fred equals Mum. And beside Mum her brother (Uncle David whom
they hardly ever saw) and then a line joining them up to Grandpa
Saunders equals Granny Saunders who was called Lucy Jones until
she married Grandpa and became Lucy Saunders.

The Saunders side of the family was quite plain sailing: Harriet
had managed to fill in quite a lot of cousins – Uncle David's children
for instance – and there was a useful family Bible which Grandpa
Saunders had left them when he died. It had ever so many dates of
births and deaths going back about a hundred and fifty years.

Fred's forebears were another matter and if it were not for Great
Grandma Jobling, Harriet did not know where she would be. Even
so, there were many gaps. She had Alastair Jobling (this was Fred's
real name, though everyone called him Fred) and Mary, his sister,
who lived in London. And then above that Grandfather Jobling
equals Granny Jobling, who was dead, so she had a black † by her
name. And beside that, great-uncle Harold, Grandfather's brother
(1915–1976) and great-aunt Joan (1918–   ) who had married
and gone to Canada. They were Grandpa's brother and sister.
Grandpa was a widower: that meant your wife was dead. It must
feel odd when your wife dies and your mother still lives on. Harriet
worked out that if *her* mother lived to be as old as Great-Grandma
Jobling she herself would be seventy-three. Unimaginable. Still, she
not only liked her great-grandmother – whom she called Grandma
as opposed to Grannie (who was dead) she was proud of having such
a thing. Some children at school hardly knew their grandparents,
let alone their greats. Still, in spite of having her about and loving
her. Grandma was not as useful with the Family Tree as Harriet
would have liked. She was very vague about dates. She was born
in 1889, she knew that much, but although both her parents died
when she was very young she could not remember the dates. She
had married Great-Grandpa in 1908, when she was 19. Until that
she was brought up by *her* grandparents, in this very same house
in Augustus Road. It was odd, because of family Bibles and things
perhaps, that Grandma could remember her grandparents' dates
and their wedding day and everything. but not that of her parents.

As it was, the Tree on the Jobling side looked as shown on the next page.

It had not been easy getting all this information out of Grandma. She had been funny about giving away her maiden name. When Harriet had heard it, she had spluttered with mirth. Fish! And Grandma had said, 'There was a time when you wouldn't have laughed at the name of Fish, my girl. The Fishes were powers in the land here once upon a time.'

'It's just funny to think of you as Miss Fish, Grandma.'

Grandma had given her such a funny smile when she said this.

It was fascinating to think that Grandma had been born in this house where they now all lay. That was in the days when Great-Great-Grandfather Thomas Fish (died 1919) was alive if not Great-Great-Great-Grandfather Fish (died? born? the whole thing???).

Folding the greaseproof paper carefully and returning it to her sock, Harriet looked at her watch and realized it was time she had eaten breakfast. She hated the unnecessary rush in the mornings, caused by her parents' habit of staying in bed until the last possible moment in order to drink tea.

'Harriet, you really mustn't hit Sam,' said Jen, putting her dark fringe round the door. She had combed her hair back behind her ears. Harriet noticed that her mother's ears stood out like handles. If she had been a doll you would have picked her up by those ears. But she was saying, 'He's younger than you are and you could easily hurt him. Without meaning to, I know,' she added.

Harriet *did* mean to hurt Sam; very much. Not all the time because sometimes it was very nice, when Debbie was not available, or there was no possibility of getting further with the family tree, to have someone to play with. But when he grabbed or shouted, or curried favour with his parents (favour Harriet felt, which had never been so spontaneously lavished on herself) then she wanted to hurt him all right. And most of all she wanted to hurt him when Mum spoke up on his behalf and made her feel half angry, half ashamed, and at the same time victimized, as though the whole family were ganging up against her, as though everything was her fault. And so, for the second time that day, she had that thick salty taste in her mouth and felt her chest heaving. She drew back the corners of her mouth and tried to smile herself out of it. 'Save me washing my face,' she tried to joke. But Jen was sitting on the edge

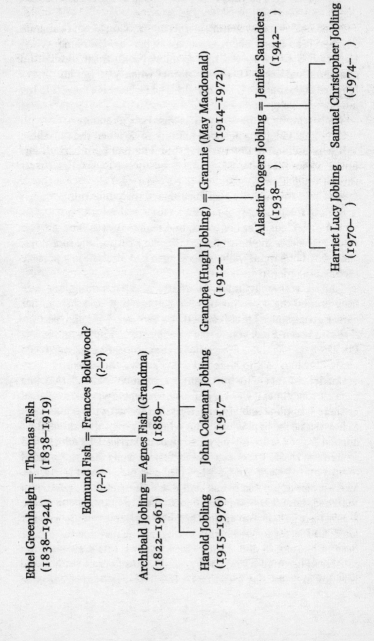

Ethel Greenhalgh = Thomas Fish
(1838–1924)   (1838–1919)

Edmund Fish = Frances Boldwood?
(?–?)   (?–?)

Archibald Jobling = Agnes Fish (Grandma)
(1822–1961)   (1889–)

Harold Jobling
(1915–1976)

John Coleman Jobling
(1917–)

Grandpa (Hugh Jobling) = Grannie (May Macdonald)
(1912–)   (1914–1972)

Alastair Rogers Jobling = Jenifer Saunders
(1938–)   (1942–)

Harriet Lucy Jobling
(1970–)

Samuel Christopher Jobling
(1974–)

of the bed and hugging her, and it *was* good, once in a while, to feel those buttons and that pendant thing she wore, and beneath, the comfortingly large breast, pressed against her face.

His toe still tingling with the scalding tea, Fred lay in a bath of tepid water at the end of the corridor and continued his murderous ruminations.

On reflection, it might be cleaner, kinder, less dangerous to others, if he could somehow fix up an electric charge of deadly intensity on one of the gadgets in the kitchen. It would have to be something the children never touched. The handle of that blender thing, whose banshee shriek filled the house whenever Jen played with it. Why should making soup involve making noise? It should be a nice, quiet activity: a little gentle bubbling, the faint scrape of a wooden spatula against a copper-bottomed saucepan, no more: not all this whirring and banging and electronic screaming. Electrocution by blender. She deserved that.

He twiddled the hot tap with his toe and wondered why the water was so luke-warm. Nothing came out of the tap. He leaned forward and twiddled it with his hand, uncertain, since nothing was happening, which way was OFF and which was ON. Experimenting with the cold tap refreshed his memory, but that made the bath even colder. Evidently the hot water tank had emptied itself, or else one of the children had left a tap running somewhere else in the house.

Despondency threatened. A hot bath had become a necessary part of Fred's routine. 'Fred's waking up in his bath – he'd never wake up without it,' Jen would say if they had friends who stayed the night. It was partly true. What was much more important was that a great deal of the bad temper which he so mysteriously and uncontrollably felt at the hour of waking, seemed to be purged by the scalding water and steam. Even now, as he lay, wishing the water was hotter, he did not know how seriously he meant the little murder joke. Jen, he would tell himself at some more rational hour of the day, was not such a bad old girl. He could have done worse. It was inevitable that some of the glamour should have faded after fourteen years or whatever it was.

On a day when the water was hot this thought would have occurred to him with more force. As it was, he lay in a state of cold and disgruntlement. He had, moreover, hoped, before the bath was finished, to have had some brainwave about how to demolish what he had come to think of as That Bloody Warehouse. The City Council had consulted *him*; put *him* in charge; the Planning Committee and the Housing Committee – everyone, or so it felt to Fred – had relied on him to manage the legal go-ahead for the clearance of the Purgstall site. He had let matters slide, not because it seemed a complicated issue but because it seemed so very easy. It had simply never crossed his mind that there would be any difficulties, and he had therefore allowed the matter to stay in his in-tray while he solved what seemed to be much knottier problems: a complaint from the Residents Association in Harborne about some bollards off Lordswood Road; an alleged breach of contract with one of the firms who regularly serviced the City buses; a wrangle about a tenancy agreement with a shopkeeper in Selly Oak. Then, when the Committee had asked him what to do, now that the Purgstall scheme was being held up by the owner of the warehouse, he had felt rather stumped. He had assumed the Bloody Warehouse was owned by the Church Commissioners. Had it been, everything would have been simplicity itself, because the Church Commissioners actually stipulated that if, after a year of standing empty no use could be found for a redundant church, it *had* to be demolished: even if it were Westminster Abbey or St Paul's Cathedral. A savage view, but one which made the lawyers' job a lot easier. When it turned out that the Purgstall warehouse was in fact privately owned he had simply advised the Planning Committee to slap a compulsory purchase order on the place. He had thought no more about it. Three or four other jobs, equally important, had occupied him during that period, and he had delayed. It was only after their next meeting, when the Planning Committee asked him to check the legality of demolishing the warehouse, that he had received a letter from Fanny Williams's solicitor, pointing out that it was a Listed Building.

This did not necessarily mean that it could not be demolished, but it looked as if it *did* mean that it could not be demolished without a fuss. Fanny Williams, as the Gladstones were ludicrously failing to recognize, was a publicist and, as far as Fred was concerned, that spelt trouble. The whole point of the Purgstall Area Development Scheme was that it should be popular. It was going to be a genuine improvement to a truly awful area. But it should also be a sign that the Council, and the Party, were concerned with the local community at (and the inverted commas were falling away from his use of the term) the grass-roots level. There was not much grass in Purgstall. In spite of its preponderant squalor, the 'ward' into which it fell was a marginal. Council Elections loomed on the horizon. As one irate member of the Planning Committee had said to Fred at a recent meeting, the last thing they wanted at this stage was any whiff of controversy – still less a quarrel with conservationists, who were notoriously fussy and tenacious. The idea that the City was not being sensitive to its architectural heritage was a damaging one: even if the building in question was an ugly little Victorian church, and the area in question was deeply in need of the amenities which the Council hoped to provide.

Why was this occupying so much of his thoughts? While the tedious details of the controversy raced and charged through his brain, he gave the hot tap one last try with his big toe and let out a howl of pain as cold water gushed out over his foot and shin, making the already lukewarm bath distinctly uncomfortable.

Cursing, he dried himself on a rather dirty bath towel and searched about in the drastically untidy airing cupboard for a clean pair of pants and a matching pair of socks. He felt cold and miserably angry by the time he had achieved this feat and went downstairs for breakfast.

In the kitchen the children had abandoned their fight and were sullenly slurping at muesli; but Jen already had her anorak on and was jangling the car keys.

'Do hurry up, darlings, we'll be *late*,' she insisted. Then she added, in no less condescending tones, to Fred. 'I hope you had enough hot water for your bath. The hand washing is simply piling up and I thought I'd put a few things in to soak during the day.'

'No,' he said quietly, 'there was no hot water.'

She did not appear to notice the challenge in his voice. She was flicking the lank hair back behind the tea-pot handle ears and ramming a woolly hat like a tea-cosy on top of it.

'I also had the greatest difficulty in finding a pair of socks,' he hissed through clenched teeth.

'And a tie by the look of it,' she said jauntily. He looked down and saw that he had forgotten to put one on. She, determined to ignore his gloomy bad temper, continued in airy tones: 'I made some coffee ages ago, and it is probably cold by now. And there's your egg and some toast. Sam, *do* hurry up with that muesli or we shall be late.'

'Not enough sugar,' Sam complained.

'Darling, it doesn't need sugar.'

'Sugar's bad for your teeth,' Harriet added. She was also ready, with her duffle coat and her satchel.

The morning routine was hellish. First, Sam had to be dropped at the Nutkin, their nearby private primary school. Then Harriet had to be driven over to EHS and then Jen had to drive to the comprehensive school in Smethwick where she taught. It only needed a mechanical fault in the mini – and they were frequent – for the whole scheme to fall into chaos. Fred had never got involved in these complicated travel arrangements. It was a source of irritation to Jen that he had never learnt to drive on the rather feeble grounds that he was too short-sighted.

'Perhaps you weren't listening,' he said. 'I said I had the greatest difficulty in finding a pair of socks.'

'I heard you,' Jen was shoving Sam's arms into his coat.

'It would help if you rolled them together in pairs rather than just throwing them into the airing cupboard.'

'Oh Fred, for God's sake, can't you see we're in a hurry?' When Jen was angry her face went quite scarlet and she trembled. 'Why should I care about your bloody socks?'

'That's typical,' he said, openly angry himself now, and enjoying the sense of release that it brought. 'You don't care. You are the most incompetent person I have ever met in my life.'

'Why can't you roll your own socks? Honestly, you expect me to do everything. You loll about in the bath while I cook your breakfast –'

'I wasn't lolling. The water was cold because you decided now was the moment to soak your filthy underwear.'

'It isn't underwear and it isn't filthy.'

'Hardly the point, is it? As for your doing everything, that's simply a joke.'

'It's true. This family would collapse if I didn't slave night and day to keep you clothed and fed and all you can do is bicker because the airing cupboard is a bit untidy.'

'A bit!'

'Oh, don't be such a baby.'

The children stared in bewilderment at their parents. Harriet wondered whether they might be about to come to blows. They were both red now, and shaking. Sweat had appeared on the top of Fred's bald patch.

'All our problems would be over if you dropped down dead,' he said carefully, and turning on his heel he left the kitchen in search of his brief case.

'Don't you want your egg?' Jen called after him. He didn't reply. She picked it up, holding the egg cup by its stem, and hurled it against the kitchen wall. The egg cup smashed, but the egg itself, being rather hard, bounced back and lay on the floor.

'Silly old thing,' she murmured in embarrassment. It was horrid having rows like this in front of the children. After a moment's pause, she bustled them out of the back door and was rather violently turning the ignition key of the mini. Still without a tie, and scarlet with fury, Fred strode past them. He did not look back once as he walked, very fast, down to the bus stop in Hagley Road.

'Have you taken your pill, dear?'

'What pill?'

'Your pink pill.'

'I didn't know I was supposed to take a pink pill.'

'You must have taken it. It was there on your plate before you came down.'

'Oh, was it? Have the children gone to school?'

Hugh Jobling sighed. His mother could be very wearing. It was hard to know whether she was genuinely forgetful or whether she simply played a game because she did not enjoy taking the pills. Dapper in his green cardigan, he went to the dining-room window.

'I can hear Jen struggling with the car now.'

Agnes Jobling laughed contemptuously. Hugh himself regarded Jen as 'hopeless' but he felt some reserve about entering into any mockery of his daughter-in-law. He had never liked the way his mother had mocked Lucy, *his* wife. She had been dead five years. His mother looked like living for ever. Already, the whole episode of his marriage, all thirty years of it, seemed to have evaporated. There had not been much doubt, when Lucy died, that he would return to live with his mother in Birmingham.

'They ought to get themselves a better car,' said his mother.

'Alastair can surely afford it.' (She never called her grandson 'Fred'.)

'All young families are finding things difficult,' said Hugh.

'And Jen is earning money schoolteaching instead of staying at home and looking after the house.' She smacked her chops as she said it. She looked like some healthy and very rare ornithological specimen; a cassowary perhaps, with a long, lean neck, and very bright, beady, almost black eyes. Her hair was scarcely changed since the days of her youth; a deep raven black, whether the result of artifice or of good luck Hugh had never managed to decide. His own hair had fallen out, most of it, in his fifties. Fred's looked like doing the same. Hugh kept what remained cut, almost shaven, very short.

'And they don't have the expense of a house,' continued his mother. 'Not that we grudge them the house. It is all much more sensible.'

Hugh, who had never had very strong feelings about his son, had been touched by his desire to come and live in Birmingham. The division of the enormous family home in Augustus Road seemed suitable to everyone. It meant that the place was occupied, and it was going to avoid unnecessary death duties. His mother still kept her dining-room and her upstairs drawing-room, furnished much as it had been before the First World War. In addition she had a bedroom and a spare bedroom. Hugh had his own bedroom, rather small, at the back of the house, a drawing-room of his own, and the use of the little parlour downstairs where, most evenings, he watched television with his mother.

'Little Harriet is a good girl,' he said tenderly, as he watched the mini back dangerously into the road. 'And young Sam will be all right when he settles down.'

'They spoil that boy,' said his mother.

'Perhaps they do. People have different ideas about children nowadays.'

'Not necessarily better ones. But yes, Harriet is a darling.'

'How is she getting on with the Family Tree?' Hugh's voice was not without a note of malice. In an entirely innocent way he liked 'needling' his mother, not because he felt any resentment towards her (he was a man of markedly subdued feelings) but merely to vary the tone of their interminable hours together. He himself had never taken an interest in genealogy and had always taken his family for granted. He was totally incurious about it. He knew that his mother's parents had died young. He knew that his father had inherited *her* father's metal works and for a short time it had been known as Jobling and Fish. It had become a munitions factory during the war. Hugh had never been interested in it. His mother, at that date, had said she wished he would take over the family firm; but she had not pressed him. The sale of the firm had scarcely been at a very profitable juncture, but the capital which came Hugh's way as a result of it had enabled him to prosper in the City. By the time he retired he had several directorships and he was still an underwriter at Lloyds, going up to town about once a month.

'It'll pass, children have crazes,' said his mother.

'Perhaps she'll unearth some skeletons in the family cupboard. Who knows?' He laughed good-humouredly and leant forward to fill his mother's coffee cup.

'Not if I have anything to do with it,' she said quite seriously.

Hugh opened his *Telegraph* and lit a cigarette. They settled into the comfortable silence in which they spent most of their days. He was startled when his mother suddenly said: 'Did you know that my father committed suicide?'

Putting down the paper, he blinked. It was oddly upsetting. He had never known his grandfather, who had died years before he was born. But there was something chilling about the discovery that the family legend was not quite as he had imagined. He wanted to ask *why* but he said: 'How?'

'I never knew about it as a child. My grandfather told me there had been an accident. It was my mother who told me.'

'Your *mother*?' Again, simply because this was different from the received family legend, it was disturbing. Hugh had always understood that both his mother's parents had died when she was a young child.

'I never really knew my mother. I met her once or twice in London after I got married. She was never mentioned in this house. I don't know why I think of it now, only little Harriet has been asking about it so much.'

'I always thought your mother died when you were a child.'

'As far as Grandpapa was concerned, she died when she left Birmingham. She was never very happy, poor woman. She died of flu in the year the war ended.'

73

'The War?'

'1919.'

Momentarily, Hugh had forgotten his mother's habit of referring to the First World War in that way.

'It was a few months before my grandfather died. He had a stroke, you know.'

'Yes, yes, I know, you've often told me.'

'You met her once, you know.'

'I met your mother?'

'Yes. It was about a year before she died. You must have been about six. Your father took us all up to London for a week one summer. The war was still on. It must have been 1916 or 1917.'

'I don't remember that.'

'You must remember. It was your first visit to London.'

'I remember *that*.'

Smiling, he was a boy again. He remembered his disappointment that Piccadilly Circus was not a circus: no clowns or elephants. He remembered the thrill of going to a matinee at the old Coliseum; a visit to the Tower; the boat-trip down the Thames to Greenwich.

'Your father and I thought it was better for you not to *know* it was your grandmother. You might have *said* something when you got home and it would only have upset your grandpapa. Do you remember visiting a lady for tea in a very dingy house on Haverstock Hill?'

He stared blankly and smoked hard on his cigarette. He strained to remember but his mind could produce no recollection of it whatsoever.

'I would like my second cup of coffee, please.'

'I've just poured it for you.'

'Have you put sugar in it?'

'Yes.'

The old lady put two heaped spoonfuls of sugar in her cup.

'You never make it sweet enough,' she said. 'I like my coffee very sweet.'

As she quaveringly brought the huge green and gold Worcester breakfast cup to her lips she appeared to be lost in concentration on the sweetness of her drink and to have forgotten the thread of their conversation altogether. But then she said, 'it somehow doesn't seem very suitable that little Harriet should know about it all.'

'I don't remember meeting my grandmother.'

'Well you did. Such a dingy little house. And she looked so worn and unhappy, poor woman, even though she can't have been sixty.'

There was a long pause. Then Hugh said, in a way which, he was aware, was painfully awkward and formal. 'Your parents were separated, then?'

'My mother eloped. There!' It seemed as if that was the end of the matter; there was such finality in her tones. Quaveringly, she brought the breakfast-cup to her lips once again.

'Who with?'

'She eloped with my father's brother. On the day after she left, my father went down to Snow Hill Station and threw himself under a train.'

VIII

In his office in the Victoria and Albert Museum David Matheson was assembling information about Oswald Fish. This alone kept him sane, he felt, after the bizarre escapades of the night before.

Although, as he had explained to Fanny, he was an eighteenth-century man, with special interest in Vanbrugh, David was good enough at his job to have recognized (just) the name of Fish when it cropped up at Fanny's breakfast table. He had seized on it, the one solid fact in a world of apparent fantasy, and been clinging to it ever since. Fish and Co., well-known Victorian Ironworks, Birmingham. Oswald Fish also minor architect, arts and craftsman. Friend of Sedding, Henry Wilson &c.

This thought had led him to look up Holy Trinity, Sloane Street, in Pevsner. Fish had not had a hand in the design of the church; as it turned out, however, he had designed the handsome red and black wrought-iron gates and railings outside. David felt pleased at the correctness of his instinct.

He had not been doing 'research' on Oswald Fish all morning, so much as fitting him into already familiar patterns in his mind. Two discoveries (like the chance of finding that Fish had designed the Sloane Street railing) had thrown light on the man's career. One had come about from flicking through back-numbers of the *Architectural Review*. He had not hoped for an article on Fish himself, but he had wanted to refresh his memory about who the major master-architects might have been who might have employed Fish. Martin & Chamberlain he knew about, but Chamberlain had died in 1883. There was Bodley, Bidlake ... and then suddenly, not in an article, but in the back pages of an issue of the *Architectural Review*, 1895, he had seen the advertisement. THOMAS FISH & SON. The names had more or less shouted for attention, *Ornamental Ironwork* in large letters; and a wide range of wares were advertised: *conservatoires, lamp pillars band stands, tomb rails, crestings, spandrels, brackets,* columns, gates, arcades, altar rails, ornamental fronts, roofing gutters: balusters, gratings, urinals, ash-bins, R.W. pipes, garden seats, cattle troughs, school fittings. The list seemed interminable. The showrooms were at 79 Porchester Street, Birmingham. This, surely, was their man: Oswald was presumably the Son of 'T. Fish & Son', a boy born into a manufacturing family who turned his hand to architecture and design.

Design, too, of an altogether more intimate, domestic kind, was revealed by happening to look up Fish, O. in various catalogues in the department of metalwork. A new Fish seemed to be revealed here. Obviously the same man as the architect – same dates, &c. But his centre of operations had moved to London not Birmingham; domestic, on the whole, not ecclesiastical. He appeared to have worked with (under, presumably) C. R. Ashbee in the School of Arts and Crafts in Upper Regent Street during the nineties.

Jeremy Tradescant, the rather arrogant young man whom David consulted in the Department of Metalwork on the subject, seemed to know a certain amount about Oswald Fish. Unlike David, Jeremy had a passion for even the most mediocre Victorian and early twentieth-century craftsmanship.

'This is Fish work,' he said ecstatically, producing a rather ugly silver-plated nickel coffee-pot with a cane-covered handle and wooden knob. '1910, I should think. A lovely piece – too thrilling.'

'Not my kind of thing, of course,' drawled David. Jeremy's rather fey mannerisms, his very soft woolly jumpers and silk scarves, the smell of very feminine scent which he always gave off, made David feel quite butch. 'Then there are these.' Jeremy's long fingers, quite hairless, with faintly protuberant knuckles, caressed a silver-plated milk jug and a copper and nickel tea-pot with spun body and turned spout. 'Aren't they heaven?'

David listened politely while Jeremy went through the catalogue with him. There was a set of cutlery made by the Guild of Handicraft and a ciborium, paten and chalice on loan from 'the Holy Ghost. Balham'. It seemed like Hitler being alive and well in Buenos Aires.

'I love Balham,' was Jeremy's only comment. 'If you want to see some really lovely Fish work, though, you should look at the rood screen in St Augustine's, Kilburn.'

'I don't really. You see, I'm just doing a bit of investigation on behalf of a friend.'

'Are you, now?' Jeremy asked, raising his eyebrows.

Jeremy had 'come out' about five years before, shortly after 'coming down' from Oxford. He liked talking about it, so David, in common with all Jeremy's other colleagues, had heard endless accounts of depressions, love affairs and erotic predilections. David had not himself 'come out'. If it had the result of tinging almost all conversation with homosexuality, and almost all areas of life with camp humour, he was not sure that he wanted to. Jeremy referred to him behind his back as 'a typical Wykehamist, they're all closet queens'. But in conversation it was never admitted that David had any homosexual leanings.

How he wished, how he ardently wished, that he did not. Apart from anything else, he was still in love with Fiona, his wife, to whom he had been married rather less than a year.

The number of erotic experiences he had ever had with men, not counting the occasional surreptitious liaison at school, was extremely small. He had gone out with, and to bed with, girls in the usual way throughout his twenties and imagined that in time, this annoying 'itch' for men would go away. Fiona, who was so clever and pretty and strong, would drive it away if anyone could. He had met her at a party of his brother's one New Year's Eve and they had fallen in love almost at once. She had a job in the Foreign Office. It was additionally delightful, after their first few passionate months together, to discover that they inhabited different social worlds. She was a brilliant entertainer and they had had most of his immediate colleagues at the Museum to dinner. He enjoyed getting to know her Foreign Office colleagues and her friends from home. New worlds were opened up for them both.

After a rather embarrassing evening when Jeremy had been round with his friend Stevie (who turned out to be a clergyman – a curate in Notting Hill) David and Fiona had rolled on the carpet aching with merriment at the absurdity of the pair, with their affected queenie voices, their habit of calling everyone darling and their too carefully elaborate *coiffure*. And as they lay there, holding hands and spluttering with laughter, David had wondered whether to tell Fiona that he, too, had a 'past' and how glad he was that she had rescued him from it. If only he had done so then, *before* they were married, he felt it would have purged the secret, perhaps even cured him forever. But some natural diffidence had prevented him from bringing the subject up again and they had married without ever needing to discuss it.

Since their marriage, Fiona had been obliged to go to Brussels about once a month for some Foreign Office work, and was gone for periods of about four days at a time. On the very first of these occasions, David had wandered into a pub from work and – in the account he made to himself (he had of course told no one of the matter) – had rather too much to drink. He had fallen into conversation with a very handsome Cypriot at the same table as himself and accepted an invitation back to the man's flat in Earls Court.

Afterwards, he had been appalled by how much pleasure this illicit evening had given him. The sheer physical pleasure was only part of it. It was the sense of having practised a deception and completely got away with it which brought such sweet delight to his heart, so that when Fiona came home and playfully said, 'Have you been a good boy while I have been away?' their lovemaking had a quality of peculiar ecstasy.

The next time she went away, he told himself that he was not going to repeat the pleasure. It was, he kept saying in the days before her flight, a single aberration, a wicked but magically delightful secret which he would keep to himself till the day he died. But in fact, he had no sooner seen her off at the Cromwell Road Air Terminal than he had plunged off in search of a mate; a search which took the inside of an hour. During this period of her absence, when Fiona was away four days, David attached himself to four different men. It all seemed so incredibly easy. They seemed to be lurking everywhere, in parks and launderettes, in pubs and amusement arcades, on tube stations and in lavatories, these mysterious fellow-conspirators with their particular freemasonic glance, which David quickly came to recognize.

He made several rules for himself. He would never do anything for which he could be arrested by the police. (He was not sure what the range of offences was but he tried to be as discreet and as quick as possible about 'pick-ups' and only to go with them if they could provide a room where security could be observed.) Nor would he ever go to any place where more openly homosexual friends, such as Jeremy, might be lurking. Nor would he ever invite them back to his own flat. The thought of these strange creatures inhabiting Fiona's bed filled him with loathing.

79

He had had many unsatisfactory experiences, and some frightening ones. But it was too late now: he was hopelessly addicted, and the number of petty little acts of adultery (not that he thought of them as such) which he had committed greatly exceeded the number he could conceivably confess to Fiona. The final and absolute rule to ensure complete discretion and secrecy was that he always refused to exchange names with his partner, and he always refused to repeat the adventure, however exciting it might have been.

With miserable bewilderment he had toiled away all morning on Oswald Fish both trying to forget and work out how he could have been so crazy as to break many of these sensible rules with Charles Bullowewo. Simple animal delight presumably played a part in it. He had never, even with Fiona (O God! he had *never* found himself making that comparison before!) had such delight. Then there had been the initial embarrassment, followed by a relief at discovering that his partner was of the same social class, higher possibly, than himself and that he had a splendid bedroom in a beautiful house rather than the more squalid bed-sits he had grown used to. Finally, in the morning, had been all the crazy delight of finding there were *women* in the picture too. For, what made it inconceivable to David that he could ever 'come out' in Jeremy Tradescant's way, was the knowledge that female companionship, of the kind he enjoyed so deeply with Fiona, would be sealed off forever. But with Charles, this was not so. It still seemed to David like a dream, when early that morning, the sheets had been drawn back and Fanny (was she Charles's wife?) had been standing there, a hair-grip between her lips as she still fiddled with her wonderful bun – telling them there were brioches for breakfast. Something had burst madly inside David at that moment. He had suddenly had a strong and completely unrealistic idea *that everything was going to be all right* – that, if Charles's wife could be tolerant of this, so might Fiona: that he could go on being happily married to Fiona while enjoying the indescribably delicious *amours* of Charles. For this was the first time in his life that David had ever felt the slightest bit in love with another man. As he lay in Charles's arms, resting his short mousey hair on Charles's great round, brown shoulder, he felt more than a little in love and it was then that he had been so indiscreet. He had not then told Charles that he was married. Even the intense joy of *that* moment could not have made him cross those insuperable barriers so fast. But he had said his real names – surname as well as Christian name; he had (*O Christ!*) given Charles the telephone number of his *flat* and told him that he worked at the Victoria and Albert.

David, toiling away at the ridiculous Oswald Fish, felt that he must have been crazy. Absolutely crazy. Every now and then fear gripped him, a quite physical sensation, a tightening of the lungs, a weak fluttering in the stomach. *O Christ.* What if Charles rang up the flat and Fiona answered? What if Charles came to the Museum? And not only Charles, because there were all the witnesses at the breakfast table – some children and someone who was presumably an *au pair* girl in jeans as well as Charles's scatty but agreeably tolerant wife.

And yet it was not simply fear which set David's heart beating. For, with every fibre of passion that throbbed through his being, David longed to be with Charles, wrapped in his reassuring strong arms and hearing his deep, cultivated voice murmuring the language of love.

'Then there are these,' lisped Jeremy. Really, his voice seemed like a parody, a stage homosexual. It can't always have been like that. Jeremy claimed to have been to Eton, but David did not know whether to believe this. Certainly Stevie, his blonde friend with a clerical collar, had not been to Eton: perhaps Jeremy had merely picked up some of his more hair-dressery conversational mannerisms.

He was holding up two bronze dolphins, heavily, ludicrously Arts and Crafts.

'Are they also by Oswald Fish?' David asked.

' 'Course, dear.'

'I wonder what they are for?'

Jeremy smirked and held them up, one for each nipple, against his yellow woolly. 'They came from a house in Bedford Park. All very William de Morgan I can assure you. Nice, aren't they?'

'Door stoppers?' David inquired, still puzzled.

Moving the bronze creatures up and down, like the tassels on the breasts of a strip dancer, Jeremy said: 'You are a thickette. Can't you recognize a pair of lovely knockers when you see them?'

IX

The chorus of Hebrew slaves from *Nabucco* was blaring out of Fanny's cassette player as the Bentley sped towards Birmingham, so that she could not hear the corgis yapping on the back seat. She felt thrilled to be approaching *her* church. The sale must have gone through months before, but it was only this morning that her solicitor had thought to tell her, and to reassure her that there seemed no likelihood of a compulsory purchase order being put on the building. He had not done his searches very thoroughly, and had been in the South of France for the whole of February, but these details had not, of course, been explained in his letter. As far as Fanny was concerned, the building was gloriously and irrevocably hers.

She was glad of the chance to be out of London for the middle of the day, even though it would be sad to miss Nana's arrival. Although she tried to be breezy about Charles bringing friends home – and it was an amazing and wonderful coincidence that his friend knew about the architect of her church – it had upset her to see them in bed together. She had absorbed, she told herself that she had absorbed, the fact that Charles had this aberration, even though she found it hard not to think it was some kind of cruel game he played to keep her on tenterhooks. What really worried her was the quite casual way he expected them to be able to stay the night without asking her permission. After all, it was her flipping house. He took her *for granted* and this morning, as he smiled at her in his lordly way, eating the breakfast which she had flipping prepared, it suddenly hurt and angered her in a way it had never done before. There he was, living rent-free in the nicest room in the house, providing nothing except wine for dinner parties and the occasional absurdly generous present (never money, always an object – 'in lieu of rent, dear girl') while he coined it in as a barrister. She loved Charles, of course she did. And if she expected him to be a suffragan husband it was hardly surprising that he lolled about as if the place was his home. But, while she loathed men to be servile or sinco-what's-its-name it was altogether another thing to be lordly.

Perhaps it was also their differences in background. Charles was used to rather seemly domestic ways. It was understandable that he should be rather condescending about her apparently chaotic mode of conducting life. She just wanted ... in her torn, rather angry state she did not know quite what it was that she did want, but she needed to get away.

Tracy, too, was another one who was getting on her nerves. Of course it was helpful to have full-time, unpaid assistance with the children and the housekeeping. And again, Fanny knew, she had only herself to blame because she had encouraged her sister to adopt this role in the household. But it was depressing that Tracy never *did* anything, never seemed to want to do anything, sat around in the kitchen most of the day with her gymshoes on the pine table, or would do if Fanny did not give her shop-business to conduct and letters to write, and named chores to perform. Sometimes she felt that she was in a household of autocars? – autocrats? – auto-somethings who just needed winding up every half day. When she was Tracy's age she had already had one successful career as a model, another as a pop singer; she had been married, had the twins, been to America for God's sake.

The children, too, were taking her more than usually for granted No one wanted clinging weedy little kids, but Fanny could have done with less slamming of doors and blaring of hideous Village People and Kate Bush, and inelegancies of diction like *no way* and *hopefully*. They after all, flip them, unlike her were having an expensive education, though you would hardly guess it to hear them talk. If only *once* Marmie would ask before leaving the table, put his knife and fork together after eating ... And why had Pandora never never never put her plate in the washing-up machine by herself? Because they expected *her* to do it, of course.

They could get on with it, the whole flipping lot of them; for one day she was going to be alone and she was going to be happy. Dear Oswald Fish, she thanked him from the bottom of her heart for providing a reason for getting out of Chelsea.

Driving along, she thought sadly, it would not have been like this, none of it, if she had been married. Properly married; not like her ludicrously ill-starred venture with the Honourable Member. She deeply envied him his marital happiness with the Girl of his Dreams. Her rather obsessive secretive friendship with him could never, she knew, intrude on that happiness. Happy marriages are inviolable. It was, though, with a deep, deep wistfulness that she had discovered, since he married and found happiness, how much she liked him. Of course he was impossible to be married to. *Quite* impossible. If they went back together again it would still, she told herself, be just as much of a disaster as the first time. But her long, rather happy conversations with him gave her a taste of what other people's happiness must be like. This largely, not wholly, accounted for the wistfulness. It sprang partly from the knowledge that she too longed to be married – solidly, properly, happily married, to a man with whom she could lose her temper and it wouldn't matter: not a suffragan husband, but a sustaining companion who would share the *responsibility*, as well as the chores and the fun.

The cassette clicked itself out – *Nabucco* was over. Verdi was a boring old arsehole.

The bottle-green Bentley had come off the motorway and was now careering towards the centre of Birmingham. She hoped that she would remember the way to Purgstall Heath or that if she couldn't she could stop and ask a policeman. The corgis yapped impatiently.

'Are you singing the National Anthem, corgis, *are you*?' she screeched at them and they yapped back enthusiastically. It was more than a joke. She had come to believe that they were in a way telepathically linked with the Monarch.

Send her victorious

Happy and glorious

Long to reign o—o—o

'FUCK' she screamed, finding herself being swirled, in the inexorable traffic system, back on to a strip of motorway which simply bore the legend NORTH, SOUTH, WEST. 'Corgis, where are we?'

She came off the motorway as soon as she could and found herself spinning round and round a roundabout. None of the signposts – and they were few enough – had names, except one which said WALSALL. And she knew she did not want to go there.

'I want Purgstall, you pimps!' she shouted desperately as she spun round again.

All the other signs said SOUTH-WEST or EAST or A34 (M), so she eventually followed one which said CITY CENTRE, and found herself skirting the concrete extravagances of the Bull Ring. Her own shop, to open in a fortnight's time, was at least in a real part of town, in Corporation Street. She had had less to do with it than her London shops simply because she had been very busy and Birmingham is not easy to get to, as she now reminded herself. When she found herself traversing the same concrete circuit, spinning round something called St Chad's Circus and whizzing yet again in the direction of New Street Station she started to scream and swear at the top of her voice, which threw the corgis into ecstasy.

This was, she decided, the most indescribably awful place on earth. How could they have built such a thing, simply not meant for human beings at all. Fly-overs, underpasses, the hideous Bull Ring tower, and inside those blocks, as she knew from previous experience, rows and rows of characterless shops with not a chink of real daylight to be seen. They might as well have been in a nuclear fall-out shelter, and for all Fanny knew they were.

Following signs to New Street Station, she eventually found herself in the twenty-minute parking space. She had no idea of the way to get out, still less of how to get to Purgstall. The corgis were scratching the upholstery on the back seat. She simply sat for a moment, staring ahead of her, shaken, dazed, and close to tears. Then, with a feeling of relief, she left the corgis in the Bentley and went to find a telephone kiosk on the station.

'Hallo.'

'Hallo, Fanny.'

'Guess where I am.'

'In a railway station.'

'How clever you are – can you hear the trains?'

'No, the loudspeakers.'

There was a pause.

'Fanny, I thought I might take the twins to the cinema on Saturday evening, if that fitted in with your arrangements.'

'Lucky things. What are you going to see?'

The Empire Fights Back.'

'They've seen it. I took them to it three nights ago.'

'Oh.'

'Marmie hated it – you know how sensitive he is. Pandora simply adored every minute. You know how she loves monsters and gadgets.'

'Well, perhaps I could take them to another film.'

'Do. Only it's a bore taking Marmie to the cinema. He always feels ill.'

'I hadn't noticed.'

'We have the two most adorable children in the world,' she said.

'I'm sure that's true.'

'But truly, truly wonderful. Cheesecake said that he thinks Marmie is going to be really good at French. *Think* of it. I can hardly string two words of French together.'

'Cheesecake?'

'The French master.'

'Oh, Mr Chisholm.'

There was an awkward little pause. Then he asked. 'How are Pandora's teeth?'

'She won't wear the brace.'

'Tell her she must. It cost four hundred pounds sending her for that course of treatment.'

'She can't wear it anyway.'

'Really, Fanny, she must. It was made to fit her mouth. What do you mean she *can't* wear it?'

'She threw it away.'

'*Threw* it away?'

'Yes. She spat it out of the car window two days ago on the way back from school.'

There was a shocked silence at the other end of the line. Then: 'But that's ... awful. What are we going to say to the dentist?'

'Don't know,' she giggled. He sounded so very solemn and serious about it.

'I don't really think it's funny, I'm afraid.'

'Don't be beastly to her about it, will you?'

'Of course not, Fanny.'

She giggled again. She loved his quiet, serious, far away voice.

'Do you ever wish you were still married to me?' she asked.

'No.'

'Never?' This was shrieked.

'Fanny, someone is calling me on the other line. I will have to ring off now.'

'Goodbye, goodbye.'

'Goodbye, Fanny.'

After the line had gone dead, Fanny spoke into the receiver: 'I flipping love you.'

X

Fred's office was on the third floor, opposite Planning.

He usually got to the Town Hall by about twenty past nine, but it depended entirely on Ivy at what hour he actually reached his office. If she happened to be cleaning the corridor outside the office door he could be delayed by anything up to half an hour.

This morning, she was waiting for him. The almost paralyzing effects of domestic irritation – the tightening of the shoulder muscles, the furrowing of the brow – had worn off while he sat on the bus and he was now prepared to be the rather jolly, amiable man that most of his acquaintances considered him to be.

'Morning, Mr Jobling.' Ivy rattled her bucket and grinned. The effect of sunken roundness was not diminished by the baggy dark blue trousers she wore under her blue nylon over-all. She looked rather as though she might, at an earlier stage of life, have been scrofulous, not to say syphilitic, but that over-eating and good humour had somehow or another seen her through. Her face sagged in fleshy folds which crinkled melodramatically into attitudes of hilarity, tenderness, shock, secrecy, as the narrative required. And there was always a narrative, sometimes several dovetailed into one conversational outpouring. Bright lipstick surrounded a mouth in which a few orange teeth danced against a background of darkness. Her whole appearance put one in mind of Hogarth's engravings.

'In 'urry dressing then, were you?' she laughed.

'Morning, Ivy.'

'I say in 'urry dressing then?'

'How do you mean?'

'Where's yer tie?'

Waves of rage against Jen threatened to well up inside him as he fingered the top button of his shirt and found that he had indeed come out without a tie.

'I must be losing my memory,' he managed to quip.

'Easy done,' she said. One of the striking things about Ivy was that she spoke with a Yorkshire accent, having come down from Leeds, motive unspecified, during the war. 'Still,' she continued, 'you're early bird. Nice and early.'

It was, he reflected, the same time that he always appeared in this corridor. The absence of a tie suddenly made him feel almost ridiculous, naked.

'It's a busy day today,' Fred said, trying to bustle past.

'You *are* in 'urry then?' She seemed affronted.

'Just a bit of a hurry.'

She plonked her bucket and mop down in his path – almost on his feet – so that further progress down the corridor would have meant actually leaping over it. With a jerk of her overpermed, slightly balding head, she indicated the door of the Planning Office.

'They were at it again Friday. Ooooh!' And her lips pursed into shapes of complete outrage. 'I were cleaning this corridor,' she took breath, 'I were cleaning this corridor so I couldn't helped have hearing them groaning and moving chairs and that and his wife's *ever* such a nice woman, you know, blonde, well as I say she probably has it dyed, rinsed you know I have mine rinsed though you wouldn't guess it they always say to me Ive you've got such *lovely* hair.' She patted her scanty curls with a fat old hand pink from scrubbing: it looked as though it had been boiled for a fortnight in disinfectant. 'Where was I? Ooooh!' and another jerk of the head resumed consideration of goings on in Planning. 'Mind you *she's* married and all.' By which Ivy presumably meant the fornicatress. 'It's the same as Mrs Riley said, she's got two ever such nice little boys.'

Fred had never worked out who Mrs Riley was. She was invoked as an authority for many of Ivy's pronouncements and presumably cleaned another part of the building. He had gone through phases of wondering whether she was like Mrs Harris in the monologues of Mrs Gamp, but decided that she was, probably, as real as Art, Ivy's husband, another oracle often quoted.

'Yeah. Mrs Riley says they're like bloody little angels. I told her I said if she goes on at this rate there'll be another bloody bun in't oven before she's done. *He's* nor only one on list – Oh *no*,' her voice sank to a whisper, 'they say she's got her eye on Whatsisname upstairs.'

'Not the Town Clerk?'

'No. Lonsdale. I don't like him, do you? I can't stand his *sights* on him. My mother would always say that she could never trust a man with side whiskers. Yeah. Funny that intit? I always remember. Oh she were a fine woman my mother: she had thirteen you know, I were youngest. There were thirteen that lived in the end and she *never* complained, she *never* gave a murmur,' Ivy had started to sway about and contort her expression into one of sentimental seriousness, quickly adding, 'not a bloody murmur: not like some of those effing sluts nowadays.'

At this point Dawn, in a tight little woollen dress which emphasized the shape of her well-developed breasts, teetered past and into the door of the Planning Department on her stilettos. Ivy grinned at her ingratiatingly, rather, it seemed to Fred, as a *tricoteuse* might smile at some aristocratic woman as she was carted past in a tumbril. He assumed, though it was never entirely clear what Ivy was talking about, that Dawn was the Jezebel under attack and he had reasons of his own for not wanting the conversation to become too specific. Once Dawn was installed safely in the Planning Office, Ivy's voice sank to a whisper.

'Have you noticed?'

'Noticed what, Ivy?'

'She never wears nothing under that skirt, not even in cold weather like we've been having, same as Mrs Riley says. Oooh and the wet. Well I'd feel it cold if I didn't wear, you know. It's the same as our Art said to me this morning he says It's that cold, Ivy, I'm going to wear two bloody vests he did, and all and I don't blame him nor did Mrs Riley when I told her she said she hadn't had her vest off all bloody summer. Well our Art feels it round his kidneys I think men do, don't you. Oh but it's a *shame*.'

Ivy was given to violent conversational changes of gear. Fred wondered what the next topic was going to be. He wondered if he was going to reach his office at all that morning before Ivy knocked off at mid-day.

'What's a shame, Ivy?'

'Same as Mrs Riley said it's worse than bloody shame it's sacrilege – that's what she said.'

'What is?'

'Knocking down our church.'

Fred blinked myopically at her through his very thick lenses and hoped he had not heard her right. That unpleasant tingling sensation of dread in the pit of the stomach, which he had come to label 'Purgstall Heath', was beginning to overcome him. Perhaps he was wrong but every word Ivy uttered made him certain he was not.

'Who's been knocking down your church, Ivy?'

'Well it's the same as our Art says it isn't right. It just don't seem right pulling down a beautiful old building like that. Our Art – that's my husband – is very fond of that church he were you know like christened in it. He says he thinks it's the most beautiful building in England. I were christened in Leeds, christened and married in't same church; my mother said to me, 'What d'you want to be getting married in a bloody church for – you'll have to buy a proper dress and a gold ring and bloody everything – why can't you get married in Whosit, you know ...'

'The Registry Office.'

'Ay, Whosit like our Glad. But our Flos had got married previous month to a sailor – ooh it were beautiful her dress, with white and veil and that and so I borrowed hers. Bugger Whosit.'

Fred felt glad that she had abandoned the subject of the Purgstall Leisure Centre. The nasty little sensation in the pit of his stomach had almost disappeared by the time she started up again.

'Not that it's being used as a church but it's standing, that's what my husband says at least it's standing and it reminds you of you know your past and that, well like how as he was brought up in Purgstall, always lived there; he were christened in that church, went to church school, even sang in bloody choir when he were a little lad. A Reverend Crisp the curate were, yeah. Our Art says he were ever such a young man but they say he were lovely and always so clean and that and then there were the bombings and people all over Purgstall in bloody air-raids their houses and belongings all just burnt to bits in front of their eyes well it's the same as Mrs Riley said and then they had Labour and to think of all that man had done for us.'

'Mr Crisp?'

'No, Winston Bloody Churchill. Our Art says everything's gone wrong since Attlee gave up India well they're all over here now aren't they and it seems a crying bloody shame to pull it down after all we've suffered just to put up another effing ugly building.'

There was no question of replying to all this. All the details of the Purgstall scheme were confidential, if not quite *sub judice*, and obviously could not be discussed with blabber-mouths like Ivy. With a little jump he transcended her bucket and was soon in his office. She was still talking but he was not listening.

There was not much of interest in his in-tray. He sat fingering his collar and realizing that he ought to go out and buy himself a tie. The desk diary said there was nothing 'on' today except a meeting of the Planning Committee at 4.15. He was not on this Committee but had agreed to sit in on some of their deliberations to give advice of a technical kind. A letter from the Town Clerk reminded him that he had not done enough homework on the Purgstall Scheme.

... possibility of a Compulsory Purchase Order? Far be it from me to make suggestions, but I am assuming that you have already:
(a) Discussed the matter personally either with Miss Williams or her solicitor to see if the whole settlement could not be made amicably and without recourse to the Law.
(b) Read the Surveyor's report on the building. This could be used to our advantage if need arose. Clearly, even if the building is to be used as a warehouse it will need a considerable sum of money spending on it before it will satisfy the Surveyor's requirements for Basic Safety (Paragraph 3 of his report).
(c) Furthermore as you are no doubt aware ...

Two sides of quarto were covered, with *cc to Mr Jobling: Planning: City Surveyor*, typed at the top.

Fred felt ashamed that he had not thought of the first suggestion – an actual meeting with Fanny Williams. Somehow he had found the whole idea so embarrassing that he had not wanted to be involved, but it was, of course, the obvious solution. She had bought St Aidan's as a warehouse. Her solicitor had made a lot of fuss about its being a listed building, but there was no reason to suppose that she would not be satisfied by quite generous compensation. Then the bulldozers could get to work and the people of Purgstall might be a little closer to getting their squash courts, playgroups and old folks' Day Centre.

The other faintly shaming thing about the affair which now occurred to him was that he had never actually seen St Aidan's. He had not even been to Purgstall Heath, although it was only a few miles from where he lived. The thought of these two details, and the absence of a tie, made him decide to have the morning out. Buzzing his intercom, he told his secretary that he would be out on official business until after lunch. As he got up to go, his office door opened, and a flabby pink arm extended the waste-paper basket in his direction.

'Ivy, what is it *now*?'

'*Her* basket.'

'Whose?'

Ivy gave a conspiratorial jerk of her perm in the direction of the Planning Office.

'My old dad's going to be a hundred in a few months.'

'Really?'

'He's in like you know home, not far from where I live Purgstall you know and the nurses well you know ladies as look after him like say as how he's as good as gold. Hundred.'

'You'll be getting a telegram from Buckingham Palace.'

'His mind's as sharp as sharp. Always were. He were clever man. Stoker on the railways for fifty years he were. Never wanted to be owt else. No, but I *say*.'

And waving the waste-paper basket she got back to more important business.

'She left it like this. She left it like this last Friday night, can you imagine last Friday night. Just look how she left it.' Ivy's features suggested outrage which might at any moment burst into a lascivious guffaw. Fred peered down at the bottom of the waste-paper basket and saw, shrivelled and damp, lying on top of the torn-up envelopes and shredded paper, a used, bright green French letter.

Fred paid seven pounds for a dark blue silk tie in the men's department at Rackhams. The extravagance brought an inner glow of peace and he knew how women must feel who derive consolation from having expensive hair-dos. Catching sight of himself in a shop window, he thought the tie improved his appearance, which was balding and slightly lumpy.

Coming back down Corporation Street, he paused and stared at the new shop front to which painters were adding the finishing touches on the opposite pavement. The single word FANNY in vaguely art-nouveau lettering was stencilled on to each gothicized window, and painted, in larger lettering of the same design, over the awning. Two men in blue overalls were heaving a large heavy object through the stained glass doors which, after a moment's puzzlement, Fred recognized as a *What the Butler Saw* machine, probably bought from some now defunct seaside pier on the south coast. The irritating thing about the shop front, even in its unfinished state, was that it was already, undeniably, the most attractive thing in the street. Fred thought, as doubtless one was intended to think, what a nice change from the chain-store men's outfitters and chemists and stationers. What a nice change from neon and plastic and plate glass. Here was fussiness, decoration, frivolity. It was annoyingly consoling.

Was the warehouse going to exercise a similar, or more potent spell? Fred, partly perhaps because of short sight, partly because of a determined desire to be sensible, gravely distrusted aestheticism, even though he was more frequently disturbed by beauty than he would like to have admitted. Birmingham in that respect was a fairly safe place to live. Less beautiful than it had been in the days of Fred's boyhood, it now seemed unashamedly, soullessly ugly. Passable industrial architecture, like his grandfather's old factory in Porchester Street, which he could still dimly remember, had been swept away by monstrous pseudo-American styles. But Purgstall, he reflected, even in palmy days, could never have been Birmingham's most beautiful quarter.

Getting there proved a depressing experience. It was not merely that the journey began with the EXACT FARE PLEASE machine swallowing his only change without providing him with a ticket, a fact the Irish bus driver refused to believe. Even after the cursing and quarrelling, the annoyance of other people behind him in the queue, the production of a five-pound note, the further cursing and the eventual purchase of the ticket, the sights from the bus window did little to lessen the gloom: the endless blocks of flats which, on an architect's drawing board, had probably looked like gleaming diamond towers, the New Britain or perhaps merely fun; but which now, after only a few years, looked as grimy and cheerless as the worst Victorian tenement. Worst of the lot were those which had been splashed here and there (in vaguely Aztec fashion, was it?) by chunks of colour, arbitrarily placed beneath windows on the umpteenth floor. Blues, oranges and reds they had been five years before: dull and dusty they were now, daubed with slogans, political.

sporting or merely abusive. Sometimes these categories, in the imagination of the graffitist, appeared to converge; sometimes the hand of a second or third person explained the puzzling emendations. ALBION RULE OK seemed a curiously old-world sentiment until side by side with FRONT RULES OK, which some wag had amended to Y-FRONT RULES: while a third hand, like a petulant schoolmaster, had chalked across the whole with the single word NAZIS. How far the anonymous correction implied preference for National Socialism, as opposed to underpants, was not made clear.

Fred was out of the bus by now and looking about him at the dismal scene. A howling north-east wind seemed to penetrate his bones. He would catch pneumonia if he stood still; but he only had a hazy sense of where he ought to be going.

It appalled and shocked him that anyone should really have to live here: indeed, it was unimaginable that anyone *could*. Were it not for Ivy's assertion that she lived in a Council Block overlooking what she persisted in calling 'our church' Fred would have found it imaginatively impossible to accept that this ghastly wilderness was inhabited. As if to contribute to the illusion, the roads were empty and there were no signs of life, except that, far in the distance, he could see an electric milk-float turning a corner.

All the street – they were not even streets, most of them, gloomy little cul-de-sacs round which the blocks were placed – had, too, such grotesquely inappropriate names: The Glebe, Wells Close. St Aidan's Crescent, Rievaulx Avenue, suggesting, if not actually Toy Town or Merrie England, at least links with some rural, ecclesiastical past. But in fact these monstrous buildings did not have links with anything. The row of shops he passed, uniformly wedged under a rectangular awning which some municipal architect had conceived as an arcade (for there was the sign: Heffer Arcade) these shops all looked as though they were barricaded, as if for a siege. Every window, even that of the newsagents, was heavy with metal grating, like an expensive jewellers: as though it was not safe to imagine that a single pane of glass could survive a Friday night without being smashed. Perhaps it was a fair assumption. The telephone kiosk, one of recent design which had been all glass, looked as though it had undergone assault by an invading spaceship full of hostile apes: the smashed receiver was actually dangling from a spiral of plastic-coated flex through the jagged edge of the huge broken pane.

Apart from the little row of shops, which were presumably open, although none of them looked open, there was nothing, simply nothing, for as far as the eye could see, which could be regarded as belonging to life: not a pub, not a cinema, not a social club. There was not even a patch of grass which had not been ploughed up by motor-cycle tyres; not even a vulgar little clump of flowering cherry trees which had not been defoliated; not a bench where old men could sit and grumble about the world which had not been up-turned, or bashed, or sprayed with the names of football teams or political extremists or the autoerotic habits of their supporters.

If ever a place needed a Leisure Centre, such as the Planning Committee was suggesting, Purgstall was such a place. Twelve months – less perhaps, if they got moving really fast – could have brought this neighbourhood a club for the old, a kindergarten, a crèche, a swimming pool, a squash court, a coffee bar, a skittle alley, rooms for table tennis and snooker, all in one complex group of buildings skilfully designed and approved by the City Architect. And now the whole scheme was being delayed, indeed was in danger of being heavily amended if not actually shelved, because some selfish woman from London refused to relinquish her ware-house.

Turning a corner, almost blown around it by the wind, he found himself at the top of a road which sloped, surprisingly steeply, downwards. And there, standing in the hollow, in the middle of what looked like a bomb-site, but which he hoped would soon become a builder's yard, stood the offending object.

The little brick chapel, for so it obviously was, however much he might want to impugn its dignity by calling it a warehouse, might once have been a church of some size, but from where Fred was standing it seemed tiny, utterly dwarfed on every side by the towering residences (Ivy's among them) of the Council tenants. It looked so puny, so fragile, that the obvious course of action was to ignore the protests of this woman in London and simply come along one day with a bulldozer. The next time she swanned up from Kensington or wherever she lived – probably she only came near the place once in a blue moon – she would find it gone. One could always use the old trick of saying that the Surveyor had opined the building was unsafe.

The illegality of such a notion thrilled him but at the same time immediately suggested its own impossibility. One could not break the law. No ... But one might twist it.

He clambered through a gap in the wire netting which closed off the site as if it were a tennis court, and clumped his way across the uneven surface, littered with brick ends, broken bottles, rusty prams, the debris of succeeding generations. At some points it was pathetically apparent that he was tramping over what had been someone's floor – tiles beneath his feet, red front steps, now dull and dusty, which had been burnished moist and scarlet: some of the bedsteads, certainly some of the fireplaces, had actually been used on that site, though now they were thick with bindweed and brambles.

As one approached St Aidan's – church or warehouse, perhaps it did not matter what one called it – the proportions of the building changed so that, by the time he had actually approached the West front, he felt quite dwarfed by it. The surrounding tower blocks were distant, and he irrationally had a sudden feeling, absurd as it seemed, that he was about to enter a great cathedral. The long lancet windows swooped up to the simple gable roof. The gutters, much rusted, were adorned with decorated drainpipes of vaguely Gothic proportions, the top of each gutter bearing the device *O.F. 1895.*

The West Doors, surprisingly, were not wooden, but like those of some great Italian baptistery, struck in metal, variegated with serpentine and floral devices, as well as more recent additions, in paintwork, of further assertions about the autoerotic practices of the surrounding inhabitants. Above it, on a placard too high for the modern inscribers to have reached, the legend proclaimed: *A MDG. For the Love of Christ and his Poor, this church was dedicated that they might worship Him in Freedom and in Truth – by one of His Grateful soldiers and servants, 1895.*

Perusal of this inscription was interrupted by a snarling at his ankles. Looking down he saw two corgis squabbling over who was to have the first mouthful of his trousers. No great dog-lover, Fred eyed the fox-like little animals cautiously. They might have meant well. On the other hand in a desolate slummy place like this, who could tell? They might only be wagging their stumpy little tails because they were mad. The slobber that was moistening his ankles might be rabid. At any moment he might start foaming at the mouth.

Something equally dramatic – more so perhaps, in terms of Fred's personal history – was about to take place. A high-pitched melodic wailing, like a mezzo-soprano about to burst into an aria, pierced the silence. The sound appeared to be coming from nowhere, a divine song borne on the winds from angelic spheres.

'COR—Geeeees! Where are my precious corgis?' And then, rising to a crescendo, 'Flor-a! Hon-ey!'

A figure appeared round the corner of the church, and Fred found himself face to face with Fanny Williams.

The vulgar conversation of the Gladstones – talk of a typical Chelsea trendy, an entrepreneuse, possibly a mistress of a Rolling Stone – had not prepared him for the vision, so that it did not occur to him to guess who she was. Nothing could have prepared him for her distinctive, immediately obvious and overpowering beauty: very bright green eyes, which did not need the mascara which dripped from their lashes, gazed out of an animated, almost an hilarious face. The fine nose was slightly retroussé; the curl of the delicate lips humorous as well as sensual. She had a firm, slightly pointed chin, and smooth long white throat, delicately adorned with bejewelled velvet choker. Her tiny ears glittered with clusters of diamanté. Her hair was piled up on top of her head in the fashion of the 1880s. Was she indeed a ghost? His flesh tingled with a cold fear and excitement which could almost have shaken his sensible scepticism. But she was not, in spite of the hair, a Victorian. Her clothes were unmistakably new, even if there was an indefinable archaism about the fluffy padded shoulders of her short black coat; the well-cut grey tweed skirt which flowed to her calves; the thick green woollen stockings which swathed her elegant legs, the expensively made crimson shoes.

As the tingling sensation continued, Fred wondered, with immediate consciousness of the absurdity of the thought, whether he had contracted some virus. The whole material scene before him seemed to shift into unreality so that the very ground beneath his feet seemed to him less real than the mysterious drug-like trance into which he was falling as he stared at the woman, framed by the iron doorway of the church. With these sensations of dizziness and fear there came a joy which shook his whole being, awakening a spiritual self long imprisoned and which he had never allowed himself to recognize. This was something much more than fancying a bird, even though the whole experience was overwhelmingly erotic and he felt almost faint with near orgasmic desire. In a way that had never happened to him before in the previous forty-two years, he had fallen deeply, hopelessly and instantaneously in love.

'Flora,' she repeated, 'let go of that man's trousers.' As she said it, she slightly bowed her head and a deep blush rose on her features and she laughed a slightly tinny laugh held back by her ring-adorned fingers. The noise of this laughter sent shivers up and down his frame as though a harpist were practising scales on his rib-cage.

'I am so sorry,' she said, 'has my dog ruined your really very charming trousers?'

It was hard to know how to take this remark: its flattering tones suggested immediately some hidden irony, concealed perhaps in the ludicrous epithet *charming* applied to trousers. They were not even smart, certainly not, like her clothes, well-cut: simply bought in a hurry from Marks & Spencer six months before. They had never fitted very well and they could never have been thought of as charming.

'No, they're – gosh! – only an old pair.' It was extraordinary to hear these ludicrously mild, antiquated expletives flying out of his mouth.

They stared at one another. Fred wondered whether she could have the slightest inkling of how he felt. When she finally said, 'What *are* we to do' any number of extraordinary replies – '*Elope!*' – suggested themselves, in disregard of the fact that they had been acquainted for rather less than a minute.

'What, my Flora, are we going to do for this poor man? You have dribbled and snuffled all over his lovely trousers.' (Lovely? This was going too far.) 'Yes, you have. Oh yes, you have. You *have*! I shall skin you alive!'

At the prospect of this fate, the little dog stopped snarling; and grinning masochistically, it began to dance round in circles. Its companion whined as though she too would like to be skinned alive by Fanny. Fred knew how she felt.

There was a Welsh lilt to Fanny's otherwise rather upper-crust voice which was unmistakable and made her utterances seem musical and strange and high. Still addressing one of the corgis, and with another rather tinny snigger, she said, 'But we might ask him what he is doing trespassing in our lovely church.' Suddenly she looked at Fred and said. 'Do you know St Adrian's?'

'St Adrian's?'

'This church.

'Isn't it St Aidan's?'

'That's what I said isn't it? A wonderful new friend of Charles Bullowewo was telling me all about it this morning. It was designed by a perfectly sweet man called Kipper.'

'Golly.'

Was one supposed to know who Charles Whatshisname was? Why had she introduced the name without explanation?

'I'm not sure I know . . .' he hesitated.

'Charles is a lawyer, fantastically clever, went to Eton and he is a sort of reproduction husband – no I don't mean that . . ..'

She seemed almost as inarticulate as Fred.

'I'm a lawyer too.'

'Oh really.' It did not seem to interest her much. She seemed more anxious to talk about her husband. 'He met this mouse-like but really very nice man called David in a lavatory and it turns out he knows . . .'

'In a lavatory?' Everything she said seemed Double Dutch.

'I *know*' – the tinny laugh turned to a squeak. 'He was flipping snooty about Kipper, I can tell you – the architect of this church. But it turns out he was really quite famous and Charles has been very firm ever since I got this place that we should watch it like *hawks* because the Church is apparently terribly unimaginable about these things and likes pulling down *wonderful* old buildings as soon as look at them. Luckily this is Listed, but Charles says that's nothing if the flipping City Council . . . do you know they want to pull it down?'

Her words poured forth in jerky, emotional, unfinished little phrases. Fred simply stared, unable to speak.

'I mean, isn't it *incredible*. Look!' She swung her arm high in a large circular gesture which seemed to indicate the surrounding neighbourhood. 'This is the only beautiful thing for *miles* and of course they want to pull it to bits.'

'They really do –' He tried in all honesty to make it sound like a statement which would explain his presence there, but it came out like a question.

'Oh yes. They really do. Where else have you seen magnificent metal doors like that?' she asked.

'Architecture isn't really my sort of thing.' He wished that her long neck and throat did not pulsate in that *sexy* way, and that her blouse was buttoned up to the top. They made it impossible for him to say what he ought to say.

'Come here,' she said and took his arm. The frisson of delight this caused made him gasp. Flora and Honey waddled ahead and they followed to a small porch and pointed arch which admitted entrance on the north side of the church.

'I've been looking at this porch and do you see how it has a sort of sawn-off look at the top? It must have been going to be a tower and then they ran out of money, I expect.' Her voice had become lower, more serious, as she pointed out detailed features of the building.

'As I say, architecture isn't really my thing ...'

'Flip that. Isn't mine – or wasn't until they started pulling down almost every beautiful building in England.'

It seemed unnecessary to point out that this was an overstatement. Normally he was irritated by conservationists. They were so one-sided and thought only of beauty and nothing of the domestic needs of the present. Even in his trance-like state he would have clung to this view if the words had come, but they would not.

'I think architecture is about the most important thing there is,' she said earnestly. 'More important than music or painting because they mean nothing to people who can't appreciate them: whereas even if you don't know why buildings are beautiful or ugly, they affect your whole life. Look at those,' she said pointing to the tower blocks. 'Future generations are going to judge us by *those*.'

'Now you mention it I can see the porch has a sawn-off look.' He was not used to looking. The bridge of his nose wrinkled at the new experience. It was hard to imagine what she saw to be so enthusiastic about. She was obviously taking no notice of him.

'He was a metal-worker,' she was saying. 'Charles's wonderful mouse-like man found it out, he worked in an ironfoundry or something and you see it all fits so perfectly, like the goldsmiths in Florence.'

He could not see anything that was remotely like Florentine gold as she led the way inside. He expected to find the warehouse packed with things for her shop so that what they actually saw was rather a shock. The roof being half off, it was exceedingly damp and musty inside. The floor was littered with rubbish of ages, accidental, ecclesiastical, ornithological. Hymn books, their covers torn off, thick with pigeon droppings, were strewn about on the broken encaustic tiles. He stopped to pick up a damp old card at his feet. In old black-letter print it read:

St Aidan's Purgstall. Easter Anthem

Then, in ordinary lower case:

Joy to thee, O Queen of Heaven.	Alleluia
He whom Thou wast meet to bear.	Alleluia
As He promised hath arisen,	Alleluia
Pour for us to God thy Prayer	Alleluia

PLEASE DO NOT REMOVE THIS CARD FROM YOUR PEW
WHEN YOU LEAVE THE CHURCH.

He tossed it down and clambered over some up-turned benches, kicking a few empty paint pots as he did so.

'The church people did their best to wreck it, as you can see,' she said.

It seemed to Fred unlikely that these ravages had been worked by deliberately recalcitrant 'church people'. It was hard to imagine delinquent archdeacons creeping down by dead of night to smash the stained glass, scatter pigeon droppings and chip-papers, or overturn the pews.

'Most of the really beautiful stuff was sold, of course, before I bought the building . . .'

So yes, indeed, it *was* her, though this was his first confirmation of the fact.

'. . . but there is still an amazing amount left. Just look at that.'

She indicated an elaborate cast-iron rood screen which seemed to dispel what little light there might have been, dividing the building into two. Close up, though, it was possible to see that it had the appearance, increased by rust, of a creeper climbing up a trellis in autumn: delicate iron leaves and flowers and fruit sprouted abundantly. Beyond, where the altar would have been, was pretty much a mess. Broken pieces of scaffolding and lengths of splintered plank were piled up against the wall.

'Did you say this building was yours?' Fred asked. Why could he not come clean and admit that he knew all about it, that Fanny and her wretched warehouse had been occupying his waking thoughts for the last two months? 'What are you going to use it for?'

'What's your name?' she replied. 'It really seems extraordinary to be engaging in *intercourse* without having introduced ourselves.' She blushed and sniggered at the word, Fred himself turning a deep shade of crimson.

'Alastair,' he said. This at least was not a lie. Alastair Jobling was his name, though now his grandmother was the only person who used it. Even Dad had adopted the 'Fred' thing. How had it started? Everyone used it, even his children, though they called Jen 'Mum'. He thought it had begun by someone – Jen herself perhaps – thinking *Al-astair* sounded like *Fred Astaire*. Now, some instinct told him, was time to break new ground. You could not embark on a love affair (he knew that this was what was happening) with a name like Fred.

'I'm Fanny Williams,' she said. 'How very American of you not to have a surname.' It now seemed awkward to tell her that his name was Jobling. 'Yes, I bought this place as a warehouse, but now it turns out to be built by this clever Mr Kipper . . . Yes, corgis, Mister Kipper. Kipper, Kipper, Kipper. Look at them, they think they are going to have dinner. Din-dins, corgis, din-dins!' She cackled at the expectations aroused by this exclamation, but showed no signs of feeding the dogs.

'So you aren't going to use it as a warehouse after all?' Fred persisted.

'You aren't from the Council, are you?' She stared at him accusingly.

What on earth prompted the next lie?

'Lord, no,' he said.

'Because Charles Bullowewo said that there would almost certainly be some little worm from the Council nosing round when I next came here. He says that their best bet is to get the surveyor to say that the building is structurally unsound and needs millions spending on it. Then they force you to sell up for much less than it's worth and before you have time to go into the matter, they bulldoze the whole lot to bits.'

Fred stared. Damn and blast Charles Bullowewo.

'I don't care if you are from the Council, really,' she added.

'Why not?'

'Partly because I like you,' she laughed at his blushes. 'And partly because if it costs me every penny I own I want to restore this place and make everyone see how *fine* it is.'

'Why?'

'Are you religious?'

'No. I mean ...' Always an embarrassing question, it made him quite inarticulate.

'Good, nor am I. That means we can both think seriously about it. I was brought up, you see, in a horrible – no, it wasn't horrible, it was marvellous. My father was the most wonderful man in the world. *Wonderful*!' (Top C: the pigeons who had been fighting over the remains of a packet of crisps in the remains of the Lady Chapel fluttered to the roof in terror.) 'But he was a very very strict and religious man. Calvinistic Methodist.' Her voice sounded more and more Welsh as she thought of her past. 'Do they have Calvinistic Methodists in England?'

I wouldn't know. I hope not.'

What a very snooty and stuck-up remark, if I may say so. The chapels were the only life people had in Neath, unless like my mother you're keen on sex. Poor old Dad. Rows and rows of little back-to-back grey houses and nothing to do except get drunk and sing hymns. Better,' she added with sudden nationalistic defensiveness, 'better than this, mind you.'

They stared over Purgstall. The icy wind was now bringing a slight drizzle which stung their cheeks.

'I think, don't you,' she said, 'that at the heart of the universe there is nothing but a deep emptiness.'

'I've never really thought about it.' He hated conversations about Life with a capital L.

'Never really thought about it?' she sniggered, as if Fred's remark had been calculated not merely to amuse but to titillate sexually. 'Corgis, Alastair has never really thought about the heart of the universe. Don't you think it's about time that he started to think?'

'How does this affect what you are going to do with the church?' he asked.

'Oh, because as I say this is the only beautiful thing in the middle of the whole ghastly place, don't you see, and I know what it's like to be brought up literally surrounded by ugliness; ugly everything; ugly bedroom slippers, ugly crockery, ugly school, ugly friends, ugly, ugly, ugly, all through the day, day after day; year after year. And I cherish anything which isn't ugly in a world like that, even if, like this church, it has been used to promote really rather disgusting fairy tales.'

Her hand indicated the crucified figure, lost in shadows, at the top of the rood screen.

'So what are you going to do?' he asked again.

Her eyes opened very wide and she replied, in what seemed unmistakably seductive tones, 'Have lunch with you?'

'I mean to the church.'

'Restore it of course. Does that mean you don't want lunch?'

'God, no.'

'Well, I do.'

'I mean no, yes, I do want lunch.'

'No, yes? What sort of answer is that, corgis?'

'Shall we go to a restaurant? Birmingham isn't exactly rich in . . .'

'Of course not. I only want a toasted sandwich in a pub.'

It felt odd to be driving back through Purgstall Heath, and beyond the gas works, in a large, purring, green Bentley. He felt too ditheringly transformed and shaken by Fanny's physical proximity to be able to give her any constructive directions about how to find her way to a decent pub. If not indecent, the place eventually selected turned out to be rather noisy, smelly, Irish and insalubrious. Rather to Fred's amazement, though, it did serve toasted sandwiches. While they waited for these (eventually unappetizing) objects they sat staring at one another across a small, round, red, Formica-topped table near the gas fire in the corner. Her eyes appeared to be surveying each facial detail in turn – nose, ears, lips, almost as though she were buying a horse; and while he returned her gaze she seemed both intense and distant, to the point where he wondered whether she might not be mildly deranged. It was the way she leant her chin on her palm, and stared and stared and stared finally bursting into a tinny giggle.

When the toasted sandwiches came appetite seemed to have left them both.

'Married?' she asked. It was a question, unspoken, which had evidently been in both their minds for quite some minutes.

He nodded, unable to speak.

She sighed, as if this was a pity. Then she giggled again and said 'Got a cigarette?'

'I don't smoke.'

'You should.'

From a distance, it looked as though she had a stand-up row with the cigarette machine. He heard her say, 'You silly flipping thing. I gave you 50p. Yes. *Fifty pee.* And what have you given me? Nothing.' She came back, scrumpled the cellophane into her ash-tray and, when her cigarette was alight, she said, 'Unhappily married.'

'Are you?' His heart thumped. The cautious reply showed he was not going to be drawn at once. But the obviousness of her ploy did not occur to him.

'No, you are, I can tell,' she said.

'How?' He felt himself blushing now and spreading his palms nervously on the table-top so that his finger-tips nearly touched hers.

'If you were happily married you would have denied the implication that you weren't.'

'Not necessarily,' he blustered, but her long, surprisingly hot, moist white fingers had crept forward and were caressing the back of his hand. 'Poor Alastair,' she said.

Never, in all the dozen years and more of being married to Jen, had he let on to anyone that things were not going swimmingly. It was partly a question of loyalty. It was partly one of stoicism. Complaining about your wife was simply bad form, like asking the referee if you could leave the football pitch at school because of some trifling inconvenience like a broken nose or a burst appendix. The decent thing to do was to press on regardless. So that now, when, stumblingly, he heard himself mention his marital circumstances to Fanny, it was almost unbelievable to him, as his own words were uttered, that they were being used to describe Jen. It was quite as if he was listening to someone else speaking.

'There's no common ground between us any more. Life used to be ... I dunno ... fun, I suppose. Not any more ...' His voice trailed away. He had not said much but he was shaking, with excitement and with partial horror at the strength of feeling behind his desire to be disloyal. Since being married, Fred had, in the strictly technical sense, committed adultery very rarely. Dawn in Planning, the

Jezebel so berated by Ivy, had, after an office party, yielded herself to him one Christmas Eve. On that occasion, questions of domestic felicity had not been under discussion. It was simply a question of unzipping and lifting of hems and unhooking and unbuttoning and leaning back across drawing boards. There had been one or two other similarly casual encounters over the years; and, after Sam's birth, a very agreeable fortnight with the Norland nanny. But never, by much as a flicker of an eyelash, had he been *verbally* unfaithful to Jen. He had never said, 'I sometimes feel that it isn't anything in particular about Jen. It's just that she *exists* that I mind.' Never had he said such a thing. Only in the earliest, blackest hours of day, had he ever *thought* such a thing, but, to his infinite bewilderment, he heard himself saying it now.

'Why not separate?' she asked. 'What a state of affairs for the children. You have children?'

'Two.'

'Same here. Much better for them. I know.'

'You don't look as though you have children. How old are they?'

'Twins. They're nine. What about yours?'

'Sam's five. Harriet is nine.' It seemed almost profane to be bringing them into the conversation. Jen was one thing, though even discussion of her made him feel oddly uncomfortable: but the children! He had never felt more mystically certain that he was going to 'have' a woman than he felt now in the presence of Fanny. Where this might lead him, what havoc it would play with the dull complexion of his daily life he did not stop to consider. But by a tug almost as strong as the enchantment he felt for Fanny, he was also aware of a desire to protect the children. He wished he had not allowed their names to escape. He wished she did not know about them.

'Sweet!' she screamed. A few heads turned in their direction and they had quite a large audience by the time she continued in rather loud tones: 'You must get a divorce as soon as you can. It gets worse the longer you leave it. The twins were only three when I realized I couldn't stand being married to Aubrey a moment longer. Three was such a perfect age. Aubrey and I went out and bought them huge ice-creams then we told them we were going to be divorced and they were perfectly happy about it. Five is older, of course and your nine-year-old – Harriet! Sweet name! – might be rather bewildered ...'

The whole thing was unthinkable. As soon as Fanny mentioned the possible effects of divorce on Harriet, he realized that the whole thing was a rather unpleasant fantasy. Of course the possibility of divorce had occurred to him, especially in the early hours of the day, from time to time, but he had never got very far with considering the practicalities. Certainly never as far as ice cream. He wondered whether she was going to come up with any of the clichés of divorce: that her former husband and she remained on very good terms: that it was desirable for grown-up people to be able to behave in a civilized fashion.

'It was the thought that You Only Live Once which suddenly got me,' she said. 'Of course it would have been lovely if it had worked out between Aubrey and me, but it didn't and it would have been *blasphemy*. Oh, is that what I mean? I'm so uneducated. You know I left school when I was fifteen.'

'What did you do then?' He wanted to stop the conversation about divorce.

'Oh, became a model. I lied about my age. I was most successful between the ages of fifteen and eighteen. You must have seen me in *Vogue* – everywhere in fact –' there was nothing boastful about this improbable assertion. On the contrary she seemed to view her former self with total detachment. 'Then I started having love affairs with people; but not serious ones and I was never promiscuous like some of the girls who slept with anyone who might help them in their career. Pop stars and film producers and . . . you know the sort of people.'

'Was . . . was your *first* husband a pop star?'

'Aubrey? Heavens no. He's an MP. That's why we all call him the Honourable Member. Opposition Front bench spokesman on something or another. He was quite incredibly solemn and pompous about it and used to say' (she assumed a pompous voice, like a bishop in a farce, not remotely like the Honourable Member's) 'I'd rather you didn't say that in front of our dinner guests, Fanny. It's rather obscene.'

Fred laughed.

'What sort of thing was obscene?'

'Oh, I don't know. We had Mr Heath to dinner once and I asked him if he'd been circumscribed.'

'Had he been?'

'He didn't say.'

She looked so genuinely as if she could not understand why this might have been an embarrassing topic of conversation. Fred found himself laughing nervously, and stroked her long white hand.

'So you left the Member?'

'The Honourable Member. Poor old thing. Yes I did. I was married to him for three flipping years. Do you know what he said when I told him I wanted a divorce? "Fanny, think of my career." And I did, too, like a twit, and I allowed him to divorce me, and then he got married again, perfectly happily, even though I should have thought I could have had him for unreasonable behaviour and lots of other things too. Anyway,' she continued with no pause whatsoever, 'that's all past history but what are we going to do about you, that's much more important.'

'Is it? I like hearing about you.'

'Let me buy you another drink.'

'I wouldn't dream of it.'

'Don't be silly.'

He let her buy the drinks. She came back with two half pints of bitter. When she returned, she smiled at him, and it seemed a knowing smile, as though they had already entered into a conspiracy.

'I think I could help you over this church,' he suddenly blurted out.

'Help me? In what way?'

'Well, you see, I'm a lawyer.'

'You said. So's my solicitor. So's Charles Bullowewo.'

'But I'm here, on the spot.'

'That's perfectly true. But am I going to need a lawyer here?'

'If you did.'

'That would be most extraordinarily kind.'

There was a grotesque contrast between the mannered politeness of her conversational formulae and the playful way in which she seemed to treat him like dirt.

'I mean, the trouble is, I've got to work this afternoon,' he said. If the clock in the pub was right it was nearly half past two. 'But it ...'

'But what?' she asked.

'It would be nice to meet again. I mean it might be –' He heard himself falling into committee language '– mutually beneficial.'

'Do you know,' she said, 'it is rather uncanny, but I realize that I have dreamt about you.'

'About me? But we've never met before today.'

'That's what's uncanny. Do I mean uncanny or supernatural? In my dream I was sitting in a pub with a tall, burly, dark man with horn-rimmed spectacles.' Was this a description of himself?

'What happened?' he asked.

'How do you mean?'

'In the dream?'

She blushed, and said with her tinny giggle. 'Something very improper. Can I give you a lift into the centre of Birmingham?'

As she said this, Fred felt her legs had seized one of his under the table and held it with a tight vice-like grip, as she gabbled on. 'Isn't it exciting, I am opening a shop in Corporation Street in a *fortnight*.'

'I'd heard.'

Her face, which had stared at him so closely earlier, now seemed indifferent, and to bear no relation to what was happening under the table, where her two legs squeezed his calf as if trying to extract milk from it.

'I'm glad you've heard. It's going to be a wonderful shop. Tell all your friends. Come to the opening.'

His heart sank when she said this. It implied that she did not think of seeing him again for a fortnight, and he was hoping to see her again almost at once.

'Where are you staying?' he asked.

'How do you mean?'

Was everything he said *so* impenetrable?

'What – I say – I mean – where are you staying in Birmingham? We might meet again for lunch tomorrow perhaps?'

'I'm not staying in Birmingham. In fact, I'm not meant to be here at all.'

They were driving back through traffic now. The corgis, unfed, were yapping in the back.

'Shush, corgis. We'll stop and buy you fish and chips on the way home. No' – only a faintly different voice was adopted for Fred – 'I should have been spending the day with my grandmother in Kensington and it's very naughty of me not to be there. Nana is the most wonderful woman. Tracy and I *worship* her, particularly Tracy. She brought us up, quite largely because our mother had to work and also because my mother is a slut who gets drunk and keeps having affairs with men. So Nana brought us up and every so often she comes to London which she adores and I always try and be there and make it a special treat for her.'

'So you aren't staying here at all?'

'No. I should at least get back to London for tea.'

'Whereabouts do you live in London? How can I get in touch?'

'I'm in the book. And here's my number.' She calmly handed him a card from a little pile kept in the glove compartment behind the steering-wheel. 'Look, will here do?' She drew up by the side of St Philip's Place. Pigeons waddled about in the drizzle at his ankles. Dazed, he stared after the bottle-green Bentley; two little foxy faces gazed back at him, their steamy breath clouding the window.

XI

'Yes,' said Jessica Owen. 'This will do well.'

She paid the taxi and alighted on the sloping pavement.

Tracy, dear girl, had cooked her a lovely little lunch, and then assumed that she would want a nap. But she had not settled. The more she thought, and the more she re-perused the faded, marbled covers of the notebooks, which she could hardly bear to open again, the more she wanted to return to the house on Haverstock Hill where she had spent her childhood. She might have the strength to find her own way home by bus, but she wanted all her energy, on the outward journey, for exploration; hence the extravagance of the taxi. How different the landmarks were as it had cruised northward. New buildings everywhere, even a mosque in Regent's Park. And Adelaide Road almost like a motorway. Even on Haverstock Hill the traffic was thick. She could remember, as a girl in 1906 or 1907, running out to the front gate and peeping through the bars at the noisy machine – almost the first she had ever seen – a Delaunay-Belleville tottering up the hill in bottom gear. She remembered the stillness which descended on the air when it had gone past. And there before her now, amid the roar of buses more than seventy years later, were the same gates, and the same steps, and the same, dreary little stucco house.

How enormous it had seemed in those days! Although it was instantaneously recognizable it was not merely her eyes that told her she was there. By some unmistakable series of impulses, sensations in her limbs and her stomach, she knew where she was. A hundred half-memories of childhood thronged back; the smell of baking from the house next door – the Trenimans. The sight of Miss Treniman, a maiden aunt of the next-door family, running out into Haverstock Hill and shovelling up the horse-shit for her roses as the drays and carriage horses heaved their way up to Hampstead. How old Miss Treniman seemed; old and mad. Probably younger then than Jessica Owen was now.

She remembered, too, the sound of her father working in the studio at the back of the house in those days, he must have had some equipment at home. The gentle tapping of his hammer on ... on copper in those days it would have been. And venerable visitors coming to the house, patting her head and greeting her mother with a distant courtliness. Later, when father had, in effect, left them, and she was older, poor Fran would enunciate the names of their distinguished guests, C. R. Ashbee and Henry Wilson, and Bainbridge Reynolds. Jessica had grown up believing that these names were something to conjure with: that saying Bainbridge Reynolds was a friend of her father's was like boasting intimacy with the Prince of Wales or the Prime Minister. Gradually, their comparative obscurity had come home to her. 'That lovely lectern at St Cuthbert's at Earl's Court,' her mother used to say, 'you know your father was really responsible for the design, even though it was Bainbridge Reynolds who got all the credit.'

How pathetic mother became, keeping up the fiction that father needed to live in Chelsea for his work. Jessica herself must have been twenty before she realized there was anything odd about her parents' ménage, and it was not until she herself married that she became aware of the fact that this was a ceremony which her parents had never actually undergone.

Emrys Owen, the man she married, was a Welsh schoolmaster, teaching mathematics in Hampstead. By that stage Jessica was twenty-two or so, and had just begun to be a teacher of infants herself. It was 1919. Fran had just died of flu. Father, who had become depressed and peculiar, and had never lately lived much in that house, returned to it briefly. She had found him a stranger. She had married Emrys to escape. She had gone to Wales in 1920. First at Swansea Grammar School, then at Carmarthen, to escape. Her own marriage had, for a short time, been happy. She had her baby, Fanny's mother, almost at once, and she had, perhaps, never really noticed what sort of man Emrys was. Perhaps the example of her parent's ménage was not helpful. With the years, she more and more believed that we learn to be married only by example. She and Emrys wouldn't have been fools, of course, like her parents, like her daughter or her grand-daughter. They would have stuck together.

As a schoolmaster in those days Emrys would have had to. But almost the most saddening thing about her months of grief for Emrys when he was accidentally run down by a tram in Swansea in 1925 was the secret knowledge that all the joy of their life together had already died.

Life since, hard to all outward appearances, had felt so selfishly happy. She had woken up almost every morning, for the last fifty-five years, thankful that she would not have to spend the day with Emrys Owen.

Unashamedly she had allowed herself to sink down the social scale. She left their comparatively genteel house in Carmarthen and set up a sub-post-office in the terraced house in Neath which had been her home for the next few decades. With such a young child, it would not have been possible to go back herself to schoolteaching. She had no shame about being a sub-postmistress. She had done it efficiently and well. Her customers had all been interesting to her. Happily, and without any sense of loss, she had abandoned her links with England and the pretensions which had kept her mother's eyes, whatever their reduced circumstances, so firmly fixed on the goals of gentility.

Besides, she could not go back. There was nothing to go back to. Father had become odd since the First World War. It was not simply mother's death, though she was afraid that had something to do with it. Her mother, anxious to the last to conceal the truth, had never allowed the nature of her father's 'oddness' to be made clear to the daughter. But oddness will out, and it soon became apparent that he had fallen into decline ever since reading in the newspaper, after the second battle of Mons, that someone called Toby Shakes-peare had gone missing. This obsession formed so big a part in the madness which finally took over her father in later life that it was hard for Jessica to know how noticeable, really, it had been in the early days after her mother died. At what date had she learnt all the details? It had come out so gradually, over a number of decades. Toby Shakespeare (if he actually existed, which Jessica had often had the temptation to doubt: the name, apart from anything else, sounded improbable) had been a natural son of her father's: the result of some indiscretion with a girl of the servant class in early manhood. The passage of the diary which she had read on the train that morning made sense, but what pathetic sense, of much that had happened subsequently to her father's mind. Annie, the servant girl, had evidently gone north. There it was in the diary: *Annie Shakespeare*. And her father's sad little encounter with Annie, years later, in the middle of Birmingham, had confirmed the existence of a son – Toby, destined to be a stoker on the railways.

Jessica's glimpse of her father's diaries – she wanted not much more than a glimpse – had convinced her of what she had always suspected. Her father had been a incurable romantic: and, as such, a fickle lover, an impossible husband and a neglectful father. But always, in the back of his mind, and rendering him perpetually dissatisfied with his present lot, was the sense that somewhere else, and with someone else, he could have been innocently happy. Annie, Toby Shakespeare's mother, had obviously been such a person. Perhaps her liaison with Oswald Fish had not lasted more than a week. For him, it was set apart; deliberately chosen (though perhaps not consciously so) as the one love which was not, could not, have been blighted. Toby, his lost son, had come to represent a whole world of lost happiness. Jessica remembered father's voice as he roared out in the mental ward, 'Toby! *Toby*! I don't want all these bloody bitches and bastards, I want my boy, my *Toby*,' and how he had wept and raved for this figment. Sometimes the ravings had become so extreme that Jessica had almost come to believe that it would have been worth trying to find Toby Shakespeare. But he had almost certainly been killed at Mons. And if not, why should a man of fifty-odd (as he would have been by the time of these ravings) suddenly be made to confront the father he had never known?

That final sad phase, the mad, unshaven old man, had obliterated all her earlier memories of her father. Standing outside the house on Haverstock Hill, earlier phases of his existence came back to her. She remembered what he had been like on the intermittent occasions, rare enough, when she had visited him in London from South Wales. His thick black hair, always parted on the sides of a bald head and well lubricated with bay rum, was brindled and dirty grey. For a long time, perhaps for the last thirty years of his life, he had had no work. He never spoke to her of her mother; nor did he ever allude to his past. He had lived on the upper floor of that stucco building, and sublet the rest of the house for flats. Usually at his side, as he sat and sat in his chair, there were drawings; designs doodled on the back of envelopes or in children's sketchbooks bought from

Woolworths. Sometimes he would draw tea-pots or chalices; at other times lamp stands or door furniture; very occasionally he would conceive architectural fancies. She remembered an occasion, when he was about seventy-five, when there had been a competition to refurbish one of London's underground stations. She thought it had been Tottenham Court Road but now she forgot. That must have been some time in the 1930s. He had never finished the drawings, of course, but the conception behind them had been so touchingly out of date. He had wanted to build a Gothic underground. The ticket kiosk, of cast iron and stained glass, was to have resembled some chantry chapel in a cathedral! It was a sign that his mind was going. How endlessly he had talked about his rivals in the field, all dead by then, or old men. He seemed to say, always, that the Arts and Crafts movement, in which he had been so enthusiastically caught up in middle age, lacked the high aspirations, the loftiness of vision of the pure Gothic of an earlier period. How she had scorned her father's work! And how amused she had been when the generation of her grandchildren (no one more eagerly than Fanny) had so excitedly returned to the aesthetic values that he had held so dear.

She had never been close to him, never close enough to hate him or quarrel with him. Whatever fire had inspired him to elope with her mother had died, been spent, before she was born. She was brought up in an atmosphere of coldness and distance.

Now, if she chose, she could probably re-read the diaries and discover the full story of her parents' romance. How her mother, at the crucial moment, had doubted, how he had gone to Bruges, hurt and angry, and most extraordinarily, contracted that liaison with a *black* woman. How her mother had, after all, changed her mind and come out to join him. At this moment, the last notebook she had read on the train had ended. Doubtless others, in the suitcase back in Neath, could further elucidate the mystery. She only had one exercise book left – it was with her now in her plastic Tesco carrier bag – and a glimpse in the taxi had shown her that it belonged to a later date when her father was nominally living at the house on Haverstock Hill. There was a long low wall opposite the house and, in spite of the cold, Jessica sat on it, perusing the little exercise book inscribed in that familiar hand. This was not a continuous diary so much as jottings:

4th January 1909. 'Are you going to finish your pudding?' 'No.' F. gives a little sigh. This is all our colloquy at the supper table this evening. Since returning from Holborn at 6, the deathly silence has reigned on our sad little house. Poor little Jessica, solemn and thin, sat reading *The Wide Wide World.* What a house for a child to grow up in!

5th January 1909. I thought today, as I taught my metalwork class, how much I would like to try my hand at a real piece of architecture again! But a man must earn his daily bread. This new man – a new name to me at any rate – Ninian Comper – has much of a future I would say. His splendid church (St. Cyprian I think) just off Baker Street achieves many of the effects that I have dreamed of in earlier days when trying to strain the airy lightness of the Gothic metaphor out of the prosaic medium of iron and brick.

15th February 1909. Yesterday F. tried to remind me that it was St. Valentine's Day. She had bought a little posy of violets from a street-vendor and laid them on my dinner plate. But I was late for dinner and did not notice them until the meal was nearly over. By then, she was half in tears and I could not be doing with tears and blowing of noses. My lateness for dinner was caused by a wrangle with a whore whom I had tupped in Kentish Town. Ah me, and if I had not done so I might have felt more amorously disposed to poor F. and so might have noticed the violets and so might have noticed F. too, trying to smile and reach me across the waves of misery and silence that separate us both. I write this in the studio in Radnor Walk where I have a divan and increasingly sleep of nights. But 10/6 for a whore in Kentish Town!! Such a price would be expensive in Jermyn Street or Piccadilly. She was a young Irish woman with red hair, in a hurry to be done so that she could pacify an infant who was crying in the next room. I gave her 5/-.

12th April 1909. Jessica, when I called at Haverstock Hill: 'Why do you not come home more often, Papa? Mama cries for you so often.'

16th April 1909. A letter out of the blue this morning from Birmingham – always a post-mark to send shivers down O. Fish's over-sensitive spine! No fears were in order, however; a letter from Pinchard the curate at St. Aidan's, Purgstall Heath! My one single architectural triumph! They believe that in the original specifications for that church there should have been a tower, where the porch is. Would I advise, since they think to raise a subscription &c. &c. I will be aware of what a flourishing &c. &c. it has now become. I write back a short note referring them to the original drawings which show a splendid solitary tower, with alternate stripes of red brick and white stone; the whole crowned by a green copper fleche or spirelet supplied by Fish & Co. Ah, those were the days. Partly tickled that they wrote, however. Partly oddly disturbed. Therefore, in part to console myself and in part to celebrate I wander down to the lower end of Shaftesbury Avenue where I meet a young lady who. for the payment of a guinea, is very willing to have a devilish excited piece of O. Fish thrust between her shapely little legs. A guinea well spent. When all was done she said, 'You're a lusty one.' which inspired me to run the course again with many interesting variations proposed by my obliging companion. How devoutly I hope that in addition to an agreeable afternoon. she has not given me some notorious bodily disorder.

18th May. I think not. All clear so far. Glorious spring day. Took J. with her hoop to Regent's Park. She is. O me, such a solemn child: I fear taught to be so by F.

Here the large sprawling hand ended. Jessica put the notebook away in her Tesco carrier bag. She remembered those walks in Regent's Park with her father. in those days rather dapper, with yellow kid gloves, and an Inverness cape; a slightly eccentric 'artistic' looking man as she later came to realize, but handsome with his very sturdy face and thick whiskers. This whoring was rather an astonishment. It was a pity. For, without these references it might have been possible to show the notebooks to someone else. Jessica did not feel prudish about the subject of sex, although it had long ago ceased to be of immediate personal interest to her. This was not true in the case of all octogenarians, she knew. But she was lucky. She had not been troubled much by sex since she was in her thirties and had had a love affair with the local policeman in Neath. No, it was not prudery that forbade her sharing these diaries with. say, her grand-daughters. It was the idea of *her father* (whom none of them had even heard of) consorting with prostitutes which was worrying. Just as it was unnecessary to imagine that the present generation were any poorer for not knowing the private details of her parents' married life, any more than they had heard of her father's metallic or architectural designs. *It was none of their business.* If he had been successful in life, or given to posterity something they still cherished – a still popular building, perhaps – it might be an altogether different matter. Great men become public property. Lesser mortals are their own masters.

Jessica sighed. How like her memories, yet how unlike, the house on Haverstock Hill had become. For one thing, the little lime trees which her father had planted, much too close together in (she supposed) 1910 or earlier had now grown to a height and thickness that guaranteed no light would reach rooms on the ground floor.

This lime tree bower my prison he used to quip. Now the trees really seemed like a barricade. The front steps. which squeezed their way through the trunks of two of them, were heavily overgrown with moss and weeds. A fat, foreign woman, perhaps a Greek, with a sallow complexion and great skeins of greasy grey hair hanging in loops from the back of her head, was peering from an upper window a cigarette dangling on her lips.

'Four trees – one for each of us.' her father had said 'One for Frances. one for Jessica and one for me.

'But there are four trees and only three of us.

'One for luck, Jessica, one for luck,' and he had laughed in his thick, rather sensual voice (or so it now seemed in her memory having read the diaries).

She had forgotten having this conversation but it now came back to her. She remembered the look of anguish in her mother's eyes. Perhaps it was later than 1910. Was the fourth tree a child her parents had never had? Or was it a foreshadowing of his obsession with Toby Shakespeare?

Another reason for not wanting anyone else to know about the diaries was that they gave such an odd impression. Jessica could never remember being a *solemn* child. She remembered being solitary, though that had been rather forced on her by circumstance. But she could remember laughing, and enjoying the company of others when it was to be had. Also. it seemed to her that her father's egotism distorted the true nature of her mother's sorrow. It was not that she was perpetually pining after him. At least, Jessica did not really think so. Undoubtedly Frances *was* fond of her father: undoubtedly, had he been more attentive to her, she would not have felt so reproachful of herself, so angry with life for having played a trick from which there was no escape.

In this respect, her parents were imaginatively, in terms of their own personal myth, alarmingly close and yet quite different. Her mother, trapped perhaps in a tedious marriage and a repressive atmosphere of respectability in Edgbaston, had determined to rebel to break out, to follow her star by eloping with her artistic brother-in-law. Something had gone wrong – any number of things perhaps. Whatever prompted her to do so, she had looked back and, like Lot's wife, been ossified in consequence. The tones of daring with which her father's diary spoke of F. and of her seductive charms entirely belied what, in reality, she had been like in life: timid, depressive, handsome no doubt, but anxious to cocoon herself in a respectability more rigid than the one she had left behind in Edgbaston. Jessica did not question the general truth of her father's account of the love affair. The subsequent elopement was to be assumed to have happened since ... here *she* was! But all that living for romance, and not being married, and having an illegitimate child only increased her mother's nostalgia for the world she had hated, kicked against and rejected.

'We never did that in Augustus Road,' she would say in tones of quiet reproach to Jessica, if some hint of domestic coarseness crept into their arrangements: if she forgot a butter knife or a tea-strainer. These allusions to Augustus Road were never made in the presence of her father, of course. Though he, like Fran, had been unable to follow his guiding star, it had been altogether for different, more complex, less comprehensible reasons. Fran had made a mistake, felt an ass, sought to compensate by displays of unhappiness and fuss about tea strainers. Father had been different. His clear vision of himself as, perhaps, a great Gothic architect had been obscured and held back by distractions: the demands and obligations of family; the need to earn a living, and (to a certain extent even after he had come to London) to appease for being the Black Sheep of the family. But the vision, though incomplete, was something she believed he had had. A final scrawl on the last page of the notebook she held suggested as much:

'It has troubled F. for months – and troubled me – that I am less famous as a metal-worker than W. Bainbridge Reynolds! F. tells her friends that it was really I, not W.B.R. who designed the lectern at Earl's Court – St. Cuthbert's Church! As though such a detail made a ha-pennyworth of difference. I admire Reynolds, of course. And I admire the church – designed by that ass Gough – rather along the lines I myself attempted to follow at St. Aidan's, Purgstall. Since coming to London, I realize that I have forgotten something precious and IMPORTANT. It was what inspired me to be an architect in the first place, and to work in old Chamberlain's office designing fire-stations and schools all those years ago when I could have had an easier time working for Pa at the works.

I know I wanted something more than ease and comfort and material success. When I saw Pinchard (who writes to say they hope they *will* raise enough money for the tower) and he told me that my designs for St. Aidan's had been accepted, I knew that something not unimportant had happened to me. I had left the apprentices. I had joined – in what minor capacity I at that moment forgot – the masters. My name – posterity could do what it liked with my name. Who knows the name of the architect of Chartres Cathedral? But I knew, and felt confident, that, when the name of Fish had been obliterated from the face of the earth there would still be my monument, my vision, my assertion that Birmingham was more than order books and ledgers and chimneys and wheels and machines and all the other appurtenances of capital: a place where *man* . . .

The hand broke off finally here. As she finished reading, Jessica was aware that the lady of sallow complexion, possibly Greek, was leaning out of the first floor window and shouting at her: 'Alla day you seeta thair and makka notes.'

Jessica smiled up at her, not quite sure what she was saying.

'You seet with the notebook and theenk I do not see you. You are all such fools. I see you arrive. I see the taxi drive away. And then alla the day you will seet with the notes.'

Jessica felt, in big cities, the constant presence of madness and delusions. There really seemed nothing odd about this poor woman, railing against her in paranoid tones, from what had been her father's bedroom window. In a way, she was grateful to the woman who yelled out, 'I know you are a communist!'

'Good afternoon!' Jessica called up to her in the friendly tone she adopted for religious functionaries, policemen or lunatics.

'You have a notebook and you are a communist!' cried the woman. 'Yesterday it was the Mafia and the Nazis and the day before . . .' her voice sank to a whisper as though anxious that even an enemy should keep the matter a secret, 'it was the IRA. So you filthy bitch scum I know who you are!' And her voice screamed loud once more.

Jessica wandered back down the hill towards Chalk Farm Station. The woman was perfectly right. She was a communist. She had joined the Communist Party in Swansea in 1931 and she had never altered her political allegiance, except once, when, in a fit of pique and adventure, she had voted for the Welsh Nationalists.

XII

The sun came out at about the same time that the children came
out of school. Jen liked the afternoon routine. If the morning rush
was all anger and agitation, 'fetching time' was leisurely, involving
leaning against the larch-lap fence near the gate of the Nutkin,
waiting for Sam to appear, while she had pleasant conversations
with the other mums about their innocent and not very eventful
lives. This was at half past three, leaving a full half hour before she
need drive to fetch Harriet at her school. Even this was hardly
necessary: since Debbie Gladstone had started to come home on the
bus, there was no reason that Harriet could not come with her.

Harriet was, it was true, always rather silly when she had just
been with Debbie – inclined to be pert and make extremely unfunny
jokes. But this could hardly worry Jen as she drove about Edgbaston
in a hazy late winter grey: a scarlet sunset in an ashen sky at twenty
to five. At this time of the year, Edgbaston was almost as beautiful
as Surrey. The air was crisp; smoke rose from bonfires, not chimneys; the avenues of well spaced, well planted trees in every road
were about to come into bud over the wide pavement. Behind high
hedges and thick shrubberies, nature richly went on being itself.
Crocuses were in flower. There were badgers and foxes and squirrels
and voles in the garden of Augustus Road, so that it seemed hardly
necessary to have the odious Ping-Pong *and* a guinea pig!

She turned the bright turquoise mini into her large drive, and
enjoyed the sensation that the wheels were crunching over fallen
cones and pine needles, giving the aromatic flavour to that whole
cedar-shaded, beech-shielded side of the garden. On such an afternoon as this, the children were happy with their own ploys. Sam
dropped his satchel on the path and ran at once to the wooden
swing, suspended from the branch of a large cedar, where perhaps
Fred himself, on visits to his grandparents, might have played.
Harriet went indoors. Jen did not know for certain what she was

doing, but this was all to the good. Harriet was getting to the age where she needed her secrets and her privacy.

Seeing the children so well occupied, Jen told them, 'I'm just going to see Grandad!' and strolled round the side of the house to the front door which led into her father-in-law's quarters.

It was a large, comfortable, reassuring brick house, with capacious bow windows on three floors and gables at the top: an architecture which expressed common sense and complete domestic self-confidence. Fred and his father between them had divided it up extremely skilfully – even Fred's Grandma had found it commendable, and she had been living there for the last ninety years. By the time the day passed by and the horrors of bad temper at breakfast had worn off, Jen often felt in a mood of great ease which was increased by the comfort and size of the house: much bigger and more comfortable than she and Fred would have been able to afford in Surrey.

'Anyone in?' she called to her father-in-law as she opened the wide front door.

'Hallo!' he called out good-humouredly. 'Just made a cuppa, care to join me?'

Jen said that she would. She had never got on with Fred's parents when his mother was alive, and when they still lived near *her* parents in Surrey. There had been something cold and brittle about Fred's mother. Only since her death had she come to revise her opinion. No one who had not been rather wonderful – so Jen believed – could have inspired so much love as Fred's dad had shown for her. He was not exhibitionistic about his grief and now, after five years had passed, hardly alluded to it. But he had obviously loved his wife dearly.

'Let's have it in the sitting-room,' he said. Tea was already made and on a trolley. He wheeled it into his own room. 'Just help yourself while I go and see if Ma's awake.' He tiptoed back almost at once.

'Still dozing,' he said. 'She's been quite silent all afternoon.'

Jen thought it was rather wonderful the way that Hugh, during his own retirement, should so willingly make light of having to look after his mother. When discussing it with Jen he always made a joke of it, but it must have been a strain.

'So,' she said, 'You've had a rather quiet day.'

'No, no, quite a chatty morning. Perhaps she's hitting the bottle. There was a tone of humourlessness about the jest. 'Poor old Ma.

I think she tired herself out talking this morning. Very interested in this family tree young Harriet's doing.'

'Don't mention it! The children were squabbling about it from the moment they woke up.'

'You'd never believe what Ma said to me this morning.'

Hugh had flushed about the gills and his eyes were wide with beady excitement as he handed Jen her tea cup.

'Of course,' he said, 'you never knew my father.'

'I hope it was nothing upsetting that your mother told you,' said Jen.

It could not have been anything very calamitous because Hugh was smiling, but he replied, 'Well, yes, it is rather upsetting. You know, I always thought that both Ma's parents, my grandparents, were dead by the time I came on the scene. How old am I?' he asked himself, replying at once, 'Sixty-nine. It makes me nine when my grandmother died.'

'And yet you never knew her?'

'Knew old Granny Jobling of course. Granny Fish is the one I never knew.'

'Granny Fish?'

'Ma – my mother's mother.'

'You're as bad as Harriet,' Jen laughed, as soon as someone spoke to her about genealogy her head started to spin.

'Blow me,' said Hugh, lighting a cigarette, 'if it doesn't transpire that Granny Fish died when I was ten. What's *more*,' he emphasized excitedly by waving the cigarette, 'I did see her, Ma took me to see *her own mother* and never thought to tell me who it was. People in the old days were damned extraordinary.'

'What was the matter with her?' Jen asked.

'Family scandal. She ran off with my great-uncle. I never knew I had a great-uncle. So Ma was brought up by her grandparents. Brought up in this house, brought her husband back here when she married my father, lived here ever since. Oddly upsetting somehow. can't say why.'

'Yes,' Jen said, 'I can see it would be.'

Actually it rather thrilled her to think of this skeleton in the family cupboard. She could not think of anything helpful to say but she drank her next cup of tea and talked about *her* day at school. Hugh thought how pretty she was, and how good-natured and personable. Fred was lucky to have found someone so suitable. Not everyone did these days, but perhaps the Joblings would be lucky. At the moment there was not a single Jobling relation known to Hugh who had ever had a divorce, or been separated from their spouse. Except his grandmother. The matter kept him musing long after Jen had left him in order to make the children's high tea and after he heard Fred's return home about six o'clock.

Fred knew that he was not drunk. Two half pints of beer at lunchtime do not make you drunk. He knew it could not be a virus. He had never felt better in his life – more vibrantly in control of all his senses, except appetite for food, which had vanished altogether. And yet, as he had bounced his way through the rest of the afternoon, having climbed out of the green Bentley in St Philip's Place, he had been in a sort of daze.

When he had got, rather late, to the meeting of the Planning Committee, for instance, he knew everyone there perfectly well: Dawn, her loose, wool-clad tits wobbling over her agenda like jellies; boring neurotic Lonsdale, puffing those rather noxious cigarettes; the Town Clerk himself; Mrs Cuthbertson who took such an earnestly do-gooding line about everything that she might as well have been Labour; Sage, whose instinct was so meanly cheeseparing that he might just as well have been Tory; Wilkins, Bilkins, Pilkins and Tilkins were all there. This afternoon they all seemed to be strangers – a circle of oddly earnest, rather ugly faces, all deeply interested in a subject which, having interested him, was now totally transformed by his visit to Purgstall and his encounter with Fanny. The voices which churned out round the table bore no relation to the foul-smelling holes from which they seemed to be proceeding. The meeting felt like an elaborate pantomime, of no relevance to the central fact that Fanny Williams was the most beautiful person in the world. Fanny's beauty made Fred feel remote but god-like; as benign as a god need be to the likes of Pilkins and Tilkins when they argued about the relative merits of a skittle alley and a second swimming pool in the Purgstall Leisure Centre; well disposed towards Wilkins and Bilkins when they read out their letters from Contractors and Surveyors and Purveyors of Dull Information: but removed from them by a golden erotic glow, the memory of having his legs squeezed under a pub table by the most beautiful woman in the world.

'Essentially as I see it,' one of the voices was saying, (though whether it was coming from behind Lonsdale's nicotine-encrusted false teeth or Mrs Cuthbertson's too-bright lipstick who could tell?) 'we've just got to give this one teeth and that means seizing the nettle and getting down to the nitty gritty.'

'It's all a matter of nuts and bolts at the end of the day,' had been the contribution of Wilkins or Bilkins or Tilkins.

'Inflation is now running at eleven per cent. The longer we leave it the more expensive this bloody leisure centre's going to be. We've already got to the point where we can't afford one swimming bath, let alone two.'

'Who said anything about scrapping the swimming pool?'

'With respect, Madam Chairman, it is, quite frankly, that or the old folks' Day Centre ...'

'Let's face it, this is an absolute tragedy,' another of the voices had interjected. 'To think that here we could be having a Day Centre for our elderly folk, we could be having somewhere for the kiddies; we could be having somewhere for the young mums and the toddlers; we could be having a youth centre for the youngsters. And the whole scheme is being held up because the space is occupied by some warehouse full of fancy goods from some frankly arty-farty shop. With respect, that's all it is.'

Someone else had declared that they would not be surprised if the warehouse was being used for marijuana; someone else had said that marijuana was less of a problem these days than glue-sniffing; another person had read an account recently which said that glue-sniffing could cause permanent brain damage and another voice had said that if his opinion was asked for (which it had not been) it was the fault firmly and squarely of the parents; a Conservative voice asked if there had been trouble with glue-sniffing in the days before comprehensive education; and another voice had asked, while on the subject of education, whether it would be possible to return to Item 3 on the agenda and draw the committee's attention to the ill-fitting windows and poor ventilation in Purgstall Middle School? Madam Chairman thought it would *not* be appropriate to draw the committee's attention to this fact, still less to take them back to Item 3. The issue under discussion was the Purgstall Area Development Scheme, with particular reference to the warehouse, formerly St Aidan's church. Madam Chairman had further expressed herself on the belief that Mr Jobling had a number of things to say on the issue.

Like an automaton, he had begun his reply. The first thing to be said was that this church was not going to be used as a warehouse.

Not to be used as a warehouse? Voices had broken out all round the table. Through the murmuring, Madam Chairman had asked what it *was* to be used for. It was, she was informed by Fred, to be restored. But restored to *what?* As a beautiful building.

Beauty? Murmuring had turned to consternation. Who was this man? A lawyer or a lunatic?

It had become, he heard himself saying, a very clear and divisive issue of principle between the conservation lobby, who felt that we had a duty to protect our architectural heritage, and those who wanted to improve the lamentable conditions at present prevailing in Purgstall Heath.

Clamour had broken out round the table. Since when had our architectural heritage brought down the crime rate? Why had the committee not been told that it had an architectural heritage? Could the committee have, frankly, a bit less high-falutin arty waffle and get down to brass tacks; or if not, it had been added, brass tacks, at least the basics? And meanwhile fingers were playing with pocket calculators and cynics were wondering if architectural heritage came cheaper than swimming baths.

Did Madam Chairman then understand, she had asked, that Fred himself was having consultations with the owner of the warehouse?

'Fanny!' someone had interrupted here, and there had been ribald laughter from the men; wiggling of the tits from Dawn; tight lips from Mrs Cuthbertson.

Stammering, blushing, Fred had admitted that informal consultations were in progress.

More laughter. Lonsdale, a cigarette in the corner of his mouth, had played with his pocket calculator. Fred had never felt more persecuted since he had left school.

Might Madam Chairman propose that Mr Jobling had more conclusive consultations with Miss Williams and report back to the committee in a fortnight's time? It had been suggested that she might be amenable (much rolling of the eyes by Dawn) to persuasion (and ribald laughter from pipe-smoking mouths). If, after all, she was not using the building there seemed no earthly reason why the site should not be cleared as quickly as possible.

The committee had moved on swiftly to Item 6, a pedestrian precinct in Shirley.

The only sensation he had felt, since the passing on of the committee to this fascinating topic, had been one of almost insane joy. They had actually *asked* him to have another meeting with Fanny. The appalling complications which this would involve lay ahead; having to admit to her that he was, after all, from the Council. All that mattered was that it gave him a cast-iron excuse to get out of Birmingham, stay in a hotel at the Council's expense, and see if Fanny was amenable to persuasion. If her excited throbbing legs under the pub table were anything to go by she was very amenable indeed.

So it was that, the tempests of the morning forgotten, he almost bounced into the kitchen in Augustus Road.

Jen looked up at her husband as he plonked his briefcase down on the unit where she had been meaning to chop up Ping-Pong's lights. The bald dome of his forehead was glistening and he looked quite red in the face. He was grinning like a zany and his eyes behind their very thick lenses were gleaming with excitement. She wondered whether he was drunk, or had been promoted, or whether Lonsdale, the one he did not care for, had fallen down a man-hole.

'Good day?' she asked. The children sat at the table eating baked beans. Sam was kicking Harriet under the table. Harriet was trying not to cry and trying to resist the temptation to kick him back even harder. Neither of them appeared to notice his arrival, even when he boomed out, with what sounded artificial cheeriness, 'Evening all! Mmmm! Beans. They look good.' In fact, he felt so well disposed towards them all and so glad that he was going to be leaving them behind while he went to London, that there was nothing artificial about his good humour at all.

At that point, unable to bear it any longer, Harriet lashed out with a well-aimed wide-fitting Start-Rite and caught Sam a nice one on his silly little shin. Instantly, his pretty, cheeky smile puckered into a scowl, his cutlery fell from his hands with a clatter and he wailed out: 'Harriet *kicked me!*'

XIII

'I can't tell you how it happened. I just found myself holding hands in the pub with this *wonderfully* handsome man from the Council.'

'He doesn't sound very handsome from your accounts,' said Tracy. 'Tall and dark and bald with thick specs and a knobbly face.'

'He was so *reassuring*. Just the sort of man I ought to marry – solid and sensible and ...' Fanny sniggered at the outrageousness of it all and stuffed another forkful of moussaka into her mouth.

They were all sitting round the large pine table in Fanny's kitchen comparing notes about their day: Fanny, Tracy, Nana Owen, Charles Bullowewo and David Matheson.

'How did you know he was from the Council?' Nana asked. She liked moussaka because you could eat it without your teeth in. She had not told them much about her day. It had awakened too many complicated and painful memories. So she munched mysteriously and rather silently, gravy attaching itself to the slight but noticeable moustache on her upper lip.

'Yes,' said Charles, 'that's what I want to know, Nana.'

She glared at him with dark furious eyes. Really, until he stopped calling her Nana it would be impossible to have ordinary, amicable conversation with the man. And it had already gone too far now. She should have corrected him at once as soon as he started it.

'When I asked him he said he wasn't,' said Fanny.

'And that made you think he was lying?' Nana asked.

'Sure of it. He blushed absolutely scarlet and anyway what would he have been doing at my *lovely* church if he had not been from the Council? Charles said there would be someone snooping.'

And does he want to pull the church down?' David drawled without looking up. He did not have much appetite and the rest of the mysterious ménage wolfing mince on every side of him was making him feel sick. It was a terribly mistake to have renewed contact with Charles. If he had simply not come back this evening it would have been possible to break himself of the habit, to consign Charles to the list of long-discarded one-night stands. Now, as he felt the large chocolatey hand fingering his knee under the table, he knew there was no escape.

'Didn't seem very certain about whether he wanted it pulled down,' said Fanny, wiping her plate clean with a piece of bread.

'Fanny, you are awful,' said Tracy. Her Welsh accent was much more pronounced than her sister's; the pitch of her voice, if possible, even higher. Her words swooped and lilted as she spoke. 'So in case he is on the Council and in case he wants to pull down your church you are going to seduce him and make him do what you want.'

'Very sensible,' said Charles. He took David's hand in his own and stroked the bony, hairless fingers. 'Don't eat any more than you want,' he murmured. David shivered.

'It isn't like that at all,' said Fanny. 'He's the sweetest most huggable giant of a teddy-bear in the world, and so *dependable*.'

'How on earth can you tell?'

'And so handsome,' she said as if in reply.

'He sounds rather a bore to me,' said Nana Owen decidedly. 'But we shall doubtless find out.' Having finished her moussaka she fidgeted in her little bag for some minty cigarettes and put one between her gravy-stained lips.

'Let me, Nana,' said Charles, whipping out a lighter.

'You have such a deep and distinguished voice,' said Nana, trying to be nice to the man.

'*Wonderfully* distinguished,' echoed Fanny, sounding as if she was going into a swoon.

'How does an African come to have a distinguished voice?'

'Really Nana, don't be so rationalist,' said Fanny.

'No one has ever thought of me as a racialist,' said Nana. 'You seem to forget I joined the Communist Party to fight the fascists.'

'When did you leave it?' Charles's voice sounded incredulous.

She realized that, apart from the irritating habit of calling her *Nana*, it was simply his *voice* which put her off.

'I never left it,' she said. 'I won't leave it until it has beaten all the fascists and the liberals and the wishy-washies.'

Charles, not wishing to be drawn, said, 'I suppose I picked up my voice at Eton.'

'Oh, at *Eton* were you?' Her reply was full of mock solemnity. 'How very nice for you.'

She had a special tone of voice, Fanny knew it well, for dealing with the forces of privilege. She had always adopted it when talking to the Honourable Member, with whom she got on rather well. It was a tolerant rather whimsical little voice, the sort of expression one might adopt to a child who said that he had been playing with fairies in the garden.

'I had been going to save my news up for a little surprise at the end of the evening,' said Charles, 'but now I can't wait to tell you all.'

'Goodee, a surprise!' Fanny jumped up with childish glee. 'Tracy, is there pudding?'

'Nana's made one.'

'Bread and butter pudding,' said Jessica.

'My favourite!' exclaimed Fanny.

The pudding was produced from the Aga – a wonderful thing, thickly encrusted on the top with yellow and brown, its soggy curranty texture beneath visible through its Pyrex bowl. They all stared at it appreciatively while Charles continued his narrative.

'Being really rather sleepy this morning when Fanny and David were talking about the church in Birmingham, I did not fully take in what they were saying.'

'No thanks,' said David, when a steaming plate of pudding came his way.

'Are you another Etonian?' Nana asked accusingly, as though *alumni* of that academy might be expected to disdain anything so ordinary as a bread and butter pudding.

'No, I went to Winchester, as a matter of fact.'

'Winchester!' Even more whimsical, as if the fairies in the garden had been pixies.

David's plate was passed back to Fanny who scooped out more

from the Pyrex bowl and made the helping twice the size. For one awful moment David thought he was going to be made to eat a double portion as a punishment but Fanny soon began to attack it with her spoon.

'You asked, you see, how I came to have what you call a distinguished voice. The answer is that my parents sent me to Eton. My father was a headmaster in Salisbury – in Rhodesia.'

'Zimbabwe.' Jessica corrected him sharply.

'He himself had received a very good education, and he was anxious that I should have the same.'

'And was he at Eton too?' Nana asked mischievously.

'No, he wasn't. My father had two pieces of very good fortune. One was his mother. And the other was the fact that his mother had kind employers. She was governess to an English colonial family who had employed her in Brussels, where the father, a Mr Mackenzie, was a diplomat. He subsequently emigrated to Salisbury and brought her with him.'

'Was she a Belgian?' Nana asked.

'No, she was born in the Belgian Congo and was taken to Belgium as the governess of a rather neglectful Belgian family who ...' a rather lascivious leer had come over Charles's face, 'shall we say left her rather too much to her own devices.'

'In Brussels?'

'In Bruges, I have been told, is where the indiscretion occurred. Anyway, she found herself to be pregnant, and was dismissed by her employers. My father's father had been an Englishman.'

'Had been an Englishman? Did he stop being one?'

'I mean he *was* an Englishman.' Charles acknowledged the correction in a way that reminded Fanny of his technique in court when there was a tiresome old judge on the bench. 'But needless to say, he could not be found. My mother went to the British Embassy in Brussels and it was there she met the kind Mr Mackenzie who took her under his wing to look after the children. And it was in Brussels that my father, her poor little half-caste child, was born.'

'I bet kind old Mr Mackenzie was really the father,' blurted out Tracy.

'Shush,' said Fanny.

'No,' Charles admitted. 'I had always supposed so myself, in spite of my father's pious account of things. I remember old Mr Mackenzie well. It was he who left the money for my education.'

'Well then,' said Tracy, as if that clinched the matter.

'I had always thought so until this morning,' said Charles. 'My grandmother had always maintained to Daddy that his father was an English artist, and it certainly would have been odd to give him the names he had to carry through life, poor fellow, if her story had not been true.'

'Don't tell us, let us guess,' said Nana. 'He was called Michelangelo Bullowewo.'

'Winterhalter Bullowewo,' said Fanny ecstatically.

'Wrong,' said Charles. 'And it was only dear David who supplied me with the clue.' He ran his large fingers through David's short mousy hair. David smiled nervously.

'Not the architect?' he asked.

'Exactly,' said Charles. 'My father was called by my devoted grandmother after the English artist who had so wickedly seduced her on her holiday in Bruges.'

There was a little silence, and then David put his hand over Charles's shoulder and laughed and they said in chorus: '*OSWALD FISH BULLOWEWO!*'

XIV

Swathed in shadows and shrubberies, the large lumpy house in Augustus Road is plunged into darkness. In the rooms, things have become indistinct shapes, as though washed in a bath of blue-black ink; children have become snoring little lumps; words have retreated into thoughts; thoughts have become dreams.

Jen and Fred, insomniac but pretending to be asleep, lie awake. Jen's eyes are tight shut. Fred's, blinking less than in daytime, stare out into the dark. Jen is thinking of her day. She is wondering if she can go on much longer putting up with the children having tantrums and Fred having moods. She tries to remember what it was like before she got married, when all her time was her own. A busy day domestically *then* was if she did a bit of ironing after a morning's teaching. Now, the grisly morning routine of getting them all up and fed, and out of the house; and then her teaching morning; and then feeding the children; and then the household chores; and then cooking supper and just hoping it was something they all liked and that Fred would not be in one of his moods.

Most people, presumably, who had fallen into this tedious matrimonial trap, muddled along somehow. Jen felt sure that if you only learnt how to muddle along it would one day get easier. People who had been married twenty-five or thirty years did not throw boiled eggs around, did they? Or anyway, much less than *she* felt inclined to. And the silly part about it was that even if he *was* impossible, she loved Fred. She had said this to Graham, the head of Modern Languages at her school, when he had rather flatteringly got flirtatious. She had loyally missed out the bit about Fred being impossible and had simply said, 'No, Graham.' And when he, with his hand still on her bottom (in the Staff Room of all places!) had asked, 'Why not?' she had replied, 'Because I love my husband.' He had looked at her so tenderly: was it admiration or was he thinking what a silly sucker she was?

It felt like ages since Fred had ever looked at her tenderly. Only rarely, it seemed, did he look at her at all . . . She closed her eyes more tightly and tried not to allow her mind to go over it all again. She would have a bit of peace and quiet after tomorrow. He was having to go to London for a few days – sent by the Town Clerk to beard some solicitor or other over this boring Purgstall Heath business. Whenever Jen heard about it, some part of her brain, with an instinct of self-protection, clicked off, so that she never took in any details. She knew it was owned by Fanny Williams, the former pop star. Perhaps Fred would meet her. She hoped that if he did he would remember to get her autograph for the children. But perhaps the name of Fanny Williams did not mean anything to the new generation. Most of those old sixties' stars seemed obsolete, like ancient monuments. What was the song Fanny had sung? There was only one which had got into the charts if Jen could remember rightly. The words drifted back into her mind, and the jerky, rather suggestive music, heavily laced, Jen now saw, with sexual innuendo.

> Baby, you'll never know the times I had
> Baby, you thought you treated me so bad:
> Now it's you who's looking O so sad
> See what I mean,
> O pussy-cat queen?

> CHORUS: Pussy cat, pussy cat where have you been?
> You made me so lonely, O pussy-cat queen!

She remembered seeing Fanny sing it on *Top of the Pops*, a long droopy rather Ophelia-like girl, with flowers stuck in her hair and young men in tight jeans pirouetting about her. That must have been all of fifteen years ago. She had been about the same time as . . . Herman's Hermits, Marianne Faithful . . . the Bee-Gees, or were they earlier?

'Jen?' Fred's voice sounded strangely loud, in the dark, after a silence of about an hour.

'Mmm?' she grunted, as if more asleep than she really was.

'Have you ever thought that at the heart of the universe, there is nothing but a deep emptiness?'

'Honestly, Fred! What an idea!'

'But have you?'

'Go to sleep, Fred.'

Shortly, he did. His artificially rhythmical breathing became the convincingly erratic breath of a man deep in the world of dreams. Ien tried to think of the next verse. She couldn't.

> Pussy cat, pussy cat, where have you been?
> You made me so lonely, my pussy-cat queen

In another part of the house, Fred's grandmother lies in the darkness. One of the disadvantages of being over ninety is that you are never comfortable. Never. Standing, sitting, lying down, it is all equally awkward. At present she is lying down; whether it is morning or night she is not altogether sure. She knows that it is dark. She cannot remember whether she has been lying there uncomfortably for half an hour or half a day.

Her mind is churning and racing about far-off, distant sorrows which she had almost forgotten. She remembers her mother's look of sadness so well, that day she took Hugh to see her. Mother would have been fifty-odd then. She had another child – Jessica – by ... by Uncle Oswald.

The memories are so distant that they have become sharply focused, like the memory of a film or a book. Is it safe to return to them? Agnes Jobling feels them to be bristling with danger, but like an enchanted traveller in a fairy castle, presses on from room to room in search of forgotten treasure. She can remember no sequences of events at all. Only scenes. They appear to be quite unconnected with each other.

Christmas Day. A huge piece of roast beef on the table. They never had a turkey that she could remember. Goose, beef, never turkey. And Grandpa stood at one end of the table, carving the meat, and, presumably, Grannie at the other end of the table – Pa in the middle, strained and unhappy; an assemblage of cousins and aunts – twenty people round the table, perhaps. And she is next to Mother. She is perhaps five years old? She cannot remember being allowed to sit up to Christmas dinner on previous years. On her other side is Uncle Oswald. She remembers the smell of tobacco and something spirituous which hangs about his very thick whiskers. As she chews away at her meat, she looks up at these bushy extravagances, so long that they cover his collar, so thick that not the tiniest speck of cheek could be discerned beneath them, as through parts of Grandpa's rather more sparse beard. Uncle Oswald's whiskers are a sensation. She is fascinated by them and dreads them. Being kissed by him is like having a clothes-brush pressed against your cheek. And while she chews her roast beef, Uncle Oswald's hand has come down and rested on her lap, just below the table. It is a large, square hand. Dark hairs cover the wrist and the part half concealed by the cuff, making you wonder whether underneath his clothes he was covered in hair all over like a monkey on a barrel organ. Some of the thick hair is sprouting from his knuckles. He lays his hand open, his palm upwards on her lap. Is she supposed to take it? But she is holding her knife and fork. And then she looks down again. Another hand has appeared, hairless, smooth, tiny and white. Agnes knows that it is tiny for a grown-up because it is scarcely larger than her own hand and she is only five. This very familiar hand has come to rest on Uncle Oswald's palm, and there for a moment they are clasped, on the blue velvet of her party frock, on her lap, on Christmas Day ... ever so long ago.

XV

What Fred did not know was that Fanny spent almost all of every day out. When she was not attending to one of her own shops, she was compulsively nosing around someone else's; buying new shoes or clothes or porcelain figurines of the Prince Consort; or varieties of dog biscuit; or expensive 'jokes' such as carefully simulated excrement or innocent-looking jars, which when you unscrewed the top exploded with a giant plastic penis; or gramophone records; or large coffee-table books which she would never read; or a new radio-cassette; or a collapsible bicycle which could be put into the boot of the Bentley; large tins of caviare from Fortnum and Mason; or pornographic magazines to read when on the loo; or, from such an amusing and clever shop further up the King's Road from her own, an old fireplace, cleverly restored; or a poster of the Village People for Marmie's room; or a perfectly hilarious handkerchief which appeared to be decorated merely with a pattern but which, when you looked closely, had FUCK FUCK FUCK written all over it; or squares of silk from Liberty's, who also sell the most wonderful tights, interwoven with lamé and which *glow* coppery or gold or silver; or new pink cellophane umbrellas, so many funny sorts of umbrellas to buy and one is always losing them; or things vaguely designated at the back of Fanny's mind as presents, suitable at some future Christmas or birthday for someone or another.

Her acquisitive instinct was so intensely strong that it would indeed have been surprising had Fred been able to guess how much time she spent in shops. Nor could he guess that on that particular day she was having coffee with her buyers, lunch with the Northern manufacturer who supplied her with reproduction Victorian lavatories, coffee after lunch with an *angelic* man who thought he could get hold of four more *What the Butler Saw* machines, formerly amusing the crowds at Margate, Ramsgate, Westgate and some-where-else-Gate; and an afternoon meeting with the auditor –

profits in the King's Road and in Brighton, breaking even in Notting Hill and Bath; he had his doubts about the Birmingham venture; the Oxford market, which began enthusiastically, had started to slump; coals, he imagined, in a way designed to sound jocular, to Newcastle. After the meeting with the auditor, a glimpse of some dear friends over on a flying visit from America who could only be seen at five o'clock, for an hour and a half, scoffing the delicious tea and sandwiches and heavy fruitcake at Brown's Hotel in Dover Street; and, after the delicious tea, she had promised to look in at a party of rather Beautiful People who lived in Ennismore Gardens. Getting from Mayfair to Knightsbridge at 6 o'clock in the evening in a Bentley was hell. Hell, hell, hell – hours and hours.

Fred knew nothing of her day. Fanny, likewise, had no inkling that he had caught an early train from Birmingham, booked himself into Bailey's Hotel in Gloucester Road, and been trying to get hold of her ever since. She did not know how anguished he felt as he called at the house in Tregunter Road and found in turn, no one at home, then a rather sexy but cheap-looking girl in jeans, and then a cadaverous old woman with very cropped white hair and a brown weathered face like the Ancient Mariner and a menthol cigarette sticking out of her mouth, absolutely horizontal. She was holding the *Morning Star* and looked at him with scorn. Fanny did not know that Fred had then wandered disconsolately in the direction of the King's Road and explored her shop, and been amazed by the powerful atmosphere it gave off, something between an antique shop and a brothel, pianola music playing *Champagne Charlie* on the ground floor in the bathroom-fitting section; upstairs, while ladies tried on long, frilly, lacy night-dresses or held up corsets in amazement and while their male escorts, if there were any, lolled on velvet sofas by the potted palms or leered over the erotic books and photographs, a baritone in white tie, swallow-tail coat and large gingery side-whiskers played and sang *The Lost Chord* at a large black grand piano on which stood a bust of the Duke of Wellington.

All this, Fred had decided, would not really go down very well in Birmingham. He was about to say to himself that people had better things to spend their money on, but when he reflected on all the hideous carpets and three-piece suites and freezers and kitchen units that evidently still got sold (in spite of the Winter of Discontent) in the Bull Ring Centre, he thought perhaps he was not the best person to judge.

The important thing, as he wandered round the King's Road Fanny' shop, was that he felt himself being kicked sideways by the force of her personality, her vision of the world. This was something which had never happened to him in his life before. He did not wonder why. When he considered the way his courtship had gone with Jen, it did not seem necessary to ask *why*. There had been nothing of romance about it. They had both rather prided themselves on how sensible it all was. For a few months before and after the wedding, no doubt, they had been conventional enough to behave, and to feel, rather lovey-dovey. Sex had been perfectly manageable on both sides, although he found her increasingly boring and had forgotten, hard as he tried, even in moods when he was well disposed towards her, what it was about Jen that he had ever imagined was attractive.

Before Jen, there had been other girls, but never in a life so consciously devoted to being sensible, slightly cynical, always trying to make everything into a bit of a joke, never this ecstatically dizzy and painful and magnificent sensation of being in love. The silliness, the frivolity of the shop somehow contributed to this seduction so that, even when not in Fanny's presence, he could feel himself wanting to discard, for her sake, his old unromantic self.

This, obviously, was quite unknown to Fanny who had had the busiest of days. She hardly had time for the very brief telephone call with the Honourable Member, thrilled and excited by his boring old General Election about to burst on the nation. The Honourable Member now thought that the sun shone out of Mrs T's arsehole; Mr Heath was never mentioned; Nana thought that Mrs T was about the most unpleasant eruption from the Forces of the Right since Mussolini and the old days. Fanny was torn between these two opinions and so found the PM rather reassuring with his specs and bluff way of speaking.

Nor had she properly had a moment for her children, who were, as she daily averred to the Honourable Member, the most wonderful children in the world. Things had been so increasingly exciting lately. Her visit to Birmingham, meeting the reassuring tubby man with glasses (The Perfect Husband, he had become known as in Tregunter Road): Charles's *fantastic* revelation (which she still found hard to believe) that he was the *grandson* of Oswald Fish; Nana's rather peculiar silence and refusal to join in this conversation; Tracy's new boyfriend, who was a plumber called Sid, which would be so very useful when the loo went wrong yet again ... Where, in all this, was she to find time for her darling Marmie and Pandora? They did not like all this change, bustle, movement, excitement. Now, even Tracy had started to be absorbed in a love affair again. Marmaduke and Pandora had secretly agreed that they rather hated love affairs. They were already bored by the Plumber. They hated the Perfect Husband, even though they had not met him yet. They despised David Matheson who was taking up so much of Charles's time. Pandora had been going through Charles's address book and had found out that David had a perfectly good telephone number of his own. Why couldn't he go home instead of taking up Charles's time? Charles was bad enough taking up Fanny's time and Oswald Fish was worse than the lot: he seemed to be taking up all the Grown-Ups' time, with his boring old buildings and bits of ironwork. What was more, the mention of him put Nana in a vile mood and she sulked and smoked and read the paper.

Charles's new boyfriend was *married*! Marmie heard them discussing it. Wet little woofter David with his pathetic voice and drawly-droopy manner had a wife! And from what Marmie could tell, hiding in the broom cupboard on the landing while they had conversation, he had become ever so soppy about Charles but did not want his wife to know and he would never have come back to Tregunter Road had he not thought that Fanny was Charles's wife!!! And now he had come back he was so much in love, etc. etc. Pandora was in stitches when Marmie told her.

And so, at the end of a rather vexing and full day, the Tregunter Road household were gathered round the large kitchen table for supper. Fanny at the head of the table, and on her left her grandmother, and on her right, Charles. Marmaduke and Pandora and Tracy and Sid the plumber were scattered about variously at the end of the table. The dish was lasagne, cooked by Tracy and very good and washed down with Rioja, again very good, supplied by Charles.

Jessica sat silent, uncharacteristically silent, as David and Fanny and Charles discussed Oswald Fish.

'To think of him seducing your grandmother!' Fanny exclaimed.

'We don't know it wasn't the other way around,' said Charles.

'He might have been one of these twisted, repressed Victorians that you find so exciting, my dear Fanny.'

'Jeremy Tradescant – that's my colleague in the metalwork department I have been telling you about.' drawled David, 'has dug up even more of his stuff. You must come and look at it. *The* most hideous teapot you ever saw in your life.'

And Fanny, who had come to rather enjoy this banter with David, squealed with fury and everyone laughed.

'Don't tell me,' Charles said, wiping his lips delicately with his napkin, 'it has a cane handle.'

And they all laughed again.

Jessica found it all indescribably painful. If she told them the truth, that upstairs in her Tesco bag she actually had the man's diaries, they would merely be passed round and sniggered over and not understood. For all his cruelty to Frances, his neglect of Jessica herself, his failure as an artist and as a man, his final pathetic lunacy, he was her *father*. The mysterious thought of the half-caste Headmaster, now dead, in Zimbabwe, shook and touched her. With him perhaps, her unknown half-brother, she might have been able to share the experience, quietly and sadly as it should be absorbed. But to disclose the knowledge of Oswald Fish now would merely cheapen the experience. There was so much, a whole lifetime of feeling and experience to convey, which could hardly be explained lightly in such a miscellaneous company.

'These beautiful black girls are lovely movers,' Sid said, the only really serious voice round the table, his mouth full of lasagne.

'Been with them, have you?' Tracy asked, putting down her fork to play with his ear, which was pierced and carried a tiny artificial pearl.

'Wouldn't you like to know,' he said darkly, shovelling another spoonful of pasta into his mouth and letting out a low 'Corrr!' in sexy tones.

Jessica would never have believed it, but after years of faintly ridiculing Fran's craving for the bourgeois, her wish for life on Haverstock Hill to resemble the old days in Augustus Road, she now felt a sense of awkwardness and *shame*. Sid was a nice young man; Charles doubtless meant well. Her granddaughters and great-grandchildren were darlings. They would not bat an eyelid, she knew, if she told them that she had been born out of wedlock. But it was a secret which she had kept up for eighty-three years and she now found herself completely unable to break it. If she could have got Fanny on her own and could have talked about it quietly it might have been different. But the idea of all those baying, jolly young people in tight dungarees and leather and pin-stripe suits laughing knowingly about her illegitimacy was unthinkable, quite unthinkable.

'It is as if we married, you know that, dear,' Fran had so pathetically explained to her about a fortnight before her own wedding. 'But your father felt superstitious about it. Felt somehow it would have blighted our happiness if we had been . . .' And she had sighed, such a quiet little sigh as if, married or not married, she could hardly have had her happiness blighted more than it was already.

'Marmie, don't read at table,' Fanny called out. Marmie, clad in a black silk blouse and tight little leather trousers, was turning the pages of a magazine called *Honcho Mail*. He had paused to stare at a photograph of two naked men astride a motor-bike. Pandora leant across to look at it and giggled. She was a pretty little girl, with the same dark hair and eyes as her brother; she was wearing a frilly little pinafore dress from one of Fanny's shops and looked like a child in E. Nesbit, with her hair tied in plaits and pink ribbons. The children ignored their mother's plea.

David Matheson was saying, 'The ghastly thing is, that people from the past can vanish almost completely without trace.' How odd it was that he spoke apparently without moving his larynx, let alone his lips, 'I mean here you have Oswald Fish – decent enough designer if you like Arts and Crafts, feeble architect by all accounts, but enough known for someone like you, Fanny, to get excited about him, and if it weren't for the extraordinary coincidence of his connection with Charles we'd know absolutely nothing about him. For instance, we don't know why he left Birmingham, we don't even know what happened to the firm of Fish & Son, though I dare say Jeremy Tradescant can find out.'

'Lovely movers, black girls,' Sid repeated. 'Whatever else we know about him we know he liked shoving it up black girls.'

'*Nag o flaen y bechgyn*,' Jessica said sharply to Tracy. She often broke into Welsh (which she had learnt to speak with her husband sixty years before) when addressing Tracy, whose father, and schools, had been Welsh-speaking.

'You what?' said Sid.

'Not in front of the children,' said Jessica. Again, it astonished her to find herself in the role of the prude, but this consistent chatter about sexual intimacies in front of Marmie and Pandora. who *were* only nine, troubled and angered her.

'Marmie, you *must* not read at table!' Fanny repeated. 'What is that, anyway? Not one of the ones I bought?'

'Charles gave it to me,' said Marmie, holding up the picture of the naked men on the motor bike.

'You mean you took it,' said Charles. 'I keep . . . those things in my bedroom.'

'It's terrible,' said Jessica.

'Really, Nana,' Tracy exclaimed, passing up Sid's plate for more lasagne, 'you behave sometimes as if we were still living in the Victorian age.'

'Wish we were,' said Fanny.

'Oh, rubbish. You would have been completely ostracized by society,' said Tracy. 'Look at the children. They would have been taken into care by now. Sent to the Parish.'

'Is it very smutty, Marmie, darling?' Fanny asked. 'Because if it is let me read it while you finish your supper.'

'I don't like lasagne,' said Marmaduke.

'It isn't right to see such things in the hands of a child,' said Jessica.

'Nana, I am nine years old,' said Marmaduke, as if this made the point. With a clatter of knives and forks, he and Pandora left the table, still holding the magazine, and curled up on the sofa at the far end of the kitchen, fondling the corgis and reading some of the printed matter of the magazine.

'Charles?'

'Yes, Marmie.'

'What does it mean when it talks about Sixty-Nine all the time?'

David blushed rather deeply and Charles said, with the air of sobriety which he always appeared to be injecting into conversations, 'I think you should do as your mother says and not read during meals, Marmie.'

'Don't you know *that?*' squealed Pandora and whispered an explanation into Marmaduke's ear.

'Oh, I remember now,' said the boy. He walked out of the kitchen, wiggling his buttocks, still flicking the pages of the journal.

'Oh my gawd, we've got a right little nancy there,' said Sid. 'How old did he say he was? Nine? Fuck a duck.'

Jessica at the same time was saying, 'Really, Fanny love, it is absolutely disgusting. You know it quite upsets me, seeing a young boy like that with his nose buried in kinky porno mags.' Normally quite English, her voice had taken on some of Tracy's Welsh sing-song when discussing this painful subject.

'What harm can it do?' Tracy asked.

'A lot of harm. It corrupts them.'

'Come on! You're sounding like Mary Whitehouse.'

Jessica bristled. She hated herself for taking this stand. She loathed Mrs Whitehouse, whom she suspected, along with all sup-porters of MRA, of being crypto-fascist. And, worst of all, she knew she would not be starting this argument if it was not a way of distracting the company from the much more embarrassing subject of Oswald Fish. Sooner or later they would be bound to find out. Charles a cousin! How many more of her father's bastard offspring wandered the face of the earth? She stared at Charles to see if any obvious resemblance could be found. There was none. She would not have guessed from his appearance that he had any European blood; but having been told, she could see that the fineness of his nose was of a kind she did not associate with Afroid facial features, and that his abundant thick hair was brushed, brushable, rather than simply being a woolly fuzz. Was his very high brow and receding hair-line at all like that of Oswald Fish? Her eyes now tried to make them so, but they were not.

She thought again of those last months in the hospital – the time after her father's last really bad attack when he had run about without any clothes on, smashing windows. By the time she saw him, the fit had passed, he was lying serenely in the overcrowded ward, his whiskers quite white, his very thick eyebrows standing out in tufts, his wrinkled brow now comparatively smooth, his eyes closed, the whitish grey of his remaining hair blending into the whitish grey of his pillows.

'Where's Toby? Frances, what happened to Toby?'

'It's Jessica, Pa.'

'Where's Annie?'

'I don't know, Pa.'

'Let me see Annie, just once, let me see Annie. O Lord God, the fires of hell – they send me all these bitches and bastards –' and he had hissed and shouted and sat up in bed, '– but I want my son, my son Toby!' And the anger had dissolved into childish gibbering sobs.

How could Sid the plumber, the drawling David, the supercilious Charles, be expected to know anything of all this? How could the story of Oswald Fish – pieced together for them by a few old bits of metalwork and a slum church in the middle of Birmingham – how could the story be understood without experience of its blankly horrible end?

'How can I teach those children manners?' Fanny was asking, while Tracy and Sid, second helpings of lasagne well tucked away under the tight blue denim of their dungarees, were fondling each other with the devoted attention of spider monkeys in search of fleas.

In the hall, the doorbell jangled. None of the grown-ups stirred. Marmie, for all his inelegancies of table manners, had the curiosity to answer it.

Fred Jobling blinked down at the strange little figure who stood before him. It was hard to guess its age or, at first, its sex. Marmaduke looked like a toy teenager; frail and pale as if he spent every night smoking and dancing, but his pretty white features were lit up with such a knowing archness that Fred did almost wonder whether it was not some dwarf or hermaphrodite, of mature age, who stood before him in black leather and satin. On reflection, and after a certain amount of blinking and nodding and grinning, he asked inanely, 'Is Mummy in?'

'Hang on,' said Marmaduke.

Fred hovered uneasily somewhere between the front step and the coconut matting just inside it. It was of old-fashioned design, the sort which normally spelt out WELCOME, only this particular example of the weaver's art bore the legend PISS OFF. He could hear Marmaduke's high-pitched spoilt little voice saying, 'There's a man at the door looking for his mother.'

Fanny's voice: 'What does he look like?'

'Big and fat and bald and rather goofy-looking.'

'Tell him to fuck off. It's probably the Jehovah's Witnesses.'

'OK.'

The boy returned, smiled politely, and said, 'I'm awfully sorry but she does not appear to be in.'

'There's been some mistake,' said Fred. He was rather cross at being ragged in this way. All right, it was rather silly to have referred to Fanny as 'Mummy' to this brat. But how else was he to have spoken? All day he had been searching for her, calling, ringing up. With the peculiar obsessiveness of the lover he felt that, having expended so much emotional energy in thinking about Fanny it entitled him to see her alone and at once. He wanted to find out if her squeezing his leg in the pub *meant* anything. One tiny part of himself, a vestige of old sensibleness, dismissed it as typical behaviour of 'that kind of women'. But *what* kind? The rest of himself knew that there was no other woman like Fanny.

The afternoon in the pub had been so strong that he was suffering from something very like shock. He knew that he could not be happy until he saw her again. Equally he knew that if he did not see her again he could not convince himself that his encounter in Birmingham had not been the figment of a fevered brain. He could not even remember what she looked like. Legs – oh yes. The smell of her scent, the texture of her long white moist hands on his own, the clothes, the hair style, but when he tried to picture the face he saw only a great blank accompanied by agonies of desire.

'I don't know why you thought your mother lived here,' Marmaduke said. His tone was deliberately, impertinently polite. Fred noticed to his horror that the child was holding in his hand an open magazine which showed a photograph of two men performing the act of buggery.

'I want to see *your* mother,' he said crossly. 'Not mine, as I think you very well know.'

There was something schoolmasterish about this last observation which caught Marmaduke on the raw.

'I am sorry, no one here can see you,' he repeated. And then he called out: 'Charles!'

A distinguished bass voice replied: 'Sugar Plum?'

'Can you come here a minute?'

'I've come to see your mother,' said Fred, 'and I *intend* to see her, so will you please tell her I am here.' He hated this rather pompous tone which sometimes overtook his voice when angry. Jen could bring it out of him. So could underlings in the office who had failed to produce work at the promised time.

At this juncture a burly, rather handsome African came into the hall. Fred was struck by the stiffness of his very white collar. It seemed to be one size too small so that the flesh of his neck appeared to be slightly overflowing on to it, like thick chocolate icing on a cake.

'Yes, Marmie darling, what is it?' His voice was gentle, cultivated, almost affected; much more upper crust than Fred's own. In spite of its smoothness, Fred felt it to be not without signals of aggression.

'This man's being really boring,' said the child.

Charles smiled condescendingly at Fred.

With the sharp, instantaneous certainty of a man in love, Fred immediately knew that the black man was Fanny's lover. Scalding pain accompanied this conviction. It made him feel helpless and shut out. It also made it seem suddenly impossible that he could openly demand to see Fanny – any more than, if she were married, he could demand of her husband that he be admitted to her presence to make declarations of love. On the other hand, some explanation of his presence, late, and on a dark night, on Fanny's doorstep, in the rain, was called for.

'I am sorry,' Charles apologized for Marmaduke's rudeness. 'Can I help you?' So this, Charles thought, is the Perfect Husband about whom Fanny had been so rhapsodic earlier in the evening. Apart from baldness, it seemed to Charles that her comparison with the appearance of the Prince Consort seemed a trifle forced. Something nebulous, and which, with his orderly habit of mind, he tried to dismiss as irrational, made him dislike Fred.

'I am sorry too,' said Fred, suddenly beaming and accommodating. He was aware that he had now awkwardly switched to the beaming liberal manner that he tried to adopt with Sikh bus conductors or Jamaican labourers, a desperate condescending niceness which seemed to defy anyone to think he so much as noticed the colour of a man's skin. 'I think I must have called at the wrong house,' he said. And then, seizing a name out of the air (did Fanny's Welshness suggest it?) he lied: 'I thought this was where Mrs Owen lived.'

'You mean Nana Owen,' said Charles.

'Is that perhaps the house next door?' asked Fred. It was becoming a ludicrous conversation. 'I'll try there then. This way or that way?' He pointed and gesticulated backing out towards the rain with exaggerated gestures, as though in addition to the brown pigmentation of his skin, Charles was stone deaf.

'I'll get her. said Charles now genuinely puzzled. 'Nana! Nana Owen!'

'What is it?' Tracy's Welsh voice came from the kitchen.

'There's someone here for Nana Owen.'

'It's quite all right,' said Fred. 'I am sorry to have caused all this trouble and confusion. Perfectly OK. In fact –' already he was blustering back into the slang talk of school stories '– spiffing.'

'Yes?'

For an extraordinary and surreal moment, Fred thought that his own grandmother had appeared in the shadows of the hall. When she stood under the glass art-nouveau lampshade he could see that the woman was in fact white-haired, slightly plumper and of a more obviously lower social class. It was the charwoman who had ans-wered the door in the morning. Her hair had been vigorously cropped, like the inmate of an old folks' home or a Russian lunatic asylum. She had a weathered, intelligent face – a moustache – what was it then? The eyes, the shape of the cheekbones, unmistakably resembled Grandma Jobling. Perhaps old women, like black men, all looked alike. At least Grandma Jobling, except in her most forgetful moods, troubled to put her teeth in before greeting strangers.

Jessica too, felt strange stirrings of familiarity as she looked at Fred. She thought how absurd it was to have been ruminating too much about her father. The bald head glistening by the front door was the same shape. But the spectacles and the ludicrous smile were different.

'Can I help you?' she said. 'I may as well tell you that I have been a card-carrying communist since 1932 and I have no religious beliefs whatsoever. Hymns,' she added as a polite afterthought, 'hymns are different. During my husband's lifetime – more than forty years ago – I went to chapel with him – *Bethel* – to improve my Welsh. But I don't believe in God, never have. And I don't believe in personal salvation. I believe in collective salvation – that the whole of society must be radically changed and altered. You people are just playing on human weakness, exploiting feelings of guilt. Of course the Salvation Army do a wonderful job of work. I know that.'

'But I don't belong to the Salvation Army.'

'I know that. Mind you, I'll say this for you people, you stood up to Hitler. Not a single Jehovah's Witness survived in Hitler's

Germany. They all died a martyr's death. I admire that. But that's not to say I condone any of the other things you teach.'

Was she mad, or was she too conspiring in what felt like an increasingly hostile practical joke? Her hectoring fluency had an almost professional ease, somehow summoning up pictures of what the suffragettes must have been like. In the parts of England Fred had been used to, such doorstep conversations simply did not happen.

'I am very sorry,' he said, 'I am not a Jehovah's Witness.'

'Why did you say you were then?' asked Jessica sharply. She seemed cross to have wasted some ripe clichés which could have been saved up for a real adversary. 'It's a funny time of night to come round grilling people about religion if you aren't a Jehovah's Witness.'

'Nana!' Tracy called out. The sexy denim-clad girl tossed back her hair and stared at Fred contemptuously. 'Fanny says she'll make you some Horlicks or you could have Bengers.'

Fred, who had walked through the rain from his hotel, would have loved a hot drink and wondered whether to say so. He simultaneously wondered what it was about the girl's face which made it obvious that she had recently been having sexual intercourse. He rather liked the look of Tracy. A resemblance to Fanny could be seen, even though her features were rather hard and her complexion was not very good. The mention of Fanny, however, gave him the chance to clear up the whole series of embarrassing confusions.

'If Fanny's in I wouldn't mind a word with her,' he said as casually as possible.

'Who shall I say you are?'

'Careful, darling,' said Jessica. 'I think this man wants to leave.'

'So do I,' Charles said authoritatively, coming out into the hall.

'I don't yet,' said Fred, again trying to be amiable; tugging the corners of his mouth back into a be-nice-to-nig-nogs grin.

'Look,' said Charles patiently. 'First you say you are looking for your mother. Then you say you are a Jehovah's Witness. Then you say you aren't. Then you say you want to speak to Nana. Come on, ducky.'

The final phrase, in Charles's deep, rather manly tones, seemed surprising. He had little time to reflect on it, however. In no time at all, big as he was, he was being bounced. Charles appeared to have no difficulty in lifting him up and actually placing him, quite gently, in the rain-soaked gravel at the bottom of the front steps. The pin-stripe form had ascended, the glossy green front door had slammed before the range of impressions had settled themselves down: the shock of physical proximity with Charles, the smell, his rather expensive unguents lingering in the nostrils; the sense that some ludicrous rather cruel jape was being enacted; the zany, almost drunken feeling given by being lifted in the air; the profound absurdity and pathos of standing hatless in the rain outside the house of the woman he loved.

Inside the house, Tracy called out, 'Honestly, Fanny, you must be out of your mind! He's not a bit like the Prince Consort.' The rain came down more heavily now, spattering the windows, rustling on the shrubs which clustered in pots in the front garden, hissing on the pavement. To Fred, as he stared up at the unwelcoming lighted windows, the sound of the rain seemed to be a humiliating contemptuous laughter blending into one with an imagined witchlike cackle of the brown old communist who half resembled his grandmother; the high-pitched almost orgasmic snigger of the sexy girl in tight denims; the silent smirk of the fey little boy in leather trousers. Fred felt angry, miserable and a complete fool. It was all so completely unlike the evening à deux which, once envisaged in his brain, he had been certain was going to take place.

In a daze of paranoid melancholy, half certain now that the whole of the natural world was mocking him and laughing at him, Fred ambled to the end of Tregunter Road, through The Boltons and out into Old Brompton Road. Buses, cars and taxis hissing down towards Knightsbridge sniggered at him as they passed. The trees, shaking with half suppressed mirth, scattered him with drips of rainwater, carefully aimed at the back of his neck. Strangers, passing him on the pavement, or lurking for shelter in shop doorways, appeared to be giving him furtive glances of derision. Sodden and miserable, he turned into a pub, with the determined intention of making himself drunk. The pub in question was not far from Bailey's Hotel, indeed, was only a hundred yards or so away up the Gloucester Road. but the kind of drinking he had in mind was not the kind you did in hotel bars. He ordered a pint of beer and a double whisky; he asked if they could sell him a quarter bottle of whisky over the counter. They could. He went and settled himself in a corner, and after a quarter of an hour or so, warmth was returning to his chilly limbs and a foolish sense of well-being to his heart.

XVI

'Have you taken your pills?'

'Which pills?'

'Your pink pills.'

'My pink frills? Is there going to be a party?'

Agnes Jobling smiled a determined, satisfied smile. Hugh sighed. For the last day or so, ever since their disturbing conversation about the suicide of Edmund Fish, his mother had been off-colour, difficult, funny. She seemed to have been far away, lost in her own thoughts. He had tried to talk to her, but she had made vacant, non-committal replies. Leaving her to her own devices, nodding in her arm chair, or clambering about her rooms like a drunken passenger during a storm at sea, her mottled hands clasping furniture as she creaked about the carpet, he had also found his mind on the coming Election. The Socialists had done for themselves now; the country was not going to put up with another winter like the last one. If they couldn't even control their own people – everyone on strike – it seemed fairly certain that the country would throw them out. The Liberal Party, thrown into disarray by more bizarre disturbances than industrial unrest, would be equally unattractive to the electorate. There was only one way that the Election could go, when it came. In a quiet way this pleased Hugh Jobling. He was not a rabidly political man. But the present outlook seemed good to the City and good to the *Daily Telegraph* and that gave him a warm glowing sense of inner peace, akin to the consolations which others looked for in religion or affairs of the heart. He had a quiet belief that the country was coming to its senses and this enabled him to get through the tedious hours with his mother.

Hugh had always loved his mother. As a child, being the youngest, he had been her pet. There had been something quite natural, after May's death, about his decision to come back and live with her. It struck other people as an odd and cruel quirk of Fortune that a man of nearly seventy should have lost his wife but not his mother. It never occurred to Hugh to view things in that way. Mother would go on forever. How often, having the other half in the club-house bar, or chatting with cousins on the patio of his house in Surrey, he had pronounced that unshakable truth.

He had forgotten, until he returned to Augustus Road five years before, that durability did not guarantee a high level of interestingness. In fact, for the last five years he had been bored. The days when he once took positive pride and pleasure in his mother's company, admired her distinctive looks and sharp tongue and strong character, were all in the past. Being an unobservant man, it had taken years for this fact to catch up on him. 'My mother is a very witty woman.' He still told people this part of the family creed, even though it was probably a quarter of a century since anything recognizable as wit had passed her thin rat-trap lips. 'My mother is a very keen gardener – pretty good for ninety-something.' But it was ten years since she really took any notice of the garden, and two or three since she could tell the difference between a lupin and a delphinium. All that had remained of his mother's good looks was her abundant dark hair and her beady, glossy black eyes. For the rest she was a powdered, shrivelled old doll. It was a miracle of nature that under the moth-ball-scented clothes which hung so loosely on her withered frame, and beneath the caked floury layer of powder on her nose and cheeks, the heart should trouble to pump blood around. All that remained of his mother's bright conversation was lodged in the memory; and the memory had time enough to work while she sat, or clambered about, smacking her chops in silence for the greater part of the day.

The decline had been so gradual that he had not noticed it, but now, since her momentary return to coherence and her revelation about her father's suicide, even Hugh had noticed a decline.

'You could take your pills with the last of your milk.'

'What pills?'

'Oh, really, mother. I can see them there. On your little tray.'

But with her now declined, semi-demented persona, there had come a hideous sprightliness that made Hugh, in a completely childish way, want to giggle.

'I think I *am* going to give a party,' said Agnes. 'Perhaps it should be a wedding party. I shall ask little whatsername next door to be a bridesmaid.'

Hugh laughed, for relief. not amusement. It was like the laughter that had seized him at moments of life's solemnity. He laughed at May's funeral. He even had the need to leave Board meetings in the City. his handkerchief almost stuffed down his throat, laughing and laughing.

All the same. hurry up and take your pills.' He was anxious to get her into bed in time to watch the *News at Ten*.

'I must look out a hat to wear,' said Agnes. 'Something with flowers on it.'

'That would be nice.'

'What would?'

'A hat with flowers.'

'What would I want a hat with flowers for? To get married in, do you suppose?'

'Very likely.'

'Very likely! You must be mad. I am ninety-three. How many men of your acquaintance want to get married to a woman of ninety-three?'

'If you say so, mother. But do take your pills.'

He held out two pills in the palm of his hand.

Agnes took them, tossed them into her mouth and brought the cup of milk to her lips with a quavering hand.

'There,' she said, triumphantly.

'Oh mother, really!' Hugh said, now genuinely cross. 'You have spat them out.'

Floating on the surface of the warm milk like little pink submarines surfaced for air, the pills bobbed about while Agnes laughed.

Next door Jen put her feet up on the sofa and watched television. The children were, at last, asleep. Staring down at her nylon-swathed toes she smiled, satisfied by the peace of solitude. Other families managed. So, she supposed, must she. Why was every single little action of daily life an occasion for Sam and Harriet to quarrel? If you gave them both an apple Sam wailed because Harriet had the apple *he* wanted. If Sam sat on a chair, Harriet protested that she had wanted to sit there. If Sam wanted to watch *Animal*

Magic. Harriet would find an excuse for wanting to do a jigsaw puzzle or crack nuts in front of the television set. If she wanted to read quietly in another corner of the room, Sam would want to go and play there with his ghastly ack-ack plastic machine gun. Perhaps, Jen reflected, she and Fred, had, as ever, timed things wrong. The gap between the two children was just too long for them to be satisfactory playmates; just too little for them to be able to lead independent lives. As it was, the atmosphere in the house was one of perpetual warfare.

In more paperback-psychology moods, Jen wondered whether the children's inability to play amiably together was a reflection of her own ropey old relationship with Fred. Time was when she would have pined for him when he went away to London. On this occasion, she could not wait for him to be out of the house. She felt that if she did not have a few days on her own she would scream, or start throwing more dangerous projectiles than boiled eggs. Fred's all-consuming egoism was getting her down. She used to have a sunny, equable character. Now she heard herself snapping and shouting at the children, as well as at Fred. And, at school, she really took it out on the worse-behaved or more dim-witted children. Only that morning she had reduced a child in her French class to tears and been horrified to discover that this gave her real pleasure.

Why in hell's name *should* she look after his socks? He had never done any of *her* washing or ironing. He had never listened when she had tried to tell him about her working day, but he had expected her to spend evening after evening hearing about committees and plans and departmental feuds and traffic systems and litigations and the Rates people. If she named to him a colleague from school that she had mentioned twenty times before he almost always said, 'Who's that?' But *she* was expected to know about Wilkins, Pilkins and Tilkins, Dawn and Lonsdale – even to listen to the rehashed monologues of the cleaning-woman on Fred's corridor. It was not a question of fairness or rights and wrongs though perhaps those came into it. Much more, it was the overwhelming boringness of it all. Jen had always thought boringness was a negative thing, something which would be dispelled by picking up a book, playing a game of tennis, having a cup of coffee with a friend. But this marital boringness had an acrid, positive flavour, threatening to wash over her, drown her like some huge roller on the shore, threatening to obliterate her very existence. Perhaps Fred had always been a bore and an egoist. Perhaps it was merely that when he told her about work in the solicitors' office in Godalming it had all the freshness and immediacy of local gossip whereas the groaningly dull affairs of the Planning Committee had no personal appeal. But it was not just that. Fred had got worse. They had all got worse, and, as she knew, they were increasingly bad for each other. The brave and sensible thing to do would be to try a new way of life – but what and where and how? Nice as it was to live in a large house in Augustus Road, they were trapped there now until Fred's dad kicked the bucket and, if Grandma was anything to go by, the Joblings were a very long-lived breed.

Trying to forget these things, Jen concentrated as hard as she could on the television screen, where the Prime Minister was talking about inflation. Jen rather liked him. She thought that if the Unions were to be bashed, an evidently desirable thing to happen, it was better that the hand to bash them was Labour rather than Tory. Jen had been brought up Tory, of course. But in the first flush of being married to Fred, she had got rather keen on Labour. Some of them were brash and horrible, but this was true of all parties. There *were* all kinds of hardships and injustices still and she felt that Labour was the party to deal with them. All the same, it was reassuring that the Prime Minister, with his round chops and bluff manner and nice grey suits, seemed so reassuringly like a Conservative.

The Prime Minister was moving on to the Common Market, with a certain awkward rubbing of his nose and shamefaced smiling, when the telephone rang.

'Jen?'

'Is that Fred?'

'Jen, my darling, hallo.' It was years, if ever, since she had been his darling, anyway for conversational purposes.

'Fred, are you drunk or something?'

'Not very.' An inane laugh accompanied this assertion.

'What have you been up to?'

'Oh, this and that.'

'Boring old business?'

'Yes. Yes, boring old business.'

'How's the wicked temptress?' she quipped.

'Who's that?'

'Fanny Williams of course.'

'Good God no. Haven't seen her ...' The next word sounded like 'solicitors'.

'Don't forget to ask her for her autograph for the children.'

'How are the children?'

'Awful, as usual.'

'Give them a kiss for me.'

'You *must* be drunk.' She hung up and laughed. The television news had suddenly turned interesting. Typical of Fred to ring up just when Jeremy Thorpe had appeared on the screen.

XVII

Fiona Matheson finished her Euro-business a day early and decided to return to London and give her husband David a pleasant surprise.

Fiona was a well-bred girl with a fine bone structure. She smelt of soap. She had quite thick chestnut hair, which she kept trimmed fairly short. Her intelligent face, slightly freckled about the nose, slightly fleshy about the cheeks, firm in chin and jaw, brought, wherever she went, a breath of the English shires. It was a face which, on an older woman, one could imagine appearing on a bench of magistrates; further back in history, tanned by the Indian sun, barking beneficent instructions to some underling in Simla; further back still, pale and stiff in brocade and velvet, her children even paler and stiffer in their best buff worsted, sitting or rather standing, for Stubbs, a savagely well-groomed horse harnessed to her diligence, a well-trimmed park lolling in the background beneath a well-ordered sky. As it was, being born in 1948, she had gone to Wycombe Abbey and LMH, only just missed her first in PPE, done jolly well in the Civil Service exam, and stood quite a chance of becoming a principal before very long.

Some of her friends had been surprised by her marriage to David Matheson less than a year before. It was not that they expected her to come up with some toy version of Captain Mark Phillips: Fiona was not that sort of girl. It was just so obvious, to the friends, that she could have done a bit better for herself. There had been a handsome naval sub-lieutenant before she went up to the University who had worshipped the ground she trod on. Then, when an undergraduate, several very eligible boyfriends, one from Wadham who was now a BBC producer; a fellow economist (from New College) who had done frightfully well in his degree and was now a don; an Hon. from the House who had only got a pass in History but had pots of money and the most heavenly flat in Rutland Gate as well as a nice house in Northumberland ... She had, in the opinion of the friends, been mad to let these opportunities pass. Then, in London, there had been two or three Civil Servants who had been fairly besotted, and a full-blown love affair which lasted four years, with a terribly dishy merchant banker.

But the truth was that she had never known what it was to be in love until she met David Matheson. The friends said that it was her bossiness; she wanted a little weed that she could dominate and control. They did not realize how totally he enchanted her. She found his conversation endlessly interesting, and his physical presence completely captivating. She had never known a man before the very smell of whom sent her into a swoon. And so it was that, the previous June, it had been David, and not the don or the banker or the BBC producer or the naval officer, now a commander, who stood in a morning coat and striped trousers, replying to the toasts in the marquee on her parents' lawn, the rain dripping down on the white canvas in an endless patter. Not for a single second had Fiona regretted her decision. Other people talked endlessly about the difficulties of marriage, the little frictions gradually wearing you down like Chinese torture. It had not been like that for her. There had not been a single boring day. She loved her work and David liked hearing about it; she in turn liked the fact that he did something rather different from the usual run of her friends. She did not entirely share his interest in architecture, but her vision of the world had been enhanced and transformed by it. London – the most obvious truth in the world – was full of buildings: she had never really looked at them until she met David. And although she did not have the kind of mind that remembered whether a column was Doric or Ionic, nor whether a building was 18th-century classical or 19th-century Greek revival, she had begun to notice texture, symmetry, proportion. Whitehall, she now saw, was not just thrown together by accident – nor Horse-Guards Parade – nor the Mall (her usual route to work, having crossed the park on a bike). Someone had thought it all out. And since meeting David she had experienced the thrill which always accompanies a meeting with the intention behind a work of art – a satisfaction akin to seeing a play well interpreted, hearing a piece of music sensitively performed. That was only the tiniest part of her love for David, though. Never before, with any of her previous suitors, had she felt so physically intoxicated, so that, even in company, if she felt his fingers on her arm, she wanted to throw herself on top of him in an ecstasy of passion.

Not that she did, in public. She had always found public gropes rather off-putting. In front of their friends, she and David kept up an almost icy distance, which made it doubly exciting when the door of the Rosary Crescent flat finally closed, and they were alone.

It was almost entirely the prospect of these connubial intimacies which brought her back from Brussels a day early. It was quite late, just after 10.30 when she finally got to the Cromwell Road air terminal, but Rosary Crescent was only a brisk eight minutes' walk away.

Turning into Gloucester Road, she thought how unhappy everyone looked, surely not simply because it was still raining. Disconsolate Latins were coming out of the late-opening shop opposite the tube with pathetically solitary little heaps of stuff piled in their arms: one lavatory roll, one half-pint carton of milk, one individual fruit pie. Others, on the opposite side of the road, stood ambiguously in the entrance of the station itself, by the closed newspaper stall and the empty barrow which in daytime sold flowers. Perhaps they were merely sheltering from the rain. Perhaps they were waiting for a friend who had stood them up. Perhaps they had no friends and were simply waiting. The pathos of all the empty little lives in that quarter of S W 7 never failed to make Fiona grateful for her wide circle of friends; her healthy happy love life; her wonderful husband. She walked past Bailey's Hotel, turned into Hereford Square and fumbled in her bag for her front door key.

The Mathesons' flat was on the second floor of a rather lugubrious row of large red Edwardian houses. It had the advantage of being wonderfully near David's work, quiet, spacious and oddly cheap. They rented it, putting a large proportion of their income aside every month in order to buy a weekend house in the country. Fiona always proudly said to people that it must have been the last flat in London (of reasonable price) to be let unfurnished. They had decorated the three rooms cheerfully and tastefully and borrowed a whatsit one weekend to polish the floor-boards, and furnished it sparsely but beautifully with their very few things and with handsome bits of stuff from both their parents. David's mother had given them a magnificent Georgian bureau for the sitting-room. The dining table and Sheraton chairs came from *her* people. The Habitat chesterfield and the spindly Georgian bedside table they had bought themselves.

Fiona pressed the timed light switch in the hall, ran upstairs swiftly before it switched itself off, put her key in the lock of their flat and called out, 'I'm back!'

The whole flat was plunged in darkness. She switched on the light. Perhaps David was already in bed. But no. For there on the mat was a pile of post which he would surely have picked up had he been back. She went through it idly as she walked into the sitting-room, and then into the kitchen, turning on lights. There was a post-card from David's brother in Los Angeles. Letters from his parents and from someone else which she left unopened; one from her bank, another from her mother. She read this carefully while she put on the gas and looked in the fridge for milk.

... and the narcissi are a real delight! Any chance of you and David coming over the week after next (the 14th)? I've got the Norbrook-Holmeses coming to dinner and thought Gerald would enjoy talking to David about old buildings ... What about the election? Your father is talking of nothing else and I must say I shall be rather glad when it finally happens. Mrs T. is bound to win by all accounts. Then perhaps at last one will get the Unions to see sense ...

There was not much in her mother's letter. Fiona shook the milk carton over the saucepan. She could feel it was full, but there was nothing coming out. Raising the carton to her nose, she discovered the reason. It was halfway to becoming cheese. With disgust she tossed it into the rubbish bin, turned off the gas and went round the flat for evidence of David. If his parents were ill, or he had suddenly been summoned away for museum or architectural work, he would surely have left a note. She looked on the table in the hall, then on the chimney piece in the living-room. Finally, she went into the bedroom. Nothing.

How bleak and empty the bed seemed. David, poor old thing, had often had to sleep alone since this boring Brussels lark began. She had never had to sleep alone in the flat. The idea of doing so was not merely depressing, it was slightly frightening. How was she to know that David had not been run over by a bus, or taken ill? Since she had been away, they would not have been able to tell her. What if he had gone out without any identifying object like a chequebook or a driving licence? He might be lying in a hospital bed, even a morgue, no one knowing who he was. She looked at her watch. Eleven fifty. It was too late to ring up his parents. There was anyway no point in creating unnecessary alarm. She lay back on the bed, still fully dressed. and decided to wait. David had not been expecting her back tonight and would almost certainly have gone round to see some friends.

XVIII

In Bailey's Hotel, Fred wondered what impulse had made him want
to ring up Jen. It was almost as if, ludicrously, he wanted to get her
permission before committing adultery. She sounded her usual
bloody, breezy self on the other end of the line. If anything, slightly
cross to be disturbed. Perhaps she had a lover. The thought had
never crossed his mind before. Normally it would have grieved him.
He now wished that she had. Surely that would be the best way:
for her to bugger off, ears and all, with one of her colleagues at the
comprehensive, leaving him free to pursue Fanny.

The pursuit of Fanny had been, so far, dazzlingly unsuccessful.
When he left Birmingham that morning, he had not foreseen any
complications at all. He had assumed that he could simply call, pick
her up, take her out to dinner, and then back to his hotel bedroom.
This, surely, had been implied by her squeezing his leg under the
pub table. Now, he cursed himself for the nervous bumbling way
in which he had mis-managed the visits to Tregunter Road – the
final one particularly. That nasty little brat Marmaduke gave him
the creeps. So too, did the smooth-talking blackamoor. The place
seemed crowded with weirdos quite deliberately keeping him from
Fanny. It was not merely annoying, it was deeply painful.

Fred knew, more than ever, that he was horribly and seriously
in love as he had never been in his life. All previous sensations of
being in love now seemed either tawdry or ridiculous. He now felt
ashamed of the time he had spent drooling, some years before, over
the thought of Dawn's woolly, floopy breasts in the Planning
Department. The poignant self-pity which had overcome him after
the departure of the Norland nanny seemed equally remote from the
sensations of delicious longing, of near-madness, which now over-
came him. The commonsense self had not been put so far behind
him that he was unable to see what was happening quite clearly.
He recognized, transparently, that the whole Tregunter Road set-

up was beyond belief terrible. Only being wildly in love would explain or justify his desire to enter the house. People said Love was Blind: quite untrue. Love saw the whole woman, warts and all, and was still intoxicated. In ordinary circumstances, as he could still recognize, he would have thought that people ought to be sent to prison for giving their children whimsical names like Marmaduke and Pandora. It was only because Fanny had done so that he thought how charmingly different and amusing it was. Had anyone else done so, he would still regard it as inexcusable. Only Fanny was allowed to behave in that way because she was Fanny. Her deliberate defiance of things which he either held dear or took for granted, actually increased her attraction. He could see now that he was thrilled by her determination to thwart the Purgstall Area Development Scheme into which he had put months of desultory office house – hard work, as he saw it. If she had shared his passion for the scheme, and travelled back to St Philip's Place with him on a bus, he would not have been nearly so excited by her flagrant aesthetic desire to preserve that boring little church, or by the Bentley or the expensive clothes or the corgis. With perhaps grandiose and certainly uncharacteristic poeticism, he regarded himself as suffering from more than a touch of the Antony and Cleopatras.

At least she had not seen him being thrown out on his ear at Tregunter Road. As he sat in his hotel bedroom, it occurred to him that she would not necessarily know that he had even called. Her acolytes and retainers seemed so universally kinky, bonkers, senile or otherwise unreliable, that there was no knowing what account they would have given, if any, of The Man at the Door. Even if, from their batty account, she had surmised it was him, there was no reason to admit it. The more cool, impressive thing would be to try again, as if for the first time. First thing in the morning? That would be the best time.

Alas, he knew that he was completely unable to wait until first thing in the morning. Reaching for the white telephone, he rang her number.

It was answered so quickly that at first he thought he was speaking to the operator on the hotel switchboard. Just as he had forgotten her face, he found it impossible to tell whether the voice at the other end of the line was Fanny's or not. He tried to recall her timbre as she wandered around St Aidan's but all he could summon up were a series of externalized descriptions which he had since made to himself: Fanny's voice was loud, lilting, musical, hysterical, a touch of London, a touch of Welsh, a touch of Upper Class: but he could not hear it with his inner ear. In the two most important identifying features, face and voice, she was a blank in his mind: a dark hole of agitation and pain and delight.

'Hallo?' the tinny voice was repeating. It was definitely too Welsh for Fanny. It must be Sexy in Denims, or it could be even that mad old witch, obsessed by Religion, who had reminded him so curiously of his grandmother.

'Hallo,' he said.

'Oh, it's you,' said Fanny, her voice dissolving at once into its metallic laugh.

'Yes.' Yes, definitely censor the visit to Tregunter Road and start afresh. 'The thing is, I've just arrived in London and I was wondering if it would be possible to call – I mean, for us to meet, or . . .'

'I'm sorry Marmie was so appallingly rude to you.'

'Not in the least. There must be some mistake.'

'*Appalling!*' Elizabeth Schwarzkopf, given the same poor materials of rather crackling telephone receivers, could hardly have delivered a more wounding assault on the eardrum. She continued in a rapid gabble, 'He was. He said you were boring which was really most uncivicated of him, but it was only because I have been boring them all rigid telling them about a man I met in Birmingham who looked *superbly* like the Prince Consort.'

'Who?'

'You do. If you had whiskers.'

'Not really.'

' 'Course.'

Once again, the stainless steel laugh gave no clue as to the seriousness or even the truth of those assertions.

'So. I can see you?'

'Do. Oh *do*.'

'When?'

'Whenever you like. Some time tomorrow.'

'I was thinking we might meet tonight.'

'*Tonight! How Romantic!*'

'Seriously.'

The noise at the other end of the line sounded anything but

serious. At first he thought she might be having a fit. Then he recognized the noise as the yapping of corgis and he could hear Fanny saying, 'Honey, my Honey, shut *up*!'

'Please come tonight.'

'Couldn't possibly.'

'Why not?'

'Because I can't.'

Because that big black bastard is going to bed with you tonight, thought Fred. Oh, God.

'It's too late and we ought to talk and we want to ... Oh I dunno ... we want to do it all properly, don't we, Prince Consort?' She was cooing now.

'I suppose so.'

'Do you feel you've met the girl of your dreams?'

'Yes.'

'I can't *believe* it! God, it's exciting. You mustn't come here tomorrow.'

'Why not? Is it ...' he could hardly bring himself to say the name '... Charles?'

'Charles? He's got nothing to do with it. He is absolutely besotted on his new boyfriend. No, it's Marmie. And Pandora, come to that. You see he was rude because he could tell.'

'Tell what?'

'He's telephonic.'

'Do you mean telepathic?'

'If you really are the Prince Consort he will have known absolutely at once.'

'But you told them all. You've just said.'

'I'm always telling them all everything but it doesn't usually mean a thing. Marmie gets frightfully jealous when it does mean something.'

'And do I ... mean something?'

'Oh Prince Consort, it's so dangerous. Think of your lovely children!'

'I'd rather not just at the moment.'

'But we must.'

'Where are we going to meet tomorrow? Can you come to my hotel? I'm staying at Baileys, just round the corner.'

There was a silence. At first he thought she had rung off.

'It's so dangerous,' she repeated. 'Perhaps we shouldn't meet.'

'Why not?' he tried to sound jocular.

'I can feel it's dangerous. Supposing you really are the Prince Consort. Supposing I really am the Girl of your Dreams.'

'You are,' he groaned.

'Then it will change everything. It's dangerous.'

'I can see that.'

He suddenly felt the seriousness of her tones and although they brought an indescribable sense of happiness at his good fortune, they also chilled and worried him. He felt as if they were standing together on the edge of a dark cold chasm.

'We ought to talk first,' she said quietly. 'We might be just going mad.

'I'm glad to be mad.'

'No. but listen. We must meet. In some open space and walk. And talk.

'Is that all?'

'Yes. At first.'

'Where shall we meet?'

'Half past nine tomorrow morning. At the Albert Memorial.' She said it suddenly, and immediately put the receiver down.

XIX

Pandora sat on her heels by the hissing gas fire in her bedroom, an Edwardian *Grimm's Fairy Tales* illustrated by Edmund Dulac on her knee. In her lacy nightgown, and her thick, brushed mane of hair, she looked more than ever like a child in E. Nesbit. Marmaduke knelt opposite her in his dark-blue silk pyjamas. He belonged to an altogether later era in history – perhaps one waiting to be born. The pyjamas had been intended by Fanny to be in the style of a sailor-suit, but, after he had cut off the white collar, the outfit half recalled a Chinese cabinet minister, half some astronaut in a science-fiction movie.

'Light, John?' asked Pandora as her brother put a cigarette to his lips. In spite of his rather silken, her somewhat frizzy, hair, their faces were identical.

'Please, Jane.'

When on their own, the twins always called each other Jane and John in protest against the whimsy of their chosen names. They also affected a strange accent, which had been improvised and changed over the years, but which though now wholly idiolectic, had once borne some relation to stage Cockney.

Pandora tore the illustration of Hansel and Gretel out of her book and smiled at it scornfully. Then she tore it in half and carefully made it into a spill. When applied to the gas fire it was slow to catch light.

'This fucking paper's too thick,' she said, with great emphasis of the glottal stops.

'Try the page then,' said Marmaduke.

Greedily, his sister tore at the page of the book, thick, slightly yellowed paper printed with a large handsome typeface. She sniggered as she did so.

'Guess 'ow much she pide for this,' she said, glancing back at the end-paper.

'Fiver?'

The spill was alight now and Pandora leant forward to ignite her brother's turquoise Sobranie cigarette.

'Eighteen quid, jus' for a fucking children's book.'

'Mikes yer sick, dunnit.'

He chuckled and handed her the cigarette for a puff.

'Where did you get this cigarette?'

'That shop in the Haymarket – you know, the fancy tobacconists.'

'Cost you a packet, I bet.'

'That's what they were, stupid – a packet.'

'No,' for a moment there was a flicker of her normal outside-world voice, 'they must have cost a lot.'

'Couple of quid,' said the boy nonchalantly. 'That father of ours is just stoopid.'

'Fuckin' stoopid,' added Pandora.

'D'you remember last week when we went to the Planetarium with him, he asked if we wanted sweets?'

'Little sweeties for the sweet little children,' she now put on a baby voice. Both the children had been outraged by being taken to the planetarium and 'treated like kids' by their father and his wife, Liz.

'Our darling step-mother offered to buy us sweets or a toffee apple while we watched Punch and Judy in the hall,' he said contemptuously, smoke pouring from his nostrils. 'And she rather foolishly lent me her purse for five minutes while I went to the sweet counter.'

'You've got a fucking cheek.'

'I only removed two fivers, didn't I?'

'I don't know.'

'Well, I did.'

Downstairs, the clock struck the half-hour, half past midnight.

'Anyway, John,' Pandora felt slightly outdone by this piece of cool, and apparently successful, villainy, 'what have we got cooking tonight?'

'I've found out wet little David's telephone number,' he spat out.

'Fucking little David. Good. What can we do with it?'

'Ring up. Or find out where he lives and go round.'

'Ought we to blackmail fucking David?' asked the girl. 'Or just hurt him?'

'Just hurt him, Jane, just hurt him.'

They laughed and laughed.

'Ssh,' she whispered. 'Someone might hear. What else?'

'Wasn't that man foul this evening?'

'The fucking fat man who wants to come and fuck her?'

'I know. He was really awful.'

'Let's fuck him up,' said the girl, with sudden intensity. leaning forward and putting her hands on those of her brother.

'Like to suggest how, Jane? I mean, we only know as how he's called Alastair and lives in Birmingham, right. Isn't exactly a lot to go on, see what I mean?'

'There must be a way. Won't she write down his telephone number when she starts fucking him?'

'She might. Depends how long she wants him to last.'

'I don't want him to last, do you, John?'

'Not really, Jane, not really. Give me that book a moment.'

'This fucking book?' she held out the *Grimm's Fairy Tales*.

'It'll do,' he said. 'I need an ashtray.'

Opening the book at a clean page, he carefully turned back the tissue paper which covered another Dulac illustration and ground his cigarette stub into the face of The Sleeping Beauty. There was a momentary smouldering and then, as he shut the book tight with the stub inside it, the smoke subsided.

'I found something really funny this evening in Nana's bag,' said Pandora.

'What was that?'

'Her diaries. It goes right back to 19 something. Fucking good don't you think, John?'

'What sort of thing are they?'

'The writing's hard to read.' From under her nightdress she produced a small marbled notebook.

'*13.xii, 16. No word from Annie about my last bay.*'

'Your last bay?'

'That's what it says. Oh, no! *No word from Annie about my last boy, tho something something to be he that I saw something last in the something.*'

'Let me try,' said the boy. He puzzled over the book. 'God, it's sprawling, illegible.'

'Fucking illegible.'

'Not really like her writing now.

'Perhaps she disguised her writing. Her last boy.' Pandora giggled. 'That was the last boy she fucked I expect.'

'*No word from Annie,*' Marmaduke was still struggling to read it, *about my lost* – not last, you nit – *lost boy though it is most certain to be he that I saw Thursday last in the Dispatch?* – something beginning with a D. *There can't be many boys with the name of Toby Shakespeare ...*'

'Toby Shakespeare! It can't say that.'

'I'm reading more of it than you are.'

There was nothing remarkable perhaps about the little book. Neither of the children could read much of it, and what they did read was impossible to understand, but because it was in some way secret and forbidden every word made them splutter with mirth.

'Try another fucking page.

'All right. Let's see.' In an exaggerated gesture, he licked a finger and turned the pages with it roughly.

'*Perhaps a man does truly only ever love one woman,*' he read falteringly.

'That's fucking better, said Pandora.

'*Something ... something.*'

'No, read it all – fucking all of it.

'*Oft have I strayed &c. and yet found no one to satisfy. Not even F.* – wonder what F. is for.'

'Lovely fucking I expect.'

Almost unable to speak for laughter, Marmaduke carried on, '*It was so strange to me that F. did not merely accept my love all those years ago but was actually eager for it* – gorblimey!'

'Carry on, she might talk about lovely fucking.'

'*... I felt so grateful to her for giving me all this love, I needed it so badly, that I somehow did not notice ...*'

'*Her?* Fucking her?'

'That's what it says.'

They rolled on the ground in front of the fire. hugging each other with the hilarity of their discovery.

'Wet little David fucks men and Nana fucks ladies,' wailed Pandora. 'Oh, oh, I shall burst!'

XX

To his shame, Fred had never, properly speaking, had a love affair. The women in his life had either been people vaguely designated girlfriends, whom he took to dances and the pictures and managed to fondle, with differing degrees of intimacy, on the front seats of cars; or there had been Jen, another of these girlfriends who had hung around for longer than most and eventually married him; then, after marriage, there had been a range of little misdemeanours which all demanded some rather comic euphemism: a bit on the side, a piece of crumpet, a spot of the old How's-Your-Father?

In the course of these varied adventures, goodness knows how many times he had technically committed acts of fornication, how many soggy little French letters he had dropped, or dripped, out of car windows; into the waste-paper-baskets of offices or motel bed-rooms; how many times his faltering drunken fingers had unhooked the straps beneath a woman's blouse, or crept uncertainly up the thigh to the top of the tights, and crept down to the knickers and beyond that to the always reassuring feel within. Goodness knows how often it had been, but, by the standards of many men, it was not that often. What struck him most the next morning, waiting by the Albert Memorial, was the oddity of having done these things so comparatively often and never fallen in love. The Norland nanny should have made him fall in love if anyone could, with her curling, almost imploring lips and her slightly Irish voice. And yet, he had found himself capable of going through the whole routine during the week Jen was in hospital without feeling anything – into her room, nightie off, pyjamas off, fondle around, up it goes, more fondle, in it goes, clasp, writhe, grunt, gasp – lots of kisses. Those lovely thick lips meeting his own again and again – a whispered inarticulate 'Well ...', up it goes again; a quickie; then he got dressed in his pyjamas, out of the room; made sure landing light switched off; slipped back into his own bedroom. Not once during this strange week, had he felt in love; not once since had he felt a twinge of guilt about the girl ...

Now, standing on the steps of the Albert Memorial, he felt himself shivering like a goof. It was a bright cold day, late March, a gusty wind, a deep blue sky. From where he stood, the Albert Hall was so clean and bright and pink in appearance that it could have been a child's toy. Behind him, Kensington Gardens were about to burst into spring. Already crocuses and snowdrops had been in flower; daffodils and narcissi were about to come out under the trees.

Fred wondered what he was letting himself in for. The strength of feeling terrified him so much that he had very nearly not come this morning. On waking, it had seemed terrible, not delightful, that he had a tryst with his beloved. He shook with the danger of the moment. With anyone, it would be unsafe to feel so strongly so suddenly. With Fanny it was truly terrifying: anything could happen. And yet it was precisely this thought, of course, which had lured him to, of all places, the Albert Memorial, at, he looked at his watch, twenty to ten.

She was ten minutes late. Perhaps she was not going to turn up after all. Perhaps she had already appeared, hidden, at some suitable vantage point, and was mocking as he stood there moving from foot to foot and blowing on his knuckles. As the thought dawned it turned to certainty. Their last venue had been a piece of indifferent nineteenth-century architecture. It would be appropriate if she 'stood him up' in so ludicrous a place as the Albert Memorial. He walked round it, at the same level, about half way up the steps, his eyes roving through the trees in Kensington Gardens. The distance, the Palace, were lost in faint avenues of feathery mist. Somewhere far away, a band was playing. No. The music, anyway, was orchestral – even his untrained ear could tell that – punctuated by cries now and again, as if supporters wanted to join in.

The sound became louder and louder, finally seeming quite near. Turning a corner of the Memorial, he saw the large green Bentley parked on the road, music blaring from its open door. Fanny was running towards him, corgis at her ankles. Her arms were folded and when his eyes met hers, she looked almost ashamed.

'*Embarrassing!*' she shouted.

'Hallo.'

'Oh, Prince Consort!'

'What?'

'Don't come down from the Albert Memorial. You look so wonderful up there.' She was at the bottom of the steps, bawling up at him now.

'I want to talk to you,' he said.

'It is *quite* the most beautiful thing in London, isn't it?' she said. 'And you look like one of the statues come to life – if not *the* Statue, dear Prince Consort.'

Some early Japanese tourists had collected at the foot of the steps to listen to her harangue, obviously under the impression that they were at Speaker's Corner.

'Can't we go somewhere private?' Fred shouted back.

'Oh, Darling Prince Consort, is it safe? Mightn't we find ourselves eloping or something awful?'

'It might be nice to elope.'

'Sssh! So foolish! Think of your darling *children*!!'

'Hadn't you better switch off the car radio?'

'Verdi is this week's composer.'

He came down the steps to join her and took her hand. The experience of standing there, in the open, with her cold, smooth hand curled up in his own, and the padded shoulder of her fluffy coat pressed against his own, brought a feeling of intense preternatural joy.

'I thought you'd prefer pop music to opera,' he said, as they walked back to the Bentley.

'Pop music?'

'You were ...' His voice trailed away. It was absurd to be talking about music instead of the Matter in Hand.

'This is *Simone Boccanegra*,' she said, in her low gabbling voice, 'which I once saw *beautifully* done, even though the plot was horrendously complicated and you are quite lost if you don't know about Medieval Italy and Doges and the Grimaldi and the whole thing is a bit like *The Gondoliers* with a mix-up about babies ... But the pops, good heavens, I just did that for a bit of fun and to make some money years ago – and if I could have been a great singer, I mean like Callas – of course I would have been. Tracy, my sister, you met her briefly, wants to be a real pop singer like, oh I dunno, but she's not had much success so far. Anyway, what are we going to do about *us*?'

They were standing by the kerb, the open doors of the Bentley still giving out loud noises.

'We could either part now for ever, and realize we could have had an absolutely wonderful life together, or we could get into the car, she said melodramatically.

'If we don't get into the car the Police and the Noise Abatement Society will come and move us on.'

'You're from the Council, I keep forgetting.'

'But I said ...'

'You are, though, aren't you?'

He grunted, in vaguely affirmative tones.

'It was mean saying you weren't.'

'Sorry.'

'And you were snooping around my church –'

'Hardly snooping ...'

'What other word do you think would do?'

'Looking.'

'Snooping around my church in Birmingham, because you want to pull it down.'

'It's not so simple as that ...'

Suddenly she took both his arms and looked into his face imploringly.

'Please, Prince Consort, tell me the truth – you must, don't you see? It will be so awful later on if you don't. I would think you were trying to get round me to persuade me to demolish St Aidan's and you would be afraid that I was just trying to seduce you to make the Council change their mind ...'

'Are you trying to seduce me?'

'What's happening to us, Prince Consort?'

The Japanese tourists, about twenty of them, had now clustered quite close. They were an appreciative audience, bowing and smiling at Fred and Fanny quite a lot, and, at the last question, breaking out into spontaneous clapping.

'Catch Flora, will you. She's gone to do a wee on the Memorial.'

'Flora?'

'The corgi.'

The little dog was crouching at the bottom of the steps, a hot yellow stream emerging from its hind haunches. Fred left Fanny momentarily and ran up to it. He wondered if they were, after all, going to have a love affair: whether they would even have a conversation about it which lasted more than two minutes without interruption. He wished that it was possible to meet her without reference to Purgstall Heath. He wished that he did not work for the Council. And yet, ludicrously, if it had not been for Purgstall, the most nightmarish problem yet to occur in his Birmingham career, Fanny would never have come his way.

He stooped down and grabbed Flora roughly from behind. The corgi turned its foxy head savagely and took three fingers from his left hand into its mouth. The pain was instantaneous and horrible and the shock, instead of making him drop the dog, made him squeeze it all the harder, so that it bit him again and snarled.

'That's not the way to hold a corgi,' Fanny said, when he delivered it back to the car.

'Not really my sort of thing.' He shook his hand free as the snarling creature scampered with an angry smile on to the back seat.

'Heavens, has she flipping bit you?'

'It's nothing.'

'Poor Prince Consort.'

It was as a matter of fact, not a very deep bite, although the wound extended across three fingers. Fanny held his hand gently and looked at it, as they sat on the front seat of the car. Then, very slowly, she lowered her head towards the wound and began to lick it and suck it until it was clean. He stroked her head as it almost lay on his lap. He wished he could undo the elaborate arrangement of her hair. There was something laughable about the way it stuck out at the sides.

'Is that better?' she asked, looking up at him.

'Yes.'

He continued to stroke her head.

She sat up again, and leant against his shoulder.

'I want to lick you all over,' she said.

'I love you.'

When she looked up again, he sealed her lips with a kiss. Inside her mouth the taste of breakfast coffee lingered, somehow adding to the delight of stroking her tongue with his own. Then her kiss became violent, and he could feel her teeth closing on his tongue. One of her hands strayed deliberately to the zip in his trousers and crept inside. His eyes closed in near ecstasy, but then opened again to see a red, very closely shaven face looking sternly through the window at his left. Above the red face was the yellow band and black peaked cap of a traffic warden.

'You can't park here, you know,' said the man.

Fanny, her hand still fondling inside Fred's trousers, leaned across and rolled down the window.

'You can't park here,' the man repeated, raising his voice above the Verdi.

Fred felt himself blushing. He hated scenes of any kind and he was afraid that he was about to be the centre of one.

'You smell!' yelled Fanny.

'There's really no need to be abusive, madam.'

'You really stink. I hate you. When did you last look in a mirror? You have the most horrible face I ever saw in my life.'

'Steady on,' said Fred.

'I see, madam.'

A pocket book had been produced. A biro was at the ready. Withdrawing her hand sharply from Fred's trousers, Fanny turned the ignition and shot off northwards over the Serpentine bridge in the direction of the Bayswater Road. She drove the Bentley as if it were a motorbike.

'Horrible, horrible little man,' she said, putting her fingers in her mouth and sucking them gently. 'Do you see what I am doing?'

'Yes.'

'Is it sensual?'

'Very.'

He had been amused and at the same time frightened by her outrageous rudeness to the traffic warden; but he was afraid of saying anything about it in case his words smacked of Town Hall officialdom. The Affair, with extraordinary lack of prelude, had now begun and he did not want to interrupt its progress with further references to Purgstall Heath. Fanny was still licking her fingers, as though she had just finished a doughnut.

'Now I can taste you. Are you in love with me, Prince Consort?'

'Yes.'

'God, it's flipping exciting.'

The car was zooming over Bayswater Road now. He wondered

whether she had any particular destination in view or whether they were just drifting.

'I've ... I don't know what's happening to me,' he said. 'I have never felt like this before. It's just all so ...' His voice trembled with emotion as he spoke. To his amazement he felt himself on the edge of tears. He was not unhappy. Indeed, he was trembling with a happiness he had never known before and which was too strong and too enormous to contain.

'It's so difficult to explain,' he continued. He wished she would turn the opera down so that they could talk quietly.

'I want to be the Girl of Someone's Dreams so much, Prince Consort. Am I going to be the Girl of your Dreams?'

'You are, you are.'

'Will you make love to me, Prince Consort?'

'Oh yes, oh yes.'

Perhaps the exaggerated emotional atmosphere was increased by the noise of Verdi. Perhaps it was indeed True Love, of a sort he had hitherto imagined to be the creation of film producers and the publishers of third-rate romances. But he trembled with her beauty.

'Why did you say you weren't from the Council?'

'I don't know. Because I wanted to –'

'To impress me?'

'It wasn't that. Oh God, Fanny. I love you. Men must be saying it to you all the time ...'

'Why do you say that?' she asked sharply.

'Because you are so beautiful.'

'Don't be sincophantic, Prince Consort. Please don't be sinco-phantic. I just can't bear it when men are sincophantic. I want to trample all over them and destroy them.'

'It's true.'

'Well, shut up about it. I want to know why you lied to me. The very first time we met. I was looking round my church and you were coming to see if you could pull it down.'

'Don't let's go over all that,' he groaned.

'But you were. It was your job. Nothing wrong with that. I hated and despised you for wanting to pull it down. I still hate and despise you for it, but that doesn't explain why you lied.'

'I fell in love with you as soon as I saw you. I didn't want you to think I was just a man from the Council. I wanted –' he took her hand '– this – not a lot of boring talk about that building.'

'It's flipping not boring. I told you it was built by a man called Kipper,' she sniggered.

'Hang Kipper.'

'He wasn't. He was called Fish. Oswald Fish. And you will never believe it but by the most *extraordinary* coincidence, Oswald Fish was the *grandfather* of my *darling* Charles Bullowewo.'

'The ... the man I met.'

'My lovely nig-nog.'

'Doesn't sound very ... I mean *how?*'

'He explained it all so angelically. His grandmother was a serving maid or a governess in Belgium and met Oswald Fish in Belgium where they had the most *romantic* attachment which led to the lady giving birth to Charles's father.'

'In Belgium?'

'In Africa, I think.'

'So Oswald Fish went to Africa.'

'Must have.'

The Bentley passed into the Harrow Road, the huge concrete overpass of West Way roaring above them to the left like some space-age fantasy, on which lorries thundered towards Acton, Northolt and Uxbridge. Beneath, the environs of the Harrow Road had something of the atmosphere of a small provincial town: terraced houses, corner shops and a gas works were visible; little brick churches, which had once soared above their squalid sur- roundings, were now dwarfed by the gargantuan road systems, and reminded Fred uncomfortably of Purgstall Heath.

'That's Kensal Green Cemetery,' said Fanny. 'Just about anyone you can think of is buried there – Trollope and Thackeray, flipping everyone. Let's walk around and have a look.'

Fred did not reply. He had hoped, now that the Affair was unequivocally under way, to go straight back to his hotel bedroom, but perhaps a walk in this ghoulish spot had always been part of Fanny's plans. A cool breeze blew as they walked through the gateway, Flora and Honey scampering ahead in defiance of a notice which said that dogs should be kept on leads. Once inside, they gazed about them at the monuments: stone slabs, angels, marble crosses, once-splendid mausoleums now patched up with brick; the

London dead of more than a century stretching as far as the eye could see in every direction. Fanny clasped his arm with both of hers, and they walked along rather awkwardly in the bright, cold sunshine.

'If you lied to me about the Council,' she persisted, 'how do I know you haven't lied to me about being happily married?'

'What do you mean?'

'Lots of men do it.'

'Do what?'

'Tell a hard-luck story. Say their wives don't love them ...'

'That's not what I said.'

'I know you didn't. But you admitted you were unhappily married.'

'Did I?'

'Yes, you did, you did. There you go again lying. Oh, Prince Consort, please don't lie. I want to make love to you but I want it to be *love* that we make – do you see?'

'But I have said that I love you.'

She sniggered.

'What's so funny about that?'

'Do you realize that we have known each other for rather less than three days?'

'I don't see what difference it makes.'

'We could be making a terrible mistake, that's all.' She withdrew her arms and stalked on independently. He quickened his pace and took her hand.

'We've got to talk about it,' she added.

'We are talking about it.'

'What's your wife called?'

'Jennifer.'

'Is that what you call her?'

'No. I call her Jen.'

'Then why did you say Jennifer? There you go again, Prince Consort. You keep trying to conceal things. Don't you understand that if this is going to be terribly important we have got to be *absolutely* honest – flipping well honest. Not just say things we think will please each other.'

Fred did not fully understand this. He wondered why she was making this point so insistently. It was unimaginable – so much so that he did not entertain the notion for a second – that she felt as strongly about him as he did about her. She was self-evidently a highly sexed girl who liked a good time. He had never met anyone before who, after only a few hours' acquaintanceship, and stone cold sober, had deliberately put her hands inside his trousers. What then did she want? What was the meaning of all this apparent sorrow and morality?

'I don't really know what you want,' he said.

She sighed and paused.

'You've heard me talk about the Honourable Member – Aubrey,' she began.

'Your husband?'

'Do you know what his mother called me once? *A trendy little prostitute.*' She adopted a parody of an English County voice. 'She really shouted it at me. *You are nothing better than a prostitute.* God, she's a foul old bag.'

'She sounds awful.'

'She's not, she's great fun. How she gave birth to that bore ... *still*, that's nothing to do with *us*. The point is, by *their* standards, I have been a prostitute ...'

'Rubbish.'

'What do you mean *rubbish*, you don't know anything about it.'

'Everyone sleeps around nowadays.' He tried to sound knowing.

'Do you?'

'Well ...' He laughed.

'I don't want to be a prostitute, Prince Consort. If you're just a bit bored with Jen and are looking for a nice sexy girl who can give you a good time ...'

'Fanny, it isn't that. I've said it isn't that. I love you. I've never felt about anyone the way I feel about you – this is all so different. God, it's making me feel quite ill. Do you realize that since we met in Birmingham I haven't been able to eat or sleep or think about anything except you?'

She stopped walking and turned to him, her face glowing with a radiant smile. Her white blouse was slightly open at the neck and, beneath, her breast heaved with excitement. Her eyes sparkled so vividly that they seemed to be on fire. He put his arms around her and drew her to himself.

'I want you,' he said.

'Hug me tighter, Prince Consort,' she said.

'God, I want you.'

Their lips met in a long and tender kiss. Then she rubbed her cheek against his own. Then she began to nibble at one of his ears.

'I'm not just a bit of crumpet, Prince Consort.'

'I know you're not.'

'I want to be the Girl of your Dreams.'

'Darling Fanny.'

Holding his arm, she led the way, down off the main avenue of the cemetery, between the rough grasses of the graves. Low-lying, like a moss-covered divan, they found a flat tombstone shaded by yew trees. With deliberate slowness, she lay down on it and drew him on top of her.

'I want you so much,' she whispered. 'Put your hand in my skirt.'

It was the sort of skirt which is split at the sides almost up to the thigh and buttoned at the hip. She undid the buttons for him and he unfolded the thick grey tweed to reveal complete nakedness.

'Your hand, your hand,' she said urgently.

He reached out to touch. She lay so still, her legs and belly were so smoothly, marbly white, that it was almost as if some effigy on the tomb had come to life and was beckoning him, an effigy on which warm, dainty and deliciously rough moss could be felt beneath his finger tips.

'Shouldn't we go somewhere more private?' he whispered.

She responded only with contented animal murmuring. Her eyes were half closed, but with her hands she gently undid his trousers, and soon he felt the sharp cold rings pressing against his buttocks as she groaned and squealed and writhed beneath him in a dizzy magic which seemed to lift them both from the scenes of time and space. For Fred, all too soon, it was over. He tried to murmur some apology, but she was still smiling, in what looked like an almost trance-like joy. Then, very vigorously, she gave one last series of manic gyrations and screamed 'OH, OH, OH!' Then she was silent, and still.

Shocked by the intensity of the experience, no longer fully hers or his, but a shared ecstasy, they lay tightly in each other's arms, still and bewildered: exhausted, and half frightened by the joy of it.

'There is such honour in it,' she murmured at last. 'It is *so* beautiful.'

His 'yes' was husky, scarcely audible. He did not know how to respond or what to say. He felt as if his entire being, his whole former self had been lifted up, shaken and thrown to the winds, and that he lay, like Adam on the dawning of his first day in Paradise, a new creature, with a new life before him.

'Girl of My Dreams,' he managed to say.

'Prince Consort,' she replied. Adding, with the old sharpness which at once declared that this particular episode was over, '*Flip!* Where are the corgis?'

She slithered off the tombstone, buttoning herself hastily while he made the necessary adjustments to his person, and stood up beside her.

'I feel dizzy, she said. 'that was so *beautiful*.'

'Beautiful.'

'But where is my *Hon–ey! Flo–ra!*'

Long grass and graves stretched in interminable yards in every direction. The dogs could have been anywhere. Fred managed a ludicrous whistle. In no time at all, the ecstatic moment on the tombstone had evaporated into the hectic comic melodrama which was perhaps, after all, Fanny's natural milieu. The cemetery had become a maze. The two lovers had turned into anxious children playing an absurd game. Having once quit the main avenue where they had walked at first, all paths looked alike. They passed the graves of soldiers, grocers, aldermen and minor poets; grandiose memorials and humble. A huge, fantastical lumpy red construction, the size of a house, commemorated Astley, the great theatrical manager. Hard by, prosperous obelisks recorded the lives of East India merchants, war heroes of the Crimea, well-connected deans and long-forgotten editors of defunct newspapers.

'Look at this one,' called Fanny, momentarily forgetting the dogs. She was peering through the battered door of a mausoleum. He came up behind her and caressed her shoulder. Staring through the hole in the rotten wood he could see eight coffins, four on each side of the mausoleum, arranged like bunks in a wagon-lit. They were large, dark coffins, far more elaborate and capacious than those of modern design, with great rusted metal handles. One of them had been ripped open, revealing the grinning skull within.

'Are you frightened?' she asked.

Suddenly he was. Frightened by the rank, musty smell, the

darkness, the damp decay the sense that these eight boxes contained beings who had once been sentient, capable of hunger and
sorrow and love.

'Is this what we are all hurtling towards?' he asked. 'Is this where
it all leads – just to damp and mould?'

'Now you know what I mean about emptiness at the heart of the
universe,' she said. 'And why I couldn't stand being married for a
single instant longer than I was. Poor old sausage,' she said,
peering in through the door again at the skull, 'you haven't really
much to smile about, have you? I bet you had a flipping boring life.'
She turned back to Fred. 'Most people do, and then, on the few
occasions when a chance of *real* happiness and joy is presented to
them, they pass it by. We mustn't pass by our chance of joy, must
we, Prince Consort? However silly it seems, and I know we've only
known each other five minutes, this is so *beautiful* – we mustn't –
Flora! where have you been?'

Her reflections were interrupted by the waddling corgi which
came into view round the corner of the path where they stood. She
stooped down and held it by the collar.

'What can we use as a lead?' she asked.

He had a handkerchief but he had already blown his nose on it
that morning. He somehow, for all Fanny's talk of complete
honesty between lovers, did not want her to see bits of his snot.

'Could you bear to lend your lovely blue tie, Prince Consort?'

Reluctantly (love made him do it) he said, ' 'Course,' removed the
thick silk from his own collar and watched her fasten it round
Flora's.

'Don't you look *pretty* my Flora? You must never bite Prince
Consort again after he's given you such a beautiful tie.'

Only when the exchange had been performed did it occur to Fred
that he could have suggested using his belt. They ambled hand in
hand, the corgi trotting at their heels, past endless graves.

'*William Makepeace Thackeray* – look at *that*, Prince Consort.'

Fred looked.

'Honey will turn up,' she said.

Some of the graves they passed were modern ones, bright with
green gravel. They had touching garish inscriptions picked out in
bright gold: VERA JINKS – THE BEST MUM IN THE WORLD. They
passed mounds of freshly turned brown earth, covering the recently

dead. Some still had their cellophane-wrapped flowers lying on top of them; one, from which Fred tried to avert his gaze, had a teddybear and a tricycle fashioned out of wire and red and yellow flowers.

'God, how awful to lose a child,' Fanny said. 'My children are the most adorable creatures in the world. They are the most important things in my life . . . I know Marmie was rude to you the other night, but he is *quite* the most extraordinary and delightful person – wonderfully odd and wonderfully himself. How can people believe in a God who lets their children die, Prince Consort, how *can* they?'

Fred was silent. Her love of Marmie was something too remote for him to enter into. He felt chilled and frightened, even more than by the grinning skull, by the sight of the floral teddy bear. He agreed with what she said. The loss of a child was the most horrible thing that any parent could contemplate and he felt suddenly tugged by a homesick feeling of longing for Sam and Harriet – a paternal feeling stronger than he ever thought he possessed. It comforted him, in a way, but he did not want to have it *now*. If he cast in his lot with Fanny, became her Prince Consort, she would gain a lover, perhaps one day a husband, and lose nothing. He longed for her with all his heart, but he had not contemplated the reality of the thing in terms of his own domestic arrangements. At home, when he was in a bad mood, and Jen's ears were showing and his shirts had not been ironed, he felt such helpless seething fury that the children were just another pair of irritants, noticeable only for their constant squabbles, and the noise and mess they created. The vulgar little yellow teddy bear shocked him into thinking what it would be like without them. The irritation, he now saw, was something merely on the surface. Beneath there was an attachment too deep to be articulated, but unshakably strong. And the realization of this made him wonder, for the first time in his married life, whether this was not what he also felt about Jen. Hellishly, maddeningly infuriating, she was. Did it really matter? What was there to show that irritations for worse might not also develop, when they actually lived together, with Fanny? And was he, for the sake of Romance, about to throw away fourteen years of solid, rooted, much of the time affectionate, shared experience?

'What are you thinking, Prince Consort?'

'This place depresses me.'

She squeezed his arm, and nibbled his ear. The gesture brought comfort. Yes, everything she said was right. Affections were easy enough to feel when away from home. The reality of life in Augustus Road was joyless. And if we could not find joy before we died, might we not just as well speed up the process, swig down a bottle of pills and wait until the flesh fell from our faces and our hollow skulls grinned in their coffins?

'I love you,' he said.

'I wish we could find Honey,' she said. As she walked she hummed the march from *Aïda*. When she sang quietly the notes came in the jerky unnatural rhythms of 1960s pop music.

'Have you always liked opera?' he asked.

'No.' She said it as though slightly affronted to be asked, as if he had said, 'Have you always had fleas?' 'I'd never been to the opera until the Honourable Member took me – didn't know the difference between Callas and Caruso. It was *Lucia di Lammermoor* at Covent Garden and God it was beautiful. I was still half hoping to make a comeback as a pop singer. I'd no idea how *exciting* music could be. By the last act my knickers were just oozing with excitement. It's the only form of music which is as good as sex.'

'As good?'

'Nearly as good.' She laughed. 'People scream and have orgasms at pop concerts – or they used to. But I never did. I never even knew what it felt like until I sat there oozing, really flipping oozing over Donizetti. Then I went to everything I could, bought all the records and couldn't do without it. It's like a drug. I think poor Aubrey didn't mind me smashing things, or losing my temper.'

'Or being unfaithful . . . ?'

'I wasn't being unfaithful. I was faithful to him for three flipping years. Just *think* of it. Even when I wasn't I don't think he'd have minded. It was the opera which did it.'

'Presumably he quite liked opera or he would never have taken you to it in the first place.'

'*Liked it?*' Again a tone of outrage. 'He's *completely* unmusical. Tone deaf. Someone had given him complimentary tickets. I think he was asleep by the end of the overture.'

'I liked the famous song you sang.'

'Me?'

'When you were a pop singer.'

He wondered whether now was the moment to ask for her autograph as Jen had suggested, for the children, but the thought of the children choked him with despair and fear.

She sniggered her tinny laugh, but as they walked along in the bright spring sunshine she began to sing –

> You left me lonely baby, why-oh-why –
> But I ain't one to sit alone and cry:
> And I've been dancing with another guy
> I've changed my scene,
> O, pussy-cat queen!
>
> He took me shopping round the Knightsbridge stores
> His Mayfair house is built on fifteen floors
> But I ain't staying any more because
> I'm only sixteen
> O, pussy-cat queen!
>
> Pussy cat, pussy cat, where have you been,
> You made me so lonely O pussy-cat queen
>
> Baby you'll never know the times I had
> Baby, you thought you treated me so bad:
> Now it's you who's looking O so sad
> See what I mean
> O, pussy-cat queen?
>
> Pussy cat, pussy cat, where have you been,
> You made me so lonely, O pussy-cat queen.

For Fred the song brought back strange memories. He had just finished his articles at a London firm of solicitors when it was in the charts. At that stage he had been rather keen on a girl called Joanna who had a flat off Holland Park Avenue. She always seemed to be playing it on the gramophone when he went round there. These irrelevant memories transported him for a moment into an earlier self and he was silent. The next words he spoke were, 'There's the dog.'

Honey was at the far end of a path, about eighty yards ahead of them. She was not alone. She was scampering about the heels of an old woman: white cropped hair, a belted navy blue gaberdine mackintosh with a hood, like a schoolgirl's, brown stockings over her skinny legs and blue canvas shoes. She carried a plastic Tesco bag.

'Good heavens, it's Nana,' said Fanny.

Fred sighed. His body still tingled with the delights on the mossy tombstone, but they had only whetted his appetite for more and he longed to be alone with Fanny and indoors where traffic wardens could not interrupt and she would not be lured away by dogs, grandmothers, black men or any other member of the travelling circus with which she chose to surround herself.

'Nana,' Fanny called, 'what on earth are you doing here?'

Jessica Owen looked up. Her face was grave and set. Perhaps it annoyed her to be discovered. Perhaps she was merely reflecting on the sad fact that it was almost impossible to see her granddaughter unaccompanied by a man. Perhaps it was merely habit and the shape of her false teeth which gave her mouth its look of rigidity.

'Nana, have you met Alastair?' Fanny's voice faltered and then she sniggered. They had declared undying love for one another, even made love on a tombstone, but she could not remember ever having heard his surname.

'We met yesterday evening,' said Jessica politely. 'You were trying to convert me to the Jehovah's Witnesses.'

Was this a joke or was she senile? Fred nodded inanely.

'What brings you here, bach?' she asked Fanny. 'I didn't tell Tracy where I was going.'

'Isn't it the most wonderful cemetery in the world, Nana? Have you seen Trollope and Thackeray and goodness knows who else – Dickens, Shakespeare probably.'

'No,' said her grandmother. 'I don't know why. I must be getting sentimental, but I had not been here for years. As you can see.'

With a brown, wrinkled finger, she pointed to a grey, rather unkempt gravestone beside which had been laid, evidently by Jessica herself, a bunch of fresh florists' daffodils. The three of them silently read the inscription

FRANCES ROSEMARY FISH   1861–1919
'I am my beloved's and my beloved is mine.'

Song. Sol. vi.3.

For Fred and Fanny the inscription meant nothing: although Fred felt certain, with a recurring sense of dread, that all this had something to do with the subject he wanted most of all to avoid.

'My father chose the inscription, Jessica said. 'Funny, isn't it? They never really got on, you know, and yet at the end I suppose he felt he had lost someone precious to him. I don't think it was just sentimentality.' Her voice trailed off. It was evident that she was trying to tell them something. Fred felt awkward to be there. 'I don't really mind people knowing now, only it's everything coming at once,' she said. 'I wanted them buried in the same place, only I never had the money to have the inscription added to, do you see? So there he lies.'

She gave a little smile.

'I still can't get over what Charles was saying last night,' she said. 'I suppose it must be true. It's so strange I never knew about it. Still, there was a lot I never knew – never will know now, I suppose. There they are though ...'

'Nana, who was she – Frances Fish? Was she something to do with Oswald Fish? How did you know about her?'

'It's my mother,' Jessica said simply. 'She died of flu, do you see, in 1919.'

'I never knew you were called Fish.'

'I'm not – haven't been since I married your grandfather. You never thought to ask me what my maiden name was. I never thought to tell you. To tell you the truth, I was a bit ashamed of it. And you won't tell anyone, will you, pet? I don't want everyone talking about it – even though now that church turns out to be important. Funny, isn't it? He often talked about that church ...'

'Who did – not Oswald Fish? Nana, you don't mean to say you *knew* Oswald Fish?'

Jessica smiled at her granddaughter, a dark impenetrable smile. Then she looked at Fred.

'I've been thinking and thinking about it,' she said. 'I couldn't decide. I knew someone was bound to start guessing sooner or later, but I don't want to talk about it.'

'Why not, Nana, why not?'

'He wasn't a happy man, pet. I think he was really clever in some ways. Not book clever. Not ideas clever. But he had a wonderful eye and a real creative flair. For one reason and another he never got the chance to exercise his gift. That was why that church meant so much to him – the one you've bought. It may not really be anything so wonderful.'

'But Nana, it's wonderful. Tell her, Prince Consort, it *is* wonderful, isn't it?'

Fred looked abashed. For love's sake, for an old lady's sake, he said, 'Absolutely wonderful.'

'I never got very interested in architecture for some reason. For him it was a passion – it meant everything to him.'

Oswald Fish?' Fred asked.

Assuming that explanation was unnecessary, Jessica continued, 'I saw it coming out in you, Fanny, you see. I noticed it when you were quite a little girl. You cared about the way things looked. You remember me taking you to see the castle at Cardiff on the train?'

'Wonderful pre-Raphaelite interiors!' Fanny exclaimed.

'How old were you? About seven I should think. I don't know what your mother was doing at the time.'

'Getting a new man, I expect,' Fanny said, crossly, as though such activities were unknown to her.

'And then all the excitement you've had over getting your shops right – he'd have loved them,' she said with amusement. 'Of course my generation thought it was something to laugh at – pointed arches, tracery. What have you. We wanted clean, clear lines. We used to laugh at the Victorians.'

'Nothing to laugh at,' snorted Fanny.

'I never really noticed buildings though, not the way you do. Living in Neath there aren't many buildings to notice except the chapels and the station. But it was his passion, d'you see. He thought he could find satisfaction with women and I daresay he treated them badly. In a funny kind of way she never minded, you know.' She nodded towards the grave. 'Oh, it made her unhappy, same as it would anyone, but I think she felt he loved her, and perhaps he did. But it wasn't his chief love. He thought he'd find perfect love if he went on chasing women, but he couldn't, do you see? Women weren't the love of his life. He was an artist. Women were really just comforts, distractions, I don't know the right word. I've never seen that church of yours in Birmingham and I don't believe I'd like it if I did.'

'Nana, how can you say such things?'

'But it was a kind of dream, a vision, that made him build it. He really thought he might be able to build great buildings – I don't know, Chartres Cathedral or wherever it might be. That was the thought that kept him going. And when it vanished, it was too much for him, do you see?'

Neither of them saw. They could not fully understand what she was talking about. Her ramble seemed full of unexplained hints and memories.

'He went mad, you know,' she continued bluntly. 'Absolutely mad. There was nothing we could do for him – raving and shouting much of the time, running about, I don't know. It's terrible to see a man like that.'

They murmured as though it must have been terrible.

'I don't know why people go mad, do you?' she suddenly addressed her question to Fred.

'No,' he faltered, 'no, I don't.'

'He kept talking about a girl he'd loved long ago – long before her,' she nodded to the grave. 'I don't think it was girls. People don't go mad because of girls. I think it was because he had a vision and he had no way of passing it on, no way of giving it shape. He died in the madhouse in Carmarthen. Terrible it was. I never told you before. Your mother, even, never knew the half of how terrible it was. I don't know why I tell you even now, only you seem to be interested in him all of a sudden. I didn't have much money then. Well, you remember the post office in Lammas Street. But I knew I wanted him buried here. So we put him on the train and had the funeral here.'

'You buried him here?'

'In the same grave.'

'*I am my beloved's and my beloved is mine.* It seems funny now, with both of them lying here. I've never been back. Besides, I never had the money to get his name inscribed on the stone.'

'So Frances Fish was Oswald Fish's wife?' Fred asked.

'I think the person who buried him there with her thought they were married.' For the first time Nana gave a truly gleeful smile.

'Nana, I still don't understand. Do you mean to say that this is Oswald Fish's grave?'

'That's what I said.'

'But ... but ...' Fanny's voice had become uncommonly quiet. 'But who was Oswald Fish?'

'My father,' said Jessica simply.

There seemed to be complete stillness in the air. Not even bird-song or distant traffic could be heard.

'Then he . . .'

'Yes,' said Jessica. 'Oswald Fish was your great-grandfather.'

Without a word, they all of them turned to walk down the main avenue and back to the car. The morning spring sunshine cast long shadows of themselves ahead on the path. Jessica, walking slightly ahead of the others, saw their separate shadows, the shapes elongated and exaggerated on the path – Fanny's piled-up hair and padded shoulders, Fred's bulky form, even the spectacles caught in silhouette. As she gazed down, Jessica wondered whether she had done right to tell them. What harm could come of it? None in a way. She had wanted so much to pour the whole story out, and yet she would almost have preferred an anonymous hearer. She wanted to tell, but did she want it known? Perhaps nothing much mattered any more. Almost forgotten, and past caring, her father slept in his grave. Soon, she would die herself: if not that year, soon enough. The dead feel no pain. The shadows behind her, hitherto separate, were coming together. She watched the shadow hands join. She saw the shadow heads come together in a kiss. Their surreptitious lovemaking made her feel isolated, out of things, but the moment passed. She felt strangely removed from the present scene, trans-ported back to the days of her own youth, to her memories of her parents, to the muddle of contradictory thoughts and emotions they aroused, so that Fanny and her new lover, treading gently behind her, seemed to her as insubstantial as their own shadows.

XXI

Fiona Matheson did not go to the office that day. She was not expected for another twenty-four hours: there was nothing to go there for. She had imagined a day devoted to David; a long night, naked and rapturous in his arms; breakfast, which he always prepared himself and brought to her in bed; a happy little morning tidying the flat and shopping: meeting him perhaps in a pub for lunch, either on his own or with one of his amusing colleagues like Jeremy Tradescant. Perhaps she might even have persuaded him not to go back to the museum after lunch.

As it was, she had spent a morning of tense, lonely, anxious misery. His absence filled her with panic. It was inconceivable that he could have gone away without leaving a note. The only explanation for his absence was that something had gone wrong. She felt chilled by a sense of foreboding, as though a shadow was creeping over the hitherto uninterrupted sunshine of her existence. The dread was nameless. She did not specifically think, as she had done at first, 'He has been run over,' 'He has appendicitis,' 'His mother is dead.' She felt merely depressed in a way that was quite unlike her usual nature; cold, and afraid, a dull ache locating itself just below her rib-cage.

The flat was horrible to her. The delight she normally felt in it was quite vanished. She did not notice the Sheraton chairs, the Chippendale bureau, the little neo-classical oil paintings of the landscape near Turin, the spindly occasional tables or the Chinese bowl on the rosewood chest of drawers. She noticed only a half-finished cup of coffee, ice-cold on the mantelpiece; David's shoes higgledy-piggledy on the bedroom floor; the odour of sour milk in the kitchen. These very faint symptoms of disorder – a copy of the *Guardian* untidily thrown on to the sofa, biscuit crumbs on the hearth-rug not hoovered up – were almost more dispiriting than if the flat had been done over by burglars, and completely messed up.

They suggested a sudden vanishing. His coffee and biscuit half finished, his paper thrown down, he had *suddenly* gone. But why? He was usually so punctilious about keeping the place tidy.

She rang up his mother at nine o'clock. It was an absurd conversation. She said that she wanted to let them know she was back. Where was David, she had been asked. And, instead of saying, 'That was what I was going to ask you,' she had merely said, 'Oh, he is out at the Museum – he's so fearfully busy at the moment I hardly ever see him,' and, with tinkly laughs, the conversation had ended.

She had dialled the number of her local police station, but when the voice answered at the other end of the line she felt unable to say that she was worried about her missing husband. She had merely apologized, said she must have the wrong number, and put the receiver down.

She had rung up Jeremy Tradescant. There, she had been bolder, though trying to sound sprightly.

'Jeremy, you haven't seen David, have you?'

'Yesterday, why?'

'Where?'

'*Al Museo*, dear, why do you ask?'

'Only I've got back from Brussels and he doesn't seem to be around.'

'Probably working his little fingerines to the bone *à l'office*. What's the time?'

'Quarter to ten.'

'Darling, it *isn't*?'

'A bit after.'

'In that case I'm deeply late. I blush to tell you where I am.'

'In bed?'

'Too awful, isn't it? I must have an instant bathette and go to work myself. I'll tell David you were worried.'

'Don't bother, it's nothing.'

'I'm sure he's all right, Fiona.'

'Thank you, Jeremy.'

'Not a bit, bye now.'

'Good-bye.'

'Be good.'

With a little squeal, Jeremy had rung off. Probably he was right.

There could be nothing to worry about. And yet the sense of dread persisted. She unpacked her things, washed some smalls, ironed a blouse, hoovered every room in the flat, and still it nagged at her, this combination of disappointment and fear. She knew that the sensible thing to do would be to forget about it, to go out and do something and to come back this evening when she was expected. She put on her coat twice, intending to adopt this course, but each time she did this something held her back. He might *ring*, call, return, and she could not bear the prospect of missing him. By now, the desire to see him again battled with the almost equally strong wish to have the mystery explained.

At about eleven o'clock, the key turned in the lock and she heard him come in. She ran to the hall and hugged him. For the first time in their married life she felt impulsively angry with him, but she knew it was a reflexive anger, only caused by her previous fear.

'I got back early,' she said. 'Where have you been?'

'Fiona.' He kissed her. She could feel his heart thumping violently beneath his donkey jacket. When she unclasped herself and looked at his face, all its colour had vanished, he looked ashen and terrified.

'I thought you weren't coming back till tonight.' he said.

'David, what's the matter, you look awful.'

'I'm ... I'm all right.'

He brushed past her into the bedroom with his shoulder bag. She stood at the doorway and stared at him.

'Are you sure you're all right?'

'I'm perfectly all right.' He snapped the words out. 'I've been at work – just popped back for ten minutes or so. I can't stay.'

'What's the hurry?'

'There isn't a hurry, but I'm meant to be at work.

'Then why did you come back?'

'I ... I've done some shopping.' He opened his shoulder bag and produced a pint carton of milk and a loaf as evidence. Fiona noticed a toothbrush and his electric razor in the side pocket of the bag.

'Have you been away?' she asked.

'No.' Again, his answer was snappy. 'What makes you ask that?'

'Because I got back last night and the flat was empty.'

He twitched as though in pain, turned to the dressing-table and unpacked his toothbrush and razor. Without turning to her he said,

'I . . . had dinner out – stayed rather late, decided to stay the night. It's a bit lonely when you aren't here.'

'Poor old thing.' She came up to him and clasped him from behind, her chin on his shoulder, looking at the reflection of both their faces in the glass. 'I *hate* going away. That's why I came back early. I'm going to ask them how much longer I need to do it. They could always send someone else. The trouble is that the two or three other people in the department who could be sent come up with better excuses than I do – babies or sick mothers or something – can't be left three days.'

'And what will your excuse be?'

'That I love my husband too much to be parted from him ever again.'

She spoke the words slowly and solemnly, punctuating them with kisses on his neck and ears. As she said them, his face relaxed into a smile and he reached up to stroke her hand which rested on his shoulder.

'I love you too,' he said.

'Anyway,' she said, with mock tones of shock, 'who were those exciting friends of yours, luring you away from the marital bed as soon as my back was turned?'

'Oh, just colleagues from the museum.'

Her face still stared towards his, but he avoided her glance. She was surprised at how quickly she picked up the tones of hesitancy and fear in his voice that betrayed the lie. She knew she would be happier to let the lie pass. Perhaps, after all, it was true. Or, if not true, perhaps there was some quite innocent explanation. But she could not resist the next trick question.

'With Jeremy Tradescant?'

He laughed before replying. Jeremy, although they both liked him well enough, was always something of a joke figure. In his own words, a figurine.

'Yes,' he said, 'Jeremy was there – and Stevie. And a girl in the metalwork department called Alice. The dinner went on rather late and they persuaded me to stay the night – so I did.' This little speech, spoken hastily, was delivered as he walked towards the door with his back towards her.

'Was Jeremy . . . on good form?' Fiona was trying not to allow her voice to crack.

'Quite. I'll see you this evening, Fiona, but I've really got to go now. Shall I buy supper, or will you?'

'I'm quite happy to.'

'You then.'

'I don't know.'

'We'll have a lovely celebration dinner. I'm so glad you're back. I can't tell you how glad I am.' He turned in the hall and gave her a long, lingering kiss. She stiffened awkwardly as he did so. She watched him walk out of the front door. She watched the door shut. The scene was misted with her tears, and she returned to the bedroom, threw herself on the bed and sobbed.

There was something compulsive, but not really comforting about the sobbing. She cried until her breast and throat heaved automatically with the movement of weeping; an almost forgotten sensation from childhood. She felt that she could have endured anything except his dishonesty. When the sobbing at last subsided and she lay, hot and weary against the pillow, she itemized the things she could have tolerated. If he had left a note, she would not have minded so much. If he had come out openly and said: I am in love with another girl – a girl in the metalwork department called Alice . . . If, if, if. But nothing could make the situation bearable. She had loved him, and still loved him, so deeply. She had, unthinkingly, *trusted* him. This single, stupid lie spoilt everything. She hated herself for having forced it out of him. If only she had let things be, he would have thought of a better one in the course of the day. Had she asked him what he had been doing during her previous absences in Brussels? Not that she could remember. It was only her foolish early return, his absence at night, which had prompted the question. If only, if only, if only . . . As she lay there, not merely their present, but all their past happiness, seemed to trickle away. If he could lie now what was there to show that he had not been lying on other occasions? When she went away to Brussels, what did he do, who did he see? When he said he loved her, had he meant it? Was their whole marriage a farcical mistake, as friends and relations had suggested at the time? Someone, a malicious cousin, had said, 'David is marrying you for reasons of pure snobbery. All art historians are snobs.' She had laughed at the time. Her people weren't, after all, so very grand. True, they had a nice house in the country, knew all the right people, her mother was the daughter of a marquess. But this could be said of dozens of families. Snobbery had never come into her view of David. Now the cruel sentence, spoken in jest months and months ago, jabbed at her brain and would not be ignored. *All art historians are snobs.* She had certainly noticed it in most of the V & A people that David had introduced her to. Jeremy Tradescant appeared to collect duchesses. Fiona, who had never needed to be snobbish, thought of it as a merely ridiculous fad. It did not mean anything. Always tasteless and embarrassing, it could not do any harm: that had been her line. Could middle-class people mind so much about that sort of thing that they would actually *marry* for the sake of it? It seemed inconceivable and yet one so often heard it said. 'She did rather well for herself?' – it did not refer to money or good looks in a husband but horrible, horrible *class.* 'He came from a perfectly ordinary family, but you wouldn't think so now.' Her mother had said it quite recently about a coal merchant's son who had married a cousin of theirs. How *foul* people were. *Nowadays.* When it meant *nothing.* When lords and ladies had no more position in society than the ornamental guardsmen in sentry boxes outside St James's Palace; when dukes were as likely to be businessmen or market gardeners as those more lowly born; still it went on: this baying, insinuating, hateful awareness of Burke and Debrett, or, if you could not manage those, Kelly's *Official and Landed Classes.*

Why was she suddenly thinking about it, suddenly so sure that this was her attraction to David? It had never crossed her mind before. David's people seemed no different from hers at the wedding. Her grandfather, Lord Seton, had made a speech: and David's best man, an old school friend. They both had the same toffee-nosed voices. Only now did it obsessively occur to her that she came from a higher drawer, and had been a good 'catch'. The thought sickened and appalled her. She had been so besotted, enchanted by David for the last two years, so deliriously happy in his company, that she had assumed that he was quite as much in love with her. He had always seemed so. Every hour had been delicious since she met him. And yet, it was unthinkable that she could ever go off on her own for a night and lie to him. Unthinkable. It made everything false, shallow, empty. It could only mean that he had not married her for love, as she had thought. *All art historians are snobs.* Burying her face in her pillow again she gave herself up to paroxysms of weeping.

How long she lay like that she did not know. Perhaps she lay in a trance of torment, perhaps she had fallen asleep. The telephone was ringing. Let it ring. And yet, after six rings, she felt a little dart of hope and lifted the receiver. There might, after all, be a quite innocent explanation. It might be him: her David.

A childish snigger was all she heard at the other end of the line.

'Hallo? Who is that?' Her voice shook as she spoke. Children's laughter so often sounds cruel. Almost certainly it was some prank. Some children, she knew, dialled numbers at random on their parents' telephones for a dare or an adventure.

'Is that David Matheson's number?' It was a funny, high-pitched little Cockney child who spoke.

'Yes, yes it is. Who is that speaking, please?'

There was more helpless laughter at the other end of the line.

'Don't be silly,' Fiona snapped, coming to herself.

'May I come round to see David?' said the voice.

'He's out at work – who is that, please?'

'When will he get back?'

'He's usually back about 5 or 6. Who are you? What do you want?'

'I'm not sure of the address.'

'23 Rosary Crescent.' She wished she had not given this information. It came tripping off her tongue automatically. 'Please tell me who you are.'

'David left something behind, d'you see,' said the child. 'I thought I'd call and give it back, see what I mean.'

'What is it?'

'Just something what I think he'd like to have.'

'You must tell me who you are. You must, you *must*.'

But the threatening little voice gave nothing away except another peal of scornful laughter.

XXII

'Is that the children?'

'I didn't hear anything.'

'Oh, Prince Consort, I don't want them to know you are here.'

'Why not?'

'Why *not*? In *bed*! With their mother! In the middle of the afternoon!'

'I suppose not.'

Fred had just passed the most rapturously exciting and wonderful two hours of his life. The little moment on the tombstone had given almost no hint of the delights that were to follow. Fanny had suggested driving Nana Owen back to Tregunter Road, but the old woman had insisted on being dropped in the middle of the town. She wanted to be on her own, to collect her thoughts, she had said. They had watched her toddling off down Piccadilly. In the car, on the way back across the park, Fanny had talked of nothing but Oswald Fish, jabbered and jabbered about the man, of how she was hardly able to contain herself until Charles got home to tell him that they were *cousins*! The coincidence was remarkable, improbable enough. Fred could not work up much interest in it. In so far as he had an opinion of Oswald Fish, the man had been nothing but trouble. And yet, mysteriously, if it had not been for Ōswald Fish, he would not have met Fanny and the chaotic adventures of the past few days would never have happened.

At Tregunter Road, the house had been empty. Tracy was out with the mini. Sid was at work, so was Charles. They had wandered about undisturbed. Though so full of things, the house had a curiously empty feel about it: Medici Society angels flapping their way up the stairs, every windowledge adorned with busts and ferns and figurines, clutter, of the kind which filled her shops, crammed in everywhere. Fred had never seen a house like it. His own grandmother's drawing-room in Birmingham was, by his standards, over-furnished, but it was nothing to Fanny's house, and not such a riot of colour. The art-nouveau glass lampshades glowed blue and red and gold. The Staffordshire figures glistened in multi-colour on mantelpieces. The patterns on chairs, sofas, curtains and table-cloths splashed about in polychrome anarchy. And yet the whole place seemed dead, like the set of a film from which the actors had mysteriously drifted away. In his grandmother's room, the multi-farious metal photograph frames contained armies of Joblings, all known to her by name. The faces which in Fanny's house peered from chimney-pieces and table-tops had the sad look of displaced persons – soldiers in First War uniform, and self-important men in frock coats posing by potted palms in photographer's studios, had obviously been bought in junk shops with the portraits of Queen Victoria.

'Isn't my house *lovely*!' she had exclaimed.

'Wonderful.' But it gave him the creeps, and he had almost dragged her upstairs.

'We mustn't make love here, Prince Consort.'

But she seemed to like the way he pulled her through the door and on to the huge, soft four-poster bed. When the velvet curtains had been drawn about them and their garments discarded, she had seemed to have no more thoughts of discretion. There had been apparently no limit to her appetites or her powers of invention.

'Talk to me, talk to me all the time Prince Consort – tell me how it feels – is that nice, Prince Consort, is it – put your fingers inside me – no, more, more – open your eyes, Prince Consort, your eyes, I want to see you. I want to see you being excited – *God* your eyes terrify me, don't stare so, they seem on fire, no don't shut them. No don't come inside me yet, Prince Consort – put your hand there – and there – am I hurting you? – but I want to hurt you – you feel so excited when I drive my rings into your shoulder blades – turn over, Prince Consort, I want to come on top of you – now you can come inside me – Now – Now – Now.'

Even at his most flagrant and adventurous in the past, he had not imagined that there were so many variations on this activity. The more it went on, to his amazement and delight, the more he seemed capable of, her excited running commentary providing fresh stimu-lation when it was needed. There was not an inch of her body he had not explored, nor a part of his which she had not worshipped with finger, tongue or eye. Drunk with *eros* they had writhed and crawled and cavorted themselves until the sheets were twisted about their ankles like corkscrews and they lay, peaceful at last in each other's arms, covered by a blanket.

'It makes such a difference,' she murmured.

'What does?'

'Doing it with someone you *love*.' The last word was whispered. It was the first time she had used it of her feelings for him.

'Yes.'

'*I am my beloved's and my beloved is mine.* It must have been so wonderful for them, mustn't it?'

'For who?'

'For my great-grandparents. To have found real, true lasting love. Nothing else matters, does it, Prince Consort?'

'How do you explain the existence of Charles?'

'How do you mean?'

'If Oswald Fish – your great-grandfather – was so much in love with your great-grandmother . . .' He let the sentence finish itself.

She was silent for a moment and murmured, 'It must have been earlier.'

'Perhaps.'

'It seems like Fate, doesn't it? My being his great-granddaughter – Charles being his grandson – my buying the church. Do you believe in Fate?'

'Not really.'

'I don't believe in God, but I believe in Fate,' she said. 'I think certain things are *meant* to be, to happen, have to happen. Like my meeting you.'

'Perhaps.'

'What was that?' She sat up suddenly in bed, her face flushed and sweaty, her hair tousled and falling thickly over her pale shoulders. At the sight of it Fred wanted to reach out and start making love to her all over again. It was amazing, how much more sexy she seemed with her hair down.

'I didn't hear anything,' he said.

'Go and look, please Prince Consort. I heard a noise in the bathroom.'

'It was nothing.' He put up a hand to stroke her breasts. They were quite loose, and not very full. He had always thought himself choosy about breasts, minded deeply the way Jen's had sagged after feeding Harriet. But Fanny's were more beautiful in that moment than the firmest, roundest breast of a sixteen-year-old.

'Please go,' she whispered, firmly removing his hands.

'Oh, all right, but it's nothing.'

Naked, he jumped out of bed and walked across the room to the bathroom, moving slightly awkwardly, for he was once more erect and it wobbled about in front of him like some ungainly pink tropical plant. The bathroom led off the bedroom. He flung open the door and said 'There's no one there!'

He was wrong. Pandora, her face contorted with merriment, scampered to his side and held out her hand to his member.

'What the hell?' she asked. But before he finished the sentence, he looked down the bathroom and saw Marmaduke, his mouth grinning beneath a camera. Blinking myopically, he was so shocked and appalled that he could do no more than stand stupidly while the flash-bulbs popped.

'Go away you *horrors*!' Fanny screamed from the bedroom. 'Prince Consort come back *here*!'

Another flash-bulb popped as he turned his back to the whoops of childish laughter.

Red, flustered, furious, he made for his clothes which were scattered over the sofa by the window and began to dress. He could not speak. The moment was too bewildering, too awful. Fanny had got up and thrown on a dressing gown and was shrieking across the landing – '*Marmie! Pandora!* Where *are* you?'

Fred heard the colloquy on the landing while he dressed.

'It was only a bit of fun, Fanny.' Marmaduke sounded at his most reasonable.

'We thought we'd catch a picture of you on the loo,' said Pandora. 'It would have made a funny picture. We could have used it for Christmas cards.'

'We weren't to know there'd be a *man* in your bathroom,' said Marmaduke.

Fred could hardly believe his ears. Still less could he believe his own credulity. It at once seemed harmless and simple and obvious. Any child might want to take a picture of Mum on the bog for a bit of fun. But then, seeing it was him, why had they taken so many – and with Pandora in the picture too?

'I'm sorry, darling, it was awful for you,' he heard Fanny saying. 'I'm sorry, I'm sorry.'

Marmie sounded as if he was crying.

'I shouldn't have shouted at you,' Fanny said. 'It was a joke, I can see that, and you've had an appalling shock.'

When Fred, slightly dishevelled and fully dressed, emerged on to the landing, she said, 'You'd better go.' He stood and stared and put on his specs. She repeated, 'Just go.'

Marmie's sobs were now loud and red and terrible. Pandora had disappeared into her room.

'But when will I see you again?' Fred asked.

'Just go,' she said. 'Can't you see Marmie's upset? I'll ring you up. Go, go.'

All her earlier tenderness had gone. It was as if he did not exist and the lovemaking with which they had occupied so much of the day had never been. He trotted downstairs as quickly as he could. Nana Owen was coming in through the front door when he reached the hall.

'I hope you haven't been trying to convert Fanny,' she said. 'It isn't fair because she's less used to arguments than I am.'

'I'm not a Jehovah's Witness.'

'I do hope you aren't a Moonie. They're the worst.'

'I am not a Moonie.'

The old woman walked past him with a suspicious glance and said, 'I think I'll see if anyone has made a nice pot of tea.'

Fred let himself out quietly and walked back to his hotel.

XXIII

'Fanny, I'm very busy. There's a no-confidence motion coming up before the House and . . .'

'The most awful thing has happened . . .'

'Not one of the children.'

'Yes, it's the children.'

There was a worried silence.

'Oh, we have the two most *adorable* children in the world.'

'Are they all right?'

'You see they wanted to play such a funny trick on me, they hid in my bathroom, thinking they could take photographs of me while I sat on the loo . . .'

'On the *loo?*'

'Well it would have been hilarious, wouldn't it?' She sniggered, relieved at last by how funny it would have been, relieved by the quiet, slightly disapproving voice of the Honourable Member.

'Was Pandora doing this or was it just Marmie?'

'It was both of them and they thought it would be such fun, and now *this* had to happen.'

'What happened?'

'Well, you won't approve, but I have fallen in love with the most wonderful man in the world. Really wonderful.'

There was a pause. Then, with the formality of a Foreign Office delegation congratulating a visiting potentate on his forthcoming engagement, the Honourable Member said, 'I hope you will both be very happy.'

'It's bound to make Marmie jealous, isn't it?'

'He will get used to it. I have always found him to get on extremely well with Liz.'

'They loved going to the Planetarium the other day.'

'We enjoyed taking them. Liz thought they might be a little old for the Punch and Judy show afterwards.'

'I love Punch and Judy.'

'I'm glad they appreciated it.'

'Are you very busy at the moment?'

'Yes. As you are probably aware, the Government is bound to fall. It can hardly rally enough support for the no-confidence debate tonight.'

'Is that a very good thing?'

'Of course. It means there will be a General Election.'

'Do you think you will be a Cabinet Minister this time?'

'There is always that possibility.'

'How *exciting*.'

'Possibility, Fanny, possibility. We mustn't count our chickens.

'I feel so reassured talking to you. It was simply awful. There was poor Marmie, expecting to get a good shot of me having a pee and in walked a big hairy man with no clothes on.'

The silence lasted some time.

'Are you still there?'

'Yes. It must have been a great shock to them both.'

'It was flipping awful. He cried and screamed and I lost my temper and we both ended up in tears. Pandora was wonderful and took control of the situation. They've both gone out for a little walk. But what a shock for them.'

'Indeed.'

'Rather a shock for the Prince Consort too,' she sniggered.

'The Prince Consort?'

'Alastair.'

'Are you and Alastair going to be ... married?'

'I don't know. We've only known each other for three days. Less actually.'

After another long silence, the Honourable Member said, 'I see.'

'You don't approve.'

'I didn't say so.'

'Don't you sometimes wish you were still married to me?'

'No.'

'Not *ever*?'

'I must ring off now, Fanny. I am really meant to be in the Chamber.'

'Watch out for photographers!'

'What?'

207

'In the *chamber*.

'Oh.'

'But wasn't it awful for them? Poor children. We do have the most *wonderful* children, don't we?'

Yes, Fanny. Yes, we do.'

XXIV

David Matheson dreaded returning to the flat. He did not know *how* she could have known, but Fiona had instantly discerned that he had been lying to her. Anything, now, would be preferable to the truth being known. Thank God he had never written down Charles Bullowewo's address or telephone number. They must never meet again. The episode was irrevocably over.

It was unlikely that Fiona would press for details. He could pretend that he had got drunk, had a brainstorm, had a trivial little one-night stand with a girl. Anything. But he knew that he could never survive it if she discovered the truth.

Sometimes, in the course of his day at the Museum, the opposite idea had seized him as a crazy, alluring temptation. Quite unable to concentrate on the cataloguing which he should have finished the previous week, his mind kept returning to the problem as the tongue strays inexorably towards an aching tooth. Why not tell Fiona the truth? She loved him. Moreover, she was so sturdy, so strong-minded, so independent, she could probably take it. Perhaps, even, it would be less wounding and insulting to her than allowing her to think that he had been with another woman. But then Jeremy Tradescant had come mincing up to him to suggest a lunchtime drink and the idea had vanished.

Reeking of scent, his eyelids pencilled with blue, his cheeks delicately rouged, Jeremy had seemed at that moment like an embodiment of one of the deadly sins dancing on the stage at a Mystery Play. His strong masculine mouth – was he wearing lipstick? – was smiling. Leaning a fluffy yellow woollen sleeve against the shelf by David's desk, he had said, 'You look in need of a drinkette, darling,' and whisked him off for gin and sandwiches at a rather *chic* little pub in a mews behind the Brompton Oratory.

Jeremy was in many ways an admirable person. David could see that he was clever, good-looking, competent at his job, and kind.

But. even had Fiona never existed, even if he was free and single, David could never have taken the plunge and been 'a gay' in the same sense as Jeremy. It was not just the make-up, not just the elegantly coiffed blonde curls, not just the tight brown corduroy jeans which seemed designed to emphasize the shape of buttocks and groin, not just the scent, or the silly way of talking. 'Being gay' on Jeremy's terms seemed to involve a complete transformation of personality which, while funny enough to observe, was too grotesque to contemplate as happening to oneself. David knew, and privately he could accommodate the fact, that it was possible to be attracted to members of one's own sex, without being limp-wristed about it. But if it were once known that he had this aberration, he could not live with the idea that his friends – Christ, his *wife* – were bracketing him in their minds with painted dolls like Jeremy Tradescant.

The lunchtime drink had been depressing, too, because Jeremy had taken up the idea of Oswald Fish with great enthusiasm.

'We've got positive *mountains* of his stuff in store, you know,' he had said, wolfing the pickled onion from his ploughman's lunch. 'Goodness *knows* how many bits and bobs there are, lying all over England. There's something rather beguiling about what I've seen.'

'They're not my kind of thing.'

'You're too pure.' The hair-do had been patted. 'Baroque my big cock. But I'm more than grateful to you for drawing my attention to old Mr Fish-Wish. Ill-making to think of all his lovely bobs and boobs gathering dust for absolute *yonks* and no one giving them a blind bit of notice.'

David had come to hate the idea of Oswald Fish. If it hadn't been for Jeremy's dear old Mr Fish-Wish, he would never have foolishly given so much of himself away to Charles and Fanny. He hoped and prayed they would respect his wish to be discreet, simply allow his mad tumble with Charles to sink into seemly oblivion, and not come round to the museum bothering him for professional advice about the wretched man. With luck, Fanny would lose interest in the Birmingham church sooner or later and Jeremy would find some other mediocre metalworker with which to busy his curly yellow head.

'I rather thought it might be a giggle to have a little exhibition – just a bishette, a Fish-Bish – of dear Oswald's things. We could have other Arts and Craftsy *objets* too – Bainbridge Reynolds is quite a dear old fluffy and then there's Henry Wilson. Of course, what's so interesting about Wish is that he had this touching Gothic nostalgia. That coffee-pot I showed you is extraordinarily eclectic. And the ciborium from Balham looks sheer 1862 until you turn it upside down and see the date on its botty.'

'Which is?'

'1909. Drink up, we need another.'

When he had returned from the bar. Jeremy had said, in graver accents, 'How's the lovely Mrs Matheson?'

'All right.'

The conversation had ended there. Jeremy's face had been kind and worried. David did not want to talk about it. He was not to know that Jeremy spoke openly of him as having a touch of the floating voter, not to mention the liberal, about him. He regarded his problem as secret, unique and obscure; he had been relieved when Jeremy had gone on to boast about being invited down to stay at Long Barford with the children of the Countess of Bayswater, a woman he had described as 'sheer HMS *Dreadnought*'.

That had been lunch. But at the end of the working day, there was no getting round it. He must go home.

The flat was so silent when he went inside that he thought she must be out, even though the light was on in the drawing-room. He put down his shoulder-bag and called out: 'Fiona!'

There was no reply. He looked in the kitchen, the bathroom. Both were empty. Then he put his head round the bedroom door.

She was lying on the bed, her head propped up by pillows, reading through some typed memorandum in a cellophane holder.

'Hallo,' he said. The atmosphere was terrible; so icy and angry that it seemed impossible to penetrate. His feigned good humour died on his lips.

She looked up at him furiously. In the course of the day, she had overcome her grief. Although her eyes were still smarting and red, she had made herself up to conceal the tear-stains on her cheeks.

'Hallo,' she said. 'Did you get the food for supper?'

'Hell, I forgot.'

She made a little grunting noise and returned to the perusal of her documents.

'We could go out,' he tried. 'We could go and have a curry or a pizza or something.'

There was a long silence. She put down her papers and stared at him contemptuously.

'Why did you marry me?' she asked.

He sat on the edge of the bed and tried to take her hand. She snatched it away. He said 'Love!' – not as an answer to her question, but as a remonstrance.

'I trusted you,' she said quietly. 'I'll never trust you again.'

'Just because you get back a day early and find the flat empty ... Honestly, Fiona, I didn't think ...'

'Where *were* you then?' She said it sharply, like a magistrate interrogating a delinquent boy.

'I *told* you I went out to dinner, I stayed the night.'

'But why did you tell me you went to Jeremy's? Do you think I am an absolute idiot? I got back here, found the place empty, no note, no message, anything could have happened to you, you might have been dead.'

'Come off it.'

She continued in the same cold, authoritative voice.

'Naturally I was worried. I nearly rang the police. I rang up your mother.'

'Oh, God, Fiona, what did you want to do that for?'

She stared. He had never flown off the handle before. Nearly a year of something very like Paradise, and now this.

'I rang your mother because you had not left a message to say where you were.'

'And so you decided to worry her about it. Christ, you're an interfering bitch. Why didn't you say you were coming back early ...' He was appalled at his own words. 'I'm sorry,' he said in a crestfallen little voice. 'I didn't mean it.'

'All right. I am an interfering bitch. I had the ridiculous idea that it might be nice to know where my husband spends his nights when I go away. I did not "worry" your mother, as you put it. I told your mother you were at the museum.'

'Well, I was.'

'I wasn't to know that, was I? Then I rang Jeremy.'

She stared at him, awaiting some kind of response. None came.

He had gone pale – paler even than he had been in the morning when he came back to the flat and found her there.

'Jeremy said he had not seen you since yesterday at the museum.'

She paused. Still no response.

'Now, I may be foolish, but either that means that Jeremy was lying or that you were lying. What cause would Jeremy have for covering up the fact that you went to dinner with him?'

'I don't know why I *said* it. I'm sorry. OK, I told a lie.'

'Are you going to tell me where you went?'

'I wandered out on my own. Got drunk I suppose.'

'Where did you sleep? On a park bench? David, when I got back to this flat the whole place reeked of sour milk. I don't believe you've been back here since you saw me off at the air terminal.'

'No.' He was quiet. He could feel himself shaking all over. Although the inevitable confession stared him in the face, he felt determined not to make it.

'Now, I am sorry, but I don't believe you have been wandering about on your own for three days getting drunk. Is it this girl Alice from the museum or someone else?'

'Shall we have a drink?' he said. 'I think we both need it.'

'I don't want a drink. I want you to tell me the truth. Is it Alice?'

'Yes.' He clutched at a straw.

'How long has it been going on?'

'It isn't Alice,' he said. It was absurd to pretend that it was. Alice was a nice enough girl, specs, freckles, Lancashire accent and a bit of a dyke, but why drag her into it?

'Is it or isn't it?'

'Let's drop this,' he said. 'I want a drink even if you don't.'

He left her and went to the sideboard where they kept the whisky decanter. He poured himself a goodish slug and gulped it down. Then he refilled his glass. Normally he drank the stuff with water, but now he was glad of the way it burnt his mouth and throat. Fiona had followed him into the room. She was being so calm, so cool, so steely, that he was almost worried that her mind was becoming unhinged, an impression not diminished by her next remark.

'I'll tell you why you married me.'

He poured some whisky into another glass and offered it to her. She ignored it.

'Pure snobbery. You are nothing but a nasty little snob.'

'Fiona!' This was too bizarre for words. She had turned hastily and gone back to the bedroom. Her vaguely uppercrust connections had nothing to do with his desire to marry her, as he would have hoped was abundantly obvious. If anything, he always thought she made rather too much of being Lord Seton's granddaughter and he had been embarrassed by their trundling the old boy out to make a speech at the wedding, rather than having her own father. 'Fiona!' he called. 'I can't *think* what you mean.'

She did not reply. While he was calling out, the door-bell rang and he heard her go and speak into the buzzer thing.

'Who is it?' he called.

'I'll come down,' he heard her say. He heard the latch click and then her heels clonking down the stairs.

Someone must have been getting at her. That was the only explanation. He had never known her behave like this. He could not for the life of him see the remotest connection between his absence from the flat and his alleged snobbery.

She was gone for what seemed an age. Then he heard the front door slam below and wondered whether she had gone out and left him on his own. He did not know what he wanted, but in a way he would have been glad if she had gone. Then he heard the clonk clonk clonk of her heels on the stairs. She was walking slowly. He poured himself another drink. The whisky was going to his head fast. When she returned to the room he had the impression that everything was swimming before his eyes and her voice seemed to be coming from far away. She no longer sounded like a JP in a bait. She spoke softly, sadly, almost croaking.

'I believe this is yours,' she said.

She held out a glossy magazine called *Honcho Mail*. He recognized it instantly. The children had been reading it the previous evening at Fanny's house.

'I don't understand,' he said.

'Take it,' she said.

'But how can it be mine, I've never seen it, I . . .'

Her voice was full of tears now as she said, 'Oh, *David*.'

'Honestly. Fiona, I've never seen it . . .'

She ignored his feeble, silly attempts to make excuses.

'That was a *child*,' she said, brokenly. 'A little *boy*, David. O *Christ*, how horrible.' She was crying openly now; tears streaming down her cheeks, her voice jerky and pathetic. 'Don't lie. Please don't make it worse. I know where you were now and –' her voice sobbed – 'what you were doing.'

'Please, Fiona!'

'I can see now why you had to lie.'

'Yes.' So the truth at last was out. They could not look at each other. He turned abjectly towards the fireplace and felt himself beginning to weep.

'I wish you'd not married me,' she said.

'But ... but I love you.'

They listened to each other's moans and sniffs.

'Fiona, it won't happen again.'

'I could almost take it if you were an honest-to-goodness queer like Jeremy,' she sniffed. 'Queers make very good husbands sometimes, or so they say. I always suspected you had a bit of it about you ... but this ...'

Her words burnt through him like poisoned darts. He could hardly believe she was saying them. She had always *guessed*? At the same time, having himself patronizingly thought of as a 'queer' who might 'make a good husband' was bitter and awful. It summoned up an image of kind, domesticated creatures in frilly aprons. And yet that was not what she had *said*. If he had been an honest-to-goodness queer ... ?

'You know I like Jeremy,' she persisted, 'and I take a sympathetic line. I hate queer-bashers like my awful old uncle Ralph.' She contrived a smile for a moment at her uncle's awfulness. 'But *children*!'

'*Fiona!*' He reached out to touch her. 'What did he say, who was it, was it Marmaduke?'

'Don't touch me, please David. I think I can survive if you don't touch me.'

'Was it Marmaduke?'

'No. He wasn't called Marmaduke. It was a funny little Cockney boy called John. He had dark hair and – but of course I needn't describe him to you.' She shuddered.

'But dark hair sounds like Marmaduke.'

'How many little boys have there been, David, since I went away?'

'None.'

She looked at him imploringly. 'I don't really want to know the details, but *please*, I would much rather you didn't lie about it.'

'But I'm telling you the truth.'

'Like you told me about Alice.'

'Look, what did that little brat tell you?'

'He told me what happened. Not very elegantly, but then I don't suppose he knew any better. Funny little chap.' She smiled again through her tears. 'A cigarette sticking out of his mouth. He asked if I was your sister. He seemed so surprised when I said I was your . . . wife.'

Again, the tears came uncontrollably.

'A Cockney boy called John who knew me and said I'd given him this magazine? I tell you it's impossible. It must have been a child called Marmaduke . . .'

'Perhaps you were drunk. Perhaps you couldn't tell the difference between John and little Marmaduke. Perhaps there were others . . .'

'Fiona, please. What did he tell you?'

'He said he was touting for trade, as he put it, at Piccadilly Circus and that you offered him ten pounds if he would let you come and – "do him over" was the phrase I think. He said you liked Sixty-Nine, whatever that is. He said that when you left in the morning there were only five pounds on the dressing table.'

'He *didn't*.'

'I gave him the extra five pounds.'

'You *what?*'

'Japanese women are expected to pay their husbands' brothel bills, I believe.' Her voice was cool and emphatic again. 'Usually, I imagine, for female whores.'

'But . . . how did he know this address? Really Fiona, if you believe his cock-and-bull story . . .'

'He knew your address because I gave it to him. He – or another child – rang up today when you were out and asked for the address. I asked him how he got hold of your number just now. He said you'd given it to him and that he was to ring occasionally. Rather rash of you I should have thought.'

He stared at her stupefied, and gulped down his whisky.

'And you believe that,' he said. 'You take the word of some horrible little urchin who comes ringing our bell but you refuse to believe *me*?'

'I don't know what to believe any more.'

'Fiona, let me explain. All right, I have been to bed with a man. He is *thirty-five years old*, Fiona, I've never laid a finger ...'

'I'm rather fed up with all this,' she said, trying to control another bout of crying. 'I simply don't want to hear any more. I'm going to bed and I don't want you to join me. You can sleep in the spare room – or any other dingy little male brothel you might like to go to.'

The last words were something between a yell and a sob. David stood frozen with horror as she slammed the drawing-room door. He was not thinking. At that precise moment he was not exactly feeling anything either. It was as if he had suddenly been snatched up into another world and his present surroundings had no reality. How long he stood there he did not know. Perhaps he was already rather drunk. Total silence had descended.

Either it was a mistake, a terrible mistake, or it was a nasty practical joke which had hideously misfired. It was intolerable that she should think him capable of paying little boys. He must clear the matter up. The only way of doing it was to make a clean breast of things and get hold of Charles. Charles was calm, strong, sensible, reassuring. Fiona would believe him.

Yet, even as he walked towards the telephone, he saw the impossibility of this course. The blank horribleness of the child's lie had momentarily blinded him to the reality of the situation. Could he really face telling Fiona the truth? She had said she would not mind if he was an honest-to-goodness queer, whatever that was. She might not mind, but, Christ, *he* did. Whatever happened, their lives were wrecked. Perhaps if they were different people it would have been possible to explain, to muddle on, to put up with the messy unsatisfactoriness of his temperament. But they weren't like that. Their happiness, like the furniture in their flat, had been exquisite, perfect, unblemished. A single blow, it seemed, could destroy it.

In any case, now was not the moment for talking things over with Fiona. It appalled him that she could be so hysterically unreasonable. The knowledge that she was lying, sulky and disconsolate, in the bedroom, made it intolerable to stay in the flat any longer. Without taking his coat, he walked out, down the stairs and into the street.

He stalked along the pavements fast, as if he had somewhere to go in a hurry. In fact he had no destination in mind. It was twilight, the end of a beautiful, cold spring day. Windows were lit up all over Chelsea, but only about half of them had the curtains drawn. Flitting past like a tormented ghost striding through the shadows, he half absorbed the dozens of human vignettes the windows mockingly displayed. Here an old man, quietly sipping wine, and watching the last glow of light disappear from the sky; there a young couple, proudly holding up their baby; elegant little groups of people sitting down to dinner; a girl with a coral necklace smoking a cigarette: all of them ignorant of him, removed from him, cut off by glass and light, and happiness.

It was dark by the time he found himself in Cheyne Walk. He crossed the road by the traffic lights and walked up along the Embankment in the direction of Westminster. The tide was high. Black and mysterious, the river glowed to his right with the yellow reflection of street lamps and barge-windows. Across its inky surface, on the south bank, the coloured lights of the fun-fair danced playfully against the blue-black sky half lighting up the lumpish beauty of Battersea Power Station.

Everything, everything was wrecked and ruined; ruined through his own blind folly. Even the particular nastiness of the child's joke – if such it had been – seemed only part of it. Marmaduke's little prank had merely punctured a floodgate of misery which he had been keeping at bay ever since he first became aware of his own consciousness. One day, one day – he had always known – the curse would come, the nemesis would catch up on him. Now, it had happened, and he no more belonged to the world, no more had anything in common with humanity, with the people who flitted past him on the pavements, or zoomed along in cars and taxis towards Millbank.

The darkened Thames, like a country pond attracting flies at evening, seemed to have drawn other lost souls to its banks. Meths drinkers staggered from lamp-post to lamp-post, some silent, some roaring out incoherent snatches of songs and hymns in broken Scotch voices. With them, more than with anyone else he had seen that evening, he felt an affinity, and as if they sensed it too, they called out as he passed. 'Hey, Jumma! It's a luvla nicht.' He scuttled past. One of them, beetroot-faced, stubbly, trousers half held up by string, a ragged Government surplus mackintosh draped over his shoulders, stood in his path and slapped a hand on his shoulder. David reached in his pocket for small change.

'I wadna take your siller, Jumma, iffa hadna sair need.'

David pressed two fifty pence bits in the man's hand and tried to hurry on, but his friend was not to be deflected.

'Do you know something, Jumma?'

'I'm in rather a hurry.'

'You're in nae hurra, Jumma. D'you know something?'

'What?'

'I used to be a gude laddie. I went to a gude schule. Are ye a Catholic, Jumma?'

'No.'

'I was fostered ba the nuns ya know, Jumma.'

'Really?'

The stench, the absolute degradation, was awful, fascinating. David stood for a moment and in the light of a street lamp he stared into the bloodshot eyes.

'I know poetra, Jumma. Do you know poetra?'

'A certain amount.'

'Say some to me.'

He smiled awkwardly; with half of himself he wanted to comply with the request. Why was he staying with this revolting man? In normal circumstances, he would have hurried past, but he wanted to linger a moment from his purpose like a wanderer in the outer regions of hell before he plunged into the abyss. In a strangely haunting, deeply sonorous voice, his companion had begun to sing.

'Ye banks and braes o' bonie Doon
  How can ye bloom sae fresh and fair;
How can ye chant, ye little birds,
  And I sae weary fu' o' care!'

The song was interrupted by a splutter of belches and coughs and by the roar of passing traffic.

'I must go.' said David.

'God bless ye, Jumma!'

As he walked briskly away down the Embankment. the croaking voice had started up again and wafted towards him over the cold air.

> 'Thou'll break my heart thou warbling bird
> That wantons thro' the flowrring thorn:
> Thou minds me o' departed joys
> Departed never to return.'

It was the last human encounter David was to have on this earth. Grimly, he acknowledged the fact to himself. He felt no guilt any more, no regret, merely an impatience to be gone. He almost ran down Millbank. Some last flicker of aesthetic sensibility, perhaps a faint wish to dramatize the moment. made him pause when he finally reached Westminster Bridge, and gaze up at Big Ben in its flood-lit, fantastical Gothic tower, across the crowds and the statues in Parliament Square, and the trees nearly blossoming with life.

'Where to?' asked the booking clerk at Westminster Station. He had pushed twenty pence through the window. Only at that moment did his resolution falter.

'Where?' he asked.

'Make up yer mind,' said the man.

'Just a ticket for twenty pence please.'

The machine did its work. The little piece of green card came slithering down the chute. Absurdly, he regretted the extravagance. He could have bought the cheapest sort of ticket. He descended the stairs and followed the trickle of people on to the nearest platform. Rush hour was over. He wandered about the dusty platform kicking the ground. Would the train never come? ALL TRAINS GO TO VICTORIA read the sign. Not this one. He had wandered to the far end of the platform, standing as near as possible to the circular cave from which his deliverance would come. The station clock said five past ten; six, seven, eight minutes past ten. Then he heard the train, like the roar of the sea in the distance. The mysterious wind which heralds the arrival of an underground train blew newspapers and sweet packets along the platform. Further down, near the exit, people were gathering their things. He was ten or twenty yards from the nearest person. No one cried out. His timing was perfect. He jumped just before the steely grey engine came through the cave entrance.

XXV

'It was a nasty shock for the poor little things.'

'I can see that.'

'You're not cross with them, are you, Prince Consort?'

'Of course not.'

'How were they to know that a great big man was going to walk into the bathroom with his John Willie sticking in the air.' She sniggered.

Several heads turned in the lounge where Fred and Fanny were having coffee together before he caught the train back to Birmingham.

'Marmie is a terribly jealous person, always has been. Even when he was three years old he couldn't wait to get the Honourable Member out of the house and have me all to himself. Pandora's different. She always seemed much more independent, an altogether sturdier character. Marmie still comes creeping into my bed at nights to be cuddled.'

'Every night?'

'Not every night, but often. It makes things flipping difficult and that's why he does it.'

'But you've had other lovers . . . I mean, I'm not the first.'

'Charles is the only one to stay the course and that's because he has a room of his own. Besides, Marmie is devoted to him – even goes into his bed sometimes, instead of mine. It makes me feel quite jealous.'

'But if I . . . I mean if we . . .'

'If you came and lived with us it would be different, I suppose. But Marmie would put up a fight. Poor little squirt. You must try and win his confidence. Won't it be lovely, Prince Consort, just by living together we'll gain two extra children each. You'll have Marmie and Pandora and I'll have your two who are sweet, I'm sure.'

'Yes, yes they are.'

'Won't it be wonderful, Prince Consort? To be happy *at last*, to have a real, warm happy family after all the misery we've both been through . . .'

Her words were wild. They bore no relation to the elaborately complicated practicalities of the case. For a start, his job was in Birmingham. He could easily enough set about looking for another. Indeed, there was an opening on the Law Commission which he could pursue if he was prepared to drop everything. But dropping everything was easier said than done. Could he really abandon the house in Augustus Road? He had allowed his father to have it expensively divided so that they could be near one another. What would be the point of Jen hanging on there after he had gone? What would happen to their children? Where would they go to school? These things could not be decided overnight. He was fairly sure that his love for Fanny was not an ephemeral flash-in-the-pan affair. But it would not be easy to imagine taking up immediate residence in Tregunter Road, even had that prospect seemed an alluring one. After his two experiences of the place – first being taken for a Jehovah's Witness and secondly being snapped, as if by KGB agents, in a compromising position in the bathroom – the heart did not exactly leap up at the prospect of living there. Augustus Road might have its pains; it was at least secure, and solid, and reassuring. Tregunter Road could have only one pleasure and that was the company of Fanny herself.

'It will all need a lot of thinking out,' he said.

'Of course. I don't want to rush things, Prince Consort. Tracy says I am absolutely mad to be thinking of setting up house with you. She says that as soon as you get back to Birmingham you'll be perfectly happy with your wife again.'

'You've discussed all this with Tracy?'

'She doesn't know the hell you've been going through. I do. I've been married, I know what it's like. Anyway, Charles has the right answer, which is that we'll just have to wait and see. Give it a few weeks and see how it sorts itself out. Quite possibly we're making a flipping great mistake, in which case there's no harm done. But I'm sure we aren't, are we?'

'Fanny.' He fingered her hand gently. She was looking, if it was possible, more beautiful than ever. Everything about her was alluring, even features which would have been a blemish in others, such as her very slightly too thick calves, or the almost imperceptible down which grew on her upper lip. But it was above all her eyes, her wild eyes, which explained the powers of the enchantress. They were the brightest, liveliest eyes he had ever seen; eyes whose hypnotic magic could make a man do murder or go mad. 'I don't much like you discussing all this with Tracy and Charles,' he managed to say.

'Why not? I tell them everything – flipping everything. If you want it to be kept a secret for the time being you needn't worry. They're very discreet, they'll never tell anyone.'

'It's silly, I suppose. I just don't like you talking about it.'

'I don't see why not.'

His real reason was that he thought it was unfair to Jen. If anyone was to be told of the upheaval in his life, he knew that it ought to be her, and that she should not come in at the tail-end of the matter after it had been chewed over by people who did not even know him. For better, for worse, she had been his closest companion, even in an odd way (God, he was getting sentimental about it) his best friend, for the last fourteen years. She had come to irritate him beyond endurance. He probably got on *her* nerves now and again: it would be understandable. But if it was all to be wound up and smashed and changed, he felt, at that moment, that she should be in on it. He could not explain this to Fanny. He said merely, 'It won't hurt, I suppose. Discuss it with Tracy and Charles if you like.'

'Poor you. There's no one you can discuss it with.'

'No ...'

'I wish you weren't going away, Prince Consort.'

'But we'll see each other soon.'

'A week.'

Fanny was coming up to Birmingham and spending much of the following fortnight there in connection with the opening of the new shop. As she said, it seemed a heaven-sent opportunity.

'My train's in three-quarters of an hour.'

'Flip it. Go on a later one.'

'I can't. Fanny ...'

'Yes?'

It seems silly to ask you this after all that's happened between us, but even if I do give up my job in the Town Hall and get something in London –'

'I do *wish* you would.'

'No, but even if I do –'

'It would be *wonderful*.'

'I'll have to carry on at the Town Hall for the next few months.'

'We'll manage.'

'No. But what I am trying to say is, they'll expect me to do my job.'

'Of course they will, Prince Consort.'

'And at the moment, part of my job is to persuade you to sell St Aidan's, Purgstall Heath, to the City of Birmingham.'

Her eyes suddenly flashed with anger and her high cheeks became pink.

'But we've agreed all that. I'm *not* selling it just so you can put up a multi-storey car-park or whatever it is you want to build –'

'Fanny, I am only doing my job in *asking* you –'

Doing your job? That's what Eichmann said when he murdered all the flipping Jews, isn't it, that he was only doing his job. I don't see how you can be so immoral.'

'Listen. Fanny, you aren't listening.'

'Why *should* I flipping listen?'

'Because I am not saying what you think I am saying.'

'What are you saying?'

'I used to mind about Purgstall Heath,' he said clearly and deliberately. 'I don't any more.'

'Well you should.'

'I don't. I don't care if you keep St Aidan's or sell it. I don't care whether you pull it down, or double its size and put a spire on it the size of the Eiffel Tower. It's a matter of absolute indifference to me.'

'How can you *say* such a thing?'

'Because I don't want your quarrel with the Council to get in the way of . . . us.' He kissed her hand. 'But you see, don't you? They are going to ask me if I persuaded you.'

'And you are going to have to go to one of your boring old committee meetings and say that after hearing all my arguments and discovering that *my flipping great-grandfather* was the architect of that church, you'll pull it down over my dead body. And yours too, I hope, Prince Consort.'

XXVI

The sun was making its way back to the Tropic of Cancer: the horse-chestnuts were nearly in blossom; spring had returned to the earth, and Mrs Thatcher was about to win the General Election.

It was polling day. In Neath, it was drizzling. There was no chance of the Tories winning there, but Jessica Owen went to vote. She went out without her reading glasses, read CON as COM in the darkness of the booth, and for the first time in her life, voted Conservative. She emerged with the satisfied feeling that a gesture for truth had been made.

There would be no chance of continuing her garden bonfire that day. Instead, she sat by the glowing grate in her little parlour with the last suitcase of her father's diaries.

Ever since Fanny had found out about her relationship to Oswald Fish, there had been no doubt in Jessica's mind that the diaries must be destroyed. The children had even got their hands on one of the notebooks. Nothing of consequence, luckily; some incoherent ramblings, jotted down during the First World War, shortly after Toby Shakespeare had been reported missing. Charles had been really fierce with them for reading it, but they were not to blame. They could hardly make out the handwriting, let alone understand the tormented workings of Oswald Fish's brain.

No one could understand. Until the discovery of the diaries, Jessica had had a rather clear notion of what her father had been like. She had thought of him as a faintly seedy figure who had never realized his great potential; someone broken by failure; above all a man who had needlessly made her mother miserable. Since reading and re-reading the notebooks, the picture had become increasingly blurred. Not long after their discovery, she had thought that the best thing she could do with them was to lock them away in their suitcases and leave them for another generation to read. But it was no good. She could not stop herself returning to them, and they were merely upsetting. It was pathetic, of course, that he went on thinking of himself as a potentially great architect. It was pathetic, in another way, that he never found love and went on and on searching for increasingly illusory sensual satisfaction. But the details of the quest were surely too tawdry to leave behind. The madness was venereal disease. Funny that she had not guessed it at the time. One or another of the tarts – perhaps several of them – who dominated so many of his London notebooks had evidently infected him. After Fran's death, there was no constraint, even had there been before.

'If only we had more documentary evidence about what the man was *like*. Surely there are letters surviving, or *something?*' The young man from the museum, Jeremy something, had said it. They were having an exhibition of her father's work in the autumn; even moving the rood screen and metal doors down from the church in Birmingham specially. Fanny, with her genius for publicity, had pressed her.

'That can't be the only notebook, Nana – the one Marmie pinched.'

'Well, it's the only one I know of, Fanny bach.'

'It's so *tantalizing*.'

Let the public go along to a museum in London and look at her father's metalwork if they liked. They seemed to have unearthed all manner of stuff Jessica never knew existed. They had even made contact with the Joblings in Birmingham. She did not want to meet them herself. Agnes Jobling, her half sister, still alive at ninety-something! Hugh, the son, had been enthusiastic about the idea of an exhibition, promised to lend them a couple of fenders and fire-tongs and allowed them to see all the old Jobling Fish catalogues. Jessica would never forgive the Joblings, though: so rich and so stand-offish. In the 1930s when she, from her funny little sub-post-office, had been struggling to keep life going, visiting her father in the asylum, how easily the Joblings could have helped. But, no, her father remained firmly the black sheep of the family. Now, when there was a chance that he might enjoy a faint flicker of post-humous fame, they came clamouring round. That plump dark bald man, who so oddly resembled Oswald Fish (though she had never told anyone that) and who had called at Fanny's house in the spring, absurdly pretending to be a Jehovah's Witness, was really

Hugh Jobling's son. Fanny had got all excited about it of course, as she had done when Charles's ancestry had been revealed. Jessica did not know whether the two of them were having a romance. He was married or so Fanny said.

So they all buzzed about, collecting stuff and sticking their noses in. She bore them no ill-will really, the younger generation. They could not know how much her parents' suffering had blighted her own life in material terms. Let them assemble their exhibition, but she would keep her hands on the diaries.

It was not simply prudery, though she really did not like the idea of the public being allowed to read of how her father contracted syphilis. It was her feeling that the diaries gave such a false impression. Many of them were written when she was not born: she could not vouch for those. But whenever, even with a child's memory, she could recall the days recorded by her father, she felt that they gave a ludicrously distorted view. They only ever recorded the bad days with Frances for instance. But really, she could remember days, even at quite a late stage, when they were more or less living apart, when her father and Fran had laughed together or had enjoyable meals. Jessica herself was always described as melancholic, lonely and miserable as a child. This was quite untrue. She had been self-absorbed, but many of the days of her childhood had been deeply happy – the wonderful day when her father bought a kite and tried to fly it on Hampstead Heath; the two or three happy little holidays he had been on with her and her mother to Sidmouth; the hilarity of pantomimes before the First World War; the excitement of tram-rides up to Highgate through Kentish Town. These days had all come back to her as clear as day as she perused the notebooks. But her father had not recorded them. He only ever seemed to write in his diary when he was obsessed by women or by Toby, his lost phantom of a son. Of course his life had been unsatisfactory in all sorts of ways, and life with Fran had not been the paradise he had dreamed of when he first seduced her in Edgbaston ninety years ago. But what life ever has been a paradise? Sometimes the revelations of the notebooks disgusted her. Sometimes she felt merely bored by their self-importance and childish egoism. In an odd sort of way, she had loved her father. That was much more important than the figure he would cut for posterity. Since the diaries threatened that love so deeply, she felt glad that they were nearly all destroyed.

One last case. The fire burnt brightly now as she sat by the hearth and opened it. Some of the notebooks she tossed in without opening them. Now and again she looked inside.

One limp black exercise book was written in a childish hand.

January 1st 1871. New Year Resolutions. 1. To say my prayers night and evening. 2. To write in my dairy (*sic*) every day. 3. To be kind to my brother Edmund.

January 2nd 1871. Went to the works with father. Watched gate hinges being made. Beef suet pudding for lunch. Went walk by canal with Ed. Played with hoops.

January 9th 1871. I lost this diary. Edmund hid it, I believe. I have now broken all three of my New Year Resolutions.

January 10th 1871. The first day of school. I am in a new form. We are doing German this term. The German master is called Mr. Addington.

She tore it in half and threw it into the fire. Was it really worth keeping? There were so many of them.

12th November 1876. The most solemn day of my life. I was confirmed by the Bp. of Lichfield today in St. Martin's Church. Father gave me a new prayer book and mother gave me a watch.

The part that religion had played in her father's early existence had struck Jessica as merely quaint, a period detail as ludicrous as the pride in his whiskers. Clearly, even during the period of the Annie misdemeanour, he had tried to be rather holy. Then he had 'lost his faith' and tried to re-write his own history as though he had always been a hedonist and a pagan. The obsession with Gothic architecture remained, a last vestige of his outworn creed. Jessica found it merely boring.

She waited for the fire to consume its load, prodded the cnarred notebooks with a poker and threw on another handful.

3rd March 1919. F. with a high fever in bed. Jessica nursing her. I returned to sleep at Haverstock Road tonight and will remain now.

4th March, 1919. F. rallying. The doctors say she will certainly pull through, although people are dying of influenza all over London. They say it gets better, F. and I should be married. As I sit by her bedside and watch her sleep, it comes over me that she has put up with much suffering and embarrassment over the years since she first cast in her lot with me. The marriage bond is not one for which I have ever held a high regard. But, watching her sweet, tired face, blissfully peaceful, even as I write, I am glad to think of her recovery. Our future together will be different, as man and wife. I must give up the whores. Leaving London would facilitate this. We could move out to some pleasant rural spot up the Metropolitan Line. Now that the war is over, they are building again up there. I have already begun sketches of the house I would like us to have. None of your folksy cottage stuff, such as friend Voysey has built near Chorleywood. Mr. and Mrs. Fish must have a proper residence. Latticed windows with pointed arches. A fine Gothic portico: a version in miniature of the great porch of Westminster Abbey. In the hall, perhaps, a fluted column to remind us of the chapter-house at Wells; good lancet windows on the staircase; a fine drawing-room which would have all the antiquated charm of a monastic library. Gables on the roof. A tower perhaps, could cap the whole, so that our house could stand out like a little Gothic castle. They say the Gothic has had its day. They have not yet seen the Fish Mansion! I will call it New Place, after my lost Shakespeare.

5th March, 1919. F. feverish again. I fear I exhausted her by telling of my plans. But she seemed so pleased by the idea that we would at last be married. I felt myself blubbering at the thought of my former profligacy. She has been such a kind good wife to me already. In her pale, haggard face, I saw all the light and excitement of the young woman I first loved when she was my brother Edmund's wife. Mrs. Fish she yet is. Mrs. Fish she shall be again. She is so pleased by the idea of New Place. She says she would like a summer house. Admirable! I have been sketching a rough plan of how it should be, a convent arbour in the fourteenth-century decorated mode. O, my darling F. I almost feel grateful for this influenza. Until I nearly lost her I did not know how much I valued her. I had forgotten all my love, but it had not gone away, and now I am in love again, feeling at 52 like a boy of 18. I do not see her grey hairs nor the lines on her face, only her bright eyes, so young and gay, and happy once more.

6th March 1919. F's fever worse. Jessica has sat with me at her side all day, sponging her forehead. The doctor has been. He thinks her very ill but that she *will* recover. For the first time in years this evening I prayed for F's recovery, with the fervency and simplicity of a child.

7th March 1919. She died at six o'clock this morning, all alone. The nurse had found her when she came in about 7. I have seen her. Where has that animated lovely creature gone, who has given me such happiness in the past, such hope of future bliss? Where is she? The form that I have seen is not my Frances – the hideous stiffened waxwork that Death mocks us with by leaving in the place of our loved ones. Oh my God, if only she had not died alone.

Jessica read this notebook slowly, and felt unable to burn it. It was sentimental to retain this and destroy the others, but she remembered the day of her mother's death so vividly that to burn the account of it would have seemed like killing her all over again. She put it on one side, and as if to punish herself for her soft-hearted duplicity, she tossed the remaining contents of the suitcase into the flames. One thing remained at the bottom: an architectural drawing on a piece of stiff card. It was faded now, almost to the point of being invisible, but it had once been coloured and delicately drawn in pencil. Was it one of the great continental cathedrals? There was a splendid tower and a spire stretching up to the clouds. Beneath, delicate flying buttresses swept out on to the lawn. Behind the church, and on each side of it, thick trees threw their shadows, as in Constable's painting of Salisbury Cathedral. He had drawn a few rustic looking characters in the foreground, large caps and tall hats, clay pipes, dogs. Underneath was the inscription: *Architect's impression of proposed Church of St. Aidan's, Purgstall Heath.*

XXVII

Immaculately big in his pinstripe, his round face glowing like melted chocolate, Charles got out of the car with his briefcase and umbrella. He flicked a piece of ash from his lapel, whence it had fallen from Tracy's cigarette.

Tracy was in her usual denims with a badge in the shape of a baked-bean tin pinned to her breast. She looked different since she had put henna in her hair. With her totally colourless, sharp little face, and the red coppery tresses surrounding it, she might almost have undergone some weird chemical transformation or been scorched by a nuclear explosion. She held down the driving seat of her Renault to let out Sid, her faithful plumber who was sitting in the back.

They had just dropped the children at school and were going to vote before work. Children at state primary schools had the day off because of the Election, but at Pandora's and Marmaduke's exclusive little establishment off Queen's Gate it was business as usual.

Sid yawned and stretched himself. He had rarely had a girlfriend who was more sexually demanding or who gave him better meals. As a result he was always half asleep these days and bursting out of his dungarees. Tracy loved the way he gave off a plumberish smell of lead putty.

They queued up outside the booths and eventually were able to cast their votes. Sid voted for the National Front. Their policies seemed to him forthright, well-argued and intelligent. His acquaintanceship with Charles did not shake his view that he did not want the country over-run with spades: let alone bleeding black poofs. Tracy had got really uptight when he had mentioned this point of view to her, so he had since kept it to himself. For Sid it stood to reason. Look at all the harm this black bugger had done already – there was that poor little creep David who had obviously committed

232

suicide, and whatever Tracy said about it there was something nasty about the way Charles and Fanny were letting Marmie grow up. Girlie mags. well, that would be different. Never did any harm to anyone to see a bit of tit. But all this kinky stuff for a nine-year-old. Besides, Charles was clever and should have known better. Sid did not mind them so much on the buses, hospital orderlies and that. but it gave you the creeps seeing one all dressed up like he was a gent – a bit like one of them bloody tea advertisements when you get the chimpanzees all dressed up in top hats and that.

Having firmly cast his vote for the Front, Sid left them and went off to mend a leaking cistern in Thurloe Square.

Tracy, in the next booth, voted for the Workers Revolutionary Party. There were three reasons for this. She would have voted communist, out of deference to her grandmother's views, but there was no communist standing. The WRP were surely the closest to the kind of thing Nana believed in. Secondly, the Labour candidate, who had come round campaigning on the doorstep, was really pathetic and had dandruff. Thirdly, in her fantasy life she continued to gaze towards the bright lights. She would be there now, she told herself, if she was not Fanny's domestic drudge. If it wasn't that she felt so tired, after shopping and cooking and looking after the children, she might even get a few songs down on tape. She had a much better singing voice than Fanny. She would have liked to have showy friends of her own, instead of simply those brought home by Fanny. She had never met Mr Redgrave but she thought he was absolutely wonderful. She loved the thought of fervent oratory, scuffles with the police, street battles: the whole idea of it thrilled her to bits. She knew how bloody awful politicians were: she had met plenty when her sister was married to one of them. She rather liked the idea of giving them all the boot and having the country dominated by the anarchic stars of stage and screen.

When she had voted, she said good-bye to Charles and left him to make his own way to work. With Fanny in Birmingham today, she had a lot to do in the King's Road shop.

Charles had thought hard about his vote. Although so happy, and so much at home in London, Zimbabwe was never very far from his thoughts. His mother was still alive out there. He did not think much of the Bishop; Nkomo was a blustering old buccaneer but had no political know-how; Mugabe was obviously the cleverest, but came out with these terrifying slabs of undigested LSE Marxism. If the British Government did not do something soon, the war would get worse. Labour had been consistently feeble and ignorant about the whole matter. Besides, it went against Charles's temperament to support them in other matters. Their educational policy was lamentable, their foreign policy non-existent. In the past, he had voted Liberal. In moments of frivolity he thought he should do the same now, to show solidarity. But a vote cast in Kensington was not going to change what happened in North Devon. There was only one course, then. He voted Conservative.

Still not wholly certain that he had done the right thing, he hailed a taxi and made his way towards the Temple. He was driven past the public lavatory where he had first encountered David Matheson and gave a little sigh. Poor dear boy. No one seemed certain exactly what had happened. He had not seen the wife, of course, but Jeremy Tradescant, who had become so thick with Fanny over this iron-man great-grandfather – Fish! – had told them all about it. Charles's first thought had been that David had committed suicide. But Jeremy thought it was just an accident, that he'd been under the influence or something. The coroner's verdict was death by misadventure. The wife had given nothing away at the inquest, except that David had been drinking whisky on the night of his death. Jeremy was sure she would have *said* if she had any inkling about David's love-life. Not at the inquest of course, but to him. Jeremy had been flabbergasted when he was told that David and Charles had been lovers.

'My dear, I always knew David was a bit of a closet queen but it never crossed my *mind* that he ever did anything about it. Fiona and he were so happy. Pure Arcadia – blisseroo. It will take us all *years* to get over it.'

Charles could not bring himself to pry further. Jeremy obviously knew Fiona pretty well, and still saw a lot of her. Of course, it would have emerged if she had guessed what David had got up to when she was away. We assume that because we are in something up to our necks that it must be obvious to other people. It so rarely is. Charles took refuge in this observation. Why should Fiona

Matheson have heard of Charles Bullowewo? And if she had, why on earth should she suppose he was her husband's lover?

He would never know the truth, but he would go on for the rest of his life hoping it had been an accident.

XXVIII

In leafy Edgbaston, there was victory in the air. The Socialist Winter had waned, and brightness and light and life seemed to be on the way. Hugh Jobling had been round the garden in Augustus Road at break of day. He had seen a couple of fox cubs dragging an old meat joint they had found in the dustbin across the dewy lawn. Housemartins swooped and twittered in the top gables. The herbaceous border was about to blossom. The delphiniums and lupins would be a few weeks yet, but they were wonderfully sturdy, and this year he had managed to keep off the slugs. Tulips still lingered, even some late daffodils. The bulbs had been wonderful that spring.

He pottered indoors, made the tea and took a cup up to his mother in bed. It was damned hard to live with, the way she had gone downhill in the last few weeks. Physically, she seemed as strong as ever. That was the cruel thing about it. Half the time you weren't sure she knew you were there. Then she'd start off on some gibberish; sometimes Hugh could not make head or tail of it. She seemed to think she was a little girl half the time, sat there, pretending to play with her toys; upset poor little Harriet by asking her if she would like to come out with her to the circus – or to a party or pantomime. Then, just as you were humouring her and asking if she'd like jellies or funny hats or conjuring tricks, she would say 'Really, Hugh, you treat me as if I was a child.' It was very wearing.

That girl Jen had been wonderful. Hugh felt he would not have survived without her. She had relieved him of most of the cooking now. He and his mother ate with the young family next door, or, if mother was dozing, Jen would take her something on a tray. He would have gone round the bend without Jen. She had got friends to invite him out to dinner, and looked after the old woman fulltime for three days while he went up to London. He had begun to think he would never see his friends in the City again. He had stayed at the Club, seen to quite a lot of important little matters at Lloyds which were easier dealt with in person, and enjoyed a little London pottering.

He had even met this Fanny Williams woman – for tea at Brown's Hotel in Dover Street. She'd seemed interested in a lot of old catalogues from the works. There was going to be an exhibition of his great-uncle's work in London. They were even going to cart down some ironmongery from this church there was all the hulla-baloo about. People in the old days were damned odd: to think he'd had this great-uncle Oswald and his mother had suppressed all knowledge of it. Run away with his grandmother apparently. But you'd think that they'd have decided to let bygones be bygones. Not a bit of it. His mother had never mentioned it once to him – until shortly before she went so funny. It was only a few weeks ago. She would not be capable of such coherence now.

He had not much liked Fanny Williams, to be honest. Jen, bless her heart, had been awfully excited and told him to get her auto-graph for the children, which he had done. She said she'd asked Fred time and time again and he'd always forgotten. Hugh could see that it must have been difficult, in the middle of technical legal discussions, to suddenly produce a kid's autograph book. As a matter of fact he did not think the children had ever heard of her. He certainly had not, until she turned out to be so interested in Jobling and Fish ware.

'I should think that woman's a difficult customer,' he had said to Fred, when he got back to Birmingham.

'How d'you mean, Dad?'

'Hard as nails, wouldn't you say? And something – I don't know, brash, vulgar. There was something I didn't quite like about her anyway.'

Fred was non-committal. Hugh supposed he had to be. Technic-ally, the Council were still trying to buy the Church but they'd never get enough money for their hare-brained development scheme once the country had come to its senses and voted for all the cuts in public spending promised by the Conservatives. Fred did not see it that way. But it was always hard to work out how Fred *did* see things. Hugh had come to realize, since his wife's death, he had never really got to know Fred. He really felt closer to Jen. They said blood was thicker than water but Hugh doubted this.

He turned the knob of his mother's bedroom door, a tea-cup in his other hand, and entered. He never did go in nowadays, without wondering whether she had gone in the night. It would be a mercy when she did really. It was pathetic to see someone go totally ga-ga.

'Tea!' he called out in a silly little jaunty voice he had begun to use since her decline. It was a bit like the tones some people adopt with pet animals.

'Is it raining?' asked his mother.

'Oh really!'

'I've got my umbrella just in case.'

She had heaved herself out of bed and was sitting, bolt upright at her dressing table, her raven hair loose down her back in a plait. She was holding a little parasol over her head, but otherwise she was completely naked.

'If you carry on being naughty we'll have to get you into hospital,' he said, 'and you wouldn't like that.' She presented an extraordinary sight. Her arms and shoulders were surprisingly young seeming. But in other parts of her body her skin was shrivelled and discoloured. She was completely flat-chested. Where her nipples once had been there were just two mushroom-coloured discs, about the size of an old penny.

'Besides, you'll get cold,' he added.

'I'm going to be married today.'

'Oh, really, who to?'

'I've forgotten his name, but he is quite a nice young man. He lives next door. Fish, I believe.'

'Put this on at least.' He draped a shawl round her shoulders. 'Shall I get Jen to come and help you dress?'

It embarrassed him profoundly to see his mother's nakedness.

'I want to carry my parasol.'

'Well, careful where you put it.' She narrowly missed poking him in the eye. 'We're going to vote today.' Really, it did not do to pander to her, it only made her worse. It was as if she was playing a silly sort of game. 'We're going to vote Conservative.'

'I'm not,' she said.

'What are you going to vote, then?' he asked.

'Liberal,' she said. 'I don't know what you mean by saying you are going to vote for the Conservatives.'

'I always vote Conservative.'

'You said only the other day that you liked Mr Asquith.'

'I'll leave you to finish your tea,' he said. 'Mind you don't spill it everywhere.'

He went down the landing shaking his head. The hall clock was striking seven. He could not very well knock up Jen till she'd got the children up and dressed. He went to the kitchen and listened to the radio. The commentator chappie seemed fairly sure that Mrs T. had got it in the bag.

XXIX

While Jen teetered upstairs with her tea-tray, she wondered why everyone expected her to do everything – the shopping, the washing, full responsibility for the children, remembering to pay the milk money, booking the summer holidays, remembering to get the car serviced – *everything*. And now that Grandma was failing, she was expected to look after her, too. Jen thought it was a bit much. But there again, it was for Fred to talk to his father about it. Hugh was a mean old so-and-so, always was. He could easily afford a nurse for his mother. Most people would have had one months ago. With this new addition to her routine ('Jen m'dear, could you just come and lend a hand with Grandma?') she felt that the last vestiges of independence had drained away from her. She was now wholly a Jobling slave, a mere appendage to varying forms of Jobling egoism – a washer of Jobling socks, an ironer of Jobling shirts, a maker of young Jobling beans on toast (*exactly* equal portions or a battle broke out); now, a helper of aged Joblings to dress, eat and go to the lavatory. How had it happened? In Surrey, she was always aware of herself as a separate person. She had time – glorious time. She could remember walking down the main street of Godalming and looking at her watch and going to have coffee – not particularly because she wanted it, but to fill up half an hour of the morning. She might have said she was bored. She did not realize then that it was perfectly possible to be bored all the time and yet not to have a free moment.

Not that Jen was bored all the time. The children had become *less* fractious in the last few weeks – that day at Dudley Zoo with her mother really seemed to have done them good – and she had started to feel a return of pride and pleasure in their company. Harriet was going to be very bright, obviously. Not perhaps a 'gifted child' of the kind they talked about nowadays, but obviously jolly good. She had terrific powers of concentration. This family-tree thing she'd been doing. They all thought she'd lose interest after the first few days but not a bit of it – she had gone on and on and on, found out all kinds of fascinating things. She had wheedled out of Jen's mother that there were some cousins in New Zealand that Jen had never heard of: and could now explain, which Jen had never been able to, exactly how the Saunderses related to the Lewis-Wards, and who 'Aunt Jessie' had been. So much for Jen's side of the family. On Fred's side, Harriet had nagged away at Grandma (Jen secretly wondered whether it had not speeded up the process of her going barmy) and got nowhere. Then Hugh, one day when his mother was dozing, had taken Harriet to one side and tried to fill her in with all the details: Edmund Fish = Frances who ran away with her brother-in-law Oswald Fish.

Jen had thought a lot about Frances Fish since she first heard the story from Harriet and had it confirmed by Hugh. That great brick house in Augustus Road, the very scene of Frances's elopement, had become for Jen a prison house. If Fred had an artistic brother who offered to take her off to London, Jen thought she'd leap at the chance. It seemed an awful thing to say to herself, but she'd really come to hate Fred in the last few months. Perhaps she had hated him for much longer, and it was only lately that she had allowed herself to admit it. When you looked at it coolly, as she now tried to, during drives back from school or the launderette (Fred had promised three times to chivvy the men to come and mend the washing machine and in the end she had gone round to the Electricity Showrooms herself but of course no one had come yet and it was *still* broken), there was nothing to like about him any more. He went on about how boring the Gladstones were, but he was worse. The only thing he talked to her about was bloody Town Hall business. He had become so self-important about it.

This Fanny Williams business, for instance: Jen had been thrilled to bits when she found out that Fanny Williams was a sort of cousin. Harriet had wanted all the names to put down on the family tree. And it really lent a bit of glamour to this boring old Purgstall Area Development Scheme. Jen had said, 'To think if it hadn't been for knocking down that church we'd never have found out about her.' Fred had snapped at her, said she didn't understand the first thing about PADS and then given her a little lecture about how essential it was, for the future of the scheme, for Labour to win the Election. He was so *stupid*. He must have been the only person in

England who thought that poor old Uncle Jim had a chance against Mrs T.

And why had none of them been allowed to meet Fanny? It was surely rather fun, being related to someone who had been on Top of the Pops and known all the stars. Hugh had met her in London, but Hugh was so unnoticing. He'd said she was brash and vulgar. Jen could have guessed that for herself. She wanted to know what Fanny was like. Fred had pompously said it was much better not getting to know her socially while the future of Purgstall lay in the balance.

This morning Jen managed not to drop anything off the tea-tray. She dumped it on her bedside table and turned on the news.

'Election day,' she said, trying to be cheery.

'I know that,' he said.

'It would be fun to live in a marginal seat, wouldn't it?' she said. 'If the Conservative candidate in Edgbaston was a baboon it would still get in.'

'You don't know what you're talking about,' he said. 'That's just something you've read.'

Sam came scampering in after a few moments in his green velour pyjamas, and his endless supply of not-very-funny riddles prevented his parents from openly scrapping.

'Knock knock.'

'Who's there?'

'Granny.'

'Granny who?'

'Knock knock.'

'Who's there?'

'Granny.'

'Granny who?'

'Knock knock.'

'Who's there?'

'Granny.'

'Granny who?'

'Knock knock.'

'Who's there?'

'Aunt.'

Aunt who?'

'Aren't you glad I've got rid of all those grannies?'

When he had extracted the desired polite laughter from his parents he went back to his own bed to re-peruse *The-Crack-a-Joke-Book*. Jen noticed that even towards Sam, formerly his favourite, Fred was now distant, moody, cold, he didn't seem to be *there* half the time, just silent and staring.

'Talking of grannies,' said Jen.

Fred had got out of bed now and was ostentatiously rummaging in his top drawer for clean socks.

'There are some clean socks in the airing cupboard,' she said.

Without responding, he stalked out to the landing. She could hear him throwing towels and sheets about in his search for socks. She had spent three-quarters of an hour the previous day tidying that blinking cupboard.

'On the lower shelf,' she said.

He came back, hardly looking at her. She found it hard to interpret the way that, recently, he had always tried to avoid her gaze. On this occasion she assumed it was sheepishness. He had obviously half-hoped there wouldn't be any socks so that he could moan and bluster about it.

But she repeated, 'Talking of grannies, don't you think it's time your grandmother had a nurse to look after her?'

'Knock knock,' said Sam, coming in again.

'Who's there?' said Jen loyally.

'Cows go who?'

'Cows go moo not who. Knock knock.'

'Not another just now, darling, I want to talk to Fred.'

'That makes news,' said Fred gloomily. If you are a tubby man, turning into a very fat man, it is hard to look dignified when you are wearing nothing but socks, and very baggy underpants. Fred's face, however, showed a furious desire to be taken seriously.

'Do listen, Fred, I want to talk.'

'Listen, that's a fine thing. Since when did you ever listen to me?'

'Your grandmother *needs a nurse*.' She said it directly into his face. She had not cleaned her teeth. He turned away in disgust at the combined smell of foul breath and strong tea.

'Talk to Dad about it. Don't talk to me,' he said.

Silence ensued while she sat on the edge of the bed and pretended to drink tea. She thought of lots of things to say, sentences beginning 'Why should *I* be expected ...' but it was no use talking any more. Instead, she quietly thought about the day ahead. Drive Sam to the Nutkin, Harriet and she both had the day off because of the election. Melanie Gladstone had very kindly said she would have Harriet. They were going for a ramble on the Malvern Hills. A bit of a drive but Melanie did not seem to mind it. The only disagreeable feature of the arrangement was that it meant *they* had to have Debbie Gladstone for the day at some future date . . .

Jen, with her free day ahead of her, had rather hoped to cycle into the town and look at the shops. Almost certainly, though, Hugh would need help with Grandma. Probably she would have to help them drive to the polls to vote.

'Oh by the way,' Fred said, adjusting his tie as casually as possible, 'I'm probably having to go to London tomorrow.'

'Lucky thing.'

'That's all right by you then?'

'I don't seem to be able to stop you doing what you want, do I?'

'It's not a joy-ride, Jen, it's to clear up . . . some business.'

'Oh. Will it take long?'

'No. No. I'll be back by Monday, I should think.'

'So you are going to London for the *week-end*.'

'Yes. Yes I am. I've got work there on Friday, work on Monday. I thought there was no point in nipping backwards and forwards . . .'

'No. None at all.'

Fred blinked at her, unable to tell why she accepted those feeble lies, faintly wounded that she did not question him more fully.

Jen looked at Fred. Her only sensation was relief that he was to be gone for three days. She was not sufficiently interested in him to wonder whether he was telling lies. And, at that moment, he looked so fat and ridiculous that it never crossed her mind that he might be having a love affair. During some of his earlier jaunts away she had thought it – or wondered it – naturally. But she did not do so today.

'Mummy,' Harriet called, 'come and help me to do my plaits.'

Jen went next door to Harriet's bedroom. As she wove her daughter's plaits, she could see her animated, flushed cheeks in the glass, happy and over-excited at the prospect of a day with the Gladstones.

XXX

Fred voted Labour on his way to work and then caught the bus. He had not had his usual bath that morning and was aware that he was rather smelly. But after making love to Fanny, he was always unwilling to wash too thoroughly for fear of losing *her* smell along with his own. It lingered with him for several days: not merely that scent she wore, but the much more delicious smell of her. Sometimes it would take him by surprise. This morning for instance, when putting on his shirt, he realized that the whole of his chest was permeated with her. These little details consoled him during their periods of absence from one another.

What had begun as a mad adventure a little over a month before had developed into an all-absorbing and exhausting romance. Given its geographical complexities, it was astonishing how the romance had flourished, how often Fanny and he had been able to meet. She had been coming to Birmingham quite a lot to see about the shop. He had been down to London once or twice since and stayed at Bailey's on 'business'. On other occasions, they had made crazy assignations and met half-way in station hotels in the middle of the day. He had spent pounds on hotels and train fares.

Since the discovery that he and Fanny shared a great-grandmother – and were something like second cousins – the atmosphere of fantasy which initially hovered around their relationship had been at once heightened and removed. Removed, because anyone might get to know, even fall in love with a cousin, heightened, because he had almost come to share Fanny's belief that it was all *meant*, that he really was the Prince Consort and she the Girl of his Dreams.

Sex, initially an explosion in his consciousness, had become no less exciting. But it had now developed from being something merely thrilling into something which was a genuine expression of their feeling for one another. It had become unimaginable that he could ever live without her, but the form this realization sometimes took in his mind was the thought that he could not do without *that*: and sometimes some dizzying moment of delight in bed with her would come flooding back into his memory.

He found himself thinking about her all the time. In day-dreams he would simply be playing over conversations they had had; long, adoring walks around London in which they could hardly move because they were clutching each other too tightly; bed, bed, bed.

Things about her which he had found repellent initially – her brashness, the loud noise, the hectic bustle she surrounded herself with, the blatant vulgarity – no longer registered. He knew they were there. He did not mind about them. If he thought about them, they made him laugh. At first, for instance, he had been scandalized by the conversational sophistication of the children. They were younger than Harriet, and yet their main form of amusement seemed to be perusing pornographic magazines. He had not yet 'got through' to Marmie and Pandora. Fanny said he must give them time and she was almost certainly right. But he had come rather to admire the way they could talk about sex so freely. It could well be that, when those two children grew up, they would have a less hellish adolescence than he had done. Simply because they were in the know. There would be no surprises left for them, except the nicest surprise of all, the discovery of what sex was like between a man and a woman when they were in love.

Fanny had broken it to Marmie the previous week that she intended to marry Fred. They had not been sure how the little chap had taken it. He had been rather quiet. Pandora, when told, had simply burst into hysterical laughter. Charles said it would take some getting used to and had privately advised Fanny not to rush things. Fred still bitterly resented every aspect of the affair being submitted to Charles for comment and approval. When he finally *did* move in with Fanny, he rather hoped that Charles would have the decency to move on; but he had not yet managed to say this.

There were a lot of things he had not yet managed to say. To Jen, for instance, almost nothing. Fanny had been impatient, but under-standing. It was not merely the forthcoming Fish exhibition which had made her want to meet Fred's father. Unknown to Hugh, she had been sounding out a future father-in-law. He had been perfectly sweet, and she knew they would adore one another. She wished that Fred would let her meet Jen and the children; she had said it would all be so much better if it all came out in the open and they could *talk* about it, but he had been adamant that the right moment was not yet.

Fred just could not bring himself to tell Jen that he was in love with Fanny. For one thing, she always tried to make a bit of a joke of everything and he was genuinely afraid that when he actually sprang the news on her, she would laugh. For another, she seemed perpetually preoccupied. It maddened him that she never had any time to talk to him properly. She was forever fussing about domestic arrangements, or seeing to the children. And now his grandmother had gone downhill she had found yet another reason to be morally one up, by helping out and 'being marvellous'. Of course she was right: grandma needed a nurse. But why the hell couldn't Jen and his Dad organize this themselves instead of bothering *him* about it?

This morning, for instance, he had been going to tell her about his business in London. He had been going to say that on Friday he had an interview at the Law Commission and that he was almost certain to be offered the job. He had the whole conversation planned out from there. Jen was meant to say, 'Are you thinking of giving up your job in Birmingham?' He would say, 'Yes.' She would say, 'Are we moving to London, then?' He would then have been able to say, 'No, I thought I'd move to London and you'd stay here. Let's face it, Jen, we've come to the end of the road. We don't get along any more. It's absolute torture for me living with you and it can't be much fun for you either.' (Actually he thought Jen was so *unnoticing* that she was perfectly happy, but he had been going to say it to make the balance seem right.) 'Then we're going to separate, is that what you're saying?' 'Yes, just for the time being.' That was how he was going to break it to her. Then, a bit later, he might get around to mentioning Fanny.

He thought doing it this way would be the most painless. Fanny had been pleased when he explained why. If he had told Jen all at once that he was in love with Fanny, it would make it look as if Fanny was breaking up his marriage. And he wanted to make the point that there wasn't much of a marriage to break up; that really Jen and he had no future anyway; would have eventually separated even if Fanny had never come on the scene. It all seemed neater like that.

But of course, Jen, damn and blast her, had not spoken the lines which had been written for her. She had not even *asked* what he was doing in London, and had seemed more anxious to nag him about getting a nurse for his grandmother. He felt now that, even more than the ears, he hated her stubborn bone-headedness. Any other wife in England would have asked, *surely*, how her husband was to spend the weekend in London. Perhaps she suspected all kinds of things and was too shy to say. He had gone through phases of hoping that she would intuit the fact that he was in love, which would conveniently let him off the hook. In this imagined scene, she had been rather nice, and said, 'Fred, I know what's the matter. It's Fanny Williams, isn't it?' But she had got nowhere near saying anything of the kind. She never did know what was the matter. That was the trouble.

When he got off the bus and walked up Cambridge Street in the sunshine, he reflected that Brum was not such a bad old place. In an odd sort of way, he was going to miss it. Of course, they had made some mistakes, but it had a sort of reassuringness that London lacked. Edgbaston was a nicer place to live than Chelsea any day. No one could dispute it. But even the centre of Birmingham had its points. He breathed the air and surveyed it all with affection.

Today was the day Fanny was having the screen moved down to London from St Aidan's, Purgstall Heath. She probably wasn't going to be there herself, and they had made no arrangements to meet until the next evening, after his interview at the Law Commission. The wrangle with the Council over the compulsory purchase order was still, technically, alive, but luckily there were a thousand other things going on in the town hall and Purgstall Heath was only one of many areas in the City which would be affected by the day's events. Facilities for the disabled, buses, playgrounds, libraries, road schemes and the hospitals would all suffer if Mrs T. really did win and implement the threatened cuts. Fred was fairly certain, in spite of what the pundits said, that she would not win the Election. The Labour record, on average, had been remarkably good. In spite of the troubles of the winter, they did at least have *some* rapport with the Unions. He dreaded to think what would happen if the Iron Lady decided to try fisticuffs with the TUC. On the whole, he thought, people had too much sense to risk it. The opinion polls showed that Callaghan continued to be popular. A solid conciliatory policy was what was needed.

On this particular day, the Town Hall was buzzing with all the rather bizarre administrative bustle of democracy. This side of things did not directly affect anyone on Fred's corridor, and neither Dawn in Planning, who was today almost unbuttoned to the waist, nor Ivy, mopping just outside his office door, seemed much affected by the atmosphere of excitement downstairs.

'Intit hot though?' Ivy asked, her bucket as usual forbidding entrance to his office.

'Not really.'

She dabbed her face and neck with exaggerated stabs of the Kleenex.

'Heavy. Same as our Art said when he got up – Ive you sweated like a bloody pig last night been to vote then?' The switch of subject was, as ever, unpunctuated and unannounced.

'Same as Mrs Riley says you couldn't do worse than they've been doing already why not let a woman have a go for a change well our Art's voted Conservative all his life, yeah, met Mr Macmillan when he come here ooh he were ever so nice shook hands and that·and he's secretary of the local Conservative Association.'

'Mr Macmillan?'

'No. Our Art.'

She never responded to banter. Not that she was unprepared to make jokes herself, but when in full conversational flight she had a manic eagerness to talk which nothing short of a bomb falling on the building would have prevented.

'No, but I think she's lovely, don't you and what do these effing people expect. I mean if you haven't got it you can't give it them can you?'

'Which people?'

'Unions. If you haven't got the money to give them you can't pay them more same as Mrs Riley says and they're all drinking and smoking and that all the while, it's not as though they were real poor like we was in t'old days well then it's different my dad says they looked after the working man *then*. He still votes Labour has some real old set-tos with our Art, well they're friendly like did you see him in t' paper?'

'Your husband?'

'Me dad. Hundred. I *told* you.'

'So you did.' Had she done? He used to half listen to Ivy's monologues. He used to listen to everybody. Now he wandered about in a silent daze listening only to the voice of Fanny inside his head.

'He had a telegram from the Queen and that and you know party up at the home and we were all there our Floss and our Glad and Daren that's her little grandson oh he were that sweet and Leslie that's his mother ...'

From the pocket of her blue nylon overall she produced a cutting from the *Birmingham Post* and continued to talk as Fred perused it.

'Well after tea he got tired like, they let him have a glass of stout though well you can see it in the picture and then we all went out to you know celebrate and that, there was Floss and Glad and our Art and Bert, that's Glad's son he's done ever so well he's a pilot we went to the pub first and then you know had drinks and we didn't eat till quarter past bloody nine even though as Art booked the table at the Berni ooh it were smashing Mrs Riley says it was just the same on her wedding anniversary they keep you waiting don't they and I was so blown out I couldn't eat the sweet – oh we had chips and peas and steak lovely bit of steak but quarter past nine. Course we'd been to the pub first for drinks sherry and that but we weren't sat down at that table till quarter past bloody nine.'

Fred stared at the newspaper cutting. It all meant nothing to him. Ivy, hideously grinning, was sitting in a circle with a lot of overweight people in the day room of an old folk's home. She was holding up a telegram from Buckingham Palace. A wiry old man, evidently her father, hair cut so short that he looked almost bald, held up a glass of stout and grinned towards the camera. CENTURY PINT! was the headline:

Mr Toby Shakespeare, 100 years old today, still enjoys his pint. Family and friends joined him yesterday in St Aidan's Home for the birthday celebrations. These ranged from Mrs Ethel Weatherborne, 71, of Hudders-field, pictured to the left, to little Daren Hardwick, 6, one of Mr Shake-speare's six great-grandchildren!! Mr Shakespeare (no relation, he thinks, of the famous man!) was for fifty years a stoker on the London and North

Eastern Railways. He told a Post Reporter yesterday, 'I preferred the days of steam.' Mr Shakespeare, a Yorkshireman, has lived in Birmingham for twenty years, to be near his daughter Mrs Ivy Yardsley. He fought in the First World War and was reported missing after the second battle of Mons. 'My family all gave me up for lost,' he quipped yesterday. 'But here I am.' Asked if he had a recipe for long life he said that he had smoked twenty cigarettes and drunk his pint every day for the last eighty-five years. Cheers. Toby!

XXXI

As she had anticipated, Jen did not have much of a free day. When it emerged that Harriet was having a day out in Malvern, Sam threw a tantrum and said he refused to go to school. When he had finally been dragged into the Nutkin, scarlet and screaming, Jen felt drained of energy, and almost contemplated spending the morning in bed. But an agitated Hugh awaited her on her return. His mother was much worse, completely round the twist.

Jen had gone next door to see. Old Mrs Jobling was not in the state of undress Hugh had described. That was one thing. She had contrived to stagger into a very light, flimsy and most unsuitable summer frock. She proposed to wear a hat trimmed with flowers and to carry a parasol because it was her wedding day.

'Besides,' said Agnes, 'I've had a letter from my mother.'

'Your *mother*?' Jen was still unused to the degree to which Grandma had gone batty.

'Oh *really*, mother,' Hugh protested.

'This gentleman doesn't believe me,' she said to Jen, as if in confidence. 'I think he is a police officer. Don't speak too loud. It would be so sad to spoil things on my wedding day.'

Hugh was making a number of agonized facial gestures to Jen which she could not interpret, an exaggerated drawing back of the corners of his mouth, a repeated raising of his eye-brows, up and down, up and down.

'Do you think I should call for a doctor?' Jen asked.

'Suppose so,' said Hugh. 'Ask for old Young,' he added confusingly, 'I don't like that junior chappie they send round on visits.'

'Doctor Fraser is perfectly competent,' Jen said.

'Dare say he is. Young knows my mother and ...' Hands and eyebrows finished the sentence for him.

'I don't know what you two want with the doctor. Are you

feeling ill? Hugh is going to take me to vote for ... Where are your children?' she suddenly asked.

'Sam's at school.'

'Is he, though?' she smiled mysteriously. 'What about dear little Jennifer?'

'Harriet's out for the day. She's gone to Malvern with Mrs Gladstone. You remember the Gladstones?'

'Poor child,' said Agnes Jobling shaking her head and looking pityingly at Hugh. 'It's Mr *Asquith* now you know, not Mr Gladstone.'

'Yes, mother,' said Hugh.

'And I was going to read you a letter from my mother but I have most foolishly mislaid my spectacles. You, my dear,' she said to Jen, 'we've never been properly introduced. My son has no manners.'

'Mother, this is Jennifer.'

'That's no way to introduce her, dear. What's her surname?'

'You know me, Grandma,' Jen interjected, holding her hand.

'She's as mad as a hatter,' said Agnes Jobling. 'She thinks Mr Gladstone is the leader of the Liberal Party and she thinks I'm her grandmother. Now where was I? Oh yes, my letter from my mother. Jennifer-whatever-your-name-is – I wonder if you would be so kind as to read it to me.'

She handed Jen a neatly folded wedge of thick blue writing paper. Jen wondered what to do? Was it all some kind of elaborate joke? She had been noticing Grandma getting funny for some weeks but she had never been as bad as today.

'You'd better read it,' said Hugh.

Jen stared down at the pages. There seemed to be a lot of them but they had been written over hastily in a large feminine hand, with few words to the page.

'*Dearest Agnes*,' she began. 'Er ... *53 Haverstock Hill, N.W. Dearest Agnes, It was so strange and so wonderful, my dearest, to see you the other day, and to meet your nice husband and your fine boy Hugh ...*'

'She's muddled,' glossed Agnes, and tapped the side of her forehead to suggest her mother's senility. 'I never had a boy called Hugh.'

'But mother,' Hugh protested.

'Let Genevieve go on,' his mother snapped.

'. . . *to meet your nice husband and your fine boy Hugh. He has quite a look of the Fishes about him.*'

'A great compliment!' interrupted Agnes sarcastically.

'. . . *and although so shy and quiet it was a pleasure to meet him and see my grandchild and hold him in my arms for the first time.*'

'All right we've got the idea she was pleased to see him,' snapped Agnes again. Then she sniggered naughtily, 'Don't know *who* she thought he was. Probably thought it was that *little visitor* of Uncle Oswald's.'

'Little visitor?'

'Oh, we weren't supposed to know. We were children. But everyone *did*. It was a serving girl called Annie. Her mother still helps in the kitchen when the cook's busy, but she used to be cook-housekeeper. Mrs Shakespeare. Funny name, but many people in Birmingham are called Shakespeare.'

'Shall I go on with the letter?' Jen asked.

'Mother writes such boring letters. When she *does* write, that is,' she added grudgingly. 'No, we all knew about the little visitor. Annie went north. Worked for Cousin Godfrey I believe. Cousin Godfrey's a bit common,' she whispered gleefully.

Even though it was all so clearly Double-Dutch, Jen felt furious with the whole world conjured up by Agnes's fantasy. It made her determined to vote Labour. These *tradespeople*, she thought in snobbish exasperation (proud that, on her father's side, her family had been Surrey professional men for at least two generations) giving themselves such *airs*. Why was Cousin Godfrey *common*? Who was Agnes, the child of some manufacturer of lamp-posts, to make such a pronouncement? And all this sly, malicious gleeful talk about little visitors and serving girls. She had all but used the odious expression 'on the wrong side of the blanket'. Was it all a fiction dreamed up out of the wastes of a senile old brain or did it relate to some actual event, lost in the mists of Grandma's childhood? Jen boiled to think of it. That poor girl, shoved out – at what age? – to work in Yorkshire as a stranger, to bring up her 'little visitor'. And who was he? Scarred for life, probably, by knowing that he was a bastard, or perhaps by not knowing, and always wondering and then finding out at the most fragile time of his adolescence.

'Mother was probably thinking of *him*,' continued Agnes, smacking her chops and munching slightly as though something un-

254

comfortable were stuck in her false teeth. 'She is a little *casual* about little visitors from the wrong side of the blanket. Hardly surprising since she *has one of her own.*'

'Shall I go on with the letter?' asked Jen.

'What letter?'

'Your mother's letter.'

'You can if you like.' It now seemed a matter of indifference to her.

'*I must write this to you, dearest Agnes, because I know you must have grown up to judge me harshly. It is too late to hope that you will alter that judgement now, but now you have grown to womanhood, and a mother, I feel that I can explain to you why I deserted you all those years ago. You probably do not know that I tried constantly to write to you and to see you when you were a child but that your grandfather's solicitors at length put an end forever to all converse between us. It was one of the most horrible blows of my life, my dearest girl. Believe me. When I ran away from your father to be with the man I loved (and still love) it never occurred to me for an instant that I would need to be parted from you for more than (at most) a few weeks. When I realized that they were determined to keep us separate I could not believe such cruelty was possible. I even came to Birmingham and pleaded with your grandfather but he was obdurate. I was not allowed to see you. Please believe this, Agnes dear. I have so much missed you, as only a mother could miss her darling child, over the last twenty years. I have another daughter, Jessica, as you know. And through all the joy of watching her grow up has been shot the thread of sorrow that she can never know her sister — and that I have never seen you, my darling, first mastering a cycle or flying a kite . . .*'

'Ridiculous,' interpolated Agnes, 'never had a bicycle, couldn't ride one. Never had a kite. Can't think what she's blathering about.'

'Perhaps mother's had enough of the letter now,' said Hugh.

'She may as well be allowed to finish it,' said Agnes, as though reading the thing had been entirely Jen's idea.

'*. . . Now that you are a woman and a mother, dear child, imagine what I have suffered for the loss of you — what torments of guilt and abandonment and self-questioning. And try to forgive me. Try to forgive your Uncle Oswald too. One day, Agnes, the world will come to recognize his real distinction as an architect and designer in metalwork. Only the other day, a chalice of his design was bought by a Church in Balham.*

This may seem a small beginning. But many great men have waited quietly in the wings of the world's stage until they were past middle age before treading the boards in the leading roles that nature assigned them.'

'Has Uncle Oswald become an actor?' asked Agnes with gleeful sarcasm.

'I believe in his greatness ..

'So we've gathered.'

'... and one day you will too, and perhaps will understand why I wanted to stay by his side as a helpmeet and support. I cannot explain myself or ask for your forgiveness now. my dear child, and this letter has gone on long enough.'

'Telling me.'

'... But believe me, darling Agnes, to be ever your devoted Mama.'

The whole experience of reading the letter brought down a heavy, deadening depression into Jen's bosom. The revelations it contained, largely unknown to her, about these former Fish skeletons, fishbones in the cupboard, did not excite her. She was merely overwhelmed by the air of misery given off by the letter, not decreased by Agnes Jobling's demented, cackling interjections.

'She never usually writes,' Agnes said. 'Don't know why she bothered to write today.'

'Perhaps she wanted to get it off her chest,' said Jen simply.

Agnes looked at her contemptuously and tapped the side of her head as if to indicate that someone in the room had lost their mental faculties.

'Bit late for that,' she said. 'She's been dead sixty years,' and she quietly rocked with mirth.

'What are we going to do?' Hugh asked despairingly, as he and Jen walked round the large lawn afterwards.

'She really ought to be seen,' Jen admitted. Oh dear. Bang went her lovely peaceful morning. The self-indulgent cup of coffee and pastry at the Danish Centre, the browse round Hudson's bookshop, the search for a really nice curtain material for her bedroom, possibly even a glimpse at the new 'Fanny' shop which she had not properly explored. Instead it was to be telephone calls, waiting for health visitors and doctors, painful interviews, and perhaps at the end, a painful scene of bundling a protesting grandma into the back of an ambulance: far worse even than the experience of leaving the howling Sam at the Nutkin.

'Could you do it?' Hugh asked plaintively. 'Ring up, I mean.'

'All right,' said Jen. She was about to offer to make him a coffee, but she thought, Why the hell *should* I make telephone calls about *his* mother? He has nothing to do except potter about in a cardigan reading the *Financial Times*.

She did not enunciate the rest of her objections. She just went back to her own kitchen, slamming the door furiously.

It was all Fred's fault for leaving Godalming. She kept thinking over and over again, as she dialled the doctor's surgery, why the hell shouldn't his father and grandmother manage their own lives? She thought of Godalming with bitter nostalgia and regret: the friends she had had at the tennis club, Cathy and Barbara both married now of course: Barbara still living nearby – Guildford – and very happy with Graham, her husband who was a civil servant; Cathy had married a doctor and gone over the border into Kent, but only as far away as Sevenoaks.

Why couldn't *they* be like this, Jen wondered, as she angrily listened for the dialling tone, instead of this wretched life in Birmingham, and Fred not even a proper solicitor any more, just some ghastly man from the Council?

'Hallo?'

The receptionist at last got round to answering. All the doctors were either out or unavailable, of course. But could Jen leave a message. Well, it was rather urgent. She explained that Grandma was finally round the twist. There was a pause.

'We'll try and get Doctor Fraser to call some time this morning.'

It was better than nothing. Indeed, being a doctor's daughter, Jen knew that it was jolly short notice. Grandma was not actually breaking up the furniture. It could scarcely be thought of as an emergency that she thought Mr Asquith was still the leader of the Liberal party. Hugh would complain when he heard that it was Dr Fraser. Jen actually preferred him to Dr Young. He was younger, cleverer, jollier. Without telling anyone else she had sometimes 'been to' Dr Fraser to pour out her troubles. He offered her pills, but she did not really want them. It just helped to have a safety valve. Otherwise she really could imagine herself losing her grip.

In spite of the awfulness of it all, the thought of Mr Asquith had the combined effect of making her giggle and reminding her that she must go out and vote. She still had not really made up her mind but she thought on the whole Labour simply because she disliked the notion of change.

She was just about to set out for the local polling-station when scrunching on the gravel announced the arrival of the post van. The door bell rang.

'It said "Do not bend",' said the postman.

'So it does. How exciting.'

Jen was always childishly elated by post.

'Don't forget to vote Liberal,' said the postman, climbing back into his van.

Jen waved her package and smiled. She liked their second postman, though the one on the bike who brought their first post was a rather grumpy Irishman that she felt she couldn't quite trust.

She wondered what on earth her parcel could be. Well, package, hardly a parcel. It was addressed to MRS JOBLING in a very childish hand, and decorated with orange and pink felt-tip pen – Jen wondered whether it was meant for Grandma, but on the back it had TO JENIFER JOBLING WITH LOVE AND KISSES. She knew her own children's writing too well and her sister's children were too old to send such a greeting. Debbie Gladstone was such a horrid little thing that it would never cross her mind to think of giving a grown-up pleasure with an unexpected present through the post.

It was so carefully stuck together with Christmas Sellotape all covered in holly, and real care had been devoted to its design. Trying not to injure it, she sat at the kitchen table with a knife, gingerly turning back its folds so as not to tear the paper or damage the writing.

The first thing that fell out as she held up the packet, was a photograph. She looked at it with incredulity and disgust. It appeared to be a most revolting-looking man, leaning towards the camera, totally naked, while he allowed a rather pretty little girl in Victorian fancy dress to finger his erect ... well, Jen hardly liked to say the word. The joy of her anticipation in opening the package had changed immediately into one of the cold, cruel, terrifying sense that someone was playing the vilest of practical jokes on her.

The next thing to come out of the package was a little bundle of cotton wool. It contained a single gold cuff-link, but she recognized it at once. There was the monogram G. V. S.: Gilbert Victor Saunders – her grandfather, who had been a medical man too. When he died, Daddy had very kindly given Fred these valued cuff-links and it had been moving for Jen to think of these links almost being literally made between Fred and Surrey, between the rather brash business world he came from, and the more sedate world of the professions, between Birmingham and Godalming. But how on earth had the cuff-link, and a pornographic photo-graph ... She now tore at the package and shook it. A letter fell out and she read it. It was written in pink capitals with felt-tip pen.

DEAR JENNY WENNY. DO YOU LIKE THIS PICTURE OF ME PLAYING WITH ALASTAIRS MISTER WILLIE. HE HAD JUST BEEN FUCKING MY MUMMY. BUT YOU KNOW ALL ABOUT THAT DONT YOU BECAUSE HES GOING TO MARRY FANNY. HERE IS ONE OF HIS CUFFLINKS THAT HE LEFT BEHIND IN FANNYS BEDROOM. I THREW THE OTHER ONE IN THE RIVER AND MADE A WISH THAT ALASTAIR WAS DEAD. LOTS OF LOVE FROM JANE.

There were several other photographs. Jen surveyed them with horror. The disgusting lascivious-looking man was indeed Fred. Why did they call him Alastair? On the other hand if they did not really know Fred how could they know that his real name was Alastair? The cufflink moreover confirmed it.

Photographs could be forged, couldn't they?

But the cufflinks confirmed it.

Jen's brain was not functioning properly any more. She felt more lonely and desolate and miserable than she had ever felt in her life. More lonely, even, than on her first day at Cheltenham. It must, surely, all be some horrible joke. She did not understand it. Some-one must have hated her, hated her terribly – perhaps for years – without her even knowing about it. Was it one of her pupils? The one she made cry? And now they had decided to pounce with these disgusting pictures and this cruel letter. Alastair. Fanny. It surely could not have anything to do with Fanny Williams. Fred had hardly met her. Hugh was more voluble on the subject, which was why they now had to collect up all the old ironwork in the house for the Oswald Fish exhibition. The hall was already cluttered with fenders, fireguards, pokers and tongs, ready for the museum man to inspect when Fred got round to telling them they were there ...

HERE IS ONE OF HIS CUFFLINKS THAT HE LEFT BEHIND IN
FANNYS BEDROOM ...

That was what it said. In spite of the disgusting photographs, Jen,
for several hours, did not even begin to think that any of it was true.
It was too absurd. Old Fred having a love affair with a pop star!
Fanny Williams had all the men in London to choose from, it was
well known. Until the full terribleness of the package dawned on
Jen, much later in the day, she was merely transfixed by the
horrible knowledge that someone hated her and wanted to hurt
her. This thought nagged at her, never left her, all through the
hours of letting in Dr Fraser, hearing his advice about Grandma,
cooking Hugh his lunch, and fetching Sam from school. Somebody,
those stabbings in her stomach kept reminding her, somebody
hates me.

XXXII

In the large green Bentley Enrico Caruso and Louise Horner sang a duet: *Gia i sacerdoti adunansi*. It was from a cassette called *Voices from the Past* and for all its technical accomplishment, the famed Caruso magic crackling through reprocessed wax on to further recycled celluloid had a peculiarly spectral quality, like a ghost bricked up a long age in some discarded cellar, and screaming to be let out.

It even silenced the corgis and Jeremy Tradescant. Fanny unable ever to be wholly silent, tried to join in the duet with her own, jerky, very pop-sounding approximation to what Verdi had intended.

She was full of quiet contentment. At last, everything, flipping everything, was turning out all right: a happy ending like in a story. Charles said that if Mrs Thatcher won this election they would stop the money supply just like that. Like what, Fanny had rather wondered, and besides, she had not really liked the idea of money being in less ready supply. Charles had smiled, like a tolerant schoolmaster explaining an elementary point of mathematics to the stupidest child in the class, and tried to tell her about public spending cuts, and it was awful, quite like one of the most boring evenings, suddenly, with the poor old Honourable Member. And then Charles had explained that the long and the short of it was that the Council were very unlikely to get enough money for their Purgstall Area Development Scheme, even if, after the next Council Election, they turned out to be a Labour-dominated council.

The way that Charles was so sort of grown-up made Fanny's head spin. Fancy *knowing* about Public Spending Cuts. Tracy had treated this observation with scorn and asked, did Fanny *never* read a newspaper? Well of course she did – the murder trials and the chatty little columns and the letters and all the proper news. She simply could not imagine allowing her mind to dwell long enough on public spending cuts to know what the implications of them might be. Luckily, though, it meant that the Council would not have enough money for that ghastly skateboard rink or whatever they wanted to build, and so could have no reason for buying, or demolishing, St Aidan's.

Terrific support had been drummed up for the little place. She felt almost guilty if it was going to be unnecessary, but it was as well to be on the safe side. She had got Donald Sinden to say it was a 'Victorian gem'; and the Poet Laureate said he would help – rather surprisingly, turned out to know more about Oswald Fish than anyone, asked her if she knew he'd done the railings of Holy Trinity, Sloane Street, and told her a nice story which, maddeningly, she had forgotten, about Oswald Fish going to supper with William and Evelyn de Morgan. It was odd that she had forgotten it, because usually the very mention of William de Morgan made her so excited that she thought she was going to be sick. Perhaps this was why the story flew out of her head.

Anyway, the church was saved, and now Jeremy had stepped into the gap left by David (poor old David; Charles said at once that he thought it was *suicide*, but Fanny felt he wouldn't have the nerve) and organized this wonderful Oswald Fish exhibition in London for the autumn. When she first met Jeremy she thought of him as one of those rather far-fetched people who take refuge in High Camp as an escape from something or other – a middle-class origin, a fear of women, a social conscience, or whatever it was that people called reality. Then she had come to see that for Jeremy High Camp *was* reality, the air he breathed. He would have choked, ceased to exist without it. She had quickly developed rather a crush on Jeremy. She loved his crisp blond curls, and his very playful eyes, and the fact that under all the hilarious posing he had a serious, rather manly face, with a firm chin and a rather well-bred nose and mouth. She could imagine it being quite marvellous, positively scrumptious, making love to him. He hadn't always been what he called a card-carrying queen, and had told her about quite a lot of his exploits with girls. He claimed that he had once been engaged. He even said that he had once had it off with his sister who was divorced from a perfectly beastly-sounding Scotch businessman . . .

Fanny had confided her crush on Jeremy to the Prince Consort during their last encounter and he had been flipping sniffy about it. Taken it quite seriously. Dear me, she hoped he wasn't going to be a jealous sort of husband. What she had tried to tell him was that to her it did not really *mean* anything, but that she would never stop wanting to hug and pet other men: even go to bed with them if they wanted it, because men were so scrumptious and life was so short and anyway why shouldn't she. Poor old Prince Consort's face had crumpled so that she had almost imagined he was about to cry. So she had knelt on top of him in that *particularly* unpleasant motel near Daventry the day before yesterday and told him not to be *silly* and that she was in *love* with him, *love, love, love*, and would stop at nothing until she *had* him. And his dear Mr Willie had perked up no end on being told this and slipped inside her easily for the ump- teenth time: and because they had done it so often she had been almost jokey, very casual about it, and done a sort of dance or gyration on him while he played with her boobies and it had all been so nice.

The Prince Consort frightened her a bit saying that he had *never* been in love with anyone the way he loved Fanny. After all he was forty-flipping-three, and you'd think he'd have been in love by now. She had been in love dozens and *dozens* of times, and almost every time to someone who seemed in some lights or at some moment to be Mr Right. So often she had been mistaken, but on this occasion she just knew she was not. He was so *dependable*, so solid, so practical. It seemed brilliant, to her, to think of changing his job to London; and it was a great relief, that, even though he had not spelt out *all* the details to Jennifer, he was so sure she would take it all in good part – might even be relieved. Fanny longed to meet Jennifer. The PC had really been very good about *not* blackening her name *too* much. He wanted to talk about her hardly at all. Whereas she, after their delicious surreptitious lovemakings, would lie in his arms on hotel beds and go on for hours about *her* life, the Honourable Member, Marmie and Pandora.

The poor children were going to take it awfully hard if she married again. She wished now that she had braved it out after the incident of poor Prince Consort bursting into the bathroom with no clothes on. It had made the children so hysterical, and her so *embarrassed*, that she had just wanted him out of the house as soon as possible. And since then, she had hardly had the courage to allow him back to Tregunter Road, unless she knew it was empty, for fear of some awful exposure being repeated. She had talked about him endlessly of course to the others, but since they had only met him very briefly once or twice, they could not comment much. They did not see his *qualities*!

He was so bear-like and furry and cuddlable, so seemingly soft and gentle and yet so firm, so stiff yet so funny. They found themselves laughing much of the time and that was surely a sign that everything was going to be a success.

The objections to it all were obvious – they had only known each other a few weeks – how would it affect his *poor* children: *her* poor children, etc., etc. And Charles was right when he said that it was mad to consider a man when you'd never lived with him.

'Fanny, sunshine, you don't know what he's like on an ordinary day of an ordinary week.'

So sensible! How marvellous Charles always was about everything. He was quite right about this. She and the Prince Consort *ought* to spend a week or two just living together, doing ordinary things (in so far as she ever had done ordinary things) and having conversations which involved other people. All their talk had been of themselves, ninety per cent of it to do with the actual drama of their romance. Who knew? Who should be told? How much longer could it go on before the whole thing burst on the World? Should they run away together? This was usual in the early stage of love affairs. Fanny was fairly used to it, one of the things, indeed, which she liked about them: they made the whole of life like some exciting serial: one was absolutely dying to know what would happen next. Usually the drama was increased by one or other of the parties thinking it was all too much and they must break it off because they could not bear all the uncertainty, or the secrecy, or the cruelty to a spouse or something else. This had not been an element of her love for the Prince Consort even though she had been pretty firm that she was not a strumpet and that he must make up his mind between her and poor old Jennifer. But he had never said, 'We can't go on meeting like this,' or 'I can't stand the lies any longer,' or any of the other wonderfully romantic clichés which every day were spoken all over the world a thousand times by unhappy couples caught in Love's potent grip.

During this visit to Birmingham, they had thought, they would not meet. Prince C. had not quite taken to Jeremy and been rather *silly* about this crush thing of hers. He was, moreover, going to be very busy, it being Election day. Erection Day as she called it this morning when *sweet* Marmie woke up beside her in bed. (How *was* it going to be when she married PC and the little chap couldn't come and cuddle her in the mornings?)

And Erection Day it certainly was. She assumed the Honourable Member would be fairly chirpily sailing to victory and that everyone would vote Conservative. She had not bothered to vote, hardly ever did, didn't like the smell inside the polling booths and couldn't use red telephone-kiosks for the same reason. Perhaps, even, the Honourable Member would become a member of the Cabinet – thrilling if so – Mrs T. surely wouldn't hold against him those years of sucking up to poor old orange sailor-boy Heath, with no very conspicuous success.

Jeremy Tradescant had not voted either. He found the people who wore Anti-Nazi League badges so appalling that he would have voted Nazi. But none seemed to be standing in his part of London and he had, besides, been only too anxious to get this stuff from Birmingham. When last glimpsed, and only glimpsed, the rood screen at St Aidan's was in a very poor state and would need a lot of work done before it was ready for the exhibition. It was to be the focal point of the whole thing. You would walk through the screen to get to the exhibition, only instead of being rusty brown, it was to be perfect matt black, with the flowers and fruit which climbed up it picked out in gold and possibly even red. He also wanted to take the doors which, oddly, would need much less doing to them, in spite of the fact that they had been exposed to the weather for the last ninety years.

When the Caruso tape clicked to an end, the car had reached Birmingham and they were soon trying to find the way to Purgstall. Fanny, even with Jeremy reading a street map and calling out directions, found the same problem as before and they whizzed and whizzed round the same faceless new roundabouts without the slightest idea of where they were going.

'This is sheer Gormenghast,' said Jeremy.

'How do people who live here manage?' Fanny asked. 'It's literally impossible to find one's way about.'

'Hellette on toastino,' he agreed, adding quickly, 'left, left, left turn left.'

'How clever of you – what made you know ...'

'Slow down.'

His directions had suddenly become quite specific, and the car now found itself cruising along a side street.

'Isn't he lovely?' Jeremy asked, pointing to an Indian youth in jeans. 'Sorry to make a detour but couldn't resist a further glimpse.'

The change of route appeared to be directed entirely towards getting a better glimpse of this oriental botty.

'Do slow down, honey treasure,' Jeremy said as they passed. He rolled down the window of the Bentley and smiled. Then said, in the purest Mae West, 'Hallo.'

The boy smiled back, evidently amused by the attention.

'You're the very person I wanted to see,' Jeremy said.

'Oh yes?' He spoke with a pure Brummy accent.

'We're in a state of the most utter perdition.'

'Come again?'

'Too too lost.'

'You're lost?'

'Up to a very serious point.'

'Ask him how to get to Purgstall Heath,' interrupted Fanny who was amused and at the same time irritated by this flirtatious exchange.

'Purgstall Heath?' asked the boy.

'That would be fun,' said Jeremy.

'Not my idea of fun,' said the boy.

'Purgstall is sheer laughsville. The Monte Carlo of the North, the Polke Street of the Old World, the biggest giggle and shriek since the hanging gardens of Babylon, or wherever they had hanging gardens . . .'

Instead of annoying the boy, all this seemed to amuse him, but all he said, was, 'You'll never find it. I'll come with you if you like though.'

'That would be most extraordinarily kind,' said Fanny in her nervous polite manner.

'A pure rapturette,' Jeremy agreed. 'But isn't it out of your way?'

'Purgstall Heath? I live there.'

The boy turned out to be called Ahmed and to work in his father's shop. In the car he did not, as Fanny feared, turn out to be a criminal, demanding money with menaces or an aeroplane to Karachi; nor did he, as Jeremy had been hoping, show the slightest sign of wanting to follow up the encounter with any amorous engagement in the afternoon. With quiet efficiency he guided Fanny to a spot where he said he could walk home and by following his directions they found themselves surveying the familiar skyline of Purgstall.

'What a nice boy,' Fanny said. 'Should we have given him something?'

'A kiss?' Jeremy suggested.

As he said it they laughed, but Fanny leant forward to place her own lips on Jeremy's and their embrace became hard and intense for a moment.

'Beautiful, beautiful,' she murmured.

'Kissing beautiful women gives one such a wickedly awful thrill – so deeply unnatural,' he said, this time fondling her breasts as he kissed her.

'Oswald Fish has brought so many wonderful things my way,' Fanny murmured, 'Nana, because she was his daughter; and the dear old Prince Consort, whom I'd *never* have met if he hadn't wanted to demove St Adrian's.'

'Demolish.'

'And then *wonderful*, beautiful you, who know all about him.'

'Only about the giggly things like rood screens.'

And now, in the May sunshine, they stood and surveyed St Aidan's. A van had already pulled up outside and they could see that men were heaving one of the great doors into the back of it.

'Isn't it looking *beautiful*?'

'Wonderful. It's pure *Altar Steps.*'

'Actually I never noticed them.'

'No – I mean the book by Compton Mackenzie – faintly dada goings-on in wonderfully bricky little high churches. Boat boys in frilly lace – too thrilling – only of course outside ought to be Coronation Street and it looks like something in Science Fiction – all these dusty glass blocks *dwarfing* the poor little church.'

'Just what I keep telling everyone – in *proportion* the thing would be lovely – well it's *beautiful* as it is, but not doll's-housey as it looks from here.'

Arm in arm they walked towards the church. The men at work were known to Jeremy. Even though he did not have very great administrative responsibility at the museum, he had more than once in the past been involved in heavy haulage operations of this character.

'We've got one door in, Mr Tradescant, now we're taking down the other.'

LIFT UP YOUR HEADS, O YE GATES, was the inscription on the door. In the sunshine Jeremy could see that it was even finer than he had remembered from his previous visits and the photographs. In the centre of each door was the Lamb in Glory; around, angels trumpeted in bas-relief, and the whole was framed with rich and varied foliage, leaves, flowers, abundant in their profusion and almost organic in their seemingly natural contrivance. It was, it seemed to Jeremy, a work which would not have disgraced one of the great medieval master masons.

'It's absolute sugar and cream,' he said to one of the workmen.

'The builders are in there now, sir,' was the reply, as though Jeremy's remark had been a purely rational inquiry. 'They're having trouble moving that fucking screen, I can tell you.'

'Isn't it *beautiful*,' Fanny crooned, laying her head on Jeremy's shoulder as they walked into the church. Chaotic, musty, filthy, damp, decayed it obviously was. But it was its beauty which, as on previous occasions, arrested Jeremy.

It was so obviously designed by a man with a real eye, a real sense of proportion. There was gracefulness about the way in which the scalloped capitals, supporting pointed arches, led the eye inexorably onwards, upwards towards the Holy end. And when the eye reached there, what a screen! Not so much a clever piece of metalwork as a miracle of organic life, frozen, like the dogs and citizens of Pompeii, in some magical stillness which did not remove them from the world of nature. Even in its rusty state, the screen was magnificent. It was as though a mural by Burne-Jones had come to life and then suffered the curse of the Sleeping Beauty and been frozen, dust-covered and neglected for a hundred years. For here were angels, climbing and wafting through the thickets of jasmine, wild strawberry and briar, the whole creation like a defiance of the metal that made it, a magic which came close to greatness. The figures at the top of the screen, as you could tell at a glance, were not Fish work. Jeremy imagined they were made of fairly thin painted wood and had been added by some artist like Martin Travers in about 1926. Martin Travers was all very well when allowed to let rip in full Baroque queeny camp as in the churches of St Magnus the Martyr, London Bridge, or St Mary's, Bourne Street. But it was out of place here. In its way St Aidan's was a little Gothic masterpiece and it was astonishing no one had made anything of it before.

Jeremy, when he first heard of it via poor David, and then met Fanny, had started out by being frankly sceptical about the merits of Oswald Fish. He wanted to get to know Fanny because she was, if not famous, on the fringes of those who were: and, when met, turned out to be a giggle and a shriek. Her accounts of the church made him feel enthusiastic, but partly because he was charmed by her and amused by her enthusiasm and it tickled him to support her pride in her great-grandfather's work. He had only made two very brief visits to St Aidan's before – both times in bad weather, and on each occasion he had been increasingly admiring of the place. But it was only his third sight of it which transported him. Fanny, the Indian's Boy's nice bottom, the whole fluffy old world of Camping was silenced and forgotten as he walked up the rubbish-and-pigeon-shit-strewn aisle in a daze of love and admiration.

'We must get this place properly restored, Fanny.' he said seriously.

'That's what I keep telling everybody,' she called back, 'isn't it Flora, Flo—ra!'

The corgis scampered to and fro in the rubble.

'I wonder what happened to all the other fittings, Jeremy said. 'Sold, I suppose.'

'Wrecked by the excresiastic people.'

'It's not going to move, sir,' said the foreman coming down the aisle towards them, where work had started on dismantling the great screen.

'But it's got to,' said Fanny, 'it's the foetal point of the whole expedition.'

'Hang on, pie,' said Jeremy. Then, turning to the foreman he said, 'You poor fluffy, what's the difficulty?'

The fluffy was a scarlet faced man of about fifty with very brilliantined hair and a hand-made cigarette half alight in his mouth. The extraordinary thing about Jeremy's social manner was that it was of a kind almost everyone, in actually meeting him, found beguiling. The workman did not seem to mind being called a fluffy.

He thrust his hand into his dungaree pockets and tried to explain the technical difficulties of moving the screen, as though Jeremy and Fanny were rational beings. They could not follow all he said but it appeared to involve joists and a sense that the whole enterprise was misconceived.

'We've got to have the screen, you see, sunshine, for our bishette,' Jeremy explained. 'So if you could be pure gold, an absolute Judy Garland, and do your best for us.'

'I'll see what I can do, sir,' said the man. 'Bert,' he roared up the church to his assistant. 'Judy Garland here wants his bloody screen so we'll start drilling at your end.'

There was no reason to suppose that it would be a very long operation, so Fanny and Jeremy decided to watch. They wanted, moreover, to supervise the dismantling of the screen before it was loaded into the vans and driven down to London.

'Will you be our special friend when Prince Consort and I get married?' Fanny asked, holding Jeremy's hand.

'If that would amuse.'

'So many marriages come unstuck because no one will be *friends* with married people. You can't imagine how lonely it is being married.'

'It's fairly lonely not being married.'

The seriousness of the remark, so uncharacteristic of their normal tone, plunged them both into silence, so Fanny plunged her hand into Jeremy's trouser pocket and tried to find Mr Willie.

'Is it really as big as that?' she asked, pleased that he was allowing her to do this. Her fascination with penises was, always had been, almost inexhaustible.

'Well, I haven't got a banana in my pocket, darling. Oh, do look, they've got the screen away from the pillarene. At *last*.'

'They're being too rough, too rough!' squealed Fanny, squeezing the object, banana or otherwise, in excitement.

'Yarouch, do leave my poor old prick in peace. They've got to be rough. We'd be here two thousand years if they took it all down gently. It'll survive. It's ironwork, not Limoges.'

Jeremy left her and went to talk to the workmen. Now that half the screen was down, it was more possible to see the ways in which it could be conveniently dismantled. The chancel gates had already been removed from their huge spiky hinges. The bangs and clangs and echoing crashes and clouds of plaster dust did indeed seem alarming but it was only to be assumed that the men knew what they were doing.

'I think the reason we both get on so well is that we are both absolutely free and open and demonstrative about physical things,' said Fanny. 'I mean people are so terrified of touching each other – really flipping terrified – and you and I like it, find it only national. If I want to reach out and touch a man's Mr Willie why shouldn't I? It doesn't necessarily mean I am in love.'

'How disappointing,' said Jeremy.

'You don't mean *you're* in love with *me*? God how exciting! Me in love with the Prince Consort, you in love with me, Charles I suspect in love with both of us, it's like a play.'

'Sheer *Severed Head* I agree, but I'm not in love with you, I'm just trying to see what the men are doing to our screenette.'

'Do you think they should be yanking all those bricks out?'

'They can't help it, the screen is more or less built into the fabric of the church.'

Much of it had already been dismantled and it was able to be fitted into quite manageable sizes for the enormous vans provided by the museum. The church became so full of noise and dust and fumes that Fanny and Jeremy had to have several little walks through the bleak Purgstall cul-de-sacs to enable them to cough and clear their lungs. When they returned to the church, nothing remained of the screen except the great metal beam, running across the chancel arch, on which the Travers wooden rood was now so precariously balanced.

'It'll cause a bit of a shake, this,' said the foreman. 'If I was you I'd watch from up the way.'

Fanny and Jeremy distanced themselves in a nasty little precinct called Glebe Close where they could look down on operations with advantage. Clearly, the removal of that top beam was causing difficulties because the men came in and out of the church several times with troubled expressions on their faces. The corgis had taken it into their foxy little heads to follow them into the church in spite of Fanny's soprano injunctions to the contrary. On Jeremy's insistence, she did not follow them. He seemed to sense that danger was in the air.

Then the men came running out, panic-stricken, and shouting, 'Get away, get out of the fucking way.'

'But my babies, my corgis, my darlings, they're still in there,' wailed Fanny.

Ignoring her plea, Jeremy took her arm and ran further up the hill. On the brow they turned. A false alarm, it seemed, unless the falling masonry was only affecting the inside. The men had all taken refuge in the van and the quietness of the air was disturbed by the racing up of the engine and the rumbling of the great pantechnicon away from the building. But when the van stopped, the rumbling did not.

It all happened so fast that it was hard to believe that it was really happening. The little building seemed to be groaning, almost in pain. Before their very eyes, the central part of the roof began to cave in; the walls, with astonishing rapidity, cracked and bulged outwards and fell. Dust and rubble rose to the air like smoke. So strange was the moment that even Fanny said nothing. She simply stood, staring, with Jeremy and holding his hand. After a long silence he said, with a dull obviousness which seemed almost sinister in his voice, 'I suppose that beam was a crucial part of the structure.'

She did not answer. When the dust had begun to settle, what had been a church now had all the jagged picturesque appearance of something which had been a ruin for years.

'At least we saved the doors and screen in time,' Jeremy said. 'Thank God for that.'

Fanny's grief was too deep for screams. She wanted to yell her head off but she could only whimper. Tears poured from her eyes and she thought she was going to choke.

'My lovely church,' she said, 'and my Flora, and my Honey ... my poor, poor babies.'

For it was indeed true: the corgis, caught by the falling rubble had been squashed flat.

XXXIII

Fred's day at the office had not been unduly taxing. Since he had made it clear to the Town Clerk that he would be leaving soon, he had not been given any very interesting or long-term pieces of work. He had dictated quite a lot of letters, and drafted a reply to the Equal Opportunities Commission about an accusation that not enough jobs in the City Transport Department were being given to women. He had spent the afternoon boning up on the law relating to burial grounds, because there was a proposal, questioned in many quarters, to cut off the corner of a suburban cemetery in order to widen the clearway. He could not concentrate on it. The thought of cemeteries merely made him remember, with delighted intensity, copulation in Kensal Green, the ecstatic figure of Fanny beneath him . . . But it was much more than *just* sex. He was drunk with her, his ears full of her music, his body not just lonely but really only half-existent without her. Now he saw the force of her assertion (scarcely original) that we only live once. And the kind of life in prospect with her was in the most urgent way irresistible. He felt closer than ever in his life to being able to guess what made people religious. For not to pursue Fanny would seem almost like a blasphemy, a betrayal of a vision of something brighter and more glorious than anything he had ever dreamed life could offer or afford.

So, confidently returning to Augustus Road, he felt strong enough at last to explain everything to Jen. He would be gentle, sensible, kind. Sometimes in the past when he had heard of marriages breaking up, he had thought, rather loftily, what fools people were. Once the excitement wore off, he had believed, sex was more or less the same whoever you had it off with, and everyone in the end turned out to be dull. Perhaps that was true in the majority of cases – but he knew it was not true now. Without Fanny, he would shrivel up. The ghastly greyness of his existence, in which he found no interest, no incentive to effort or laughter, would eventually overwhelm him in a cloud of irritation and cynicism. He must not allow this to happen to himself. One day, he felt, he could explain it to Jen. It was all so much more than just leaving her for another woman. She would not make a fuss. There was nothing she could do to stop him. Their marriage had been dead for years anyway. And the vestige of the old Jen, the Jen he still regarded as a friend, would surely see that he *must* be allowed his chance of making a sort of poetry out of life. It was all so much more, he repeated to himself as he walked up Augustus Road, much more than just sex, or an infatuation, or an affair, It was a choice between life and non-life, between joy and death: and no human being had the right to deny another human being the chance of joy ...

He wanted to communicate all this to Jen at once, but she hardly looked at him when he came into the kitchen and did not reply when spoken to. As usual, the chaos of family life went on around him, making conversation impossible. Sam had the television on rather loud. Dad came round from next door and explained about Grandma's condition. The doctor had given her some pills and said she should be kept under sedation until arrangements could be made to take her into a 'home'. The explanation of the Grandma crisis took up about half an hour and then the old boy began to talk about the General Election until Harriet came in, thrilled by her day out with the Gladstones and determined to make Sam jealous by a catalogue of the number of ice creams she and Debbie had scoffed. High tea wore on. The children were bathed and put to bed. Fred and Hugh watched television. Supper was slammed on the table and then Hugh withdrew. It must have been nine o'clock before Fred and Jen were actually left alone together.

'You seem a bit quiet,' he began.

'Do I?'

'Jen, there's something we must talk about – something I have been meaning to say to you for weeks now ...'

'Only me,' said his father popping his head round the drawing-room door again. The old man entered, carrying a large cardboard carton which had contained wine bottles. 'Next time that woman asks we might offer her some of this.'

'What is it?' asked Jen. Fred had never seen her look like this. She was pale, shaking, and every word she spoke, on average about three every one and a half hours, had been measured and careful as if she was having difficulty with the language.

'More Jobling and Fish stuff,' said Hugh. 'Can't imagine there's anything they'll want for this exhibition but you go through it – fire-tongs, pokers, that sort of thing.'

'Have a drink.' said Fred. He was suddenly losing his nerve about the big showdown with Jen. A cowardly voice inside him was saying, *Another day, tell her another day, when she looks less tired . . .*

'No thanks, old boy, it's very kind, but you two don't want me round your necks all the time.'

Fred protested, but his father had made for the door. 'I'll go and hear what that Robin Day chappie's got to say for himself. They say it's going to be a landslide.'

And once again, they were alone together. Fred nervously unpacked the things from the box and spread them on the carpet – a couple of metal dishes, a door-knocker in the shape of a dolphin, three pokers . . .

'You were saying,' Jen said.

Fred could tell she was in a cold fury. What was it this time? He so wanted, if he had to have the showdown now, that it should not be muddled by some trivial piece of petulance about the washing-up machine or something of that order.

'Ah, well,' he stumbled. He tried to smile at her and said, *'Jen, love . . .'*

She looked away crossly. 'You said you had something important to talk about.'

'I'm thinking of getting a job in London,' he blurted out. 'I thought it was only right to tell you.'

'How kind of you.'

A long silence ensued. She wasn't going to make it easy for him. She stood by the fireplace, staring down at him where he sat with the pile of old ironwork, a look of cold contempt in her eyes.

'Probably on the Law Commission,' he added.

'What are you proposing? We've all got to move to London now, have we? We've just got settled here. Your Grandmother is round the bend – you're so hopeless you haven't even noticed all the things I've had to do for her over the last few weeks. Well, she's moving into a home now, but there's still your father. I thought we were meant to be having separate households but he's in and out all day long wanting me to do things for him. How *typical* of you,' she suddenly flared out, 'to go and get a job in London without even asking me.'

'Well, it isn't settled yet . . .'

'I never wanted to come to Birmingham and be a nursemaid to your relations,' it was as if she wasn't even trying to listen to him, 'but at least we're settled now. Harriet's starting to do really well at EHS and I've got my job – not that *that's* ever been any concern of yours. But you don't ask us before wanting to uproot us all over again, oh no . . .'

'Jen, you don't seem to understand.'

'No,' she said, 'I don't.'

'Jen,' he added, 'I've fallen in love.'

There was an awful silence. They listened to the hall clock ticking outside the room. Slowly she paced the room. Was she going to ask nothing? You couldn't just tell your wife that you had fallen in love and be greeted by silence. It was unnatural. She did not seem to be listening. Why didn't she ask him *who with*? Why didn't she at least say *something*?

At length, she paused and looked at him. She crouched down on her haunches where he was playing with the pokers and snatched one angrily out of his hand.

'My God, I was a fool to marry you,' she spat out.

Still holding the poker, she continued to pace the room.

'I said I'm in love,' he repeated.

She did not reply.

'I'm in love with Fanny Williams and she is in love with me. I should have told you before, I'm sorry, but somehow it was always . . . difficult.'

Even now, nothing but silence. She was not looking at him at all. Just walking slowly up and down the drawing-room with the poker. When she came to the round table by the window she stared at it for a moment: she could see her face reflected in the polished mahogany. A vase stood there, full of daffodils. Raising the poker casually, Jen gave the vase a sharp rap; it skated off the table in several pieces, scattering water and flowers.

Little beads of water skidded across the mahogany like ball bearings and began their slow drip, drip, drip on to the carpet.

'There was really no need,' he began.

'Oh, no?'

Was she drunk? Had she, too, like Grandma, become unhinged?

'There was no need,' she continued slowly, spittingly, deliberately, 'to throw my *father's* gold cuff-links in the Thames.'

Oh hell. She'd cracked. Fred would never have thought it of old
Jen. What he had come to loathe about her was her reliable same-
ness, and now she was going to do a Mrs Rochester act. Cuff-links?
In the Thames?

'I never threw —'

'No, but you left them lying about and someone else did. Not both
of them. I've got the other safe. They were kind enough to post it.
But the other — Daddy's gold cuff-links — grandfather's — just —
threw — away.' She was crying now. Fred was so taken aback, so
slow to grasp what she was talking about, that he felt no pity for
this display of emotion, merely disgusted by the ugliness of her
face when contorted by tears, and more than ever before by
those bloody ears. 'Just to throw one away — deliberately,' she
blubbed.

'This is all Double-Dutch to me,' said Fred.

'Is it?' Her tears subsided and the coldness returned to her voice.
'Is it,' — and then she added, with a meaning glare — 'Alastair?'

That made things clearer. He had never been Alastair to Jen,
always Fred. Throughout his married life, except to his grandmother, he had been Fred. She did not have to say any more than
'Alastair' to show that she knew about Another Woman: probably,
by some means, knew about Fanny. Well, it would make it easier to
talk about it now.

'I was going to *tell* you,' he said. 'O God, Jen you know what it's
like — Harriet and Sam hammer and tongs all day long: Dad in and
out: the telephone ringing. And I've been busy ...'

'So I gather.'

'I mean we just haven't had the *chance* to talk. I didn't want to
deceive you ...'

'So, it's true,' she said quietly after a pause. He stared at her. How
much, really, did she know? Was she merely fishing?'

'Yes,' he said. 'It's true, Jen. I *love* Fanny, it's the most wonderful
thing that has ever happened to me. There's no good pretending
any more. You and I have never got on particularly well — and the

last few years have been hell, sheer hell – for me, at any rate. I dare say for you.'

'Thanks.'

'Listen, Jen, we've got to talk about this properly. I don't know whether you've been in love the way I'm in love at the moment. It isn't something you have to apologize for. It is so full of joy. It feels so pure. Fanny and I are so happy. You wouldn't want to spoil our chances of happiness ...'

She had stopped pacing about the room, and although the poker was still in her hand, there was no evidence that she was about to smash anything more. She said, in her more usual tone of voice, 'You make me *sick*. SICK!' she repeated.

'But Jen ...'

'Oh come on, Fred, grow *up*. You're talking like a kid of sixteen.' She put on a baby voice to throw his own words back at him, '*It's so full of joy, it feels so pure!* How *can* you sit there and be so *hypocritical?*'

The accusation wounded him.

'I'm being perfectly frank and fair with you. How dare you call me a hypocrite?'

'I don't know what you've walked into, Fred. I don't want to know any more about it. But the idea of your calling it all pure and lovely makes me absolutely sick. I never want to see you again. I never want you to see the children again . . . . .'

'*What?* But come *on*, I've come clean and –'

'Clean? Clean? How could you? That child's not much older than Harriet. She ... but I can't even talk about it, it just makes me feel so sick. If you want to throw in your lot with a *woman* –' the word on her lips sounded stronger and more vile than the worst insult '– a *woman* who uses her own *children* as sexual toys ...'

'Jen, I don't know what you're talking about, you've never met Fanny ...'

'Oh, my God!' No longer listening, she seemed to want to catalogue his apparent misdeeds. ' "Jen *darling* I've got to go to London to see this awful Williams woman, such a bore – wish we could get this Purgstall business out of the way and forget about it." ' When she imitated his voice, Jen puffed out her chest and assumed a ludicrously pompous stance. 'And of all the times to choose!' she went on. 'Oh, yes, you've been honest, you've come *clean*. Going off to London for God knows how many weeks for – for that!' She shuddered. 'While I stayed here and minded the house and the children and looked after your father and your *grandmother*, for God's sake.'

'Don't start all that over again.'

'You can leave tonight. Go to bloody Fanny.'

'Jen, you don't understand.'

'No, and I don't want to understand. All I know is that you are never going to see those children again. How *could* you? With a little girl – and then come home and cuddle Harriet on your knee and – Oh my God, it's *disgusting* ...'

Fred blinked at her stupidly.

'We must be talking at cross-purposes,' he said.

'Go to the bureau,' Jen said quietly.

What was this? Some trick? Game? Punishment? Bewildered, he did as he was told.

'Top drawer,' Jen said.

He opened the drawer.

'Take out the envelope.'

He did so and began to peruse its contents. He groaned as he read Pandora's letter and saw the photographs.

'Jen, I swear to you –'

'Don't try to lie your way out of it, Fred. That only makes it worse.'

'But let me explain. There's a perfectly innocent explanation.'

Perfectly –'

'All right, I admit. I was in bed with Fanny. We had been making love ...'

'Fred, I *don't want to know*. Can't you get that into your thick skull? *I do not want to know*.'

'But you must let me explain.'

'You are not going to claim that it is trick photography?'

'Of course not.'

'That is a picture of you and a *little girl*, Fred.'

'Yes. I don't deny that.'

'Then I don't want to know any more. How can you stand there and be so cool about it? Don't you see how vile it is? I don't want anyone who can be so *vile* in the house.'

Suddenly, and to his surprise, Fred became angry. All right. He could see she was bound to be upset. Pandora's trick had been horrible and disgusting. Perhaps the news that he was having an affair came as a great shock to Jen, and combined with the letter, she was, inevitably, going to react in an emotional way. But it was not the emotional reactions which angered him. It was her stubborn air of moral superiority. She always had to be morally one up and by God she was *glorying* in his disgrace now. At last she had found something she could really taunt and squash him with.

'You don't want to listen, do you,' he suddenly flared up. 'You've never wanted to listen. You've never taken the slightest bit of notice of me all the time we've been married. All right. Be morally superior if you like. You're welcome to it. Be as moral as you *fucking* well want. Grow some angel wings to match those fucking ugly ears of yours. But I've got something I want to say to you and you're jolly well going to listen whether you want to or not. Being married to you has been unmitigated hell for the last fourteen years. I thought you'd be reasonable when I told you about Fanny, but you can't be reasonable because you're just a stupid stuck-up ugly bitch. I hate you, Jen. Do you hear that? I hate you and I have always hated you and I think I must have been absolutely mad to put up with it for as long as I have done. But now I've found somebody that I *do* love I'm not going to let you spoil it for me as you've spoiled everything else . . .'

He stopped.

She stared at him. He was red, sweaty, shaking. She had never noticed before how disgustingly ugly he was.

He, looking at her, was having the same thought too. She had gone quite scarlet, but she was not going to cry. His words had silenced her. He felt a hideous kind of pleasure at the look of shock in her eyes.

'Christ, be careful,' he suddenly yelled.

She had raised the poker and hurled it at him with a furious force. It struck him between the eyes, and he fell to the ground without uttering a sound.

For a moment she stood, just looking, looking, not quite sure what she had done. When she ran over to him, she was only half fearful, still partly furious with him. Now was no time to play absurd games. She knelt down by his side and looked at his fleshy, lumpy face. The specs, unbroken, strangely, had fallen down to the end of his nose. The poker had not made much of a mark on his brow. There was a bump, but it did not seem to be anything much.

'Fred?' she said, now less querulous and quietened into alarm. 'Fred, don't be *silly*.'

His lumpish form was still.

All at once Jen's common sense came to the rescue. She realized that she might have hurt him really badly. What was she going to say when she rang up Doctor Fraser? She *couldn't* tell the truth. What if Fred *died*? They could hardly call it murder, just throwing a poker. Could they? What would happen to the house, the children?

Thoughts and actions now came fast. Before ringing up the doctor, she must contrive to make it look like an accident. She tried to heave him up by the armpits, but she could hardly move him. She knelt on the floor and listened to his heart. She was not sure. Yes, it was still beating. It *had* to be. One more heave. And this time, she did manage to move him a little. She had never dreamt he could be so heavy. Inch by inch, and now sweating profusely herself, she got him to the hearth. There were metal baubles on each corner of the fender, not so different in size from the head of the poker. She rolled Fred over so that his head rested against the fender. Then she shook him, as though he was simply being lazy about getting out of bed.

'Come on, old thing,' she said.

She went to the drinks cupboard and got out a bottle of Rémy Martin. With her foot she turned Fred over; stooping down, she forced his mouth open and poured quite a lot of the stuff into his mouth. Most of it just came slopping out again, the way it did with teacups when she filled them too full. A curious calmness had descended on her, the horrible sense that she could quite easily do without Fred, and a thrill, quite new to her, that she might be able to get away with it.

She corked up the brandy bottle and went to telephone the doctor.

XXXIV

Next morning, Jen sat in a horrible waiting-room in the Queen Elizabeth hospital. There were several other people there, but no one was talking because all eyes were glued to a television set in the corner, giving out the Election Results.

They had let her see Fred, he was in a coma in the Intensive Care Unit. Doctor Fraser had been very kind and seemed to accept entirely her version of the previous evening's events: that Fred had removed his spectacles, tripped over the cardboard carton of ironwork in the middle of the drawing-room floor and dangerously concussed himself on the corner of the fender. The hospital seemed to think his chances of survival were fifty-fifty, but described his condition as critical.

Jen thought it was a fairly good description of her own condition too. She would neve be able to forget, or to forgive, Fred's speech of hatred to her. It was so monstrously untrue and unfair. She had wasted her life for his sake, uprooted herself from Surrey, slaved for him, nursed his grandmother ... The catalogue of grievances went on raging and raging in her brain, so that she could feel no compunction about having thrown the poker. Only yet more rage that he was now causing all this worry and inconvenience by being in the hospital. Melanie Gladstone had kindly taken the children to school for her that morning. Jen had rung her own school to say she would not be coming in. She was sad to be missing a teaching morning.

If he died, what would happen? She would take the children back to Surrey, but what would happen inside to herself? Would all the shock and rage subside? Would she be tormented by guilt for the rest of her life? None of it was quite real to her yet. She felt heady, in an unaccountable way, excited.

'The crowds are gathering outside Number Ten,' said the television. There they all were. As everyone had predicted, the Conservatives had won.

'It wasn't *murder*,' Jen said to herself. The idea of herself in the same league as Doctor Crippen or Adelaide Bartlett was almost laughable. Even in death, if he was going to die, there was something you could never take seriously about old Fred. She should have married Mark, she saw that now, the chartered accountant who had been so keen on her when she went so much to the tennis club.

The children had been puzzled by their father suddenly being taken off to the hospital, but not in the least upset. They had caught from their mother the habit of not taking Fred seriously. Bonking your head on a fender seemed such a foolish thing to do. And Harriet had hardly mentioned it, just been thrilled because it was Friday and Friday was the day they had gym. Fred's poor old father was the only one to mind, but the seriousness of the accident had so far been kept from him. He had other problems of his own, keeping Grandma under sedation.

'And now here's the moment they've all been waiting for,' said the television commentator. A cheer had gone up in Downing Street. There was Mrs Thatcher, neat as a bird, in her recent perm and her trim little blue suit, with Denis, waving, by her side.

At that moment the doctor came in and sat down beside Jen and took her hand.

'I'm afraid he's died,' he said quietly.

In Tregunter Road, Fanny also watched the dramatic scene on her television set. Tracy was gathered round with the char and various other friends. Charles had gone to work and Jeremy was at the museum, so it was a largely female gathering.

Tracy's reaction to the appearance of the new Prime Minister was voluble and predictably horrible. She screeched with hatred when Mrs Thatcher had said that the Queen had asked her to form an administration.

Fanny was less thrilled. It was still too soon to know whether the Honourable Member would get a place in the Cabinet even though he had comfortably increased his majority. She was too shaken to care. The horrible, horrible turn of events in Birmingham had almost broken her spirits. Her wonderful church destroyed – and not by the Council, but by her own idiotic efforts to restore and beautify it. Her darling Honey and Flora crushed in that brutal and disgusting way. She knew that people had worse things to endure. People could live through the deaths of their children so she would be able to live through this. And God she was lucky and had more or less flipping everything that a woman could want: Charles, being angelic; her two adorable children; and the wonderful Prince Consort, to whose visit this evening she so eagerly looked forward. Tonight they were going to brave it out and sleep together in her large four-poster and poor old Marmie would just have to lump it. How she looked forward to the Prince Consort's embraces. They would console her as nothing else could for the loss of the church and the corgis. It was to be a night of love, not a wink of sleep, over and over again that tubby, furry body dominating her own so *excitingly*. For, yes, she did love him; and yes, in spite of the warnings and cluckings of all the others, she had found Mr Right.

Mrs Thatcher had come forward through the crowds and was making for the cameras. Tracy was prevailed upon to stop booing while they listened to the product of goodness knows how many elocution lessons enunciating the prayer of St Francis of Assisi:

' "Lord, make us instruments of thy peace. Where there is hatred, let us sow love; where there is injury, pardon; where there is doubt, faith; where there is despair, hope; where there is darkness, light; where there is sadness, joy." '

FOR THE BEST IN PAPERBACKS, LOOK FOR THE 🐧

In every corner of the world, on every subject under the sun, Penguin represents quality and variety – the very best in publishing today.

For complete information about books available from Penguin – including Pelicans, Puffins, Peregrines and Penguin Classics – and how to order them, write to us at the appropriate address below. Please note that for copyright reasons the selection of books varies from country to country.

In the United Kingdom: For a complete list of books available from Penguin in the U.K., please write to *Dept E.P., Penguin Books Ltd, Harmondsworth, Middlesex, UB7 0DA*

In the United States: For a complete list of books available from Penguin in the U.S., please write to *Dept BA, Penguin, 299 Murray Hill Parkway, East Rutherford, New Jersey 07073*

In Canada: For a complete list of books available from Penguin in Canada, please write to *Penguin Books Canada Ltd, 2801 John Street, Markham, Ontario L3R 1B4*

In Australia: For a complete list of books available from Penguin in Australia, please write to the *Marketing Department, Penguin Books Australia Ltd, P.O. Box 257, Ringwood, Victoria 3134*

In New Zealand: For a complete list of books available from Penguin in New Zealand, please write to the *Marketing Department, Penguin Books (NZ) Ltd, Private Bag, Takapuna, Auckland 9*

In India: For a complete list of books available from Penguin, please write to *Penguin Overseas Ltd, 706 Eros Apartments, 56 Nehru Place, New Delhi, 110019*

In Holland: For a complete list of books available from Penguin in Holland, please write to *Penguin Books Nederland B.V., Postbus 195, NL–1380AD Weesp, Netherlands*

In Germany: For a complete list of books available from Penguin, please write to *Penguin Books Ltd, Friedrichstrasse 10 – 12, D–6000 Frankfurt Main 1, Federal Republic of Germany*

In Spain: For a complete list of books available from Penguin in Spain, please write to *Longman Penguin España, Calle San Nicolas 15, E–28013 Madrid, Spain*

WISE VIRGIN

Life has not been kind to the medieval scholar Giles Fox

His inexplicable failure to win a Fellowship at King's, the unfortunate loss of two wives and now the onset of blindness, have merely sharpened his resolve to astound the world with his interpretation of the Pottle manuscript, a little-known thirteenth-century tract on virginity.

But when Miss Agar, his academic helpmate, impetuously proposes marriage, and when his daughter Tibba discovers the precocious, and quite unmedieval charms of public schoolboy Piers Peverill, an intriguing new light is shed on Giles's investigations into the manuscript . . .

'A delight, a book of acute observation and delicate ironies' – *Listener*

'He is a hypnotic storyteller who leaves in his wake a trail of curiosity and unease' – Anita Brookner in the *Standard*

'Clever, calculated and very funny' – *New Statesman*

THE HEALING ART

WINNER OF THE SOMERSET MAUGHAM AWARD, THE SOUTHERN ARTS LITERATURE PRIZE AND THE ARTS COUNCIL NATIONAL BOOK AWARD

Pamela Cowper is facing death. Not a vague probability, but a shockingly imminent oblivion from cancer. How will she face it?

Dorothy Higgs, on the other hand, is told that she will live to be one of her doctor's success stories. And, as the two women confront their destinies across gulfs of fear and hope, fate, as always, reserves the final twist until the end.

'Not a page goes by without our being astounded' – John Braine in the *Sunday Telegraph*

'I could never have enough of it' – Auberon Waugh in the *Evening Standard*

THE SWEETS OF PIMLICO

WINNER OF THE JOHN LLEWELYN RHYS MEMORIAL PRIZE

Evelyn Tradescant. A recent failure in love, with a passion for natural history, timid and rather lonely.

By accident she meets Theo Gormann in the park, an old man with a chequered, enigmatic past (baron, ex-intimate of Goebbels, pacifist, drama critic ... who knows?). A strange, quasi-erotic friendship develops as Gormann delicately and cleverly draws Evelyn into his net. Suddenly, Evelyn discovers she is controlling a balance of power, power she relishes manipulating ... Or is she?

A. N. Wilson's baroquely sparkling first novel leads the reader down paths of trickery, lust and greed to the heart of a conundrum.

A very talented, assured and intriguing new English writer' – *Observer*